HIS PATH OF DARKNESS

DI ROB MARSHALL
BOOK 6

ED JAMES

Copyright © 2024 Ed James

The right of Ed James to be identified as the author of this work has been asserted in accordance with the Copyright, Designs and Patents Act 1988. All rights reserved.

No part of this publication may be reproduced, stored in or transmitted into any retrieval system, in any form, or by any means (electronic, mechanical, photocopying, recording or otherwise) without the prior written permission of the publisher. Any person who does any unauthorised act in relation to this publication may be liable to criminal prosecution and civil claims for damages.

This is a work of fiction. Names, characters, businesses, places, events and incidents are either the products of the author's imagination or used in a fictitious manner. Any resemblance to actual persons, living or dead, or actual events is purely coincidental.

Cover design copyright © Ed James

OTHER BOOKS BY ED JAMES

DI ROB MARSHALL SCOTTISH BORDERS MYSTERIES

Ed's first new police procedural series in six years, focusing on DI Rob Marshall, a criminal profiler turned detective. London-based, an old case brings him back home to the Scottish Borders and the dark past he fled as a teenager.

1. THE TURNING OF OUR BONES
2. WHERE THE BODIES LIE
3. A LONELY PLACE OF DYING
4. A SHADOW ON THE DOOR
5. WITH SOUL SO DEAD
6. HIS PATH OF DARKNESS
7. THIS WORLD OF SORROW (early 2025)

Also FALSE START, a prequel novella starring DS Rakesh Siyal, is available for **free** to subscribers of Ed's newsletter or on Amazon. Sign up at https://geni.us/EJLCFS

And coming 30th November, FALSE DAWN, a second Shunty book – get it on Amazon.

POLICE SCOTLAND

Precinct novels featuring detectives covering Edinburgh and its surrounding counties, and further across Scotland: Scott Cullen, a rookie eager to climb the career ladder; Craig Hunter, an ex-squaddie struggling with PTSD; Brian Bain, the centre of his own universe and bane of everyone else's.

1. DEAD IN THE WATER
2. GHOST IN THE MACHINE
3. DEVIL IN THE DETAIL

4. FIRE IN THE BLOOD
5. STAB IN THE DARK
6. COPS & ROBBERS
7. LIARS & THIEVES
8. COWBOYS & INDIANS
9. THE MISSING
10. THE HUNTED
11. HEROES & VILLAINS
12. THE BLACK ISLE
13. THE COLD TRUTH
14. THE DEAD END

Note: Books 2-8 & 11 previously published as SCOTT CULLEN MYSTERIES, books 9-10 & 12 as CRAIG HUNTER POLICE THRILLERS and books 1 & 13-14 as CULLEN & BAIN SERIES.

DS VICKY DODDS SERIES

Gritty crime novels set in Dundee and Tayside, featuring a DS juggling being a cop and a single mother.

1. BLOOD & GUTS
2. TOOTH & CLAW
3. FLESH & BLOOD
4. SKIN & BONE
5. GUILT TRIP

DI SIMON FENCHURCH SERIES

Set in East London, will Fenchurch ever find what happened to his daughter, missing for the last ten years?

1. THE HOPE THAT KILLS
2. WORTH KILLING FOR
3. WHAT DOESN'T KILL YOU
4. IN FOR THE KILL
5. KILL WITH KINDNESS
6. KILL THE MESSENGER

7. DEAD MAN'S SHOES
8. A HILL TO DIE ON
9. THE LAST THING TO DIE
10. HOPE TO DIE

Other Books

Other crime novels, with *Lost Cause* set in Scotland and *Senseless* set in southern England.

- LOST CAUSE
- SENSELESS

"It is the controller of Nature alone that can bring light out of darkness, and order out of confusion. Who is he that causeth the mole, from his secret path of darkness, to throw up the gem, the gold, and the precious ore?"

— James Hogg, *The Private Memoirs and Confessions of a Justified Sinner*

1

DAY 1
SUNDAY

The Tweed was quiet this morning. The sun hung over the water, casting a dappled glow along the parched river. An Indian summer, they said, with everything all dried up. Made up for how bad the weather had been a few months ago.

The metal bridge resonated with each step. Iain Hogg cleared the end and faced a choice – follow the shore of the river, or head up the bank into the thick woods. An idiot who didn't know where they were going could waste hours in there, but he wasn't that idiot so he took the path up the bank.

As much as he tried to keep calm, sweat soaked his armpits and ran down his arms and his back. Everywhere. And it was getting worse. He loosened off his shirt, thick enough to keep warm outside at three in the morning, but way too bulky for this kind of hike in this heat. He smelled like broken biscuits. Salted caramel flavour. That stuff was everywhere now. He rounded the bend and stopped.

The groove led down a decline towards the wide mouth of the tunnel, bricked up around the sides, with an open square left in the middle. Sheer black inside.

Hogg cupped his hands around his mouth. 'Becky?'

He waited but got nothing – just his words rebounding at him. Couldn't even hear birds singing.

'Becky?'

His words sounded pathetic. Shrill. Small. Desperate.

He set off along the final stretch towards the tunnel, taking it slowly in case he fell and stopped just outside.

Some kids had brought wooden pallets up here, but left them to rot at the side. He presumed they were kids.

He tried to set off again, but it was as though his legs weren't letting him enter the spooky tunnel, no matter how much he felt he should go in. No matter how many times he'd been here. No matter how recently.

In stark contrast with the bright daylight, the tunnel was pitch black inside – just a thin shard of light crawled across the rough pebbles, soon lost in the depths of the old railway tunnel.

Weird to think there used to be train tracks running through here. Used to be trains, too, running right where he stood. Hadn't been any for yonks, mind – fifty years, *at least* – but still, it was weird to consider.

The nearest active train station now was across in Gala, meaning Peebles got short-changed yet *again*. The bus took ages getting into Edinburgh – and he knew.

Aye.

He was prevaricating, just like he'd done all his life.

Sod it, he needed to get inside.

He put his hands in his pockets, wrapping the fingers of one hand around his keys and gripping his torch with the other. He didn't know if he'd need to use either, especially defensively. Possibly offensively.

Stop thinking like that!

Hogg sucked in a deep breath. 'Becky?'

Still nothing, just a wild reverberation of his voice, the syllables crossing over and catching, but not really fading as they spread inside the tunnel. Like those old Gregorian chant CDs his gran used to listen to, everything overlapping and never ending.

All of a sudden, it just stopped and Hogg was left in a wall of silence.

Despite his brain telling him it went straight to hell, the tunnel didn't go very deep at all. Everyone called it the half-mile tunnel, and half a mile was nothing. And he'd been here tons of times, with Becky and others, but that was all years ago.

Sod it – the quicker he went in, the quicker he'd be out the other side.

Then he'd head to that bakers in town, get one of their millionaire shortbreads. Ah, it was Sunday and they were shut. It'd have to be a slice of cake and a hot chocolate in that fancy place.

Aye – that'd be his treat for doing this. His reward.

Hogg clicked on his torch, then shone the light into the tunnel, casting the beam off the sludgy pebbles on the ground and the curved brick vaulted ceiling, damp and uninviting.

Becky wasn't here.

Aye, maybe he'd just go and get that cake now.

He turned off the torch, then set off back the way he came.

Then stopped.

The patch of grass, sitting under the pallets, just outside the tunnel mouth was darkened. He switched the torch on again, then shone it over it.

Not just shadow.

Blood.

And a *lot* of it.

Hogg wasn't an expert, but it looked way too much to be compatible with life. He had no idea how much you could lose and still survive. Was there that much on the ground?

Shite.

Took him a few seconds to catch his breath, then the realisation hit like a baseball bat to the face – he wasn't looking for a survivor, but a corpse...

He rubbed away the salty sweat on his forehead.

He could pretend to himself it was from a rabbit, that maybe a fox had got it. Kid himself about how they'd reintroduced some eagles nearby and maybe one had caught a fox. Killed it, then dropped the body and something else had taken it.

But that was all nonsense.

He knew where the blood came from. Whose it was.

He should get back to Peebles, get his slice of cake, then have a think.

But what if Becky was still alive and in there?

Like she just needed someone to take her to hospital?

Or at least call for help?

He could save her life.

He should. He needed to do this. He needed to see if she was okay.

Hogg turned around, sucked in a deep breath, then stepped into the tunnel, scanning his torch across the walls and the floor as he walked through the darkness. Water dripped from the ceiling, despite it being dry for weeks.

He set off into the darkness, keeping his torch on a wide beam.

'Becky?'

His own words seemed to whisper back at him.

Or was there someone else in here with him?

2

MARSHALL

Not for the first time in his life, Rob Marshall felt massively underdressed. The number of times he'd driven through Gattonside recently and he'd never ventured down the lane to this place. When he'd been at school in the village, this had been a knackered old pub, the sort that turned a blind eye to such trivial matters as the ages of the patrons ordering pints of snakebite, especially when they'd been at the nearby high school.

And he'd kind of assumed it'd stayed the same.

Wrong.

The interior had been gutted and reworked, like a central London eatery or one of those places on George Street in Edinburgh he'd taken Kirsten to. Tiled walls and floors. The ancient beams had been stripped and sealed in a dark colour. A fire roared away in the far wall, despite the heat outside. The long bar had a coffee machine and wine fridges instead of beer taps and there was a new wall just opposite it, blocking the espresso maker's hiss from diners through there.

God, the coffee smelled good, though.

Despite his look, Kirsten had won a competition she hadn't even known she'd entered. Her summer dress was still valid in early September, with her hair tied back in a ponytail. Such a difference from when he first met her. She walked up to the maître d' in his shirt and slacks. 'Hi, we've got a table under Jennifer Marshall.'

Marshall shuffled over, each step making him feel even more underdressed. He looked down at his navy jeans, black trainers, brown leather jacket and black Aphex Twin T-shirt – at least that was niche enough to appear stylish, even if the material was more a grey now after repeated abrasive washes.

You had to just act like you owned the lion's den, even if the lion was getting ready to savage you.

'Follow me, madam.'

Marshall followed Kirsten and the maître d' through the doorway then past tables of well-dressed diners sipping away at wine and slicing into roast beef.

Jen sat at their table, her fingers wrapped around a glass of white wine seeded with droplets of moisture, staring off out of the window towards the Tweed and Melrose, the posh houses mounting the hill across the river. She turned and noticed them, then gave the mildest of smiles.

Kirsten leaned in to do a double kiss, then took the seat next to her.

Marshall just gave a smile as he sat opposite his twin sister. 'Happy birthday, Jen.'

She smiled back – at least it was fully formed now. 'Happy birthday, Rob.'

'Another year, eh?' Marshall let out a deep breath. 'I feel old.'

'You look it too.' Jen stared into her glass, twitching her nostrils.

Marshall had seen that look on her a few times over their shared life. Her exams, her wedding day, when she was pregnant with Thea, Thea's exams, her divorce, Thea leaving for university. 'You okay, Jen?'

'I'm fine. Why do you ask?'

'Just seem a bit preoccupied with something, that's all.'

'Long story...' Jen reached over for the menu and started running her finger down the page.

So she wasn't going to talk about it, whatever it was.

Magic.

Marshall sat back. 'Quite a nice place, this.'

'I like it.' Jen glanced up, then looked at what he was wearing. 'Sorry, I should've told you it was fancier. You've dressed like we're meeting in that grim pub up in Stow.'

'The Stagehall Arms?'

'That's the one.'

Marshall smirked. 'It's shut now. Heard someone bought it and they're renovating it. Probably end up like this.'

'Demolishing it would be a better idea.'

Marshall laughed – he didn't disagree. 'This is a bit of a long drive over from your place.'

'Nowhere near as far as for you two coming down.' She smiled. 'I appreciate it, by the way.'

'No worries. It's our turn after you came into Edinburgh last time.'

'Did you get the train?'

Kirsten shook her head. 'Rob drove.' She nodded at Jen's wine glass. 'Did you get a taxi?'

'I'm not made of money.' Jen licked her lips. 'Thea drove me.'

'She's just back from Canada already?'

'Aye. Poor thing's badly jetlagged, but she had a whale of a time. Got to get her head straight for a week tomorrow when she goes back.' Jen smiled at her brother. 'She's sorry she's not here, but she's meeting up with her old school pals from Peebles. They've gone into Edinburgh'

'Of course. It's important to stay in touch, right?'

'Isn't it?' Jen gave him a sour look that could curdle milk. 'I do appreciate you seeing her now you stay in Glasgow.'

'Haven't lived there for a while now, Jen. Kind of got kicked out of my old place.'

'Oh, I didn't know that.'

'Long story, Jen.' Before Jen suggested he moved back into the granny flat above her garage, Marshall grabbed Kirsten's hand. 'We've moved in together.'

'Oh?' Jen's eyebrows shot up. 'Since when?'

'Three months now.'

Jen gave Marshall a look. 'And you didn't tell me?'

'You've been a bit busy, haven't you?'

Jen turned her head to the side. 'How's it going with your operation?'

Kirsten frowned at her. 'Which one?'

'Is there more than one?' Jen was blushing – she'd overstepped the mark. Her special move. She leaned in and spoke in an undertone. 'The endometriosis treatment?'

'That. I'm on a waiting list.'

'You know how long for?'

Kirsten shrugged. 'Said it'll be a year.'

'This country...' Jen shook her head. 'Waiting times in BGH are through the bloody roof. My pals on the wards are constantly getting it in the neck. See it in A&E too. But that's good news that you're on the waiting list.'

'Morning all!' Bob Milne shuffled over, his detective's eyes scanning the three of them and the rest of the room. He'd tucked his lime-and-brown-checked shirt into his chinos, his belly pushing the fabric to the limit – one too many roast potatoes and it'd all flop out. He wheeled in Grumpy – his father and Marshall and Jen's granddad – into the space at the head of the table. 'See who we've got here, old fella?'

Grumpy's eyes shifted around between them, still with that

mischievous energy flashing in them. 'Well, well, well. The gang's all here, eh?'

Marshall caught a briefly arched eyebrow from Kirsten, then gave an equally brief shrug in return – he'd had no idea they were coming. His glare at Jen hopefully made that message clear to her.

Jen looked away quickly enough that it gave him some hope she'd received the message loud and clear. 'Rob was just saying how he's moved in with Kirsten.'

Milne beamed at his son, then at Kirsten. 'That's cracking news, son. So you finally got turfed out of that looney's place?'

'Like I told Jen, that's a long story.' Marshall smiled at their dad. 'Is Catherine coming?'

Milne sat between Jen and Grumpy, then started adjusting his cutlery into some arrangement that presumably made sense to him. 'Your, uh, half-sister won't be joining us, no.'

'Oh, that's a shame. Why?'

Milne smiled at Marshall, then at Jen, then at Kirsten. 'Some good news, though. I've bought a house just along the road.'

Jen snorted out a laugh. 'Good way to steal attention from our birthdays, I suppose.'

'It's nothing to do with that, Jennifer. I'm just fed up of living in Edinburgh. Too snooty. Too sharp-elbowed. Fancied a move back down to my homeland, so I sold up. On the market for *two days*, then some daft sod from London made an offer even the king couldn't refuse.'

Marshall held his gaze. 'You're moving to Gattonside?'

Milne slapped his father's back, maybe a bit too hard. 'Just along the road from Grumpy's sheltered housing, so it'll be nice to spend even more time with the old rascal.'

Grumpy rolled his eyes. 'Speak for yourself, Bob my lad.'

Milne laughed it off, but there was a flicker of hurt in his eyes.

Marshall waited for his focus to settle on him. 'It'll make your commute to Fettes a bit worse.'

Milne leaned forward, resting his elbows on the smooth wood. 'And that's the other thing. They're shutting the place. Sold it off, like my house. And...' He scratched at the back of his neck. 'I'm retiring at the end of the week.'

Jen laughed. 'You're *what?*'

'Been a while coming, sweet pea.'

She glowered at him. '*Don't* call me that.'

'Sorry. You used to love it when you were wee.'

'Maybe. But then you left us, didn't you? Didn't love *that*.' Jen clicked her tongue a few times. 'Wish I hadn't invited you along now...'

Milne tried to laugh it off, but his lips were a knot.

'Hang on.' Marshall sat back in his chair. 'You're retiring at the end of the week, but you haven't thought to tell us before now?'

'Not that I've had much opportunity, but my boss has been trying to dissuade me. He refused to put in the paperwork, trying to force my hand into staying for another two years. But I told him that was it. I'm done, Rob. I need to move on with my life. Because of the work we've done recently, I've got a few weeks' accrued holiday, so I'm off on Wednesday for three weeks.'

Grumpy cackled. 'Studs up!'

Milne frowned at his father, then smiled at his son. 'Got a few pals who stay over there full-time, then I'll have two final days in the office to wrap everything up. Last day in the office is the Thursday. Move house that Friday.'

'That'll be a huge change for you.' Marshall raised an eyebrow. 'So what changed?'

'I'm not as sharp as I used to be, son. Or as sharp as I need to be for this job. Feels like I've dropped off a lot in terms of...' Milne stared off into the middle distance.

'Are you okay?' Jen tilted her head slightly. 'This isn't your way of saying you've got Alzheimer's or a brain tumour or something, is it?'

'No, no. All my marbles are still rolling around in here.' Milne tapped the side of his head. 'I'll be like Grumpy, don't you worry.' He tapped his old man's arm. 'Clean bill of health at my last medical. Cholesterol needs a bit of work and my blood pressure could do with coming down, but the doctor says I'm doing well for a man my age in my profession.' He looked right at Marshall. 'Besides, I've achieved everything I wanted to in my career. Taken down a lot of very malign actors, shall we say, both inside and outside the police service, north and south of the border. And, I guess, the final straw is I blame myself for what happened to poor Davie Elliot.'

Marshall held his gaze. 'That's not on you, Dad.'

Christ, the word just slipped out.

Dad.

It felt *weird*.

Marshall cleared his throat, hoping nobody else spotted it. 'That wasn't your fault and you know it.'

'Someone needs to carry the can for it, mind. Might as well be the bloke who was in charge of his prosecution on the police side, eh?'

The waiter appeared, all smiles and easy cool. 'Hey, guys, do you know what you'd like to drink?'

'Pint.' Grumpy pointed back through the restaurant. 'Lager. Helles, if you've got it, Pilsner if you don't.'

'We don't have any draught beer on, sir.'

'Any kind, then, I don't care. Just make sure it comes in a pint glass.'

'Sir, we don't have draught—'

'You can pretend, son. Pour a bottle into a pint pot, then pour another until it's up to the pint mark. Then bring it through and pretend it's come from a keg.' Grumpy tapped his nose. 'I won't grass, alright?'

'Okay, sir.' The waiter smiled. 'I heartily recommend the WEST St Mungo, which is—'

'Sign me up, son! Pint of that!'

'Okay.' The waiter scribbled something down, then looked at Jen.

She raised her glass. 'I'm fine for now.'

Milne smiled at him. 'I'll have the same.'

'So a bottle in a pint glass?'

'Aye, you can split three across two pints, right?'

The waiter humoured him with a smile. 'And for you, madam?'

Kirsten looked at Marshall. 'Seeing as how I'll be driving home...'

'You have a glass of wine, if you want.' Marshall squeezed her hand. 'I'll drive.'

'Right. In that case, I'll have a glass of the malbec.'

'Sure thing. And for you, sir?'

'I'll have a coffee, thanks. Long black with oat milk.' Marshall smiled, just as his phone rang. 'Bloody hell.' He got his phone out of his pocket and checked the display.

She Who Cannot Be Named calling...

God, he really needed to stop playing that stupid game.

DCS Potter.

'Sorry, I'd better take this. The boss has probably dropped her pen and needs me to drive up to Glasgow to pick it up.' Marshall got up and stormed through the bar back to the front door. He stepped out into the sunshine and answered it. 'Ma'am?'

'Rob, hope I haven't caught you at a bad time?'

'Just having a family lunch, so you could say it's a bloody awful one.'

'Oh, I'm sorry.'

'It's my birthday. Ours. Mine and my sister's.'

'I see. Is your father there?'

'He is.' Marshall swallowed the sigh. 'Do you know him?'

'Oh, we go way back. Say hello to Bob for me, would you?'

'Will do. How can I help, ma'am?'

'Ah. Right. Listen, I need— No, I shouldn't. You're at a lunch.'

'It's okay. Seriously. What's up?'

'Look, you go back to your family, Rob. This can wait.'

'Can it, though?'

She chuckled down the line. 'You know me too well...' She paused to clear her throat. 'Someone's found a body in an old tunnel near Peebles.'

'I'm not far from there just now. I can—'

'Rob, the reason I'm calling *you* and not someone else in my vast empire is there's a slight possibility this murder might be related to those cases you've been investigating for me.'

'Oh?'

'Note the stress. *Might* be. Rob, I need you to attend, but you're there to consult, not to investigate. Okay?'

'Sure thing. I know the drill.'

'You do, but you don't necessarily follow the drill, do you? Rob, if these cases *are* all related, I need to know ASAP. Okay?'

'Okay.'

'Now, you finish your lunch and give the local cops a chance to sort out what's what, then head over to Peebles.'

3

Marshall took a final swig of his coffee as he drove past Neidpath Castle, then ploughed on towards the car park, where he found the huddle of vehicles. Seemed like half the Borders cops were in attendance, all shepherded by a lone cop. Mature and still a PC, but tall and eager. He held up a hand to stop Marshall, then motioned for him to wind down his window.

Marshall complied. Another fresh-faced jobsworth who couldn't spot a DI a mile off.

'Sorry, sir, but the car park's closed.'

'DI Rob Marshall.' He held out his warrant card. 'DCS Potter asked to attend.'

'Sorry, sir. Of course.' He brandished his clipboard. 'Your name's not on the approved list.'

Marshall laughed and corrected his earlier thought – this guy was the kind of jobsworth who didn't care who he pissed off, so long as he did exactly as he was told. Those rules were there to be followed, not to be understood and amended. 'Can I take your name, Constable?'

Using his rank made him bristle. 'PC Graeme Veitch.'

'Thank you.'

Veitch inspected Marshall's credentials. 'Sorry, sir, but I have my orders.'

'And who gave them?'

'Sir, I can't let you through without—'

'It's fine, Graeme.' DI Callum Taylor strolled over, his greying rockabilly quiff flapping in the breeze. Not quite as tall as Veitch, but he had a much bigger presence. 'I can personally vouch for Rob.'

Veitch looked him up and down. 'If you insist, sir.'

'I do.' Taylor waved him through.

Marshall took it slowly and claimed the last space, wedged between two MIT pool cars which were both still operating despite being totally buggered eighteen months ago when he'd been based down here full-time. Almost too tight a fit for his monster car. Definitely should sell it. Or get someone to exorcise it. He killed the engine and got out into the hot sun, the breeze tempering the heat a bit. He took in the area. Hills on all sides, with recent forestry work giving some of them a close shave. 'I always forget how nice it is over here.'

Taylor was already crossing the stone bridge over the Tweed.

Marshall had to jog to catch up with him. 'Thanks for that save there, Cal. Jobsworths everywhere, eh?'

'Mm.'

So that was how he was going to play it, eh?

'It's been a while.'

'Six months, eh?' Taylor gave a brief glance. 'That nonsense up in Eyemouth, right?'

'Hard to forget that. How have things been down here?'

'Same old, same old.' Taylor reached the far end of the bridge and started the descent along a well-worn path through a rugged wood that was itself ripe for forestry work. 'Can't keep away from the place, can you?'

'Me? Oh, I love it around here. Born and bred in the Borders. The hills keep calling me back as much as the murderers.'

'You've moved on to bigger and better things, though. How's Gartcosh treating you?'

'Ach, it's fine. Get my head down, get on with the work and don't get caught doing anything too naughty.'

Taylor stopped dead. 'Rob, back in April, things were a bit... uneasy between us. Just because I'm your replacement in the Borders MIT doesn't mean we can't get on.'

'Agreed, Cal.'

Taylor gave him a hard look, then a tight nod, and he was off, marching along the old viaduct and crashing through a pair of uniformed officers like a bowling bowl between pins. 'Word from the gaffer is you're here to consult, aye?'

'That's right.'

'Cool, well, I'll let you consult away.'

The path led to the tunnel mouth. A circular hole dug into the hillside, with the entrance bricked off at some point. Would've been a door in the middle, but that was gone now, leaving it wide open.

A few cops stood around, but didn't seem to know what to do. The forensics officers were working away both outside and inside the tunnel, their arc lights making the interior like Bonfire Night.

'Suit up, Rob.' Taylor tossed Marshall a suit, mask and goggles, then started signing them into the crime scene.

Marshall grabbed his trousers and hauled them up over his jeans. 'When did you get alerted?'

'About eleven.'

Marshall tugged the jacket on then checked his watch. Two hours ago. 'That's quick going, especially on a Sunday.'

'We're a well-oiled machine.' Somehow Taylor was already dressed.

Marshall zipped up his jacket, but putting the overshoes on top of his trainers made him lose his breath. He stood up and caught it again.

Taylor was frowning at him through his goggles. 'You okay there?'

'I'm fine.' Marshall snapped on his mask and goggles, which were both a bit nippit. Still, he wasn't going to complain. 'I'm following your lead here. Just consulting, after all.'

'Sure you are.' Taylor entered the tunnel first. 'You ever been here before?'

'Once, I think. Cycled over here with some pals when I was at school. Went in and they all turned off their torches halfway in. Totally crapped myself. I'd forgotten to bring mine. My sister's idea...'

Taylor laughed. 'You cycled all the way from Melrose?'

'Cal, I used to cycle down to Penrith and back in those days.'

Taylor led him through the lit-up tunnel. 'Visited here a few times myself.'

'I thought you were from Glasgow?'

'I am, but we moved to Peebles at the end of high school. Folks still live in the town, up by the wee Tesco. Used to come down here and have a wee drink of a Friday evening.'

'Over in Melrose, we preferred the local underage watering hole in Gattonside.'

'Oh, we had one too. Kids these days don't know they're born, do they?' Taylor stopped near a clump of CSIs, their lights bleaching the brick walls.

Marshall stopped. He couldn't see any daylight in both directions, just the arc lights making the moss and lichen glow. Just an old tunnel. If it wasn't for them, it'd be even spookier than he remembered.

If you didn't know it was there, you'd miss it – a little doorway was cut into the side wall. Someone had etched an upside-down crucifix and written HELL.

Marshall could well believe it went there.

A small room, though Marshall had no idea what its function would be. A storage tunnel for the railway, maybe. Storing spare coal?

Taylor nudged a pair of CSIs aside, letting Marshall see inside.

Its modern function was much clearer – a couple of cans of Stella sat in the near corner, next to two used condoms, the latex ripped open ages ago.

Over by the far wall, a woman lay on her back, staring up at the ceiling. Or she would be if her head hadn't been caved in. Her thin blonde hair was matted with blood. Red lipstick faded and cracked. Tight jeans, but her loose top was torn at one shoulder and ripped right across to expose most of a blue bra. One shoe on, the other kicked off and discarded a few metres away, where a CSI was taking great care to photograph it.

Taylor crouched by the body. 'Pathologist has been and gone. He reckons blunt-force trauma to the head.'

'No shit.'

Taylor's laugh was echoed by a few of the CSIs. 'Post-mortem is arranged for tomorrow morning and hopefully we'll find a few more things from that.' He stood up. 'We think she'd been drinking.'

Marshall felt the walls of the tunnel close in and his goggles steam up. 'Big-time drinking?'

'Very big.'

Marshall took a long look at her. He'd seen blunt-force trauma several times and found it hard to argue with it, especially the fact her skull was bashed in on both temples.

Aye. Murder.

But nothing to pin it to anything in his scope of work.

'Follow me.' Taylor got up with a creak, then walked off through the doorway and headed away from the entrance.

Marshall followed him. This end was darker and gloomier

without the CSIs' lighting. The eastern entrance appeared – a glowing hole in the blackness that quickly expanded until it was a doorway.

The daylight stung Marshall's eyes as he stepped back out into the greenery. The crime scene extended to the rise at the far end. As many CSIs worked away on this side of the tunnel as the other, focusing on a pair of pallets propped up against the retaining wall. 'What's going on, Cal?'

'Found some blood outside the tunnel there. Under the pallets.'

Marshall got as close as he could but couldn't see much. 'You think it's hers?'

Taylor held his gaze. 'We'll find that out. I'd wager someone dumped the pallets on top to cover it up. Might've looked good in the middle of the night, but's blindingly obvious in the cold light of day.'

'Assuming it's hers, do you think someone killed out here, then dumped her in there?'

'We'll see. What I will say is it's much trickier getting here undetected from this direction. It's just by the bridge practically in the town.' Taylor thumbed back into the tunnel. 'Much easier to do that from the other side.' He looked up into the blue sky. 'We just don't know what happened here, Rob.'

Marshall looked back the way. He could've done with a few more minutes inspecting the body, but Taylor seemed like a man eager to get on with his task, without having to babysit a consulting idiot. 'What do you know about—'

'Name is Rebecca Yellowlees. Most people call her Becky. She lives in Peebles. Went missing on Saturday night. Drunk, by all accounts.'

'Impressive work.'

'Peebles Highland Games yesterday. Hundreds of miles from the Highlands, but hey ho. And people say kids these days don't drink and go to the gym or cinema instead. If that's the case, the youth of Peebles haven't got that memo, judging by how busy uniform were yesterday. We think she'd been drinking from noon.'

'You seem to know a lot about her already.'

'Good reason for that. Her body was found by one Iain Keith Hogg. Her ex-boyfriend.'

'Oh. How ex are we talking?'

'A good few years now. Childhood sweethearts.'

'Have you interviewed him yet?'

'Not yet, no.'

'Mind if I watch while you take a stab at it?'

4

Taylor let out a deep sigh, impatient for Marshall to finish removing his protective suit. 'Remember the rules and we'll be grand.'

Marshall's overshoes were being a bit clingy, so he had to crouch to get them off. 'Are these your rules or my boss's?'

'My boss's, Rob. Remember – I'm the deputy SIO here and you're only here to check if this connects with your other cases.'

'One of which you worked.'

'That one in Glasgow?' Taylor dumped his crime scene suit in the discard pile. 'Aye, but I was a mere DS back then. Just had to corral the troops and do the doings.'

Marshall dumped the jacket into the discard pile. 'Whereas here, you're much more hands-on.'

'Something like that. Let's go.'

Marshall followed Taylor along the path of the old railway line.

At the rise, PC Liam Warner was talking to a man dressed in a violently orange jacket. Marshall was surprised to see Warner still in a job after many costly blunders. Living proof of how desperate the police force was for officers.

'Iain Hogg, this is DI Rob Marshall.' Warner grinned. 'It's still DI, isn't it? You haven't been promoted?'

'Haven't been demoted, either. Still DI.' Marshall flashed a smile. 'Can you give us a minute, Constable?'

'Sure thing. I'll just be having my piece.' Warner slouched off through the throng towards the bank of parked squad cars.

Marshall got a better look at Hogg.

Staring at the ground, lips pursed. Baby-faced, but wizened around the eyes. His widow's peak was lengthening, his raven hair thinning at the back with some flecks of grey at the temples. Maybe early thirties, maybe older. Ragged shorts rid below his knees. His thick lumberjack shirt was soaked with sweat and reeked of decay. He hid his left hand up the sleeve.

Marshall could smell the booze wafting off him. Bad enough to have a stinking hangover, worse still if you discovered the body of someone you knew. And loved. And maybe even still loved. So many motives in there, but that wasn't Marshall's job – he just had to see if this was a dot that connected to another.

Taylor gave him a curt nod. 'DI Marshall here works in a specialist area and has been asked to consult on this case.'

'Right.' Hogg looked away, his lip quivering. 'What's this area?'

'I investigate serial murders.' Marshall let it sink in, but Hogg seemed to be made from fairly shallow mud. 'Mind taking us through your last twenty-four hours?'

'Aye, sure.' Hogg exhaled slowly. 'Went swimming on Saturday morning.'

'You or your kids?'

'Me. Don't have any kids.'

Marshall took another look at him, but he didn't have the lean physique of a swimmer. 'How long were you swimming for?'

'Hour and a half. Try to swim three miles at least once a week.'

'That's pretty good going.'

'Taken me a while to get up to that standard, eh?'

'I can't swim myself. I mean, I learnt to swim but I just get bored when I do it.'

'I'm the opposite. Find it lets my mind drift off, so I don't think of anything. Like I'm asleep, you know?'

'Sounds good. What did you do after your swimming?'

'Went home, had some food, then went to meet a few mates in the pub.'

'Which one's that?'

'The Steps.'

Buchan's Steps.

Marshall knew the place – boy, did he know it. Maybe it wasn't as rough as it was back when he'd been chucked out as a drunk underage teen. Maybe it was. 'On Northgate, right?'

'Just by Sainsbury's, aye. Where I work.'

'You were working in Buchan's Steps?'

'No. I work in Sainsbury's. Drink in the Steps.'

'Right, with you now.' Marshall gave him a smile. 'So you went there to meet your mates?'

'Aye.' A long sigh. 'We had a couple of jars, then we walked over to the Highland Games down in the park. Had some cans with us. Decent laugh.' He scratched at his neck. 'Stayed there all afternoon and got a bit wasted, to be honest with you. Didn't even have a burger and the amount we put away...'

'The games finish up about five, right?'

'Right, aye. Went back to the pub.'

'The Steps?'

'Aye. Fair few of us in there. Out in the beer garden until it got a bit chilly.' Hogg rubbed at his arm – he had a farmer's tan, no doubt topped up by an afternoon in the September sunshine. 'Few lads talked about getting a cab over to the club in Gala, but I couldn't be arsed with that.'

'So you were in there until closing?'

'Not quite.' Hogg scratched at his neck again. 'I got chucked out.'

'What time was that?'

Hogg raised his shoulders. 'Search me. Was a bit wasted, like I told you.'

'Was Ms Yellowlees with you at the Highland Games?'

'She was, aye.'

'I gather you were an item?'

'Back in the dim and distant. We hadn't planned on seeing each other there. I mean, we hadn't seen each other for years, like, so it was pretty weird.'

'Was she with you when you left the pub?'

Hogg was reddening – either from shame or anger. Maybe both. 'Told you, I got chucked out.'

'So what, you went home?'

'Can't remember.'

Marshall stood up tall, but Hogg was even taller. 'Here's the thing I'm struggling to understand, Iain. You were drinking with an ex-girlfriend, but you say you got chucked out of the pub. Next thing we know, you've found her dead body in a tunnel outside of the town this morning.'

'How's that weird?'

Marshall almost laughed, but he caught himself. 'Explain to me how you just so happened to find her body, then?'

'I heard she was missing, so I went looking for her.'

'Who did you hear that from?'

'Went to her home, but her mum told me Becky hadn't come home last night.' Hogg nibbled at his thumb. 'Or this morning.'

'What made you go there?'

Hogg gave Marshall some side eye, then looked away to

where the CSIs were working. 'You ever get this thing when you're pished and you wake up and you're still drunk? And you can't really remember what you said or to who? And you can remember little fragments, where you've made a right arse of yourself?'

Marshall smiled at him. 'Used to call that the Onion Man when I was young. The wee guy who'd sit on the edge of your bed and whisper all the things you did last night.'

'Right.' Hogg smiled at that. 'Well, that's me this morning. Had a visit from the Onion Man. Made me worried I'd said something I shouldn't have to her last night. It was nice just seeing each other as pals, you know? Didn't want any bad feeling. So I wanted to put it right.'

'Even if there was nothing to be put right?'

'I didn't want the Onion Man whispering in my ears again.'

'And when she wasn't there?'

'I... I panicked. Started scouring the area for her.'

'Even with a stinking hangover?'

'Right.'

Taylor was rolling his eyes and thinking the same thing as Marshall – this didn't sound at all dodgy...

Marshall smiled at Hogg. 'How old is Rebecca?'

'Twenty-five. Same age as me.'

Marshall struggled to believe that. 'And she's still living at home?'

'No. I mean, aye. She does now. Lived in Glasgow, but she moved back home a few months ago.'

'Right.' Marshall took a deep breath. 'Thing I'm struggling with here is how you just happened to find her body.'

Hogg shrugged. 'Half-mile tunnel was the first place I looked.'

'Exactly. You just so happening to look in the very place she'd been murdered. That doesn't seem weird to you?'

'Right. I mean... The Onion Man mentioned something

about the tunnel. Not sure what it meant, if I was supposed to go there, or if she went there, or he was just spit-balling about old times.'

'Are you taking the piss?'

'No! Just telling you the stuff running through my head this morning. Guess I got lucky.'

'I'm not a believer in luck. What made you think this was likely?'

'We used to hang out here when we were kids. Smoked and drank inside. Even went into that wee cubby-hole, if we were brave.' Hogg scratched his neck again. 'Even, eh, had a shag in there once. Made me wonder if she'd come here after the pub.'

'On her own?'

Hogg sniffed. 'Mate of mine, Titch, he reckons he saw her leaving the Steps with a bloke.'

'You know this bloke's name?'

'Nope, sorry.'

5

Taylor drove them along Peebles' wide high street. Grand old buildings full of shops, pubs and cafés. Older couples stopping to chat. Two decent hotels too. At least. 'What are you thinking there, big man?'

Marshall smiled. 'You're bigger than me, Cal.'

Taylor pulled up at the lights just as a large brute with silver hair crossed ahead of two pensioners, walking hand in hand. 'Still pretty big, Rob.'

Marshall sat back in his chair. 'If you're asking whether I'm thinking if this isn't connected to my work, then I'm tending to agree. As far as I can see, this is just a standard case of a spurned lover going over the score.'

'Over the score?'

'Hogg isn't the brightest, is he? He probably got pissed, tried to rekindle stuff with her or just had it out with her. Then he accidentally killed her.'

'My take too. But how do you explain them getting from the Steps to the tunnel?'

'I'm just a consultant, Cal. That's for you.'

'Typical.' Taylor took the left turning down Northgate, past the old department store that was now a Costa Coffee. 'So when does your consulting end?'

'I'll sod off once we've confirmed this isn't connected.'

'Last time you did that, up in Edinburgh, you were there for, what, twenty minutes?'

'Saying I'm outstaying my welcome?' Marshall's joke didn't land. 'This is a different beast, Cal. This case is still unfolding, whereas all the cards were out on the table with that one. Besides, you were there and we agreed it didn't match your one in Glasgow.'

'Right. So that means I have to put up with you a bit longer? Great.' Taylor pulled in just past the back entrance to Sainsbury's. Next door, a few units were built into the front gardens of old houses. All four were taken up by a new shop – Northgate Hardware.

Marshall groaned – he knew the owner. Gary Hislop. Had even thought the scourge of the Lowlands had stopped spreading, but there it was. Malignant. 'I see our friend is still operating.'

'Tell me about it...' Taylor got out, then darted around the front to block Marshall leaving the car, forcing him to stay seated. 'Remember, you're here to watch and speculate, not get involved.'

Marshall folded his arms. 'Going to suggest I inhale and exhale to keep enough oxygen in my body?'

'You're a cheeky sod, you know that?' Taylor grinned as he pointed back along the street. 'You know you asked way too many questions back there.'

'They were basic ones. If you'd have asked them, I would've got out of your hair. As it is, I'm still not satisfied with what we're finding here.'

'I'm leading here, okay?'

'I'm not stopping you, Cal.' Marshall raised his hands. 'But you're stopping me getting out.'

Taylor huffed out a sigh, then let him out.

The sign for Buchan's Steps hung above the door. Barely legible and needed to be repainted.

Taylor waltzed inside like a regular and stood at the bar, resting his fingers on the scarred wood.

Marshall was as overdressed for this pub as he was underdressed for the place back in Gattonside. And it was exactly as rough as Marshall remembered from all those years ago.

A huge barn of a place, rammed full of punters and none of them were eating, just mechanically bringing their glasses up to their mouths to sip while they watched English football on the telly. Southampton against Chelsea. Might be Sunday lunchtime, but there weren't any roasts being served in here. The only food on show was bags of crisps, torn down the seams and shared with other drinkers, and a rack of peanuts between optics, advertising shots of vodka and rum for a pound. They all knew what they wanted – televised sport and cheap booze with prices scrawled on jagged fluorescent yellow stickers.

Three beer pumps offered Stella, a local 80 shilling and the safety pint of Guinness. The main feature behind the bar was the thirty-nine whiskies heaped in a display, a large number of which looked almost empty. The barman was pouring doubles of both Grouse and Bells from the optics. One fifty a shot. Probably not much profit after the minimum pricing was taken into account, but if you sold a lot of volume...

'Afternoon, Clive.' Taylor rested against the foot stand at the bar like he was ordering a pint. 'Mind if we have a word?'

'Just a sec, Cal.' Clive rested the glasses on the bar top and pointed at the punter. 'Three quid, Eric.'

'Daylight bloody robbery.' The old-timer slammed down a fiver then took his change and slumped off to join his pals. Didn't seem to have a drinking partner, so settled the two whiskies on the table in front of him like he was conducting a blind taste test of two generic blends.

Clive took in Marshall, like he didn't want an outsider drinking in his pub. 'Like your T-shirt.' He shifted his gaze to Taylor. 'What's your poison, Cal?'

'Off it these days, Clive.'

'Crying shame, that. Not many can put away what you can.'

'Which is why I'm off it.' Taylor tapped the bar like he was trying to remember something. 'You know a Rebecca Yellowlees?'

'Kathryn's lassie, aye?'

'That's her. She been in recently?'

'Last night, as it happens. Why? What's she done?'

'She on her own?'

'Hardly. Big bunch of them in. Highland Games nights can be brutal, Cal. Lucrative, but brutal. Place was stowed out.'

'You know who she was with?'

'About ten of them, Cal. They're not getting any younger, but they all seemed to be free and single. A lot of letting down their hair, if you catch my drift. Plenty sore heads this morning, I'll wager.'

'Anyone causing any bother?'

Clive sniffed. 'Iain Hogg, as per.'

'What did he get up to?'

'What didn't he? He was filthy drunk when he came in after the Games. Had a word with him and he promised he'd be a good lad. Filthy bugger wasn't.'

'In what way?'

'Usual. Being a bit of a pest. Sexually aggressive.'

'In what way?'

'Hands everywhere. Particularly with Becky.'

'She okay with that?'

'Up to a point. Then she told him to stop. And he didn't listen.'

Marshall rested his hands on the bar. 'Did you intervene?'

Taylor shot him a look, which he ignored.

'Course.' Clive took a sip from a clear glass mug, half filled with milky coffee. 'Split them apart. Final warning for him. Don't get a lot of lassies in here. Trying to do more for them, you know? Karaoke nights. Even do a book club on Tuesdays, but that's a bit of a washout most weeks. My wine's not good enough, apparently. Who needs more choice than red or white?' He sipped more coffee and shook his head. 'Even doing a wee disco like last night. First time in years. Those lights and new speakers cost a pretty penny, not to mention the DJ, so I need to keep the crowds coming in to repay the investment. And the last thing I need is clowns like Iain Hogg giving this place a bad reputation, that lassies can come in here and get felt up by a total arsehole.' He clattered the mug down on the bar. 'This game isn't as easy as it once was, I'll tell you that for nothing.'

'Can well imagine.' Marshall smiled. 'When did Mr Hogg leave?'

'Chucked him out. Fell over in the toilets, didn't he? Went in there to see what he'd done. Head in the urinal trough. So me and Big Titch carted him out. Threw up on Titch. His velvet jacket's reeking now.'

Marshall smiled at that. It tallied with the tale of woe they'd heard from Iain Hogg. 'When did Becky leave?'

Clive stared into his empty coffee mug. 'She was here for last orders at one, I remember that. Council gave me a special late licence, in case you're wondering. Think she ended up leaving with a lad, though.'

'You know who?'

'It'll come to me.' Clive clicked his fingers a few times. 'Way I saw it, she'd been hitting on this laddie to piss off Hogg. I'll say that much for nothing. After all that handsy malarkey, it was like she was trying to goad him after I'd split them apart.'

'Goad him how?'

'Kissing him. Slow dance to that George Michael tune with all the saxophone. Then they had words.'

'Becky and Iain?'

'Aye.'

'Harsh words. Shouty ones. If you ask me, there's a lot still going on between them two.'

Taylor frowned. 'They used to go out, didn't they?'

'Bit more than that, Cal. Don't you remember?'

'Way before my time.'

'Aye, those two were an item when they were at school. Broke up about five years ago, I think.' Clive clicked his fingers then pointed at Taylor. 'Jonathan Sandison. That's the lad she left with.'

'You know where we can find him?'

6

Taylor stormed out of the bar, hands in pockets. 'See when I said I was in charge of this, Rob, I expected you to actually listen to me this time.'

Marshall followed him along the pavement, then yanked Taylor back from the road edge.

Taylor shot him a glare. 'What the—'

A column of vintage cars hurtled past them.

Embarrassing for Taylor, being caught mid-strop like that and saved.

Not that he thanked Marshall.

'Cal, you didn't ask many questions, so of course I had to step in. You step up and I'll step back.'

Taylor shot him a hard look, then crossed the road and went inside Northgate Hardware.

Marshall took his time following. That whole group of cops down here who'd replaced him and his old boss put the toxins into toxic masculinity.

He really didn't want anything to do with this place anymore. Just clear this from his scope, then bugger off back to Gartcosh.

Easier said than done.

Marshall entered the shop.

Six narrow aisles of products rammed into the space. Much bigger than the other three he'd been in. The original in Galashiels, the one in Kelso and, accidentally, Morrison Street Hardware in Edinburgh. He'd assumed that place couldn't be connected to the others, only to find the owner standing behind the counter, grinning away.

Just like in here.

Gary Hislop's boyish face was accentuated by the kiss curl, making him look like a matinee idol. He looked Marshall up and down, then took off his apron, revealing a white T-shirt that simply read:

GANGSTER

'Jonty, can you deal with these customers?' Hislop limped off through to the back. He moved like he was in a lot of pain. Some wounds never healed, especially when someone drove a car into you.

The lad looked up from restocking some boxes of screws. The red T-shirt under his apron matched his eyes – this was a man who'd been drinking recently and very, very heavily. Probably still under the influence by the way he dropped the boxes onto the shop's floor. 'Bollocks.' He crouched down to pick them up and dropped them again. Looked like he was going to tip over.

Marshall held out a hand to help him up.

'Cheers, man.' Jonty gripped tight and let himself be winched up. He was skin and bone, his clothes hanging off him. His eyes were giant globes that made him look not so much like a frog but a nineties raver, still caning it years later.

Marshall couldn't tell how old he was – could be anything from thirty to a well-preserved sixty. 'Jonathan Sandison?'

'Try to go by Jonty now, but aye.' He shifted his gaze between them. 'Cops?'

'DI Callum Taylor, based in Gala.' He showed his warrant card. 'And this lump here is DI Rob Marshall, who's consulting on a case for me.'

'Right.' Jonty rubbed at his nose, then dusted off his hands on his apron. 'What can I do for you, gents?' He glanced at the stockroom, as though expecting a request to speak to his boss, or at least get some insight into his nefarious schemes.

Taylor grinned wide. 'Good night last night?'

'Depends on who's asking...'

'Come on, Jonty. We're the police. We're asking.'

'Aye, I had a good night. Bit crap I had to work today, but hey ho. My fault for answering a text from the boss when I was three sheets to the wind, eh? Double time, so can't knock it. That's how the devil drives, eh?'

Marshall smiled at him. 'Funny way of describing your boss.'

'Gary? Och, he's a good lad. Could have many worse bosses.' Jonty shifted his focus between them, as though he couldn't decide who was the bad cop here. 'To answer your question, yes. I had a decent night last night. And I'm having a shocking day today.'

'Where were you, mate?'

Jonty leaned against the pole, arms folded. His biceps barely formed. 'What am I supposed to have done?'

'Nothing. We're speaking to people who've recently been in touch with Becky Yellowlees.'

Jonty swallowed hard, his Adam's apple bobbing up and down. 'She okay?'

'Mother reckoned she went missing last night.'

Jonty shifted his focus between them. 'You guys responding to a missing person case seems a bit of overkill, if you don't mind me saying.'

Taylor clapped him on the shoulder like he was a trusty pet dog. Almost knocked him off his feet. 'Seem to know an awful lot about police procedure there, Jonty.'

'Trained as a cop, didn't I?'

'What happened?'

'Hated it. Lasted four weeks at Tulliallan. Joined the army instead. Hated that even more. And here I am, working in this place with a stinking hangover.' Jonty slapped himself on the forehead. 'Sorry. I sound like I'm moaning. I'm totally chill with my life. Love living here. All these walks around here. And the mountain biking. This gig gives us freedom to do what I want. Love it.'

Taylor stared at him. 'That what you told Becky last night?'

'Eh?'

'Tempted her out for a cycle up in the hills?'

'Mate, I've no idea what you're on about.'

'Okay, so maybe you drank so much you blacked out, in which case I'd be tempted to give you the benefit of the doubt.' Taylor held his gaze until he looked away. 'Trouble is, you were seen leaving Buchan's Steps with Becky Yellowlees at the back of one this morning.'

Jonty walked over to the counter and slipped under it, rather than raising it. He grabbed a mug of tea and sipped it with a snarl, then spat it out. 'Bloody cold.' He rubbed a hand across his lips, then looked at them and seemed surprised there were cops in his place of work 'Fine. I left with Becky. We were both banjaxed. The nips in there...' He sniffed. 'Are you allowed to call them nips these days?'

'Let's settle for shots, Jonty.'

'Right. Shot of voddy for one fifty. That's insane, right? And we had a lot of them. A skinful.'

'How long had you been drinking together?'

'Me and a pal bumped into her at the Highland Games.'

'This pal got a name?'

'Scott Horsburgh. Went to school together. Joined the cops together, actually. He even joined up. Left after a few years, mind. Works as a joiner now. Anyway, we bumped into Becky and her pals in the park. They had a bucket of alcopops and some wine. We had some beer. Wasn't just her, though, bumped into a few other pals from school too. Pretty weird, man.'

'Name any names?'

'Eh. Sam Porteous. Sam Stoddart. Sam Scobie. Chantelle Grieve. Dani Keddie. Danny Melrose. Sam Pringle. And the other Sam Pringle, the lassie. Not related. Dave Geddes. His brother wasn't there, mind. Eh, oh aye. Becky. And Iain Hogg.'

Marshall wanted to drill into the 'oh aye' but this was Taylor's interview, not his.

Taylor was nodding along with the names, writing them all down. 'You speak to any of them?'

'All of them, aye.'

'What about?'

'Bits and bobs. Know how it is.'

'Know how it is with my pals. What were you talking about? The government? Rangers' prospects in the Premiership this season? The works of Kurt Vonnegut? The notion of Cartesian duality?'

'Cartesian *what*?'

'Never mind. What did you talk about?'

'Catching up, eh? What we've been up to. What other pals are doing. What we're all up to now. Sam Scobie's working at Microsoft down near Reading. Wee Danny's a dentist. Chantelle's working at this payments start-up in London. Least I think that's what she said. Last time anyone saw Wee Titch, who just seems to have disappeared.'

'Wee Titch?'

'Aye. His brother works in the Steps. Even he's not seen him.'

'What were you saying to Iain Hogg?'

Jonty narrowed his eyes at them. 'Why are you so interested in him?'

'What were you talking to him about?'

'Nothing much, to be honest. Talking shite. He was there with a group of lads a few years younger than us. Not so much acting the big man as clowning around, like he does. Slurring his words at three o'clock, man. Shouldn't have even been let into the boozer, but Big Titch vouched for him. So obvious when he got chucked out.'

'What happened?'

'Arsehole had been making a nuisance of himself with the lassies, I think. Spewed his ringer everywhere, man.'

'Which lassies would these be?'

'Well, Becky. I mean, she wants to be called Rebecca now, so I'd better respect that, eh? Especially if I want to be called Jonty.'

'Gather you left with her?'

'That's not what happened. We left at the same time, sure, but we went separate ways. She lived down by all the posh houses. I don't.'

'So you let a woman walk home on her own?'

Jonty shrugged. 'I asked, but she didn't want me to come with her.'

'Sure about that?'

Jonty stood up tall. 'Come on, lads, level with me here – what's this about?'

'Her body was discovered this morning.'

Those massive eyes bulged even larger. 'What the *fuck*?'

'We believe she was murdered. So how about you repeat your story, but this time you tell us the truth, eh?'

'I've told you the truth, man. Been telling you it.'

'Thing is, Jonty, if we were to find evidence of your presence near to where her body was...'

Jonty wiped a thick bead of sweat away from his forehead.

'DI Taylor's not winding you up, son.' Marshall folded his arms – time to take over for a bit. 'We've got several CSIs searching for forensic traces on Becky's body and near to where she was found. If any of those belong to you...'

Jonty started sifting through some paint charts, like he was looking for the perfect shade for his bathroom. 'Look, if you want the truth, I'm giving you it...'

'But not all of it. Right?'

Jonty stayed quiet.

'What DI Taylor didn't mention was my role here. He's a common or garden murder cop, but I'm a different flavour altogether. I'm here to investigate if there any connections between Becky's death and another two under superficially similar circumstances.'

Jonty blinked hard a few times. 'You think a *serial killer* did this?'

'I hope not. But I'm seeing if one was. And if you were to be that serial killer.'

'I'm not a serial killer!'

Gary Hislop limped through. 'Everything okay, Jonty?'

'Aye, sir. Just helping the police with a murder investigation.'

Hislop shot daggers at them. 'Who's died?'

'Becky Yellowlees.'

'Never heard of her.' Hislop shot some more of those daggers at Marshall. 'He's on the clock, so if you need to ask him more, can you do it after four?'

'Sure. We won't be much longer.'

Hislop shut his eyes, then limped away.

Marshall glowered at Jonty.

He'd got the message, though. 'Okay, so me and Becky left at the same time, like I said. And I didn't walk her home, but I did walk with her. We went to Neidpath Tunnel.'

There it was.

The truth.

'Thank you for your honesty, Jonty. A lot of people would just double down and keep lying to us.' Marshall stared hard at him, hoping he would maintain that. 'Why did you go there?'

'Her choice.'

'Did she say why?'

'Weird day, man. Weird for both of us. Seeing all these people from school. People I hadn't seen in *years*, all back home. Like Becky herself. Meant a lot of reminiscing. Dave Geddes started talking about that tunnel, about how we used to drink and smoke dope there as kids.'

That supported Hogg's Onion Man story...

'Dave's got a twin brother, who used to score dope for us.' Jonty narrowed his gaze. 'This isn't an admission of anything.'

'No, of course not. Lots of people like a smoke. It's okay. So you and Becky walked to the tunnel?'

'Right. Out past where the Highland Games had been, then across the bridge and through the woods. Thought we'd got a bit lost, man, but nope. There we were. Right at the tunnel. Man, I was so pissed, I was lucky I'd got there without tripping up.'

'So what did you do there?'

'Didn't smoke anything, if that's what you're asking.'

'Did you drink?'

'Becky wanted some more. Asked if I knew any bars that'd still be open. Had to point out she wasn't in Glasgow anymore. Peebles at one in the morning, man. We were bloody lucky the Steps had stayed open so late. So, no we didn't have anything with us. And we kissed.'

'That the first time?'

'Aye, man. Fancied her at school, but she didn't seem into me, like. And she was seeing that arsehole, wasn't she?'

'Who?'

'Iain Hogg.'

'Did you go into the tunnel?'

'Aye. Torches on our phone. Went inside. That place is dark as hell in the daytime. This was at night, man! Pitch black in there. She was really up for it, like. Hands everywhere. Kissing and... Thing is, I felt a bit weird about it.'

'Weird how?'

'I'd heard this sound, which totally freaked me out.'

'What kind of sound are we talking?'

'Like a low moaning.'

'You mean, an animal?'

'Not sure, man. Weirded me the hell out. So I left.'

'You left her on her own?'

'Becky wouldn't come with me. Totally refused to. Said she couldn't hear anything, but I heard it again, coming from deeper in the tunnel. And I had to leave, man. Couldn't stay there.'

Taylor rested his hands on the countertop. 'We found her body in that tunnel.'

Jonty ran a hand down his face. 'Fuck.'

'You left her on her own there, Jonty, and she's been killed.' Taylor paused. 'Did you kill her, Jonty?'

'Of course not!'

'Trouble is, we've got people who saw you leaving together, but we don't have anyone who saw you leave the tunnel.'

'We weren't on our own.'

'Eh?'

'Someone else was there.'

'This moaning sound?'

'I'm not talking about that. Someone was watching us.'

'I thought it was just you two.'

Jonty looked right at Marshall. 'I think it was Iain Hogg.'

'What do you mean?'

'He'd been letching onto Becky in the Steps. The barman told him off, right? Then he got chucked out for spewing into the urinal. Must've hung around and followed us so he could spy on us. You know what people are like when they're that pished, right?'

Taylor shook his head, then looked over at Marshall. 'Sounds like nonsense to me.'

'I'm not so sure about that.' Marshall smiled at Jonty. 'How sure are you it was him?'

'Pretty sure.'

'Can you identify any—'

'I saw a flash of orange in the woods outside the tunnel. Hoggy had been wearing an orange flight jacket. It must've been him.'

7

Taylor pulled up in the car park, next to Marshall's car. 'What's the mileage like on that thing?'

'Better than you'd expect.' Marshall opened the door but didn't step out. 'Why, do you want to buy it?'

'Not in the market for a new motor.'

'But if you were?'

'Then we could have a discussion.' Taylor killed the pool car's engine, then clapped his hands together. 'Okay, Roberto, that's been a decent help from you, have to say. I'll let you bugger off back to Castle Grayskull.'

Marshall smirked. 'Castle Grayskull?'

'Aye. It's what we call Gartcosh. Where Skeletor lives.'

'In the *Masters of the Universe* cartoon?'

'Aye. Are you too young to remember it?'

'No, I do. Trouble is, Cal, He-Man was the one who lived in Castle Grayskull, not Skeletor.'

'You're talking shite, Rob!'

'I'm not. Skeletor lived in Snake Mountain.'

'Nonsense! It's got a bloody skull in the name!'

'I'm not having this argument, Cal. Check on your phone.'

'I'm not going to do that.' Taylor rubbed at his forehead. 'My point stands, though – you get on back up the road.'

'I'll need to speak to DCS Po—'

'She Who Cannot Be Named?' Taylor grinned. 'You almost said her name out loud, Rob. What's wrong with you?'

'Don't call her that. She doesn't like it.' Marshall needed to change her contact on his phone.

'Nobody likes their nickname, Dr Donkey, do they?'

Marshall tried to keep calm as he looked across the car park. Despite it being a murder case, a whole load of bugger all was going on. Cops just standing around and chatting rather than doing their actual jobs. 'Is Gashkori about?'

'Fine, Rob. I get it. You want to go over my head. Speak to him and *he* can tell you to bugger off back to Skeletor's lair, which is Castle Grayskull.'

'Snake Mountain.' Marshall got out and looked across the car park.

Perfect timing – Graeme Veitch and Liam Warner were walking Hogg over to a squad car. They stopped, but struggled to get him in the back. And not because he was refusing – they couldn't get the door open.

Marshall walked over and nodded at them both. 'We've got this, lads.'

Warner had a lump of something that looked like hummus around his lips. 'We'll be back in five minutes.' He strolled off and Veitch followed.

Marshall watched them go.

He caught Taylor's frosty look – this wasn't part of his plan, which was for Marshall to talk to the boss then get sent packing, not to interfere with his questioning.

Marshall ignored him and smiled at Hogg. 'Thanks for your honesty earlier, Iain. It's greatly appreciated.'

Hogg's forehead creased. 'No worries, mate.'

'Got a few more questions to ask, if it's all the same?'

Hogg reached his left hand up to tug at his ear. 'Fire away, pal.'

'We gather you and Becky had some difficult words in the pub last night.'

Hogg ran a hand through his hair. 'Can't deny it, much as I want to.' He locked eyes with Marshall. 'We used to be an item, you know?' He stared into space, lost to some reminiscence. Seemed to be the peak of his life, with everything after a descent to this point. Whether he'd murdered her... Well... 'That fanny, Jonny Sandison, kept going on about it. Prick wants everyone to call him Jonty now. Kept bringing it up. I mean, when you see people you haven't seen since school, the past is the main topic, right? But he wouldn't let it lie, for some stupid reason. Just kept needling us both about it. *Total* arsehole.'

'He was talking about how you were an item?'

'An item?' Hogg looked at Taylor, then at Marshall. 'You don't know, do you?'

'Sorry, I'm not following.'

Hogg sighed. 'You heard of Beltane?'

'Of course. The Common Riding in Peebles.'

'Aye, like you get anywhere else in the Borders. Everyone's out for the day, drinking and laughing and all that. But it means a bit more to the town than the others do to theirs, alright? There's a bit more *stuff* around it.'

'Stuff?'

'You know. Stuff.'

Taylor grinned. 'I don't, Iain. Might help if you explain it to us.'

Hogg scratched at the stubble on his chin. 'You have a Beltane Queen, right? A young lassie at school. Gala has the Braw Lad and Selkirk has... Can't remember what theirs is, but it's just a laddie. In Peebles, the day is all about her, right? But you also have a Cornet and a Cornet's Lass.'

'The Cornet's an honorary title, right?'

'It is and it isn't. The Cornet's also like the ambassador for the town across the whole of the Borders. Attends the other Common Ridings. I mean, in 1906 or 1976, you can see the point. But now?' Hogg rolled his shoulders. 'I was the Beltane Cornet in 2017. Becky was the Cornet's Lass.'

So a very solid connection between them...

'That was when you were an item, right?'

'Becky was my girlfriend, sure. Doesn't always work out like that, though. Year before us, it was a brother and his sister. Year after, same. But we were both eighteen. Neither of us even lived in the town anymore. Becky was at Strathclyde Uni in Glasgow and I was at Napier in Edinburgh.'

'So you were in a long-distance relationship?'

'Less than an hour on the train or the bus, but aye... We saw each other most weekends.' Hogg shifted his gaze between them. 'You boys went to uni?'

Marshall nodded. 'Durham.'

Taylor shook his head. 'Too thick for it.'

'Okay, but *you* know how it is, right?' Hogg was staring at Marshall with a furious intensity. 'Student life happens during the week. Big piss-up on a Wednesday night, but a lot of people go home for the weekend. Maybe got a job, or just seeing pals back home. Me and Becky spent that time together, most weeks. Until it sort of started slowing down... And I was the one going through every week. Then it became every other week, then...'

'What was Becky studying?'

'Pharmacology.'

'And you?'

'Computer science. I dropped out at the end of second year. Failed the exams, didn't I? Failed the resits too, so I came back home and...' He looked across the car park towards Neidpath Castle and Peebles beyond it. 'Here I am. A Peebles lad again, working in Sainsbos.'

'So you were Cornet when you were a student?'
'Right.'
'Was that when she broke up with you?'
Hogg stared at him, tears forming in his eyes. 'She said it wasn't working. Think she'd met someone in Glasgow, like, but she didn't say.'
'Did you ever have any confirmation of that?'
'No. She stopped replying to my texts immediately. Sometimes she'd go, like, an hour. Leaving me on read, man. *So* rude.'
'What do you mean by that?'
Hogg looked at him like he'd lost his mind. 'She'd read the message but didn't reply.'
Marshall felt the generation gap slap him in the face right there. Relationships falling between the cracks of data items displayed on a phone screen. 'Must've been a shock to see her yesterday, then?'
'Tell me about it, man. But it was good, too. Becky was on top form. Kind of felt like we hadn't split up, you know?'
'Is that why you were behaving inappropriately with her?'
'Eh?'
'We've got eyewitness reports from the Steps last night, stating you'd—'
'Man...'
'You were warned off her, weren't you?'
'Right.' Hogg leaned back against Marshall's car. 'Wait, you think *I* killed her?'
Marshall looked over at Taylor. 'I'm merely consulting.'
Taylor brushed past, muttering, 'And asking all the bloody questions.' He stood between them. 'We're keeping an open mind on all aspects of the case, sir.'
'Do you know that I didn't leave with her?'
'We do. Heard you got chucked out. Fell asleep in a urinal trough. Threw up on a barman.'

'Right. Spoke to Big Titch about that. He accepted my apology.'

Taylor stepped closer to him, so he was almost invading his body space. 'I want to know precisely what you remember doing last night.'

Hogg wrapped his hands together. 'See when I spoke to you earlier, all that shite about the parsnip man?'

'The Onion Man.'

'Right. I can't remember getting home. Woke up in my bed.'

Taylor got right in his face. 'That's complete bollocks, Iain. You waited around, didn't you?'

'No!'

'You followed her and Jonty Sandison down to the tunnel, didn't you?'

'Of course I didn't. I'm not a psycho!'

'Come on, Iain. You were spotted there.'

Hogg stared up at the blue sky, then shut his eyes. A man weighing up the cost of the truth. Or the price of a lie. 'That's right.' He looked over at Marshall. 'I just remembered. I followed them. It's all just snatches and fragments. Don't know what got into me. But I did. They went to the tunnel, went inside. And Jonty fucking Sandison was in there with her, kissing her. But he got weirded out and he left.'

'Weirded out by you being there?'

'Nope. He didn't see me. Not that I knew, anyway. But he cleared off, so I approached her, asked if she was okay.'

Marshall caught a flare of rage in Taylor's eyes, but shot him a glare to keep quiet.

'And Becky was alright with me being there. Said it was just like old times. We'd had some angry words on the dance floor, sure, but she... she apologised, said she shouldn't have said what she did.'

'What did she say?'

Hogg shrugged it off. 'We just sat there, chucking stones at the wall like we used to. Had a good chat about stuff. Regrets. All that stuff we went through. Felt like old times, man. Then she kissed me. She suggested we... uh, have sex.'

'*She* did?'

'Right. She didn't want to go to her mum's and I live with my wife.'

'You're married?'

'Right.' Hogg tugged at his hair. 'Erin's away for a long weekend in Palma. Majorca, you know? Her pal Eilidh's hen night. But she'd know if I took her back home. Neighbours would spot Becky leaving, right? And we've got one of those video doorbells...'

No thought spared to the guilt of the crime, just entirely around how he could get away with it without getting caught.

Taylor chuckled. 'Naughty boy.'

'Hardly.'

'Come on, Iain. You making the beast with two backs with your ex-girlfriend is the height of naught—'

'We didn't have sex.'

'Sure.' Taylor laughed. 'Be very careful with your next words, son, because we'll be performing a post-mortem on her tomorrow. We'll find out whether she'd had sex and if there were any indications the sex was consensual, or otherwise.'

'We didn't, man. Last thing I wanted to do was have sex. I was drunk, cold and scared. Plus, I'd been sick. And cracked my bonce off the trough in the bogs. Passed out. Didn't feel very sexy.'

'Sexy enough for her to allegedly kiss you, though.'

'I swear.'

Taylor folded his arms, smiling. 'Come on, Iain, your ex offering you it on a plate... That's a tale as old as time.'

'We'd been an item, sure, but that was a long time ago. If we were to get back into anything, I'd want it to be when we were both sober. To chat it all through, make sure it was going to be okay. A lot went on between us and I wanted it all squared away. And I didn't want just a fling. I'm married, for crying out loud. Happily. She trusts me, so the last thing I'd do is jeopardise that.'

'But?'

'But Becky... She was the love of my life. I don't feel the same way about Erin as I did about her.'

'What did you do, then?'

'I left. Went home... to have a wank.'

'To have a wank?'

'Right. I mean... The whole thing was totally messed up. But that was what I did.'

'So you left Becky there alone. In a dark tunnel. In the middle of the night.'

'I tried persuading her to leave. Told her I'd walk her back to her mum's, but she didn't want to. Just told me to go after I'd spurned her. She slapped me. So fuck it, of course I went.'

'Did you see anyone there?'

'No.' Hogg's eyes twitched. 'Not really.'

'What do you mean?'

'I heard something.'

'What kind of thing?'

'This low moaning. Becky said she didn't hear it, but...'

'Iain, you know you're in deep trouble here. You've admitted to being the last person to see Becky alive.'

'Mate, someone was there. With us. And it wasn't Jonty.'

'So, you're using the traditional "a big boy did it and ran away" defence?' Taylor laughed, his cold eyes focusing on Marshall. 'Seen that work so many times, Rob. You must've done too?'

Marshall didn't join in with the ribbing. 'Iain, DI Taylor's correct. This is serious, okay? Deadly serious.'

Hogg chewed at the nails on his left hand. 'I was attacked just outside the tunnel.'

The silence lingered for a few seconds until Taylor broke it with a crack of laughter. 'You were attacked?'

'I was!'

'Was it Jonty?'

'No.' Hogg shook his head. 'And I don't want this to sound weird, but I think it was the devil...'

Now Marshall couldn't help but laugh. 'The devil. Right.'

'Aye. Jumped on me.' Hogg held up his hands. 'See how I've got blood under the nails? That was from fighting off Satan.'

Marshall grabbed his wrists and checked them. The other hand showed the same, except for the thumbnail. He'd clearly been in a fight and clawed at someone's flesh.

Whether defensively or offensively, Marshall didn't know.

He locked eyes with Taylor. 'We need to get this checked for DNA.'

Hogg stared at Marshall. 'So now you believe me?'

'Not in the slightest.' Taylor snapped a handcuff onto his wrists. 'Iain Hogg, I'm arresting you for the murder of Rebecca Yellowlees.'

8

Taylor slammed the pool car's back door and sucked in a deep breath. Liam Warner sat next to Hogg on the back seat, chatting away to Hogg like they were old mates on their way to the football. Hogg stared at the blue gloves covering his hands and protecting the evidence.

'Right, we're done here.' Taylor patted Marshall on the arm. 'I'll follow them over to Gala to process Hogg. Get someone to run that DNA from under his nails.' He flashed a wide grin. 'We'll get him charged by teatime.'

Marshall stared hard at him. 'I don't believe he killed her.'

A frown flickered across Taylor's forehead. 'Come on, Rob. Of course he did. He's practically admitted to it.'

'Practically? Or actually?'

Taylor rested his hands on his hips. 'Only downside to our conviction is, because of you being so eager to prove your worth to She Who Cannot Be Named, we had this chat with him in a baking hot car park, rather than in an interview room, under oath. Because you know Gashkori wouldn't let you in one, don't you?'

'I don't—'

'Rob. We *know* he's done it.'

'We don't *know* anything, Cal. He's admitted he was there but that's all. He's got a solid motivation, sure, but there's no smoking gun here. Not that I can see. Besides, he claims he was attacked.'

Taylor shook his head. 'More likely he attacked her.'

'We didn't find any scratches on her, right?'

Taylor looked away. 'Maybe he got into a fight with Sandison.'

'Again, didn't see any scratch marks on him and he was wearing a T-shirt, so you'd expect to.'

Taylor looked hard at him, with mirth in his eyes. 'So you're saying Hogg got into a fight with *Satan*?'

'Of course I'm not. I'm just saying be careful what you tell Gashkori. This isn't an open-and-shut case, so don't present it as one.'

The mirth only grew in Taylor's eyes. 'Speaking of what we tell our bosses, what are you going to say to She Who Cannot Be Named?'

'Do you mean, am I going to grass on you for not knowing where He-Man lives?'

'No.' Taylor gritted his teeth. 'I mean, is this connected to the other two cases in Glasgow and Edinburgh?'

'I don't see a link yet, other than they all happened in disused train tunnels. Which seems to be a bit of a stretch.'

'Agreed. So, you're going to clear it and clear off?'

'I don't just show up and nod my head a few times. If that was the case, Cal, you could do it.' Marshall got a flicker of enjoyment from Taylor's wince. 'I'll have to parse the victimology and the method of death, including the presence or absence of a sexual factor.'

'Rob, absence of evidence is not evidence of absence.'

'You can say those words, but what do you actually mean by them?'

'I mean, do you think he shagged her?'

'The post-mortem will tell us. And presumably they'll be analysing those used condoms in there.'

Taylor brushed a hand down his arm. 'Okay. Look, thank you for getting Hogg to open up. It was a big help. But I'll ask you one last time, okay? Is this connected to your work?'

Marshall could lie, but that'd be just to spite Taylor or his boss. And it'd likely impede justice. So he shook his head. 'No, Cal. This doesn't look like it is.'

'Cool. Thanks again. And as a courtesy, I'll let you know how it goes with him. Be seeing you.' Taylor got into the driver's seat of his pool car.

The squad car drove off and that was that, then.

Marshall walked over to his car and had to shuffle sideways to the door because Taylor had parked too close to his. He got in and called Kirsten.

Taylor didn't follow the car. Just sat in his, phone to his ear. Probably grassing on Marshall.

As much as he could be an arse with Taylor, this wasn't his case. He had to keep remembering that.

Just a coincidence they happened in tunnels. That's all it was.

Kirsten answered – sounded like she was in a room full of people talking and laughing. 'Hiya, sweetheart. You okay?'

Marshall tried to cover his sigh but it still came out. 'Aye, just finished up now.'

'Did you get a result?'

'Maybe, but not the one I wanted. Just heading off now. Where shall I pick you up?'

'Me and Jen are having a cup of tea in Jack's in Melrose.'

'Excellent, I'll see you there.'

'Rob. There's…' She exhaled down the line. 'Not sure how to

say this... After you left, because I wasn't drinking, Grumpy joked I was pregnant. Your dad found it hilarious. It made me want to leave rather than explain to them what was going on.'

'Oh, Christ. I'm sorry about that.'

'It's not your fault.'

'Hang on, you ordered a malbec, didn't you?'

'I didn't touch it.'

'Right. And Grumpy spotted that.'

'Right.'

'Jesus, my family...'

'They're not all bad. Jen was great. Always is.'

'Brilliant. Listen, I'll square that off with my father.'

'You don't have to. Remember, this is my body, right?'

'Sure.' Marshall felt like he'd stepped into a minefield. 'I'll just check he doesn't go blabbing to—'

'Oh, hang on, Rob. I've got another call coming through.'

'I'll see you soon. Next stop, Melrose.' Marshall ended the call and put the key in the ignition.

A car pulled in next to him. He looked over and locked eyes with DCI Ryan Gashkori. Talking to someone on the phone. Didn't take an expert to guess who that might be. He looked as tired and jaded as Marshall felt. His shaved head had grown out so his hair was like a tennis ball a dog had been gnawing at.

This wasn't Marshall's case.

He ignored his own mantra and got out of the car.

Just as Gashkori joined him. 'Afternoon, Inspector. Thought you were on your way home?'

'That's right, sir.' Marshall gave him the courtesy of a nod. 'Just finished up here.'

'So I take it we're in the clear?'

'Hardly. All I've achieved is managing to get you a suspect who doesn't seem to fit the pattern for my crimes.'

'The words "doesn't seem to" are making me a bit twitchy here.'

'Why?'

'Well, I'm devoting time and resources to solving a murder here. If this is a serial case, I'll lose that to Edinburgh or Glasgow.'

'Why's that a problem?'

'Marshall. Is it part of your terms of reference or not?'

'Trouble with my role is I don't deal with certainties, sir, just probabilities.'

'This nonsense again. Brave way of covering your arse, eh?' Gashkori smirked. 'You're not trying to claim this case, are you?'

'Not mine to claim, anyway. It's been made clear to me a number of times how my role is to consult and not to investigate. If this is part of a serial murder case, I'll do the same to the DCI on that.'

'Right, good stuff.' Gashkori clapped his shoulder. 'Say hi to Kirsten for me.'

'Ryan!' An old guy in his seventies ambled towards them. Not a youthful seventies, capable of doing tai chi in the park every week. No, this guy looked like he'd lived through a world war or two. And moved like it. 'I need a word.'

'Sure.' Gashkori's phone blasted out. He checked the display. 'Crap. Sorry, Martin. Just be a sec.' He turned away from them and answered his phone.

'Martin Gill.' The old guy thrust out a hand to Marshall. 'Pleasure to meet you. Eh, didn't catch your name?'

'DI Rob Marshall.'

'In that case, the pleasure's all mine.' Gill waved a hand around them. 'I own all this land, you know? Not the castle, that's owned by the Earl of Wemyss. But everything down towards Ettrick. It might be due south of here, but it's a bugger to drive between because of the southern uplands. Those hills are poor for crops but perfect for sheep, though. Forty thousand of the buggers roam my land.'

Marshall hadn't met a farmer who operated on a serious

scale who didn't brag about how much they owned straight away. Probably went with the territory when chatting to others in their game, so they could understand where they both sat in the feudal hierarchy. 'That's a hell of a lot of land.'

'Not mine, mind.'

'But you said—'

'No, I mean yes, it is mine. But it's been in the family for generations. I'm merely the custodian.'

Ah, the old 'just a custodian, me' line – usually worked well with inheritance tax lawyers...

'Do you own the tunnel?'

'Indeed I do. Used to be owned by various companies. Symington, Biggar and Broughton Railway. Caledonian. London, Midland and Scottish. Then it was all taken into public ownership as part of British Rail.' Gill's snarl betrayed his disgust at the concept of state ownership. 'Not that it was ever much of a going concern. But after Beeching shut a lot of supposedly rotten train lines down in the sixties, the tunnel came back into our ownership. I've voted Tory all my life, but that just... The railways are a natural treasure, but they decimated them in pursuit of the motor car.'

'I imagine the tunnel must be a bugger to maintain.'

'Isn't it just...' Gill shook his head. 'We get kids in there all the time. Drinking and whatnot.'

'But not adults?'

'Oh, yes. During the day. Walkers and cyclists. At least they treat the place with respect.'

Marshall looked around the place. 'Don't suppose you have any security cameras?'

'What would be the point? I don't keep any livestock or plant in there. And, to be honest with you, I don't actually mind them being in there.' A dark look settled on Gill's face. 'Ryan wouldn't confirm it, but is it true it's Rebecca Yellowlees?'

Marshall had a choice to make. Either would probably piss

off Gashkori so, rather than toe the party line, he went with a nod. 'I'm afraid so, yes.'

'I knew her. Becky, they all call her. Good girl. Cornet's Lass a few years back, of course. Which is pretty ironic.'

Marshall caught a glare from Gashkori, still talking on his phone, but ignored it. 'Why would that be ironic?'

'Well, her parents live in the Beltane Inn. I mean, it's just her mother there now. Kath's a good woman. Been through a lot. Hell of a lot. Darren was a good man, God rest his soul.' Gill looked around at Marshall. 'And she's now about to go through even worse, isn't she?'

Gashkori re-joined them, putting his phone away. 'Sorry, Martin. You mind giving me a second here?'

'By all means. It's not a pressing matter, anyway.'

'Of course.' Gashkori took Marshall aside, leading him around the back of his pool car. 'Cal said you'd left?'

'I had, but then you showed up and I wondered if you'd want a word with me.'

'I'll be frank, Rob. I'd rather dip my balls in acid than have a word with you. I don't want you here, so can you kindly bugger off?'

'I was in the process of buggering off, sir.'

'And yet you're quizzing Martin Gill there?'

Marshall looked around but Gill had walked off somewhere, no doubt away to brag about the number of sheep he owned to someone else. 'He was the one doing the quizzing.'

'Right, sure he was.' Gashkori rubbed at his nose. 'Cal Taylor said you disagreed with him arresting this Hogg lad?'

'I didn't say that.'

'What did you say, then?'

'I think it's premature. Cal's getting uniform to take Hogg over to Gala in order to obtain the DNA from his fingernails. That's a good idea and might prove that he was involved.'

Gashkori nodded. 'Must be the victim's.'

'Is that what Cal told you?'

Gashkori narrowed his eyes. 'You don't think it is?'

'It is hers in Cal's view, which is why he's arrested Hogg.' Marshall left a long pause. 'Trouble is, sir, it's going to look bad if that DNA isn't the victim's. And there were no signs that she'd been scratched, nowhere near enough to get that amount of flesh under his nails.'

'So you think Hogg's telling the truth?'

'Could be. But that kind of thing only tends to happen with defensive marks, where someone is fighting off an attacker. If we'd found DNA under Rebecca's fingernail, then sure I'd buy it. But the evidence we have seems to be more consistent with Hogg's story.'

Gashkori looked up at the sky for a few seconds. 'Rob. I've only spoken to you for five minutes and you've already pissed me right off.'

'Sorry, sir. Nature of the beast when you're asked to play devil's advocate.'

'I sense a but here?'

'Just that I'm used to consulting with DCIs and working with them as an add-on to an investigation, just like this one. But they usually let me help out and make it a collaborative thing, whereas you—'

'You're saying I don't collaborate?'

'No, sir. Not at all. I've worked with DI Taylor for a few hours and it's been productive, but now you're getting rid of me. Again.'

'I got rid of you fair and square, Rob, because your particular skills are better suited to what the boss wants to do strategically, not as some kind of basic detective. So don't try and make out like I'm being petty here.'

'You insisted you don't need me.'

'You're right there. I didn't need you or your hocus pocus hours ago and now we have a suspect, we definitely don't have a use for you. This is a basic case, as far as I can tell and as far as anyone can show me. A love triangle gone wrong.'

Marshall didn't know what to say to that, so did the only thing he could – stay quiet.

'And that's your problem, Rob. When you have a hammer, everything looks like a nail. When you only work on supposed serial cases, everything looks like a serial case. And, in my view, you're trying to hammer in a screw because it's the only tool you have to hand. Actually, maybe you're trying to screw in a nail. Either way, this isn't a case for you.'

'I've been ordered to make sure it's not related to the other two cases.'

'Oh aye, the one in Edinburgh... The case of the killer lamppost.' Gashkori laughed. 'Actually, there could be a whole gang of lampposts hunting people, eh? See them practically everywhere these days. I'll get the lads to bring in all the local lampposts for questioning.'

Someone cleared their throat behind them.

DCS Potter stood there, eyes narrowed. 'Afternoon, Ryan.'

9

'Ma'am.' Gashkori plastered on a smile. 'Didn't see you there.'

Potter returned the smile with interest. Tight bob, dressed for Sunday lunch rather than in her usual uniform. 'No, Ryan, of course you didn't. And that's why you felt it okay to belittle an officer I've explicitly asked to consult on a case for me. You know very well I take that as though someone was trying to snub *me* in this investigation.'

Gashkori's smile faded. A bead of sweat slid down his temple. 'How long have you been listening to us?'

'Long enough to know you're trying to wriggle out of doing a proper job. Yet. Again.'

'Miranda, that's not what I'm doing at all.'

'Sounded very much like it, Ryan. Need I remind you that you are a DCI. As DCS, and therefore two ranks higher, you are being insubordinate.'

Gashkori gasped. 'We've got a simple case here, that's all.'

'Of course you have.' Potter smiled at Marshall. 'Rob, have you got a minute?'

'Sure.' Marshall followed her across the car park, but knew

enough to listen and not to offer anything here. She had her agenda and Gashkori had his. 'What's up?'

'I didn't hear much of that, to be honest with you, but I could tell he was being a right pilchard to you.'

'I've received worse, ma'am. Much worse.'

'I've told you before, Rob. Call me Miranda.'

'Okay. I'll try, but it's still awkward to be that familiar more than one rank upwards.'

Potter pursed her lips. 'It's somewhat unfortunate for Ryan that I just happened to be in the area, otherwise he could bully away with impunity...' She thumbed over her shoulder along the direction of the Tweed. 'I was supposed to be meeting your old man for a coffee in Melrose.'

'You're meeting Bob Milne?'

'Unless you've got another father?'

'Miranda, after the stuff I've been through, it wouldn't surprise me.'

She laughed. 'I've been asked to see if I can persuade him not to retire.'

'Just as well he told me, then.'

'Right.' She smacked her forehead. 'Sorry. I hadn't thought of that. I'm just doing a favour for the head of Standards. He highly rates Bob and knows we go back a long way.'

'Ma'am, I have no way of influencing him, if that's what—'

'No. I gather your history with him is somewhat... colourful.'

'That's one way of putting it. I'm the last person he'd listen to. Actually, my sister would be the last, but I'd be second-last. And neither of us holds any sway with the old bugger. Like I said, he just informed us he's leaving soon. He seemed pretty determined to go out.'

'So I gather. Facing an uphill battle, am I not?' Potter nodded slowly in response to her own question. 'Okay, Rob. I need your honest opinion. Do we have any interest in this case?'

'To be honest, ma – iranda, I don't know what to think. There's tons of data being collated here, but I haven't had the time to analyse much of it.'

'I gather you've spoken to a few people, right?'

'Right. I helped identify a suspect.'

'Interesting choice of words there. Not *the* suspect?'

'Well, yes. But I don't believe he killed her. Or I don't think we have sufficient evidence to know he did.'

'So he's not a good fit?'

Marshall looked around the car park, fizzing with activity – officers of all stripes milling around. 'I honestly don't know. Maybe Gashkori's right. Maybe I'm too oblique for Police Scotland.'

'God, no. You're an ideal investigator, Rob. You don't chase stats.' Potter laughed. 'In fact, you *use* statistics. You use data to inform your work. Either for BSU or before. But either way, you're here at *my* instruction and *I* don't want this investigation to ignore any possibilities because we're afraid to look or because we're too focused on a particular solution.'

'Of course.' Marshall reached back to scratch at his neck – felt like something had bitten him, but there was nothing there. 'Speaking of statistics and probability, I'd say it's about fifty-five to sixty percent likely they've got the right guy.'

She took her time assessing that. 'That's not very solid, is it?'

'No. I can see how he's got a plausible motive, and it's enough for an arrest. We're talking the civil standard of proof based on the balance of probabilities. Trouble is, as you know, the criminal standard is about eighty to ninety percent.'

'Beyond a reasonable doubt, eh?'

'Or even an unreasonable one.'

'So, what's the doubt in your mind, reasonable or unreasonable?'

'A few things don't add up for me. Like I say, I need to crunch some data with Hardeep tomorrow, then cross-reference a few things.'

'You mean with those two cases in Edinburgh and Glasgow?'

'Starting with those, yes.'

'You think they could be connected because someone's killed someone in a tunnel?'

'Isn't that the reason I'm here?'

'A large part, aye.'

'But the rest of it?'

'Making sure Ryan is doing his job.' She looked across the car park at where Gashkori was holding court with a few detectives, then she focused on Marshall again. 'I'm asking you, Rob, am I going to look daft here?'

'The problem with this stuff, Miranda, is they could be connected, but it could all just be a coincidence.'

'But why do they all have tunnels?'

'It might seem trivial to us, but if we assume these cases are all connected for a second, then you start to see possibilities. For example, someone might see train tunnels as important in some way for any number of reasons. Like they're still angry with the Beeching report in the sixties for shutting them all down. Or they're angry because people take the train instead of driving their car. Or, I don't know, they've just heard about all these old tunnels across Scotland and think that'd be a good place to kill someone. And if it is a serial killer, then we've got...' Marshall ran out of mileage on that thought, so he had to change direction. 'If someone kills *once*, there's a good chance we've got a rational killer. Like the assumption Ryan's team are making here. An ex-boyfriend sees her flirting with someone else, then leaving the pub with that someone else. So he follows them to the tunnel, where he kills her. And let's face it, disused tunnels are dark places far away from the public eye. The bottom line is they're just *really* good places to commit murder.'

Potter processed it slowly. 'So you buy it?'

'I can see why *they*'ve bought it, for sure. But if someone has killed three times, then they're psychopathic in some specific way.'

'So you're saying they could be connected?'

'They might be. At the moment, I just don't know. But if you put pressure on me to say either way, I'd suggest it's more likely to connect to the Glasgow case than the Edinburgh one.'

'Can you say why?'

'The Glasgow one was very obviously a murder. Edinburgh was deemed an accident.'

'Okay, Rob. That's good enough for me so far. I'm officially ordering you to work this case and to eliminate the possibility they're not connected to your other work.'

'What about our presentation for Wednesday?'

'Already handled.' She tapped at her temple. 'And I'll deal with Ryan. This is the kind of case we need to get Andrea Elliot off the bench for and make her do some work for a change...'

10

'You just can't help yourself, can you?' Taylor was doing that kind of angry driving Marshall hadn't seen since his dad had left home a long time ago. An explosion of rage at something other than the here and now that was targeted at Marshall.

Or maybe it was just about the here and now. And targeted right at Marshall for a good reason.

He barely slowed for the 20 sign into Peebles, then seemed to catch himself and behave like an adult.

Marshall felt his blood rushing up into his throat, his neck, up his back. He sat back and folded his arms. Anything he could do to get calm and keep calm. 'What exactly have I done, Cal?'

'Don't call me that. It's Callum to you. Cal is for my mates.'

Some people just didn't leave the playground, did they?

Marshall tried to breathe slowly. 'You're annoyed with me for insisting we do due diligence on a murder?'

'It's not just that, Rob. It's—'

'Rob's for my mates.'

Taylor laughed at that. The ice seemed to crack a little.

'Sorry. It's just... I was driving through Innerleithen, following the car with Hogg in the back, then I get the call to come back and look after you. It's frustrating. We've got a suspect in custody. He's as guilty as a cat next to a pile of feathers.'

'I get that you see that, Cal, but we haven't formally interviewed him. And the DNA under his fingernails won't be from Rebecca Yellowlees.'

'Rob, he slipped up so many times when we spoke to him. Told us stuff he shouldn't have known.'

'But you need to take it slowly, okay? Do it in the logical way. Let's start with processing the stuff under his fingernails. You can't assume it's hers. And you need to wait for the post-mortem.'

'And until then, we just waste taxpayer's money on this nonsense?'

'This isn't nonsense, Cal. Most taxpayers would like to see their money used to convict people as much as to prevent miscarriages of justice.'

'Taking yourself a bit too seriously there. There's no miscarriage of justice here.'

'Glad you're sure of it.'

Taylor eased across the bridge onto the south bank of the Tweed, following a pair of slow-moving coaches, presumably heading for the nearby botanical gardens.

Marshall thought that was in the other direction, though. Something niggled at his brain, suggesting there were maybe two.

Taylor was thumping the wheel, like that could speed anything up. 'Soon as the DNA comes back, you'll look like a right arsehole.'

Marshall laughed at that. 'Or you will.'

Taylor took the second right off the main road, then weaved between tall gateposts into the grounds of an old country house stuck in the heart of Peebles.

The sign for the Beltane Inn basking in the middle of the parched lawn would've been snazzy about twenty years ago, but now it looked tired and weathered. Another five years and maybe the fashion would return.

It wasn't just the sign that belonged to a different era, though. The hotel was a giant stone Jacobite building, with three round towers sticking out at odd angles and from unusual locations. Ivy climbed up the front, healthy and green on one side, dry and brown on the other – probably a fire risk with the wrong guests...

Taylor opened his door and planted his foot on the ground. 'You're still just consulting here, Marshall, okay?'

'I know my place. As long as you do your job, I'm content to just do mine.' Marshall got out and followed him over to the house, their feet crunching over the pebbles, overgrown with weeds. His phone chimed with a message from Kirsten.

> Spoke too soon. Been called in. Call you later x

Marshall tapped out a quick response:

> Ouch. Bad luck x

He put his phone away just as he caught up with Taylor. 'I take it someone's been around to talk to her?'

'Been around, aye, but didn't talk to her.' Taylor rang the doorbell and pleasant chimes rang out. He pointed at the Mazda on the pebbles. 'Must've been out.'

'Coming!' Footsteps thundered inside, then the door opened to reveal a flurry of activity. A woman in her late fifties, slender to the point of gaunt, untucking an apron and hauling it up over her head. 'Can I help you, gentlemen?' A soft Mancunian accent, more from leafy Cheshire than the inner city.

'Kathryn Yellowlees?'

'That's me.' She looked at them in turn, her eyes darkening. 'And you are?'

'DI Callum Taylor.' He showed his warrant card. 'We need to—'

'Have you found her?'

'Probably best if we do this inside...'

11

Kathryn Yellowlees set a large tray down on the table. 'There.'

Despite her grief, she'd made them tea. And not just tea, but a whole spread. A pot each of breakfast tea and Earl Grey, along with three types of milk, plus a giant plate covered with three scones and countless homemade biscuits.

Marshall sat in the corner of the dining room, looking out of the back of the hotel down towards the Tweed, though neighbouring houses blocked most of the view.

Kathryn took off her apron again and sat opposite Taylor. 'How do you take it?'

'Black, thanks.' Taylor accepted a cup of Earl Grey, giving Marshall a waft of the cloying perfume.

'And you're oat milk, Inspector?' Kathryn smiled at Marshall. 'Couldn't remember, so I've got oat, soya and milky milk...'

'That's correct, yes.' Marshall smiled as he took his tea and helped himself to the oat milk, tipping it all in. It never went far enough.

Kathryn sat back and nervously nibbled at a biscuit. She couldn't deflect anymore – no escaping her grief now. 'So…'

Taylor set his cup down and gave a friendly smile. 'I'm sorry to have had to bear the news to you about Rebecca.'

'Her father died two years ago.' Kathryn's lips twitched. 'Hit me for six, I have to say. Heart attack. Upshot was I've got to run the place myself when, really, we should've been thinking of retiring. All the money we'd set aside when we were younger. All the work Darren did in refurbishing this place.' She got up, walked over to the mantelpiece and pointed at a painting of a ruined building. 'See?'

Took Marshall a few seconds to realise it wasn't a painting but was actually a photo of the hotel before extensive refurbishment.

'His life's work was in fixing this place up. We sank our savings into buying it, then we scraped together enough to pay for the building work, piece by piece. It took us five years of hard work every night to make this place into a functioning hotel. We both had jobs in Edinburgh at the time, so each room took a lot longer than it should've done. But we did it and we've achieved something special. Our plan was to grow the business, then sell it off and retire on the money but now… Now it's the only thing I've got left of Darren.' She shut her eyes. 'And of Rebecca.'

Marshall took a sip of tea. 'I'm very sorry for your loss.'

'Are you?' She glared at him. 'You didn't know her, did you?'

Marshall rested his cup back on the saucer. 'That's true. But it's horrific when you lose someone you love. Especially at a young age like that.'

Her glare deepened, then something passed between them. Some deep understanding – how Marshall knew precisely what she was going through.

He'd just approached the same grief from a different angle.

And had over twenty years to recover from it.

She poured herself a cup, then tipped in the briefest splash of milky milk, as she put it. 'She didn't come home last night. Not unusual, but she'd always message me. And she'd usually be back mid-morning. So I panicked. I was at the police station to report it, but nobody was there. What's the country coming to? I had to stand in the street and phone her. Came back here. Two of your number came around and took some details. Said she'd probably turn up. And they left. So I've been out since, looking for her. Speaking to her friends.' She shifted her focus between them. 'Can I see her?'

Taylor slurped his tea. 'She's being taken to the pathology department at BGH just now. I could give you a lift there, if you—'

'I'm more than capable of driving there myself, thank you very much. I'm asking if you need me to help identify her body?'

'We've already had a positive ID from the person who discovered the body.'

Her forehead knitted together. 'Who was that?'

'I'm not at liberty to—'

'Don't give me that.' Kathryn smashed her biscuit down onto the table, breaking it into several pieces. 'My daughter has been murdered and you won't tell me who killed her?'

Taylor took a sip and drank it slowly. 'We—'

'It's Iain bloody Hogg, isn't it?'

'I can't conf—'

'No, you don't. Don't do that. You think he killed her, don't you?'

Taylor raised his hands. 'Like I said, I'm not at liberty to divulge—'

'He was here, you know? First thing this morning. That daft bugger was here. Acting all suspicious. Crafty. Like he'd done something and pretending he hadn't. Said he just wanted to catch up with my daughter after seeing her in the pub last night.' She started collecting up the bits of broken biscuit on the table. 'It was him, wasn't it?'

Marshall knew he needed to take over. 'I gather your daughter and Mr Hogg were acquainted?'

'Were. And acquainted is a bit euphemistic. They were an item, a long time ago.'

'Do you know what happened between them?'

'Iain was a bit of a loser, I'm afraid.' She raised her hands. 'I'm not saying he wasn't good enough for Rebecca, but he was... There was something lacking in him. Something missing. So if you're saying he found her body, then I'd say he's the most likely to have put it there in the first place.'

Taylor looked away from her. 'You reported her missing this morning, didn't you?'

'That's right. I told the two laddies who came around that it's not unknown for Becky to stay over somewhere. She's twenty-five, but hasn't changed since she was sixteen, I swear. She'd text me and say she was staying at a friend's in Edinburgh or in Peebles. Or if she was on a date. But she'd always message me to let me know. *Always*. Because I worry.'

'All parents do.' Taylor gave a polite smile. 'And she didn't message you?'

'No. Last I heard from her was about five o'clock last night, saying she was drinking with a few people in the Steps. She'd been at the Highland Games with her pals.' She gave Taylor a hard look. 'Have you done any location analysis on her phone?'

'We have, yes.'

'That lassie never went anywhere without that phone.'

'The network has given us an extract of all the cell site connections her phone made. Basically, it's a list of latitude-longitude coordinates. To my eye, they all looked like they were in Peebles, but we'll confirm that. It's currently off but the last-known location was in the Steps last night.'

'That's not good.'

Taylor scribbled something in his notebook. 'Did your daughter often visit the Steps?'

'It's their old haunt. Her and her pals. When they were younger, they'd be in there every Saturday night.' Kathryn narrowed her eyes between them. 'She said a few from the old crowd were out.' She stared into space. 'Funny how they all spread out in their teens and twenties, only to return, isn't it?'

Marshall met her gaze. 'Did the same myself. Went to Durham at eighteen, but moved back here from London a couple of years ago.'

'That's a long time away.'

'Best part of twenty years. When did Rebecca and Iain split up?'

'When they were at uni. He dropped out after two years up in Edinburgh. At Napier. Rebecca went to Strathclyde in Glasgow. Bit of a mess, really. He was the Beltane Cornet in 2017 and Becky was his lass.' Kathryn looked around the empty dining room. 'It was Darren's idea to call this place the Beltane Inn. Used to be a family home, then it became a wreck over the years. His family are from Peebles originally, but moved to London in the fifties. He said he felt all this local history in his blood when he got a job in Edinburgh. I'm from near Manchester, as you can tell. And we couldn't name it anything else, could we?'

'Do you know if she'd been seeing anyone in Glasgow?'

'I don't know. Her love life was a closed book to me and she never gave an inkling. So no, I don't think so. She moved to Edinburgh after she graduated for her work, so she was a bit closer to me. I could easily get the bus up. She'd come down often. We're in a hillwalking club and she'd be down every fortnight, come rain or shine. Usually rain.'

'When did she move to Edinburgh?'

'About two years ago. She worked in a pharmacy in the West End.'

'Was she the pharmacist?'

'She got her degree. An MPharm from Strathclyde. She wasn't accredited by the General Pharmaceutical Council, so she can't work as one.'

'Do you know—'

'No. She wouldn't say.'

'But she still worked in a pharmacy in Edinburgh?'

'That's right.'

'Did she live in Edinburgh?'

'She did, but she moved back home a few months ago.'

Marshall had seen a lot of that – kids moving back to stay with their folks to save up to buy their own place. 'Was this after your husband passed away?'

'No, I lost Darren the year before last.'

'Was she still working in Edinburgh?'

'No. She was helping me run the hotel. She'd lost her job but didn't want to talk about it. Ever.'

12

Taylor glanced over at Marshall. 'You're pretty quiet there, tiger?'

Unlike the traffic, which was loud and heavy. And Taylor had gone down the wrong street – Marshall knew western Edinburgh pretty well now, but this wasn't the best way to get where they were going. And might even have been the worst.

Marshall laughed. 'Tiger?'

'Anything to get a reaction from you, Rob.'

If it wasn't for the red markings at the side of the road, Marshall would've suggested dumping the car and walking. 'Sorry, just thinking.'

'Such is the nature of your job, right?'

'Something like that.'

'And is that thinking leading you anywhere?'

'Not really. Sorry.' Marshall ran a hand down his face. 'It's just making me ask more questions, you know?'

'Right. I get it. Like, why was she sacked?'

'We don't know she was. She could've left.'

'Sounds like it, though.'

'And why wasn't she accredited?'

Taylor laughed. 'Got to admit, though, it looks more and more likely that Hogg killed Becky. Showing up at her mum's place, desperate to speak to her.'

'It's completely consistent with what he told us, though.'

Taylor inched forward along the street towards the turning they needed. 'So, these tunnels. In Edinburgh and Glasgow. You can't seriously think this is all connected, can you?'

'Keeping an open mind is what my job is all about, Cal. You're flying headlong into a conviction, while I'm paid to make sure that conviction sticks and that it's the right thing to do. Right now, while we're speaking to people, I'm collating data. And it takes time to crunch that. Longer still for some flash of inspiration to connect all the various dots.'

'I won't hold my breath, then.' Taylor took a chance to sneak through a gap in the traffic and got along William Street. He pulled in then pointed at Teuchter's, one of Edinburgh's still-thriving old-fashioned pubs. 'Nice boozer, that. Not that I'm on the sauce anymore. You a drinker?'

'Have my moments, aye.' Marshall got out into the searing heat. 'Shouldn't be this hot in September in Scotland. Should be laws against it.'

'Hard to disagree.' Taylor pushed into the chemist's shop, leaving Marshall baking in the heat.

Marshall followed Taylor into Beveridge & Sons.

Taylor walked up to an assistant by the till, while Marshall hung back to take in the shop.

Empty of customers, just rows and rows of toiletries and *weird* stuff. Bath pillows, Easter eggs in September and rolls of camera film in 2024.

The assistant slipped off into a backroom, leaving Taylor on his own. He noticed Marshall's approach, but didn't say anything.

A harassed woman burst out of the back room, scowling

and shaking her head. Fizzing with energy and anger. Her smile was as real as a hamburger made from sawdust. 'What?'

'Police, ma'am.' Taylor raised his warrant card. 'Just need to ask a few questions.'

'As if I didn't have enough on.' She gave a weary snort. 'Sorry. I shouldn't take it out on you. I've had two members of staff off sick all week, so I've had to work all the shifts. And I mean *all* the shifts.'

'You run this place?'

'Own it too. My name above the door.'

'Beveridge and son?'

'Well, that was the original name. Goes back to the 1930s. I'm the fourth Beveridge to be in charge here. The first woman. Maybe if I get enough time to go on a date I might be able to have sex enough times to have a son to poison their life with familial expectation. And not die when my child was twenty, unlike my father, who left me to learn how to run a shop while studying.' She ran a hand down her face. 'Sorry, I shouldn't rant like this. It's just been one of those weeks, you know? One of those weeks.' She held out a hand to Marshall. 'Sorry. Didn't see you there. Steph Beveridge.'

'DI Rob Marshall.' He shook her hand. 'We wanted to ask you about Rebecca Yellowlees.'

'Oh.' Steph stared down at the counter. 'Her.'

'Gather she used to work here. Is that right?'

'Part of the reason I'm so stressed. When you take someone on, you might think they seem a good fit, but then you have to work with them. And you get to know them. She *left* and I've been short on staff since. Down two pharmacists this week and I'm supposed to be on a sun lounger in Rhodes.'

'We gather she wasn't a pharmacist?'

'No, but she did all the rest of it. There was a small matter regarding her foundation training. The degree is one side of it and there was nothing wrong with that, but she worked at a pharmacy in Glasgow which shut down under a cloud. So she wasn't accredited, but I was going to provide that for her, then it'd give me a third pharmacist. But she left before that was complete.'

'Why did she leave?'

'How do you not know?'

'Excuse me?'

Steph laughed. 'This was a police matter.'

'Excuse me?'

'I had to sack her. She'd been supplying controlled substances to a friend without a prescription. There was a major police investigation into this. How can you not know?'

Taylor looked like he was going to hulk out and smash up the shop. At his own incompetence, probably.

But Marshall kept his peace. Tried to keep calm. Keep it all under lock and key, in case the implications exploded outwards.

'It was sheer hell.' Steph tore off her glasses to rub at her nose. 'Part of the reason I've got a pharmacist out on sick leave is the stress it took on him. On us both, to be honest. Because Becky tried to pin it on us. Saying it wasn't her doing. But she'd faked prescriptions for both of us. And we had incontrovertible evidence to the contrary.'

'So why wasn't she in prison?'

'I couldn't tell you that. Like I said, this was a police matter.'

Taylor clenched his jaw. 'Sure it wasn't hushed up?'

'Are you accusing me of something?'

'Not at all.'

'Well, don't. Because I've been to hell over this. Journalists knocking on my door. Undercover journalists trying to buy illicit substances.' Steph pointed at Taylor. 'But I had all these safeguards in place. Goes back to my grandfather's day. It's how we identified the fraud in the first place. Whatever happened, it was entirely down to Rebecca Yellowlees.'

'Do you know the names of the officers who investigated?'

13

Taylor thumbed over at St Leonard's station, caught under a dark cloud in the late-afternoon sunshine. He looked like a hitchhiker who'd been at it for hours and was now resigned to walking. 'Sure we can't do this inside?'

'Sorry, man.' DI Craven lumbered like a wrestler, bulky muscles filling out his suit. Thick black hair slicked back, face like a sock stuffed with snooker balls. 'You know how it is, right? We let you pair in the building, next thing we know you're attending briefings and making a mess of stakeouts.'

Taylor laughed. 'We're not that bad, are we?'

'Aye, but you're not that good.' Craven looked over at his partner. 'What do you think, boss?'

'No way.' DCI Mukherjee shook his head. Balding to the point where all he had left on top was a hair island in the middle, the solitary tuft sticking up like a palm tree and no longer able to be combed over. 'I'm in complete agreement.'

Marshall leaned back against Taylor's pool car. 'I'm working for DCS Potter to determine if it's part of my portfolio of potential serial homicides.'

Craven whistled. 'She Who Cannot Be Named herself, eh?'

He clicked his tongue and glanced over his shoulder. Potter had climbed the ranks and pissed a lot of people off along the way – and in those she hadn't, the overriding emotion was fear. Craven nudged Taylor with his elbow. 'Someone's dining at the big table, eh?'

Marshall grinned. 'I'm more the sommelier.'

'Well, you can pair this wine,' Craven raised his middle finger, 'with this main course.' He raised the other one.

'Namedropping won't get you anywhere, you daft sod.' Mukherjee checked his blingy watch. 'Besides, we've got to shoot off in a few minutes. By the time we got in and found a meeting room, we'd have to bugger off.'

Marshall didn't have to charm him – the namedropping had worked. 'Where are you heading at this time on a Sunday?'

'Got two lads on a stake out in Niddrie. So, like the King said, it's now or never.' Mukherjee did an Elvis-style shake of the hips.

Taylor folded his arms. 'Fine. Let's do this here, then. Now.'

'Cool.' Craven got behind the wheel of a pool Mondeo and Mukherjee got in alongside him.

'Always the same with these clowns...' Taylor got in the back and gestured to Marshall to lead. 'Rob?'

Marshall got in behind Craven, but he left the back door open, in case the buggers tried to drive off anywhere – the bollard would take the door clean off and even drugs squad DCIs didn't want to have to explain that. 'I'm working with DI Taylor and the Borders MIT to investigate—'

'Ryan Gashkori?' Craven's bushy eyebrows shot up. 'Wow. Thought you couldn't stand him, Cal?'

Taylor shrugged, but his face had reddened. 'Ry's a good guy.'

'Sure.' Mukherjee laughed. 'Sure he is.'

Taylor smirked. 'Thought you two were in a hurry?'

'We're in the drugs squad, Cal. Never in a hurry. We're tortoises. But we always win the race.'

Marshall didn't want to let them detract from this. 'Need to speak to you about a Rebecca Yellowlees.'

Mukherjee sat back and blew air up his face. 'Aye, we know her.' He gestured at Craven. 'Dean and I did her for drug trafficking. Faking prescriptions, so she could give fentanyl to some associates of hers. Very naughty behaviour.'

Craven nodded. 'Naughty, naughty, very naughty.'

'So you arrested her?'

'Arrested, charged, prosecuted.'

'How was she not in jail?'

'First offence.' Mukherjee clicked his tongue like he was tempting a horse. 'Usual story. No previous record and she'd pled guilty, so she got off with a fine, a two-year suspended sentence with probation and a spot of community service. Two hundred hours of working with drug addicts. The General Pharmaceutical Council pulled her ticket.'

'I thought she wasn't accredited?'

'She wasn't. But she was in the process of it. No chance of her working again in that field.'

'Sounds like she got off pretty lightly, though.' Taylor flashed them a grin. 'Thought you two were hard bastards.'

'We are. But when a lassie tells you how this whole messy mess is connected to organised crime, one thing leads to another, you know?'

'You mean, she grassed?'

'She grassed. Put us on to some right nasty buggers behind this whole sordid thing.'

'And are they behind bars?'

'That's a whole other affair, my good friend. Ongoing case.'

'Isn't that always the case...' Taylor sucked in his cheeks, looking at Marshall. 'I know what you're thinking there, Rob.'

Marshall raised an eyebrow. 'Go on, Uri Geller, what am I thinking?'

'She's grassed on some dodgy people, but walked off with only a tiny slap on the wrist. It's possible this is a gang hit.'

'Had briefly crossed my mind.'

Mukherjee looked at Marshall. Then at Taylor. Then back at Marshall. 'A gang hit? She's dead?'

'Her body was found in a tunnel near Peebles this morning.'

Something passed between them. An edginess. The weary tang of disappointment. Or a case going the wrong way.

Marshall needed to get on the front foot here – and stay there. 'Is it possible she'd be killed in a gang hit?'

'Hard to say without seeing your evidence. How was she murdered?'

Taylor swallowed. 'We're awaiting the post-mortem, but it appears someone attacked her in a tunnel.'

'A tunnel?'

'Disused railway tunnel down in Peebles.'

'Mate, I can think of a million better places to kill someone than in a tunnel in the middle of the night. The kind of people we're working with wouldn't be so blatant. Make it look like an overdose. Or just disappear her.'

'Are these people connected to Gary Hislop?'

'No. Trouble with Gary Hislop is he's only connected to himself and some people in foreign climes. And he's very, very good at both covering his tracks and making sure we can't follow them. And your case sounds much more like a crime of passion than an organised hit.'

'If you want passion, mate, we've got it by the bucket-load.' Craven looked over at his boss, then got a tight nod, so he swung around to look at Marshall. 'Here's some more grist for your mill, then. One of the people she was supplying fentanyl to overdosed a week ago.'

Marshall sat back and looked across the car park. 'Which could create a personal grudge?'

'Indeed. Particularly as the family is connected to people who solve problems with their fists.'

Marshall got out his notebook and made a note of it, scribbling away against his thigh. 'Can we get access to your case file?'

'Mi case es su case.' Craven winked at him. 'But honestly, I don't think this is the likely explanation for your thing.'

'Why not?'

'To me, the obvious target for that would be her friend. Keegan McAllister. Twenty-seven. Connected to a drug gang over in Glasgow. He's on remand in HMP Edinburgh for dealing.'

'He's on remand, but she's already been prosecuted?'

'Exactly. Her trial went ahead because she pled guilty and complied with our investigation. But Keegan's maintaining his innocence, despite admitting to paying Rebecca for the drugs.'

Mukherjee rolled his eyes. 'He won't sing. Wouldn't back her up. He knows which side his bread's buttered on. Do the time, get out in a few years and be looked after by his mates.'

'But...' Taylor's forehead twisted into a tight knot. 'Think I see what you're saying. You've got an accused pleading guilty and agreeing to testify. But the other accused has a motive to get them killed, which would make her evidence hearsay and therefore inadmissible for when you go after the big bad guys?'

'Precisely. Her evidence is good, but it needed to be proven in court. Or at least it was.'

'She hadn't provided a sworn statement?'

'Statement, yes. Sworn, no. PF wanted the jury to see the whites of her eyes.'

'So the exclusion of that statement and her testimony could scupper your case?'

Mukherjee looked at Craven like the thought had just crossed their collective brain cell.

'Lads, if she didn't feel like she was going to die and the statement wasn't sworn, then you've got a massive hole in your case against this Keegan McAllister guy.' Taylor folded his arms. 'Huge motive for him to arrange her death, isn't it?'

Marshall tried to follow the logic. It intrigued him.

Necessity and reliability... need both to get the statement in without testifying... The necessity was there – she's dead – but without the jeopardy of her knowing she was going to die or giving the statement under oath, it's just words. No reliability. The prosecution would have their work cut out for them to get that past a judge.

Taylor laughed. 'Have to say, it sounds like complete nonsense to me. *Way* too complicated. Like you said, Mike, if you're going to bump someone off, you do it in an easier way. Arrange a car crash. Drown them in the river. Make it look like suicide. Not follow her to a disused railway tunnel in the middle of the night with two potential witnesses. No, this is a love triangle gone wrong. A crime of passion.' His phone rang. 'Better take this.' He got out of the car and walked away, phone to his head.

Mukherjee winked at Marshall. 'I agree wholeheartedly with Callum. This doesn't feel like it fits.'

'Drug people always think it's drugs.' Marshall shifted his focus between them. 'Thing is, I've seen suppliers and dealers charged with criminal negligence causing death, even manslaughter based on providing a known lethal drug. This is what you should've been doing with Rebecca, isn't it?'

'It was and it wasn't.' Craven made a show of weighing two things up. 'Thing is, when Keegan was arrested, the local news ran the story. TV and press. He appeared in court and instead of pleading guilty or whatever, he named Rebecca. Kicked up a big stink with the judge.' He thumbed at Mukherjee. 'Caused a bit of hassle for Mike here.'

Taylor opened the passenger door again. 'That was Gashkori. He's asked me to attend the PM.'

Marshall stayed where he was, locking eyes with Mukherjee. 'You're Gashkori's replacement, right?'

'For my sins, aye. Why?'

'No reason. Does it go back to his time?'

'Nah, this is after. And we're different streams. Three DCIs there. I was deputy on that case, but got saddled with it after Ry moved down to you lot.'

But that didn't mean Gashkori wouldn't know anything about it.

'I'll see you boys later. Thanks for the help.' Marshall got out. 'The PM's happening tonight?'

'Gashkori managed to get Leye to fast-track it, aye. But you're not coming.'

'I'm just here to consult, Cal. How can I consult if I'm not there?'

Taylor shook his head. 'Why don't you take up a hobby, Rob? Like golf or clay pigeon shooting?'

Craven and Mukherjee both laughed at that.

Marshall slammed the door and held Taylor's glare as he walked around the back of the car. 'Already got a hobby – helping inept officers become competent.'

14

STRUAN

DS Struan Liddell felt that throbbing feeling in his head and deep in his guts. He always got it before he went into battle. A heady mix of too much adrenaline and too much caffeine – a cocktail that always meant trouble. But not for him. *Never* for him.

He looked across the table. 'You okay there?'

DI Andrea Elliot was staring at her notebook, lips moving as she read. Her red eyes focused on him as she slurped her seventh coffee of the day. 'What?'

Struan hadn't worked with her that long, just the last year or so, but she'd aged a lot in that time. Bags under her eyes. A few silver threads in her thick hair, her long fringe dragged tight across her forehead and tucked behind her right ear. 'Just wondering if you're ready to interview him, that's all.'

'We're ready when I say we are.' Elliot sat back and tossed her pen on the table. 'But I think that's all I can do, to be honest. Our interview strategy, for what it's worth, is bad cop, worse cop. A lot less evidence than I'd like, but I think we have to just get stuck in and see what we can shake loose.'

Struan thought of teeth, spilling on a dark pavement. 'So we're ready to interview him now?'

'Fine. Let's do it.' Elliot got to her feet and cracked her knuckles, the ligaments rattling like ball bearings tumbling down a staircase. 'You know something, Struan? It's good to be off the bench.'

'You feeling like the gaffer's side-lined you?'

'Didn't say that.' Elliot walked over to the door. 'Sod it. Of course I do. And it isn't just a feeling, Struan, it's a demonstrable fact.'

'You taking him to a tribunal?'

'What would be the point?' She looked down at his hands. 'Have you taken up boxing?'

He looked at the giant purple lumps on his knuckles. 'No. Why?'

'What are those bruises from? Beating up the homeless?'

'Thought I'd got away with that...' Struan laughed, but felt a rash of embarrassment rise up his neck. 'It's my old man. He's in that stage of dementia where he's angry all the time. At me, at his carers, at my mum despite her being long dead. Only way I can deal with it is by punching things.'

'You're beating him up?'

'God, no. I'm punching walls.'

'Jesus, Struan. You know that's a red flag for someone being a psychopath, don't you?'

'Even psychopaths would struggle with what I'm going through.'

'Just look after yourself, okay?' Elliot left the room and marched along the corridor.

Struan fought the urge to chase after her and took his time following. By the time he entered the interview room, he was greeted only by a glower from Elliot – she'd already started.

'And DS Struan Liddell has just entered the room.'

Iain Hogg sat opposite her, looking like he'd had a skinful

the night before. Red-faced and not all of it sunburn. His eyes were too close together, like they were using his nose as a seesaw. His hands were splayed on the table.

And he'd lawyered up. A sack of broken jelly Struan didn't recognise sat next to him, scribbling away on his legal pad. Probably jotting down romantic sonnets.

Struan picked up his chair, swivelled it around and sat on it the wrong way round. He cracked his knuckles, but it sounded like someone snapping fresh twigs rather than anything particularly badass. 'Let's get stuck in, shall we?' He waited for eye contact – didn't take long for Hogg to focus on him. His left eye twitched. 'Did you feel any shame after you killed Rebecca?'

Hogg's mouth hung open. 'Excuse me?'

'I'll take that as a no, then.'

'I'm... *What*?'

'You felt no shame when you killed her?'

'No! Of course I didn't.'

'Sorry, did the shame only come afterwards?'

'I didn't kill her!'

'Oh, come on. Does that mean you're a psychopath, then?'

'What? I keep telling you lot. I didn't kill her!'

'Did she die too quickly for your liking? Did you want her to suffer longer?'

'This is outrageous. My client is—'

'Rebecca got what she deserved from you, eh?' Struan sat back, resting his arms on the chair back. 'I saw it with my own eyes. Pretty sickening, man. Brutal, man. Brutal.' He left a long pause. 'Do you feel proud of killing her?'

'No!'

'But you said you didn't feel any shame. What was it, then?'

'Nothing. I didn't kill her.'

'So, you felt nothing, then?' Struan nodded along, like he was concocting some kind of theory. 'That confirms it, then. Psychopaths don't feel anything.'

'I'm not a psychopath.'

'Sure. Of course. You murdered your ex-girlfriend in cold blood and you didn't feel anything. But of course you're not a psychopath, are you?'

'I didn't kill her!'

'Aha. I've got it now.' Struan clicked his fingers hard a few times. 'You're saying you disassociated from the event as you did it.'

Hogg snorted, then wiped at his cheeks.

Bingo – Struan was getting somewhere with this. Infiltrating his mind.

'My next question is have you ever been treated for your schizophrenia?'

'Of course I haven't.'

'Take it that means you refused the treatment? Happens a lot. It's a shame, really. It's really become a treatable condition, what with the medication available these days. Trouble is, there are loads of people who aren't even diagnosed. Worse, there are those like yourself who clearly know the bats aren't all roosting in the same belfry, but refuse to speak to anyone about it. The worst kind. You cause so much difficulty. Not for yourselves, but your loved ones.' Struan left a long pause. 'For someone like Rebecca.'

'I'm *not* schizophrenic.'

'Aye, sure you're not. Because someone who can murder someone only to push those actions into another corner of their psyche couldn't possibly be, could they?'

Hogg stared at the floor over to the side of the table, then he shut his eyes.

Decent tactic.

Shut down completely and let the whole interview happen without you. Act like you're not there. Stall the fuck out of anything. Then all you had to do was wait until the cops got fed up, then you could leave.

At least, that's how the theory went.

Time for a little wake-up call.

Struan chapped at the desk and attracted Hogg's attention. 'Do you beat up your wife?'

'My *wife*?'

'Aye. Your wife.'

'Erin? What are you talking about?'

'Have you got a second wife, Mr Hogg?'

'Of course I don't.'

'But you have been beating her up, right?'

'This is outrageous! My client is here because he found a body! And now you're accusing him of domestic abuse?'

'Trouble is, we sent a few lads around to his home address to speak to Mrs Hogg, but she's not in.' Struan left a lengthy pause. 'Where is she?'

Hogg sat back and tugged at his hair. 'Why do you want to speak to her?'

'Why do you think, Mr Hogg? Ask her what she thinks of England's performance in the recent Euros? How she thinks the new Labour government is faring?'

'There's no reason I can think of.'

'Iain. You killed your ex-girlfriend. Of course we want to speak to your current partner.' Struan drummed his fingers on the table. 'Hang on a minute. Have you killed her too?'

'Of course not! She's away.'

'Right. Sure. You mean run away?'

'No.'

'Where have you buried her, Mr Hogg?'

'My client refuses to answer that.'

Struan laughed. 'We'll find her remains soon enough. Maybe someone like yourself will uncover them and come forward.' He sniffed. 'Still, it's pretty good going to kill both your wife and your ex in the same weekend.' He looked over at Elliot, then back at Hogg. 'We could probably do with a full list of your other romantic dalliances over the years, just to make sure they're all still breathing.'

Hogg sucked in a deep breath that seemed to catch in his throat. 'Erin's away on a hen weekend. With her mates from uni.'

'When's she due back?'

Hogg looked at his watch. 'Nine o'clock this evening, I think.'

'Precise.'

'It's a flight. Might get delayed, but I doubt it. Supposed to pick her up at the airport.'

Struan leaned forward. 'Gather from our colleagues who spoke to you earlier in the car park that you admitted to struggling with erectile dysfunction?'

'*Excuse* me?'

'At the tunnel. You and Becky were kissing. But you walked away. Bit of a struggle getting the drawbridge to raise, was it?'

'That's not what happened.'

'What did happen?'

'Nothing. She tried it on and I walked away.'

'Okay. Maybe the truth is you don't fancy women much.'

'I'm fucking married.'

'So are loads of men who haven't accepted the truth about themselves. I'm thinking you were there for the bloke.'

'What bloke?'

'Come on. You told us there was another guy there.'

Hogg looked at Elliot, like she'd give him any respite. 'This is insane. How can you... How can... How?'

'Was that the allure?' Elliot grinned at him. 'Did you go there on the promise of a threesome?'

'Fuck you. Fuck the pair of you. I'm innocent!'

Elliot laughed. 'Son, you're as guilty as anyone I've seen. Deluded, maybe, but guilty.'

'You lot have…' Hogg sat back with a gasp. A broken man, further destroyed by their questioning. '*Fuck* you.'

Elliot snorted into her hanky, a loud atonal parp that wouldn't have sounded out of place on a late Miles Davis album – the kind of stuff Struan's old man still insisted on listening to. She dabbed at her nose. 'Sorry. Hope this isn't a cold.' She put her hanky away. 'Why don't you just tell us the truth here? Doesn't matter whether you did it or not, just that it's true.'

'I am!'

'Don't believe you, but anyway…' Elliot flicked through her notebook. 'We've got a couple of other cases we need to ask you about. In April, a woman was murdered in the Innocent Railway tunnel in Holyrood Park in Edinburgh.'

Hogg blew air up his face. 'Wasn't me.'

'Okay. So we're just going to take your word for it?'

'Aye.'

'How can we know you didn't do it?'

'I was in Bournemouth all month.'

'Bournemouth?'

'Right. I'm a joiner. Retrained after I dropped out of uni. Best thing I ever did. Mate of mine got us a contract on this hotel renovation down there. Decent money. So I was away the whole month. Paid for me and Erin to go to Disneyworld in Orlando in May. Got so badly burnt there, man.'

'You didn't come home for weekends?'

'Wasn't one of those gigs. Had to sign one of those waivers, you know? Just worked right through the week. No time off.'

Elliot jotted something down. 'We'll need to check this all out.'

'Sure. You do that. Got all of my receipts.'

'And what about July of last year?'

'July? I'd need to check.'

'You weren't working in Outer Mongolia? Or on Mars?'

'No, I was here, I think. At home. Working.'

'You think?'

'I'd need to check.'

'You happen to visit Glasgow in that time?'

'Glasgow?'

'You know, biggest city in Scotland. Home to Celtic and Rang—'

'I know it. I wasn't there.'

'Right. So you weren't at Kelvingrove Tunnel?'

'Never heard of it. Listen, I can categorically state that, yes. Can't stand the place. It's... Something weird about it. Like everyone hates your guts, despite seeming like your best pal. Can't stand it, man. Got really bad memories of the place too.'

Struan snorted. 'We'll need you to look out your movements for that month.'

'Sure. Let me go and I'll get on it.' Hogg looked at his lawyer, then at Elliot, then at Struan. 'You've mentioned two tunnels, other than Neidpath. Do you honestly think someone's killing people in tunnels across Scotland?'

'Are you?'

'No. I'm not. I didn't kill Rebecca.'

Struan felt a nudge on his knee.

Elliot leaned forward and shook her fringe free. 'When did you last see her?'

'In the pub, last night.'

'And before that?'

'Years ago.' Hogg exhaled slowly. 'And I mean *years* ago. Like five? It was when we broke up. When I saw her yesterday, it brought up a lot of stuff. About how our relationship had been a sham. A complete joke.'

'You were both students when you broke up, right?'

'Aye. I was at Napier. Total mistake for me to go. I just about scraped in, but I wasn't smart enough for uni. I hated school, but uni was even worse. I wasn't made for it. Lucky I got onto an apprenticeship after I left. Mate's dad's firm. Taught myself a trade.'

'And Rebecca was at Strathclyde, right?'

'She was. Not exactly a long-distance relationship, but far enough… Trouble was, I was the one getting the bus through to Glasgow every weekend. Turned into every couple of weekends, then it was once a month. Then my texts were going unanswered for almost an hour at times. At the end of one visit through there, she just told me not to come back. Told us, "I can do better than you". That was the reason.'

'How did that affect you?'

'I mean, I dropped out of uni not long after. The whole thing ending like that just crushed me. Thing is, I don't think she ever did do better than me. Not that I heard. Or saw.'

Elliot smiled like she agreed with it. 'How long have you been married to Erin for?'

'Just over two years.'

'Are you happy?'

'Define happy… We're comfortable with each other. We get on quite well. I don't mind the stuff she does. Her clubs and groups and that. Same the other way around. And we go to the pub together a lot. Two holidays a year. It's all good.'

Elliot nodded slowly, like she knew that exact feeling. 'You and Rebecca were the Beltane Cor—'

'That stuff was a total farce, man. I *hated* it. Thought I'd get respect from people, but they all just took the piss, didn't they?'

'Anyone in particular?'

'Just anyone with an EH45 postcode, eh?'

'Care to furnish us with any names?'

Hogg shook his head. 'I'm afraid to open my mouth anymore because everything I say leads to this twat thinking I did it. I didn't. And you're doing my head in.'

'Come on. Anyone who'd want to harm you?'

'My client has already refused to answer that. Given the behaviour of your colleague here, I think we should all just move on, mm?'

15

MARSHALL

Taylor could shift when he wanted to. His rubber-soled boots squeaked across the diagonal stretch of pavement across the car park to Borders General Hospital like he was a raging mouse.

The wind had picked up, casting grit into Marshall's mouth.

Taylor hadn't said anything all the way down from Edinburgh. Not so much that Marshall's name was mud, as he was made of the stuff.

Marshall managed to catch up with him as he passed the smoking shelter. His calves burned.

'Cal!' The voice came from behind.

Marshall turned.

Gashkori stood there, sucking on a cigarette, eyes narrowed to thin slits.

'Didn't see you there, sir.'

'Clearly.' Gashkori breathed smoky air across Marshall's face as he waited for Taylor to double back and join them. He didn't. Gashkori sucked another deep drag. 'Cal told me you've uncovered a possible lead?'

'Have I?'

'Drugs. And organised crime relating to drugs.'

'Right.' Marshall couldn't help but think he'd stepped on a landmine. He had to be very careful here. 'That's an avenue we should investigate, sir.'

'You mean *you* should consult on, not *we* should investigate. Because you're not an investigator here.'

Fuck this.

Marshall rested his hands on his hips. 'Trouble is, sir, it feels an awful lot like I'm the only one investigating anything.'

'That right, aye? Have you been speaking to half of Peebles? Have you attended the post-mortem? Have you found her phone?'

'Where was it?'

'In the pub. Found in the ladies toilet.' Gashkori shot him a look. 'Cal said you were meeting with Craven and Mukherjee?'

'That's right, sir. They prosecuted Rebecca Yellowlees for—'

'Bet they did.'

'There's a possibility someone killed her to silence her. Stop her testifying.'

'How big a possibility?'

'Ask Callum, he'd say fifty percent.'

'And you?'

'Five would be stretching it.'

Gashkori snorted. 'Listen, I used to run that team. Those two are good cops, but you need to keep a close eye on them. At all times.'

'In what way?'

'The way I see it, they're trying to grab hold of some glory.' Gashkori held his stare. 'Just like you are.'

Marshall had to laugh at that. The paranoia was seeping off him in waves, like booze off a drunk the morning after a heavy night before. 'There's hardly any glory here, sir.'

'Sure. But I know your game.'

'Excellent. Glad someone does.'

Gashkori frowned at that. Seemed to throw him off his stride.

Exactly as Marshall intended. 'I didn't say I thought it was a drugs murder, sir.'

'No, but you don't think it's a simple case of murder.' Gashkori inspected his cigarette. 'You ever hear of Occam's razor?' He grinned like he was some kind of intellectual behemoth. 'Basically, the simplest explanation is usually the best one.'

'Sure, but is that explanation really all that simple? And the weakness with Occam's razor is you can sacrifice accuracy when you prioritise simplicity.'

'Rob. A drunk man following an ex is both simple and the most accurate. Happens every weekend in every town in Scotland.' Another drag, held in his lungs. 'Okay, thank Cal for taking over for me. I'm heading back to the station to break some skulls.'

Marshall raised an eyebrow. 'What's happened?'

Gashkori gave him some side eye. 'Getting a load of hassle for letting Andrea Elliot interview Hogg. With Struan bloody Liddell. Talk about a recipe for nuclear disaster. Lawyer's kicking off big time. I mean, he should be grinning wide. His client denied all the allegations and gave up nothing extraneous. Still.' He waved his phone in the air. 'Good news is I've got a written instruction from She Who Cannot Be Named to bring in Elliot, so it's not my balls on the chopping block.' His sigh betrayed the feeling they were still at risk. 'Trying to cling to the fact we've got a solid suspect and he's all limbered up, so I'm going to get in there and finish the job.' He clapped Marshall on the arm then stubbed out his cigarette on the bin. 'Let's pin this on Hogg, aye?'

'It's not as simple as that, sir.'

'It can be.' Gashkori loped off across the car park. 'Make it so.'

Simple was the last thing this case was.

16

The service lift rattled as it descended, even though it was only down one flight of stairs.

Marshall knew he was a lazy sod, but it didn't stop him.

The door opened and an orderly stepped in, then did a double take and stepped back. 'Oh. Sorry.'

'It's okay.' Marshall flashed his warrant card. 'Here to see Leye.' He walked past him, then pushed through the swinging door into pathology.

The new Borders pathologist, Leye Anotade, was all gowned up and working away. Odd seeing him in here, a much bigger physical presence than his predecessor, but someone whose quiet serenity made him disappear from any room.

Taylor stood next to him, arms folded and silent.

Rebecca Yellowlees lay on the slab in front of them, like she was asleep. Except for the chaotic mess that was her skull. Hard to see where all the pieces fitted together...

Leye looked up at them, then went back to his work. 'Good evening, gentlemen.'

'Hiya, Leye.' Marshall raised a hand.

'You've just missed your boss.'

'I caught him upstairs.' Marshall joined them at the table. 'Thank you for getting on top of this so early.'

'You know me, Rob. I prefer to work late. It's much quieter. And on a Sunday, it's super quiet. Monday mornings are always insane, so I doubt I'd get around to this until afternoon.'

Taylor shifted his focus between them – seemed a bit perturbed by that, but Marshall couldn't tell what or why. 'Appreciate it, mate.'

Leye looked up at that word, then back down.

'So, doc, how's it look—' Taylor stared at his watch. 'Sorry, got to take this.' He walked off, fishing his phone out of his pocket. 'Alright, gaffer?'

Leye watched him go, then looked at Marshall. 'Do you remember that case we worked together in London? The Chameleon?'

'Will never forget it, Leye. You were a massive help. I needed a sounding board to go through some of my more outlandish theories.'

'True.' Leye's laugh was full-throated, but kind. 'Those theories could be a bit out there. But you ended up being right, didn't you?'

'We caught him. Up here. It's why I'm back on my home turf.'

'So I gather. But this is one of those cases where your weird shit might be true.'

Marshall rested against the edge of the slab. 'Is this your way of saying she's an alien with three legs or something?'

'No, my friend. I can only count two.' Leye's laugh was like a cough. 'It's just...' He looked over at the door. 'Taylor and Gashkori are hard work. I prefer when I can just get on with things in peace, but they come in and...' He looked up. 'Taylor's your typically useless cop. I've seen a hundred thousand of them over the years. But Gashkori... He concerns me.'

'In what way?'

'He's a bully.'

'Sure, but you must've seen a ton of bullies at that level in the Met, though?'

'Plenty, sure. All worse than him. Police work in general is all bullying. You just need a dose of competence to get away with it. You can be a total arsehole when you're right. He's also erratic, though. Never know what he's going to ask you to do.'

The door swung open again and Taylor strolled back in. 'Tell him once, you've told him a thousand times, eh, lads?' He stood between them and seemed to be aware they'd been talking about something, but didn't seem ready to pry. 'Okay, so what's the score here, mate?'

'Five nil, my friend.' Leye pulled out a scalpel and started cutting away at pale flesh. 'I'm not sure how much DCI Gashkori told you, but I'll be finished soon enough. I've confirmed cause of death as blunt-force trauma to the skull. Two instances of it. I gather that's consistent with the forensics work, which found blood outside of the tunnel under some pallets.'

Taylor nodded. 'And then dragged her along the floor?'

'Does a tunnel have a floor?'

'Along the ground, then.' Taylor scratched at the side of his head. 'Thing is, it's going to be hard to differentiate between her being smashed into that wall by hand or her running headlong into it. Right?'

'Very difficult.' Leye leaned forward and plunged his knife into her body. 'Except, of course, there are two planes of injury.' He pointed at her skull with his free hand. 'Yes, she could've run into the wall herself, but would she then run into it again at full speed, only to hit the same spot, but on the other side of her head?'

Taylor frowned, twisting his features up like a knot. 'Not following you here, pal.'

'I'm saying she couldn't have run into the wall the second time because the first injury would've rendered her unconscious, so she couldn't have injured herself again.'

'With you now.' Taylor started walking around the table and stopped on Marshall's side. 'You're saying someone smashed her head into the wall twice?'

'That's the only possible explanation.'

'She couldn't have run at—'

'No. The angles are all wrong. I've been inside that tunnel. An incredibly spooky place. There's no viable surfaces with a sufficient run-up to allow such an injury to take place.'

'So it *is* possible?'

'A two percent chance. But that's if you had an adequate place to do it. But it'd need someone to transport her body, which would put the balance of probability greatly on murder. This is straightforward, my friend. The killer smashed her head off the tunnel wall a couple of times and broke her skull. A subdural hematoma, which put pressure on the brain stem. The only good news is Rebecca would've been dead within minutes. Ten, the absolute maximum. Even if she'd been found within seconds and they'd somehow airlifted her immediately to the Royal Infirmary in Edinburgh where a surgical team was prepped and ready, there was nothing anyone could've done.' Leye waved around the room. 'This place isn't equipped for that kind of attack.'

The door opened and Kirsten yawned her way in. 'Alright, lads.' She stopped and looked around. 'Everyone okay?'

Marshall walked over and kissed her on the cheek. 'Didn't think you were working?'

'Nor did I. Call from on high brought me in, sadly. So here I am. Working.' Another yawn, then she smiled at Taylor. 'Been processing that guy you brought in, Cal.' She held out her fingers as if they were talons. 'We extracted the stuff out from underneath his fingernails. A couple of samples. We're running them for DNA.'

'Is it Rebecca's?'

Kirsten looked over at Leye. 'The early news is it's definitely human and definitely male. The blood type is O positive.'

'Male?' Taylor gestured at the cadaver in front of them. 'So it's not hers?'

'Nope. And it doesn't match her blood type.'

Taylor's head dipped. 'Is it the killer's, then?'

'How the hell am I supposed to know that?' Kirsten laughed. 'Cal, I'm a forensics officer, not a psychic. I can't speculate on it being the killer's or anyone else's. Your remit is to find someone, then let me do the doings.'

'Is it Sandison's?'

'Who?'

'Jonty Sandison. He was in the tunnel with them.'

'Cal, you get me his DNA? I'll do the rest.'

Taylor blew out a slow breath. 'Does Gashkori know about this?'

'Depends.'

'On what?'

'On whether he's listened to the voicemail I've left him.'

Taylor laughed. 'By the power of Castle Grayskull, eh?'

Kirsten raised an eyebrow. 'What are you talking about?'

'Just a joke between me and your man here. He reckons it's where He-Man lives.'

'And he thinks Skeletor lived there.'

'You're both wrong, you daft sods.' Leye laughed. 'It's where He-Man gets his power from.'

'That's not right.' Taylor got out his phone and checked the display. 'Huh. I'll be buggered.' He looked over at Marshall. 'Still think we've got enough to convict Hogg, though.'

Marshall raised his eyebrows. 'Are you kidding me?'

'It's rock solid, Rob. He did it. Just because it's not her DNA under his nails, doesn't mean he didn't do it.'

Marshall had dealt with cops like him and Gashkori before, but not to this extent. They felt they had their killer, and were prepared to throw everything at a conviction. Even when it didn't fit. 'Look, Cal, you stay here and finish the PM. I need to get back to base and do some thinking on this score.'

'Base, as in Castle Grayskull. I mean Snake Mountain?'

'No, Gala.'

'Right.' Taylor narrowed his eyes, but couldn't do anything but agree. 'Sure.'

'Call you later.' Marshall nodded at Kirsten. 'You staying?'

'No. Your sister dropped me off so I could grab something. Need a lift, if you're heading to Gala.'

'Sure.'

'Coolio.' Kirsten walked into the area behind Leye, then came back with a pair of goggles. 'Cheers, Leye.'

'You owe me for that!'

'Of course.' Kirsten walked out of pathology and along the corridor, but past the lifts. She took the stairs instead.

Marshall caught up with her and climbed alongside her – he really needed to get fit. *Really* needed to. He was gasping worse than Grumpy as he burst out into the foyer.

Kirsten stopped and smiled at him. 'You okay there?'

'I'm okay. Just... stairs.'

'You need to come out running with me.'

'I do.'

'So.' She set off through the hospital. 'You and Callum don't see eye to eye, do you?'

'I usually don't care, but Gashkori and him are fixating on this being Iain Hogg.'

'And you think he's innocent?'

'There's a world between innocent and guilty. Right now, we don't know anything really. Their theory was the flesh under his fingernails was hers, but it's clearly not. So now it's a waiting game with your DNA stuff. And even then...'

'I'll try and get the laws of physics to speed up.'

'I didn't mean that. I meant, that'll give us evidence. But rather than acting like an adult and waiting for that, Gashkori's ploughing ahead and trying to force a conviction.'

'Which will catch them out.'

'Will it, though?' Marshall held his gaze. 'I don't know. I've seen stuff railroaded through before, only to fall apart in court.'

'So what's your plan, Rob?'

'I'm going to have it out with Gashkori. This latest thing you've found is going to open the case wide.'

'You're a brave man, Rob.'

'Someone's got to be.'

17

Marshall stood in the open office doorway, ready to knock, but he stopped and let the scene play out.

He hadn't seen Andrea Elliot in a few months. She seemed okay, which surprised him considering everything she'd been through in that time. But she didn't look at him, just focused on her computer monitor.

Gashkori was perched on the edge of her desk, staring into his clasped palms resting on his knee. 'What you're telling me is, despite clear instruction, you and Struan signally failed to get a confession during the interview. Correct?'

Elliot ignored him and kept typing on her keyboard, eyes locked on the screen. 'Sometimes you throw everything at them, Ryan, including the kitchen sink, and they *still* don't say the magic words.' She sat back and looked around at him. 'My guess is you're thinking Hogg's either a total psychopath or you've got the wrong guy here.'

'Or it was a piss-poor interview.'

She shrugged, when Marshall would've expected her to put up a fight. Maybe even blame it on Struan. Maybe even point out how flimsy the charge was.

Gashkori stood up and sat in the chair next to her. 'How did it go with him in the interview?'

'We got nowhere. Well. He revealed they were Beltane Cornet and Lass.'

Gashkori laughed. 'What the hell is that?'

'How long have you been working down here, Ryan?'

'A while.'

'Well, you should get a better handle on the traditions here. I'm trying to get in touch with the committee. Hopefully me and Struan can speak to them tomorrow. See if there's any juice.'

Potter brushed past Marshall as she entered the room. 'There you are, Ryan.'

Gashkori looked at her, then back at Elliot, then he stood up tall. 'Ma'am. I thought you'd gone?'

'That'll be why you're suddenly on your best behaviour.' She beckoned Marshall over to join them.

Gashkori spotted him for the first time, but didn't say anything. He cleared his throat. 'I was just chatting to Andrea here about our interview strategy for—'

'I heard what you were discussing, Ryan. You're trying to throw DI Elliot under the bus, aren't you? And by extension, me.' Potter raised her eyebrows. 'Have to say, Ryan, like Shania Twain said, that don't impress me much.'

Gashkori was like a rat backed into a corner. He tugged on his nose, then cleared his throat. 'I think we all know it's Hogg who's killed Becky. It's one of those cases where all he's doing is denying everything. "Wasn't me. I didn't do that. I couldn't possibly have killed her, could I?" All that shite. But he was there when she was killed. He's got a very plausible motive.'

Potter looked at Marshall. 'Rob, you've been shadowing DI Taylor, right? Do you think it's plausible?'

Marshall took one look at Gashkori and got a severe glare. But having the big boss in the room meant he could act with impunity. 'I have to say I'm extremely sceptical Hogg killed Rebecca.'

'Of course you are.' Gashkori threw his hands up in the air. 'Care to spell it out for us?'

'Have you spoken to Kirsten Weir about—?'

'I spoke to her earlier at the hospital. Didn't expect her to come in, but she turned up all the same.'

'Did you listen to her voicemail?'

'No.'

'She's in the lab just now, so I could—'

'What did she have to say?' Potter looked right at Marshall.

'Just that she's running the DNA from under Hogg's fingernails.'

'I got that bit.' Gashkori nibbled at a fingernail. 'What else?'

'She said the DNA sample belongs to a male and it's a different blood type to Rebecca.'

Gashkori took a few seconds to think it all through. Felt like he was staring right through Marshall. 'So?' He leaned forward. 'If I was looking at DNA to do my job, I'd have quit the force a long time ago. Fail to see the problem here. It's Hogg.'

'The problem is, Ryan, you don't have any evidence of Hogg attacking Rebecca.'

'Doesn't mean he didn't do it.' Gashkori clenched his fists tight. 'Rob. You bash someone's pumpkin against a tunnel wall like that, you're going to get blood and brains on you. We'll find that evidence.'

'Trouble is, Kirsten's team didn't just do his fingernails. DCs Paton and McIntyre retrieved the clothes he was seen wearing last night. Kirsten swabbed both them and him for blood spatter and grey matter. We don't have anything.'

Gashkori folded his arms. 'You're telling me a man who used to be the victim's lover and who confessed to being at the crime scene with the victim *didn't* kill her?'

'I'm saying I think it's unlikely, aye.'

'So you come in here and—'

Potter raised a hand to shut up Gashkori. 'Rob, do you think this could match the case in Edinburgh?'

'I mean, it *could*. There's blunt-force trauma in both.'

Gashkori rolled his eyes. 'Rob, you yourself discarded that.'

'No, I said it's unlikely to be connected to the case in Glasgow in Kelvingrove Tunnel. And I still stand by that assertion. When I assessed those cases in April, we had two data points which appeared to be unconnected. Or we just didn't know how to connect them, which is less likely. But with the Edinburgh case and with Rebecca here in Neidpath, we have two victims possibly killed by a blunt-force trauma in a disused railway tunnel.'

Gashkori laughed. 'So you think it's all connected? Do all those bits of string join all sorts of dots?'

'Possibly. I haven't done the work yet to validate the whole thing.'

'Okay.' Potter smiled at Gashkori. 'Here's what we're going to do, Ryan. First, Rob and Callum will mosey on down that avenue and see where that leads them.'

Gashkori grunted. 'Are you sure about that?'

'Why, do you have an issue with that approach?'

'It's just, you're taking a DI off me to do this—'

'Are you saying I'm interfering in your investigation?'

'No, of course not. Just... Cal is one of my best cops and we're losing him to something in DI Marshall's terms of reference.' Gashkori scratched at his neck.

Potter stood there, arms folded.

Gashkori snorted. 'Fine. They make a good team.'

'I'm glad you're in agreement, Ryan.' Potter rubbed a hand down his arm. 'Now, I've got to get myself back to Gartcosh, having wasted enough of my time here in the Borders.' She slipped on a leather biker jacket. 'I'll see you all later.' She walked off out of the room, leaving the three of them behind.

Gashkori walked over and watched her cross the open plan office, then turned and shut the door. 'Couldn't fucking help yourself, Rob, could you?'

'With what?'

'You grassed to She Who Cannot Be Named behind my back.'

'Okay... For starters, I report directly to her, despite only being a DI. Unlike you, Ryan. And I didn't go behind your back. I haven't briefed her until now. Besides, she's the one who brought me in to consult on this case. That's all that's happening here.'

'Bullshit.' Gashkori thumped the door jamb. 'You were at the door with her. Of course you went to her!'

'I was standing there while you chatted to Andrea. You just didn't notice me.'

'Leave me out of this.' Elliot was working away on her computer, oblivious to the battle raging behind her. 'Got enough on my plate without you two adding to the noise with your constant bickering.'

Gashkori stepped closer. 'You were listening in on us?'

Marshall stood up tall, then gestured out into the office space. 'Can we have a word in private?'

'Fine.' Gashkori charged out through the door.

'I'll see you later, Andrea.' But she didn't reply, so Marshall followed Gashkori into his own office.

Gashkori picked up a bottle of water and strangled the lid off. 'Out with it, then.'

Marshall stood his ground. 'Sir, I'm telling you this as a friend, okay? I honestly think you need to consider other options here. Hogg is looking like a no-go.'

'Bollocks.'

'Sir. There's nothing on him. Sure, he had a decent motive to do it, but there's nothing saying he did. Meanwhile, you're in danger of getting yourself into deep shit here. Miranda's not impressed.'

'Miranda, eh?'

'I'm serious. You're focusing on the wrong suspect.' Marshall saw he was getting nowhere – time to move on. 'Callum and I met Rebecca's mother earlier. She deserves justice for what's happened. If you let us investigate these links, this case might disappear off your plate. But please focus on other suspects too. Like Jonty Sandison.'

Gashkori ran a hand through his hair and something seemed to settle in him. 'I thought it was him.'

'Been there, sir. Bought that T-shirt. Worn those shoes for a few miles. Let me be clear, though. I'm not saying it's *not* Hogg, just that you need to open this out until the evidence base is stronger.'

Gashkori finally looked over at him. 'So you think I should let Hogg go?'

'Have you finished questioning him?'

'We haven't finished validating his alibi.'

'Why?'

'Trouble is, we can't. After he left the pub, the only person who saw him was Rebecca's mother, first thing this morning. Not even his neighbours, who were also all pished because of this Highland Games nonsense.'

'Okay. Then let him go.'

Gashkori seemed to think that through. 'I hear you, but I'm going to keep him in. He's been charged, but we won't get into court until Wednesday because of the backlog in Selkirk. So that gives us a couple of days' grace.' He clapped Marshall on the arm. 'Thing is, I'm starting to see your point here.'

Finally...

'That's good, sir.'

'What you were saying has resonated a bit with me. That

thing with recovering DNA from under Hogg's fingernails. Means it *might* be a serial killer's.'

'What?' Marshall laughed. 'There's a much more rational explanation. Jonty Sandison, for instance. Rather than diving into the world of a serial killer, you should—'

'Rob. You're consulting on my case. The boss said you're not to take any active investigative work. Your job is to look into this one up in Edinburgh and in Glasgow too. While the DNA's processing and while we're hauling Jonty Sandison over the coals, you can appease She Who Cannot Be Named by reviewing these as serial killings. Think on how much glory there'll be in taking on a serial murder case and solving the whole thing, eh?'

18

DAY 2
MONDAY

Marshall yawned into his fist and watched the traffic trudge along Gorgie Road, scanning the cars for the pool Audi coming up from Gala nick, but he kept coming up blank.

Kirsten stood next to him, focusing on her phone rather than the street. Travel mug in her hand, laptop bag at her feet almost touching his. 'Bet you wish you'd driven yourself, eh?'

'Wish I could, but Potter wouldn't let me.' Marshall wrapped an arm around Kirsten. 'But this way, I got to stay in bed that bit longer with you.'

She kissed him on the lips. 'And I loved every second of it.'

'Me too.' Marshall kissed her back, deep and long, then broke off reluctantly. 'You can head off down to Gala, you know?'

'They can wait for me.' She stood up on tiptoes to kiss him again.

Marshall planted his hands on her hips.

'Get a room!' Taylor pulled up on the double yellows, window down and grinning away. 'Pair of perverts. I could arrest you.'

'You're one to talk.' Kirsten reached in and yanked his clip-on tie right off. 'That time you got caught in—'

'Give me that back!' Taylor got out and tried reaching for it.

Kirsten handed him the tie, with a grin. 'Just messing with you, Cal.'

'What they all say.' Taylor clipped it back on but it didn't sit quite right. 'Anyway. You happy for me to drive us through to Glasgow, Rob?'

Marshall shrugged. 'Suits me. I've got a bit of work I could do while you drive.'

'So long as you don't talk at me, I'm happy with that.' Taylor winked at Kirsten. 'I'll see you later, doll. Ryan's waiting for you.'

'Bet he is.' Kirsten kissed Marshall, then walked over to her car. 'See you tonight, Rob.'

'Can't wait.' Marshall waved her off, then slowly got into the passenger seat of the pool car. He stowed his laptop bag in the footwell – he'd see how the chat progressed before he decided on whether to do the work.

'Nice to see you wearing a suit, champ.' Taylor shot off into a gap in the wall of traffic before Marshall could clip himself in. 'I'd heard rumours you were seeing Kirsten, but didn't *know* you were.'

'Aye, it's been a while now.'

'Good. She's seemed happy for a wee while. Take it that's down to you?'

'I've no idea, Cal. Have you known her long?'

'We had a good working relationship back in Glasgow, when she did our forensics. Then we kind of lost touch when she moved away. Was that Edinburgh or Aberdeen? I can't remember. Weird how you find old people in new places, isn't it?'

'True enough.'

'Kirst's a good person.' Taylor looked over. 'Please don't mess her around.'

'Wasn't intending on doing it.'

'Good.'

Marshall grinned. 'So this incident where you got caught?'

'Not my story to tell.' Taylor slowed for the lights heading onto the fast road west. 'Sorry if I'm a bit grumpy today.'

'Hadn't noticed.' Marshall laughed. 'What's going on?'

'Just hate missing the briefing. You know how it is, right?'

'FOMO?'

'What's that?'

'Fear Of Missing Out.'

'Something like that.' Taylor scratched at his chin, already stubbly. 'If you aren't part of the discussion, you're the topic.'

Marshall nodded. 'When it comes to briefings, I only get Joy Of Missing Out. Usually a waste of time, in my experience.'

'Please don't tell that to some of the DCs. Either the younger ones like Ash Paton or that older useless one in Elliot's team.' Taylor drove off, clicking his fingers. 'McIntyre, is it?'

'He's okay.'

'Okay isn't good enough, though.' Taylor kicked down as he joined the fast road. 'Don't want them to think briefings are optional.'

'They're not. They're just tedious, that's all.'

'Guess you're right.' Taylor had to ease off a bit, but the traffic wasn't too bad for this stretch at this time of day. 'It'll be weird going back to my old stomping ground, though. If we'd done this last night, I could've stayed at a mate's through there.'

'The one who you got caught—'

'We're not talking about that.'

'Sorry.' Marshall struggled to hide his smile. 'But the people we need to speak to weren't on last night, given it was a Sunday, so it would've been a complete waste of time.'

'Guess so.'

'Are you living in the Borders now?'

'Staying with my ex's brother in Dalkeith.'

'That sounds complicated.'

'I was mates with him first. It's how we got together.'

'Ah, well that makes sense. Staying on a mate's sofa sounds better.'

'True. Still, it's an absolute bugger of a commute.'

'It's not that bad, is it? Thought everyone would be heading into Edinburgh?'

'Sure, they are, which makes getting out of Dalkatraz a total nightmare at any time of day.' Taylor glanced over. 'Heard you've been living with Pringle?'

'Long story.'

'We've got a long drive.'

'What's there to say? Pringle's living in South Africa now. The house is on the market and the solicitors are dealing with it. Don't expect it to shift quickly, given the market.'

'But?'

'Truth is, I'm glad to be out of there. It wasn't easy. Having to look after him when he started going downhill. And I guess this finally gave us the kick we needed. Me and Kirsten are serious about each other, so that was the push we needed to move in together.'

'Talk about a bugger of a commute... Gorgie to Gartcosh?'

'Could be worse.'

'Sure, but not much.' Taylor looked over again. 'Listen, we really got off on the wrong foot with each other yesterday. I want to just get on with stuff together, okay? No egos, just focus on the work.'

'It's what I try to do, Cal.'

'Then we're agreed?'

'Sure thing.' Marshall reached into his bag for the laptop. 'Better look over this stuff, if you don't mind.'

'Why would I mind about you shutting up?'

But Taylor's smile had a bit of cheek in it, rather than a lot of malice.

19

SHUNTY

DS Rakesh Siyal couldn't sit still, even though he knew he should. He was bursting with energy – it was like someone had wired him into the mains. Even had to check all the plugs were off in the room.

Colin Hooper sat next to him. His skin was a lighter shade of grey than his suit. As cops went, he was probably as useless as people said Siyal was. But he wasn't a standard cop – he was one of the investigating officers tasked with looking into other prison officers. And that meant he had particular strengths, like Siyal had. Disciplined, organised, efficient and did what he was told. Only downside was he didn't report to Siyal.

The red-faced guard sat opposite them, facing the door and not looking at either of them. Stephen Fields. Thick silver hair in no discernible cut, just seemed to sit there. Something horrible hung from his left nostril, tangled up in all the thick hairs. 'That's correct.' But he was getting impatient now, his fingers fidgeting harder and harder.

Siyal leaned on the table, but it wasn't like a police interview room. 'You're saying you didn't know where David Elliot was being transported to?'

A glance in his direction. 'That's correct.'

'I find that hard to believe.'

'How?'

'Listen, we've been tasked with digging into the death of David Elliot back in April. It'll make our jobs much easier if you were to play ball here.'

'How am I not?'

'We just need you to tell us the truth.'

He shut his eyes. 'Shouldn't this be a fatal accident inquiry?'

'It is, Stevie.' Hooper rested forward on his elbows. 'DS Siyal and I here have been asked to assist with preparing the groundwork for it. As part of this, we are interviewing court officers like yourself who would've known where Davie Elliot was going.'

'Told you, pal.' Fields threw out his hands. 'We didn't know where the boy was headed. Neither of us did. Know what they say about this place? We're like mushrooms – kept in the dark and fed shite.'

'That doesn't sound right.'

'Are you calling me a liar?'

'If you lie to someone's face, you're entitled to call them a liar, yes.' Hooper stayed very still. 'Now, I'll let you off with that and give you one last chance to change your answer.'

'Mate. Read my lips. We didn't know where he was going.'

'Okay. But you received an email regarding that, didn't you?'

Fields shifted his gaze between them. 'What?'

Siyal reached into his briefcase and pulled out a wad of information. 'On Wednesday the seventeenth of April, you were the recipient of an email sent by Damian Ridpath.'

'Damo's my supervisor, aye.'

'This email provided detailed technical instructions on the arrangements for transferring Davie Elliot to HMP Glenochil.'

'First time I've seen it.'

Siyal shifted to the next page. 'This is a list of the system accounts which read the email. Your account went in no fewer than six times.'

'Still don't remember it.'

Hooper laughed. 'That's nonsense. See if the email was someone asking me something stupid, I might forget. Same if it was a Nigerian prince looking to split his inheritance, if only I could meet him at a local airport with a few thousand pounds to cover some admin fees. Or someone promising me to make my willy longer. We've all seen hundreds of them, right? But this is very pertinent to your job and about a high-profile case you were tasked with overseeing.'

Siyal flipped over the page. 'Not to mention you going into the email six times, but you claim you don't even remember doing it once?'

'Sorry, but I can only tell you the truth here.'

'Okay.' Siyal sifted through the pages. 'Next, there's no sign it was forwarded to anyone, so at least you're in the clear on that score.'

'You honestly think someone's leaked this information?'

'We know they have, Mr Fields. It's just a case of identifying who and a matter of when we catch them.'

'Maybe I went to the toilet or kitchen and someone got access to it. Someone could've gained access to my computer. Like a cleaner or another officer.'

'These machines are locked down.' Hooper showed some of his paperwork. 'No screenshotting allowed, before you start down that path, and no ability to get files off there.'

Fields scratched at his neck. 'Could've taken a photo of the computer screen with their phone, right? Then they could've read it over the phone to someone...'

'Nope.' Hooper shook his head. 'The logins are constantly audited. Every use of the machine is recorded using the webcam. If your machine was left unlocked, we've only got you at the machine.'

'So you're watching us constantly?'

Hooper laughed. 'Mr Fields, you work in custody in the legal system. If you want privacy, you're in the wrong vocation.'

'Besides.' Siyal went to his last page. 'We've retrieved the phone records of every phone attached to nearby cell sites.'

'That must be thousands?'

'It was. And that was a lot of work. We've narrowed them down to people inside the building. So we know that's not possible.'

'You've gone through our phones?'

'Someone has been murdered in custody, Mr Fields. We have to treat this matter with the utmost importance.'

'Okay, but they could've called using a phone box?'

'None in operation nearby. By the time you get to the nearest one, you'd have missed the opportunity.'

'Look, lads, I can't help you. I knew Davie Elliot. Dealt with him a few times for transfers up from the Borders. He was in Melrose then Gala, right? He seemed a good lad and what happened to him was tragic. But it's got nothing to do with me or the other lads in here. We did everything by protocol.'

'So you're confirming you read the email?'

'Must've done.'

'And you're vouching for the whole team?'

'I am. Yes. We trust each other like brothers.'

So, either Fields and his mates were telling the truth or the people who got the information figured out another angle.

Siyal looked at Hooper, then back at Fields. 'Thank you for your time, sir. We'll be in touch.'

20

STRUAN

David Bowie sang about serious moonlight, but now Struan knew all about serious silence. He could handle many things, but silence wasn't one of them.

And Elliot was seriously giving him the silent treatment.

Not that he was about to break it, no matter how hard he found it.

They were standing outside a villa in the better part of Peebles. He'd fancied living around here himself, but it was just that bit too far from his old man's in Kelso. An hour with a good wind behind you. Easier to get into Edinburgh from here, though. Maybe once that was all settled, he could think about it.

The door opened and a man looked out. Mid-twenties, tall and thin. Sharp eyes. And a familiar face. 'Can I help you?'

'Hi, I'm DI Andrea Elliot.' She stepped forward, holding out her warrant card. Then she frowned. 'Hang on, you're Graeme Veitch, right?'

'PC Graeme Veitch, aye.' He shifted on the spot, like a wee lad who needed to go to the toilet. 'How can I help, ma'am?'

'You were managing the crime scene at Neidpath Tunnel, weren't you?'

'Aye.' Graeme yawned. 'Was there until midnight. Might be hot when the sun's up, but it was perishing after dark. And all those stories about the boy getting attacked by the devil... Pretty spooky.'

'I assure you, the devil wasn't there.'

'Sure, you say that, but if it's you and a clipboard against the forces of darkness...' Graeme yawned, his tongue waggling as he did so. 'Sorry. On back shift tonight, but I'm absolutely shattered.' He looked at Struan. 'It's DS Liddell, isn't it?'

'That's right.' Struan had never knowingly met the lad before. 'But call me Struan.'

'Of course. What can I help with?'

Struan smiled at him. 'We're looking for Gordon Veitch.'

'That's my dad. What's this about?'

'He was the chair of Beltane in 2017. Is he in?'

'Come on through.' Graeme led them into the house, tastefully decorated but a good while ago, then out into a conservatory at the back of the home, looking across a cottage garden filled with flowers and mature trees. 'I'm caring for Dad at home. Dementia is absolutely brutal, man.'

Struan nodded. 'I can fully empathise. Doing the same for my old man.'

'Sorry to hear that, Sarge.'

'It is what it is, right?' Struan gave a smile, then walked over to Gordon in the corner.

Dressed in a tweed suit, with lime shirt and navy tie, like he was heading out somewhere. Bare feet, though. And muttering something to himself. His hair was neatly trimmed, but his eyebrows were out of control.

Struan stepped close to Graeme. 'If you don't mind me saying, son, he looks old enough to be your grandfather.'

'He isn't, sadly. He's only seventy-four. He was a cop, as I'm sure you know.'

'We didn't.'

'Aye. Joined up later in life, so didn't get his thirty until he was in his sixties. Had me late on too. Used to play rugby for Peebles RFC. Got two Scotland caps, but they were just token gestures. Georgia and Argentina. I mean, I'm surprised they even play rugby there. Then he joined the army. Became a cop when he left. Had me when he was forty. Mum was forty-three. Lost Mum three years ago to the same horrible disease. No sooner had she gone than Dad starts going downhill.'

'Your parents both suffered dementia?'

'Right. I mean, he's mostly fine, but he has more moments of lucidity than Mum. She was way worse.'

'Man, that's brutal, if you don't mind me saying.'

'It's hit me pretty hard, I have to say. I'm only thirty-five.' Graeme didn't look anything like that age. Or act it. 'Shouldn't have to deal with this stuff yet.'

'You deal with what life chucks at you, don't you?' Struan held his gaze. 'My mum died when I was seven.'

'Sorry to hear that.' Graeme stared up at the ceiling.

Gordon briefly looked in their direction, but didn't seem to notice them. He went back to watching the blackbirds buggering about on the lawn.

'Would we be able to have a word with him? It's not about something he's done. Just about an active case.'

'Sure, of course.' Graeme walked over to his father. 'Dad, there are two people here to see you. Police officers.'

'What have I done now?'

'Nothing.' Struan kept his distance. 'We just need to ask you a few questions, that's all.'

'What time's tea, son?'

'Dad, it's only nine o'clock.'

'Right. Can I have some breakfast, then?'

'You've just had it.'

'Have I?'

'Kippers, toast and porridge.' Graeme smiled. 'Not all on the same plate, before you start.'

'Okay.' Something flickered in Gordon's eyes. 'What time's tea?'

Graeme smiled, but Struan knew that look, the sign of patience being tested way past breaking. The love he'd put into looking after his old man, but seeing his brain rot away in front of him like that. Having to endure the same questions, the same requests. And the hatred, the accusations, the bile. All coming from a place of confusion, but hard to stomach.

And you always had to smile through it.

Yeah, it was a lot to go through.

Graeme clapped his hands together. 'Can I get you two some tea?'

Elliot nodded. 'That'd be good, thanks.'

'Cheers. Milk and one.' Struan sat in the armchair next to Graeme's father. 'You okay there, Gordon?'

He looked over with milky eyes. Despite his silver hair, his skin was still smooth enough to be in his thirties. 'What's that?'

'Asked if you're okay.'

'Aye. I'm fine.' He went back to looking at the birds and muttering.

'Someone was talking to us about you yesterday, Gordon.'

'Oh, aye? Who was that?'

'Iain Hogg. You mind him?'

'Oh, him. Aye. Daft wee sod.'

'How do you know him?'

'Beltane. I was the boy for a bit. Way too long, aye.'

'What do you mean by that?'

'I ran the pigging thing, you arsehole!'

The insult slid off Struan like rice pudding off a wall. Yet again. 'Right, with you now.'

'They wanted someone to run it who'd been in the forces. Did all the marching in the army, didn't I? Looked the part. Helped put it together. Iain Hogg, eh? He was the Cornet one year. And the lassie… Becky, was it?'

'Rebecca Yellowlees, aye.'

'Lovely lass. Kind, smart. Good with the wee ones. Him, though… Went off the rails, eh?'

'Did he now?'

Life sparkled in Gordon's eyes. 'Don't you know?'

'We heard he dropped out of uni, aye.'

'Oh, is that what he's saying?' Gordon laughed. 'Some laddie.'

'You remember what happened?'

'Didn't leave. He was booted out. Still got a size nine right up his hoop!' Gordon laughed. 'What's he done now?'

'Just need to speak to him in connection with a murder.'

'So he's missing?'

'No. It's not that.'

'Son, I was a copper for thirty years. I know when I'm being lied to. What's he done?'

'Iain found Rebecca's body yesterday morning.'

'And you think he killed her?'

'Could he have?'

'Tough question.' Gordon seemed to consider it for a few seconds. That, or his blackbirds were interesting him greatly. 'Maybe. Tell you what, though, that arsehole really pissed me off when they split up. I'd vouched for him. Swore he wouldn't be an issue, despite some of the committee having reservations. I knew the boy's father, right? James. Good guy, but not when he had a drink in him. Barred from all the pubs in the town except for Buchan's Steps.' Gordon laughed. 'Hate to think what you'd have to do to get barred from that place!'

Struan joined in laughing. 'Gather Iain got himself chucked out last night.'

'What, how?'

'Hogg fell asleep when peeing then collapsed into the urinal! Headfirst!'

Gordon leaned back and bellowed with laughter. 'Headfirst?'

'Aye. Pish sloshed all over him.'

'In the name of the wee man, that's... Clive still running the place?'

'He is, aye.'

'My God, Mary'll be ages getting the stains out of him.'

'Mary?'

'My wife. She's sitting right there! When wee Graeme tripped up in the street and burst his nose, it took ages to get the blood out of his uniform.'

Ah shite, he'd slipped.

Just like Struan's old man would. The present was a confusing foreign country, the past a safe place.

'Here you go.' Graeme handed his father a cup of tea, with steam wafting up.

'That right, Mary?' Gordon looked over at an empty armchair. 'Mind, that wasn't that long ago.' He frowned, lips moving like he was counting the seconds. 'Of course. Of course.' He looked into his cup. 'There's nowhere near enough fucking milk in this, you prick!'

'I'll go get you some more, Dad.' Graeme took the cup back, then headed back into the house.

'Back in a sec.' Struan got up and followed Graeme through, leaving Elliot with his father. The kitchen was decorated like someone's idea of an Edwardian cottage. Someone in the late nineties.

Graeme was over by the kettle, shaking his head.

'You okay there?'

Graeme swung around, then dabbed at his eyes. 'Aye, I'm fine.'

'It's tough, isn't it? Losing your dad slowly like that. Day by day.'

'Exactly that. At some point, he'll be mostly gone. But until then, there are glimpses of the way he used to be.' Graeme shook his head. 'But the *rage*... it's off the charts. I know he's angry at the condition and not me, but... Last week, he was shouting at me for wanting to steal the house from him.'

'I've had that. It's not easy to listen to.'

'No. And he doesn't want to go into a home. But I really can't do this on my own, though. It's...' Veitch brushed at his eyes again. 'I mean, I've got to, haven't I? But I can't seem to make it work.'

'It's the promise you make.'

'And you don't know the cost. I was seeing this lassie, you know, but then Mum started going downhill and, with her and Dad and work, I just had no time. She's engaged to someone else now.'

'That's rough.'

'Right.'

'Did you know Iain Hogg?'

'Everybody knew the Hoggs. One of those families, you know? Five of them. Three lads, two lassies. Iain's the only one left in the town. Youngest, I think.'

'I gather he was Cornet and Lass with Rebecca?'

'Aye. Back in 2017.'

'Were you ever involved?'

'Course I was. Dad ran it for thirty years. I'm on the committee now, myself. Another drag on my time, but he wouldn't let me refuse it.'

'Were you Cornet?'

'2015.'

'I'm from Kelso, so things work a bit differently over there. Care to explain how it all works?'

'What's there to say? It's the Common Riding in these parts.

Used to be a fire festival, back in less enlightened times. Still have that up in Edinburgh. But ours got formalised, then merged with the Common Riding. All that stuff you have in Kelso and Gala and Selkirk and Hawick, we have all that too. But we've got three big roles. The Beltane Queen is a lassie in P7 at school, one of the three in the town. To them it's a one-day thing, with most of the kids put forward involved to one extent or another.'

'And the Cornet and his Lass?'

'Right. We choose him, then he chooses her, so it's usually a girlfriend or a sister. Very occasionally just a friend.'

'And yours?'

'The lassie I was seeing, Katie... she was my Lass. Loved her, but... Family comes first, eh?'

'What does being Cornet mean?'

'You're basically the ambassador for the town. Show up at all the other towns' Ridings, with your sash and rosette.'

'Then you're free after a year?'

'Nope. Three-year commitment. You both become the Cornet's right hand the next year, then left the following year. He's on the right side of the main man so he can take the flag from him. Flags are always in the right hand. You don't have to do much, just support them.'

'So there was an overlap?'

'Right. Hogg was Cornet when we were right-hand support. Same with Becky.' Veitch tipped in some milk. 'I mean, they were *supposed* to be.'

'What's that mean?'

'Hogg got stood down.'

'Stood down?'

'It's ancient terminology. Everything's a euphemism. I mean, I was twenty-five when I got the nod. Just after Dad's time, one of his old cronies, Eric, came up to me and said, "About time you got yourself on a horse, son". That's when I knew it was my turn. Thought the chance had passed me by. So when Iain Hogg was stood down, it's because he'd been a naughty boy.'

'Naughty how?'

'I mean, they were going out when they were Cornet and Lass. Then they split up, didn't they? Caused a wee stramash in the town. Dad worried it made us all look a bunch of fannies.'

'You know what happened between them?'

'He did something at the university. Up in Edinburgh. Napier. Same place I went. Easy enough to drive up there in my old Fiesta. Dad had to help out.'

'With the university?'

Veitch sighed. 'Had to write a letter of recommendation to the head of faculty at the uni. Hogg had been a stupid boy.'

'Do you know what he'd done?'

'Afraid not.'

'Do you mind me asking your dad?'

'No, but you won't get anything out of him. When he starts talking about Mum... That's it. He's gone for a few hours.'

Struan still fancied another tilt at him, though.

'But the lad Dad wrote to still works there. Old uni mate of Mum's cousin.'

'What was his name?'

21

MARSHALL

Taylor strolled down the steps to ground level and stopped outside the tunnel opening.

Marshall joined him, an aching numbness in his stomach.

The walkway hung over them, carrying cyclists and runners into Glasgow's West End. Someone darted across now, his steps like machine-gun fire above their heads. A middle-aged man, seemingly oblivious to them and to the tunnel opening.

Kelvingrove Tunnel. Yet another victim of the Beeching cuts. Just like at Neidpath, the entrance had been blocked off by bricks, probably as a result of health and safety legislation. Unlike Neidpath, the middle was filled by a pair of massive gates, heavily graffitied over in a range of tag styles. A padlock hung down – even that was tagged by the artist.

Taylor twisted the padlock up and entered a code. 'Bollocks.'

'What's up?'

'Code doesn't work anymore.'

Marshall peered through the gap between the gate and the tunnel edge. He saw nothing in there, just empty black ink.

Water poured nearby and splashed further away. 'It's just as well we visited, because I've completely forgotten everything about this place.' He took out the official police tablet from his laptop bag, yet another piece of technology weighing him down, physically and mentally. He pulled up the old case file and sifted through the photos.

A stern-looking man facing the camera. Shining blue eyes. Dark hair cropped tight, except for a loose tangle above his left ear, that swept down.

Adam Malkmus, aged twenty-nine.

Cause of death: blunt-force trauma.

Just like in Edinburgh and Peebles.

Above, a pair of students rumbled over, their bike tyres whirring, shouting at each other about a TV show. At least, Marshall assumed it was.

He let out a slow breath. 'Feel a bit stupid. We'd discounted any connection, but it's the same cause of death as the other two.'

Taylor was checking his phone. 'Thing is, it's easy to discount stuff when you've only got two cases and a likely explanation for each, right? And you're here, doing the work to validate.' He fiddled with the lock and it clicked, then swung open. '*Et voilà.*'

'How did you manage that?'

'Get a lot of kids breaking in here, so the council have to change it all the time. Texted a mate in uniform, who had to go in there last week following some urbexers in their forties and fifties.'

'Urbexers?'

'Urban explorers. People who have YouTube channels where they go to places they shouldn't, film it, then make money from it.'

'And these were—'

'Nope. These guys were novelists. Or so they claimed. One

was writing a book about urbexers finding a doorway to another dimension.'

'Like Narnia?'

'Kind of. But this was in an old tunnel rather than a wardrobe. Anyway, Sketchy let the daft buggers off with a warning.' Taylor went first, but the daylight didn't stretch far into the tunnel. 'Goes for a mile, would you believe? Twice as long as Neidpath.' He snapped on his torch and held it up like he was an FBI agent on TV, shining it against the side wall.

Like Neidpath, it was all brick, aged by a hundred and fifty years of life underground. Water was the main source of weathering, rotting some bricks and covering others in thick moss.

Taylor switched to a broad beam, which didn't reach that far in, but made more of the surface glow. 'Body was found right here, wasn't it?'

Marshall pulled up the photo of the decomposing corpse propped up against the side like he was having a little snooze. With his brain bashed in. 'Just over there.' He pointed ahead of them, then walked off.

Someone had painted '100' in yellow, presumably marking out the number of metres into the tunnel. Or feet. Or yards.

Marshall crouched beside it. 'The body was found just here.'

Taylor cast his torch over the bricks, bleaching the brown almost white. 'You thought I was trying to pass the buck on the case at the time, didn't you?'

'That's not true, Cal. I was asked to review every single murder in the UK with a view to them being the work of a serial killer.'

'But you didn't think we did a great job, did you?'

'No comment.' Marshall grinned but Taylor shifted the light away so he couldn't see it. 'It's not malicious, you know? I'm told to play devil's advocate.'

'Got enough literal advocates of Satan in the criminal defence world.'

'Sure, but they're all just doing a job for their clients and to underpin the criminal justice system.'

Taylor looked at him like he'd gone mad. 'Do you enjoy it?'

'No comment.'

Taylor smirked. 'Do you think we both might be wrong on this?'

'What, that this *is* connected to the other two?' Marshall inspected the site where the body had lain again. No trace anyone had ever been here, let alone died in that exact spot. 'This is still early days and it's really hard to say, despite what Potter or Gashkori want.' He stood up tall again. 'What I do know is this is now a cold case. Whether it's a cold *serial* case, I can't say yet.'

'But?'

'The violence could be consistent with the Neidpath one. But there's a massive difference.' Marshall tapped on a photo, showing the tunnel wall just after the corpse had been removed – it looked exactly the same as now, like the death had been erased from existence. Or had never happened, despite the pictures. 'There's a photo of a survey done the year before. Looks exactly the same, doesn't it?'

'What do you mean?'

'There's nowhere near enough blood here. And nowhere his head was clearly struck.'

'You think the victim wasn't killed here?'

'Right. Someone transported him here.'

'That can't be a hundred percent likely, can it?'

'Explain?'

'Well. The body was found after a few days and it's not exactly a sauna in here.' Taylor splashed in a puddle, as if to emphasise his point. 'So any evidence could have been washed away.'

'See what you mean, but there'd still be something.' Marshall sifted through the reports. 'And there *are* signs the body was dragged in here. Scuff marks on his boots, for instance.' He pointed back towards the light. 'And some possible signs of being hauled along there.'

Taylor nodded, his face lit up from below like a Halloween pumpkin. 'So you've got a mystery over how they got the body down here?'

'Right.' Marshall took a fresh look at the site. 'I don't know. It kind of fits and it doesn't. Thing is, Neidpath is pretty far from any roads, so it'd be hard to transport a body there. Easier to kill there. Here, it's really close to a main road. Someone could easily spot the killer bringing the victim here to be killed. Risk of discovery and release of victim.'

'You're saying they killed him first. Pull up, lug the body down here, get in, dump them.' Taylor pointed up the way they'd come. 'This is right by a cycle path, Rob. People running and walking home all day long. That's a massive risk.'

'I see your point, but it's still doable. Four in the morning on a Monday, say. Nobody's coming home from nightclubs, or hardly anyone. Too early for people going to work. September too, so it would've been dark. And you'd hear anyone coming towards you in the general silence, whether they're cycling, walking or running. See their lights too, if they had them.' Marshall stood up tall and put his tablet back in his bag. 'Thing is, Cal, I didn't work the case like you did. I just came here for a look around and ran through the MO with you to make sure it didn't match anything in my caseload. It didn't then, but it might now?'

'Or it might not.' Taylor blew out a deep breath. 'So this is a waste of time?'

'No. What we exclude is as important as what we include. And if we can determine a factor we hadn't previously known about, that might blow things wide open. The software we use continually analyses data points to look for connections, no matter how tenuous. And even ones that didn't become known until two or three cases later. As long as all of the data points are captured.'

'Okay, so now we're here again, have you found anything new?'

'I've got a few extra things I could add, aye. Then we can see what comes out after Hardeep's played around with it.'

'Hardeep?'

'Singh. My assistant.'

Taylor laughed. 'I'd love an assistant.'

'Think of him like a DS who can use both of his brain cells in the right order. And at the same time. Without starting a fire.'

Taylor laughed louder now.

The echo didn't seem to die away and it unsettled Marshall. Gooseflesh ran up and down his arms. 'In profiling, we have to play the long game because, well, so do serial killers.'

Taylor snorted at that. 'That's very cute.'

'Just like you, Cal.' Marshall pinched his cheek. 'Anyway. It's not just Hardeep working away with a pencil. Most of it is automated. The program runs in the background and pulls from all sorts of databases including ViCLAS and HOLMES. It's what we do with the output that's the most important part. Last month, I was at a conference down in Cambridge run by the software vendors – they said the next version is going to use AI. With that tech going the direction it is, maybe one day the profiler will be virtual.'

'I'd prefer that.'

'So would I.' Marshall set off back towards the tunnel entrance. 'Remind me again, who found the body?'

22

Marshall followed Taylor out onto a vertical beer garden – a patio area stuck at the top of the building, looking across rooftops towards some of Glasgow University's newer buildings. The older ones were hidden.

Two of the six tables were occupied. The nearest by a group of four lads, already getting stuck into pints of hazy beer, the citrusy smell wafting over. Probably students back early – or who'd never left.

Two men in their early thirties sat at the far table. Both with half-drunk coffees in front of them. Short hair and shades on, both painfully hip, wearing box-fresh T-shirts with slogans Marshall didn't recognise – then again, cool was the last thing Marshall was. Or cared about.

The taller of the two raised two fingers cradling his pack of cigarettes. 'Taylor?'

Taylor stood over him. 'Thanks for meeting us here, Craig. Mind if we sit?' He didn't wait and took the bench opposite him, leaving the other half for Marshall. 'Didn't expect you pair to actually show.'

'Not like we're not busy at this time of day, is it?' Craig held out a hand for Marshall to shake. So many beads and wristbands dangling. 'Craig Bell.'

'Rob Marshall.' He didn't get the offer of a hand from his mate.

'Gav Robertson.' His chubby face was soon masked behind a wall of vape mist. 'How can we help you?'

Taylor sat back, acting like he was a normal bloke meeting some pals in the sun for a morning chinwag. 'Need to ask you some questions about Adam Malkmus.'

'Right.' Craig snorted, then pressed his cigarette butt into the ashtray. 'Have you solved it?'

'Sadly not. Yet.'

Craig dropped the cigarette and looked up, eyes narrowed with hope. 'What do you want to know?'

'We've just been to where you found him.'

'Horrible place.' Craig sparked another cigarette. 'Last place we thought to look.'

Marshall leaned forward. 'How did you get in?'

'Lock was open.' Craig blew out a puff to the side, away from them. The smoke still came back. 'Must've been broken by whoever killed him.'

Marshall nodded, like he agreed with it. Truth was, he didn't know anything really – and he certainly didn't like to assume. 'And he was just sitting there?'

'More like lying. Propped up, anyway. That's where we found him.' Craig looked at Gav and something seemed to pass between them. 'Adam was a good guy, you know? Really good guy.'

'In what way?'

'What can we say?' Gav sucked on his vape pen and let it mist out slowly. 'Adam was a DJ. Full-time gig. Like us.' He gestured at Craig. 'All three of us own a company. It's a music thing.'

Craig burped into his fist. 'Used to run a club in Glasgow. Bass Cadet.' He took another drag on his cigarette. 'That's how we met him. Then we joined forces, renamed it and grew it into a chain in Manchester, Bristol and London too.' He opened his laptop and slid it around. 'Here's the flyer for our podcast.'

Marshall had a look at it.

Berghain
Hunters
Club

'Berghain? As in bargain? Because it's cheap? Or good value?'

'No.' Gav laughed. 'Berghain. It's a club in Berlin. Named after the Kreuz*berg* and Friedrichs*hain* districts. Super exclusive. Virtually impossible to get in unless you know someone or look a certain way. Elon Musk was turned away despite being on the guest list.'

'And it's in tribute to that?'

'Our whole ethos is, aye. Everything is super exclusive. We've got an app and a mailing list. If people want in, they need to queue for months beforehand. Virtually. And they pay us a monthly amount for the privilege. It's pretty lucrative.'

Taylor was looking at his phone.

Marshall nudged him and handed him the flyer, which he actually took. 'What's the link to Berlin?'

'Adam's German.' Craig sucked deep on his cigarette. 'Well, Bavarian. Calling a Bavarian a German is kind of like calling a Scotsman English. He's from Tutzing, a wee town in the lakes in Bavaria. He went to uni in Berlin and got into techno there. He moved to Glasgow for work a few years back. Worked at an investment company, but did the DJing at night and at the weekends.'

Taylor put his phone down. 'Says here it's a gay club.'

'That a problem?'

'Why would it be?'

Craig looked away. 'Just wondering where this is going, that's all?'

'Was Adam gay?'

'It's no longer a crime in this country.'

'Not saying it is.' Taylor smiled. 'Just trying to build up a picture of his life.'

'I'll take you on trust, then. We went there, desperate to get into Berghain. Turned down twice. Adam worked in a bar in Berlin. It's how Craig and I met him. He knew how to get in. Knew the door staff. We got in and had, like, the best night. And we kept in touch with him. When he moved to Glasgow, we started going out to clubs together. And we just chatted a lot. So the natural progression was to a podcast. We did it under that name. Berghain Hunters Club. Gav and I were his co-hosts. And it took off. All of us were able to give up the day jobs a few years ago.'

Taylor blinked hard a few times. 'Just from a *podcast*?'

'No. The clubs contributed a lot to it. But the podcast got people to come along. Pretty soon, we'd be making more from our Sunday night than we did from our day jobs. So we started doing a Saturday. Then a Friday. Then we bought a place and then expanded out.'

'How did the pandemic hit it?'

'This is all after that. We rode the recovery train. But we'd started getting decent Patreon money from the podcast during lockdown. People wanted to dance, so we'd stick up some mixes. We got good creator money from YouTube too. Aside from that, we just talked about music and clubs and gigs by experimental acts. And we did some daft stuff about growing beards as well as we grew a brand. That took off, weirdly enough. Went viral on TikTok. And we started doing live shows where we'd talk shite on stage, then have exclusive club nights afterwards for our members. And we could do pop-up nights anywhere. Sheffield, Nottingham, Dublin. Even Edinburgh. We saw there was an audience for what we were doing, so we started up new clubs with some mates doing the running.'

Marshall was jotting it all down on his tablet, the pen tip clacking off the screen. This didn't feel relevant, but maybe Rebecca Yellowlees had been a subscriber. Or maybe not. But she did have a Glasgow connection. And there was a drugs connection to her conviction, certainly – not a million miles from the club scene. 'Did Adam know a Rebecca? Maybe a Becky?'

Craig glanced over at Gav. 'There were maybe a couple of girls with that name.'

'Any of them Yellowlees?'

'Sorry, I'd need to check.'

'Check what?'

'The list of our Patreon subscribers.'

'Can you send it to us?'

Gav sat back and stroked his chin. 'I'm not sure we can.'

Taylor rested his elbows on the table. 'We can get you a warrant.'

'It's not that. I'm just not sure how we'd do it?'

'I can get you a guy to copy and paste the names down by hand, if comes to it.'

'Fine. We can do that.' Gav scribbled a note to himself. 'Who is Rebecca Yellowlees?'

'She went to university in Glasgow. Strathclyde.'

'Pleased for her.' Craig took a puff of smoke. 'Still don't know her.'

Taylor wafted away the smoke. 'Why do you think Adam was killed?'

Craig looked over at Gav with a raised eyebrow and got a nod back. 'Drugs.'

'That's your theory?'

'And the police's too, isn't it?'

Taylor leaned back and almost rolled off the bench. 'We believed it was a possibility. But the fact you just brought it up like that...'

'Thing is, Gav and I are straight edge. No drink, no drugs, no casual sex. Vaping and smoking are about the only stimulants we let into our bodies. And caffeine.' Craig held up his empty coffee cup. 'But that kind of mind-set is rare in the scene. You're either like us, or you're chasing absolute destruction. Booze, pills, love. Sitting in someone's kitchen at half six in the morning with an empty bag of coke, arguing about Space Raiders and Monster Munch.'

'And Adam? Was he straight edge?'

'No. Adam was a massive caner.'

'Was Adam dealing drugs?'

Gav sat back and finished his coffee. 'I think so.'

'You think so?'

'Put it this way, I know some people who bought some E from him.'

'Ecstasy?'

'And speed. And ketamine.' Gav raised his hands. 'But I don't know anything else about it. I didn't like it, but Adam was Adam, you know?'

'Did you tell that to the detectives investigating Adam's murder?'

'We did, aye.' Craig got out his phone and started fiddling with it. 'Someone called Quarrels. Didn't think that was a real name, but there you go.'

23

Some buildings had a glorious view.

Others looked at the back of an Asda.

The office lights were low, making Marshall squint at the glare bleeding in from outside. Wasn't even the car park, just the back. Right now, a delivery lorry was making a mess of pulling in, getting waved through by a gang of store employees.

Maybe not so much an office as a sweaty meeting room – the only good thing about it was the tea drum.

The door rattled open and a suited woman walked through.

Tall and feline, she looked like she should have a few whiskers on her angular cheeks. 'DI Alex Quarrels.' Even her voice was a Perthshire purr. 'Callum Taylor.'

He leaned into her hug, then broke off. 'Oh, a hug? You must miss me here, boss.'

'We do, actually. The quality of tea making has gone right downhill.' Quarrels grinned at him. 'Speaking of which, I gather you helped yourselves?'

Taylor raised his cup. 'Thanks again.'

'Right.' She started pouring herself a cup from the drum. 'How's life treating you down in the Borders, Cal?'

'Not bad. See my folks a bit more. Work's decent enough.'

'Good, good.' Quarrels gave a little yawn – looked like she was ready for a late-morning cat nap – then sipped some of her tea. 'So, let me get this straight, Cal – you're here to dig up a cold case. Right?'

'Adam Malkmus.'

Quarrels looked over at Marshall. 'Cal's last big case with us before the exalted Ryan Gashkori sent for him.' She pawed at his forearm like a cat desperate to be fed. 'Congrats on the promotion, by the way.'

'Thanks.'

'I'd say it's well deserved, but...' She shot him a crafty wink. 'Anyway. Malkmus... You're more than welcome to take that case off our hands. DCS Potter was—'

'Jesus!' Taylor raised his hands in the air. 'You don't name She Who Cannot Be Named! Doesn't that mean she appears?'

'Do you see her anywhere?' Quarrels looked around her office. 'Anyway, *the boss* was in here, asking a lot of questions about that case when we were investigating. We agreed to put it down to a gangland hit.'

'She agreed with that?'

'She wears a few hats. Back then, her remit covered all this serial malarkey as well, but aye, she agreed that drugs was the likeliest reason.'

'You don't sound convinced?'

'Short on evidence. Then She Who Cannot Be Named was back, all excited by that other case in Edinburgh, but didn't think they were connected.'

'What did you think?'

'Not paid enough to think for myself.' Quarrels laughed. 'Cal here thought it could've been an accident.'

'I didn't say that.'

'Sure. You did. In front of the whole team.'

Taylor was blushing. 'Suggested we keep an open mind, that's all.'

'Right.' Quarrels laughed again. 'Clearly a murder. *Clearly*. I mean, someone took him there.' She blew a raspberry. 'I was a bit disappointed when Potter's idiot palmed it off, though.'

'Should probably introduce myself. Rob Marshall.' He smiled at her. 'I'm Potter's idiot.'

'Ah, shite.' Quarrels slapped a hand to her forehead. 'Talk about putting your foot in it, eh?'

'It's okay. I'll forgive you.' Marshall took a sip of his tea. 'Just tell us your take on the Malkmus case.'

'My take? It's a murder.' She stared at Marshall, but clearly saw that wasn't going to do. 'What's there to say? A techno DJ murdered in suspicious circumstances. Killed in an unknown location and dumped in a tunnel. Some foreign forensic traces on him, but nothing we could match any suspect to. Like I said, She Who Cannot Be Named was interested in trying to pair it to a murder in Edinburgh back in April. I was on holiday when that came in, but I did some work on it when I got back. I agreed with your assessment. They don't connect, but I'm intrigued as to why Potter's idiot is here after all this time. Are you less sure the cases aren't connected?'

'In a way.' Marshall finished his tea and set the cup aside. 'Callum is investigating a murder in Neidpath Tunnel down by Peebles.'

She laughed, so high and shrill it ached Marshall's eardrums. 'So you think someone's killing people in tunnels?'

'Potentially.'

'Are you serious?'

'Weirder things have happened.'

'But Malkmus wasn't killed in a tunnel?'

'Right, we know that.'

Quarrels sighed like she was dealing with two particularly

difficult children. 'Malkmus was murdered elsewhere but dumped in that tunnel.'

'DI Taylor and I have just spoken to the guys who found Adam's body. Craig and Gav. They put it down to drugs.'

'Good. Because I did too.'

'Have you got anything to back that up?'

'Mr Malkmus had been warned by a local gang boss, but didn't listen.'

'You know this for a fact?'

'We have two statements to that effect, yes. The exact nature of his infraction is unknown. He'd either shorted a Mr Big on his supply, or he'd stepped into territory this Mr Big occupied.'

'You know who this Mr Big is?'

'They wouldn't say.'

'Right. That doesn't seem likely. You must have suspicions?'

Fury flashed across Quarrels's face. 'You ever had to manage multiple snouts, Inspector?'

Marshall smiled at her use of the archaic terminology. 'Back in London, aye. Had twenty on my covert human intelligence source log at one point.'

'Then you'll know that the buggers are as inscrutable as quantum physics. You can know where and when a drug deal is going to happen, but you can't know who is doing the dealing.'

'I guess so.'

'And that's the case here. Both our sources are connected to multiple organisations in this fair city. So we couldn't pin it down to one, assuming it's even true.'

'But you believe it?'

'I'm inclined to say yes. Put it this way, it wasn't a surprise he'd been killed to the two numbskulls who found him.'

'Craig and Gav?'

'Right, the very same. I mean, it's noble of them to go out looking for their mate, but to find him... And in that state?' She clenched her teeth. 'It's unthinkable. But they suggested drugs as the likely cause too. They couldn't give us anything concrete.' She narrowed her eyes. 'Why, do you think it's connected to something else?'

'We're not sure.'

'We believe a car drove up to the main road in the middle of the night, then the killer dragged him down there. We consulted with a criminal profiler, a Professor Liana Curtis. She believes the fact he was moved means we're looking at a strong man or more than one killer.'

'Did you think it was them?'

'No. They had an alibi. And not each other. They were DJing to over five thousand people at the time.'

Marshall nodded slowly. 'The fact you've homed in on the drugs angle is a bit—'

'If you've come here to tear apart my repu—'

'Hold on!' Marshall raised his hands. 'It's nothing to do with that. It's just that our case in Peebles has a drugs angle.' He gestured at Taylor, who seemed to be enjoying their heated discussion. 'We need to investigate the connections.'

'Then, by all means. But either way, we never had a suspect, so the case is just sitting there, cooling down to freezing. I'm happy to reallocate it to you, Marshall.' Quarrels looked at Taylor. 'Or to Ryan Gashkori.'

'Whoa, whoa.' Taylor was on his feet now. 'Not so fast, Alex.'

'What?'

Taylor raised his hands again. 'We need to discuss that with Ryan and... You know...'

'Detective Chief Superintendent Potter.'

Taylor winced, then looked behind him. 'Aye.'

'Thought as much.' Quarrels blew out, making her lips vibrate. 'Back in the fridge it goes...'

24

SHUNTY

Siyal stepped out of the High Court's back entrance into the warm Edinburgh morning, phone clamped to his ear but trying to look where he was going. Smelled like the place had been used as a urinal overnight. Several times. He rounded the corner. 'I'm getting nowhere with them, sir.'

'Figures.' Bob Milne sighed down the line. 'Keeping schtum, huh?'

'Exactly that. They're worse than a gang, sir. Their stories all align perfectly. No deviation.'

'Despite the evidence?'

'That evidence isn't concrete, sir. We lack corroboration.'

A withering groan down the line. 'Anyway. How's Hooper doing?'

Siyal looked behind him to check he wasn't being followed. 'Hooper? He's getting the same results as me, sir.' The Royal Mile was thick with foot traffic, but nothing like it'd been during the Festival. 'You know the way cops sort of clench when they see us come calling? It's the same with him.'

'Right.' Milne chuckled. 'That sounds familiar. Do you get the impression they're covering something over?'

'Possibly, but probably not.'

'So you think it's just common-or-garden arse-covering?'

'I'd say so, sir. But we don't have anywhere near enough to eliminate the alternative.'

Another deep breath sprayed against the receiver. 'In that case, Shunty, I'll leave it with you for now. I've got a meeting with the chief constable soon, so I'll head back to base afterwards and we can pick up then. Can you schedule some time in my diary with Phoebe for the close of play? We need to have a deep dive into this.'

'Sure thing.'

'Meanwhile, make yourself busy, as you do best.'

'Catch you later, sir.' Siyal ended the call and looked around. He was on George IV Bridge, far enough away from his car for it to be a pain. Might as well walk back home, get some lunch there, then head into the station.

The prospect of a one-to-one meeting with the boss where he'd have to schedule it in Milne's calendar, rather than just a quick 'have you got a minute?' catch-up didn't exactly fill him with confidence.

No, it felt like Milne was going to get him to park the investigation.

Not that Siyal could exactly blame him. This case was going nowhere and going there slowly, despite everything he tried to do.

He could spot the futility a mile off, but was helpless to stop it.

'Shunty!' Footsteps rattled towards him, then a hand gripped his shoulder.

Siyal swung around, reaching for his baton.

DI Andrea Elliot stood there, eyes like a hawk ready to pounce on a field mouse. She ran her hand through her hair, the fringe much longer than he'd ever seen. 'There you are.'

'Here I am.' Siyal let his grip go. 'What are you doing here?'

'Collecting a picture from a shop on Cockburn Street.'

That sounded like bullshit. 'How are you doing, Andrea?'

'Do you honestly care?'

'I do. Tell me the truth – you're following me, aren't you?'

'Fine. Aye. I saw you leaving court there. Just need a wee word with you, Shunty.'

'Oh? You don't speak to me for ages, then when I just so happen to be investigating the circumstances surrounding your husband's murder, you decide to sneak up on me?'

'We're old pals, aren't we?'

Siyal didn't have an answer for that. 'Why are you here?'

She rolled her eyes at him. 'Come on, Shunty...'

'The truth. Now.'

'Fine. There's no painting.' She looked him right in the eyes. 'I'm working for the Edinburgh MIT on a case.'

'No, you're not. I know you're working on the Peebles murder.'

Her eyes bulged. 'How do you know that?'

'Fingers in many pies, Andrea.' Siyal smiled. 'Struan told me he was working in Edinburgh on something with you.'

'Hang on. You and *Struan* message each other?'

'What's that saying? Keep your friends close, but your enemies closer.' Siyal waited but she didn't laugh. Didn't even smile. 'Stop trying to dig into my work.'

'I'm not.'

'Don't deny it. You are.'

Those words shut her up.

An old man was looking at them. Scowling. But he could just be wondering who the hell they were.

'In spite of all the stuff you've put me through, Andrea, I do sympathise with you. But I'm asking you to bugger off.'

'Bugger off?' She laughed. 'Is that a technical term?'

'It is, yes. You can't be party to this investigation and you know that.'

'Come on, Shunty. Just a little bit.'

Siyal looked past her. 'Where's Struan?'

She folded her arms. 'Trying to get hold of a witness at Napier University.'

'Nearest campus is up in Morningside.'

'Right.' She bit her lip. 'To be honest, someone let slip you were working at the High Court today. I promise to bugger off, if you give me an update.'

Siyal felt like he had no choice. That, or report it to Milne. 'Look. I shouldn't tell you this, but how they knew where Davie was being taken is still a mystery.'

'Okay.' Elliot ran a hand through her hair. 'Thing is, Shunty, I told you and Bob Milne that months ago. I'm baffled as to why you're persisting with this.'

'Because we need to know the truth. To stop others—'

'Shunty, for God's sake. There are a million ways to do it. Follow the van. Park people on the likely routes. Park them outside every prison. You name it.'

'I know there are many ways to do it, but I need to know the *exact* one. Then we can prosecute the *right* people. Otherwise, it could just be a coincidence.'

'You've got the killer, right?'

'He's being sentenced next month.'

'A lot of work going into this for a closed case.'

'Andrea, what happened to your husband was a tragedy and shouldn't have happened. You have my apologies, but—'

'You didn't do anything. Did you?'

'No. Of course not. But we need to stop it from happening. Especially as there's an organised crime element to this.'

'You think Gary Hislop did it?'

'I didn't say that.'

'You think it, though.'

'I'm paid to be thorough. I'm paid to root out all corruption here.'

'You sound like Bob Milne there.'

'He's a good man and a great cop.'

'And you, Shunty, are a bloody idiot.'

'What?'

'This whole thing is completely pointless. You've prosecuted the killer. Move on.'

'Don't you see? If they can kill Davie with impunity, what's to stop them from killing you or your children?'

She shut her eyes. 'You already have the suspect.'

'It's simple, Andrea. Basic policing. Big fish eats the little fish… Trade up a few times and you get the big fish.'

'You don't have any fish. You've got a rod covered in dog shit.'

Siyal wanted to walk off but she'd just come after him. 'I've got work to get on with. Suspect you do too.'

It looked like she was crying.

Siyal didn't know what to do.

She rubbed at her eyes. 'The reason I'm here, Shunty, is I need this whole thing over with. I'm begging you. End the investigation for me.'

Were those crocodile tears? Or real?

Siyal could drop the investigation. Hell, the case was close to dropping itself. But her asking him to drop it… Aye, it made him want to dig even deeper. He stood up tall to his full height and looked down at her. 'Do you know anything about what happened?'

'Are you kidding me? Are you *honestly* asking me that?'

'Answer me straight.'

'Of course not. And I… I can't believe you're asking me that.'

'I'm paid to ask the very difficult questions, Andrea.'

'Well, I'm not paid to answer them. My kids keep asking me a million questions. Davie's parents too. I don't have the answers other than someone killed him. And I can't sleep. Until this is all over and we can put it behind us, I can't sleep. I need to move on, Shunty. They all do. Give us that closure. Just let me have some peace and stop digging.'

Siyal looked her up and down. 'You're asking me to end an investigation?'

'No. I'm just asking you to stop digging where you don't need to dig.'

'Sounds like I need to dig into you.'

'Come on, Shunty… It's nothing to do with me. It's my kids.'

'I promise you'll be able to move on, but only once I've finished this case. Davie was never kind to me, but he deserves the respect of an investigation into what happened to him. He deserves justice. And not simply prosecuting the man who killed him. The whole organisation needs to come down, or it'll happen again.'

'Come on, Shunty, you've drunk too much of the Bob Milne Kool-Aid…'

'This is over.' Siyal walked away from her.

'Shunty!'

Siyal sped up, ignoring her shouts.

'Rakesh!'

The old man tilted his head in her direction.

25

STRUAN

Alistair Henry's office looked south across the rooftops of Morningside, Edinburgh's famously posh area. A reputation it didn't really deserve in Struan's eyes – certainly plenty other parts of the city were much posher and had more money. Murrayfield, for instance.

Still no sign of Alistair Henry himself.

Struan turned back to look out of the window. 'Just asking where you went walkies, boss. That's all.'

Elliot let out a sigh. 'I don't have to say anything, Struan.'

'No.' Struan turned to look at her. God, she looked tired, like she hadn't slept in months. He knew why that might be, but... 'Of course you don't *have* to say anything to me. The fact you're not makes me wonder what you were up to.'

'I wasn't up to anything.'

'But you won't say where you were.'

'I'm not telling you.'

'Fine. Your choice. I'll find out soon enough, anyway.'

She raised an eyebrow. 'From your pal Shunty, eh?'

Gotcha.

'So you *were* meeting him?'

She briefly shut her eyes. 'Bumped into him when I was running an errand. We had a brief chat.'

'Were you following him?'

'No. I was picking up a picture for Sam.'

'Where is it?'

'Made a mistake. It's in the Peebles shop, so I'll have to drive there to collect it.'

Struan stared at her. Aye, his little nugget of information about Shunty's whereabouts had paid off. Sneaky as.

But what was she really up to?

What skin did she have in that game? Her husband had been killed – she was as much a victim as anyone, surely?

The door opened and a large man barged his way in, stroking his thick beard, carrying two laptops under each arm. He stopped dead. 'Can I help you?'

'DS Struan Liddell, sir.' He showed his warrant card. 'Are you Alistair Henry?'

'That's me, aye.' Henry deposited his laptops on his desk. 'What's up?'

'Your secretary said you're the head of department here.'

'Well. Depends on which department you're interested in?'

'Computer science.'

'Then, yes I am.' Henry picked up a mug of coffee from the desk, took a drink, then spat it back out. 'Dis*gusting*.' He looked around, wiping his lips. 'Can I fetch either of you a cup?'

'We're good.' Elliot smiled at him. 'DI Andrea Elliot.'

'Then you won't mind me getting one myself?' Henry set off towards the door.

'We do.' Struan positioned himself between Henry and the door. 'We just have a few questions, then we'll be on our way.'

Henry stood there, lips twitching. 'Of course.' He sat behind his desk and pulled off his left shoe and sock. 'Fire away.' His eyes scanned across the desk.

'We're interested in Iain Hogg. We gather he was a student here.'

'Iain Hogg... Iain Hogg... Iain Hogg... Aha.' Henry picked up a pair of nail clippers, then set about attacking his big toenail. 'The name rings a bell. Who is he?'

'Studied here from 2017.'

'Ah. That's...' Rather than use any of the laptops he'd brought in, he logged in to a desktop PC and started working away. 'Ah, yes. I wasn't at the same level then as I am now. Just a mere lecturer, but Mr Hogg was in fact one of my students.'

'We gather he left?'

Clip. 'Did he?' Clip. 'Bugger.' Clip. 'Let me just check...' He focused on the screen. Clip. 'Ah, yes. He dropped out in 2019. Which is curious. If I remember correctly, he had a placement at one of the banks set up for the third year... Oh. Hang on, I see. I remember this case.' He looked back down. Clip. 'What's your interest in him?'

'We gather there was an incident during his time here, which necessitated someone having to write a letter of recommendation for him.'

'Indeed. One PC Gordon Veitch of Peebles. He gave a statement twice, which stayed his expulsion once, but not the second time.'

Struan looked over at Elliot, but she wasn't paying attention. They'd only heard of one letter. 'What happened?'

'The first time was during his first term here. Mr Hogg and a friend were caught stealing the stag's head from the student union at Edinburgh University on a Friday night.'

'At Edinburgh?'

'Right. Our students are permitted access to their union. We pay a healthy sum for the privilege, of course. And you know how it is with universities...' Henry shifted his gaze between them, grinning away. 'Or maybe you don't.' He cleared his throat. 'There are always these daft urban legends about how someone's cousin or brother stole the stag's head in the dim and distant, but they're all nonsense. That one is virtually impossible given the level of CCTV in the place. But Iain and David were coders. Hackers, really. So they saw it as something to hack. They caused a distraction by setting off the fire alarm. They didn't manage to get it out of the building, obviously, but they got it down from the wall, then they waited in the toilets.'

'How did they get caught?'

'Getting a stag out of a toilet when you're drunk isn't an easy feat.'

'What happened to them?'

'Now, an infraction like that would normally be enough to kick someone out, but PC Veitch's letter was sufficiently strongly worded that we changed our minds and let Mr Hogg off with a final warning.'

'Which he didn't heed?'

'Nope. Well, he did. Initially, at least. That incident was in first year, like I said, but his second incident was at the end of his second year. He'd failed his end-of-year exams, okay? And he had to take resit exams in August. He needed to pass the resits to get into his honours years, which was of course to be the placement. So he had to spend the summer revising, when he'd probably rather be travelling or working or both.'

'And he failed?'

'Failed to even turn up.'

Elliot scowled at him. 'Seriously?'

'Seriously. Then he came in here, chasing after me, running through the corridors, screaming and shouting invective at me. And it wasn't a mystery over why he'd failed to show up for his exams, was it? He was drunk. A few too many had turned into way too many. Whether he would've passed, I can't say, but it wasn't a case of expulsion, he just left without a degree.'

'There wasn't a chance to appeal?'

'There was no case to answer. He'd been given his final

chance. It might sound harsh, but universities aren't there to babysit troublesome students. The world of work presents a stark difference to school and we're there to bridge that gap. Now, if he'd been able to show the same level of application to his studies as to his efforts to steal another university's stag's head, then he wouldn't have been in that position. There's just no coming back from that behaviour. None at all. And when this Gordon Veitch character called me up again to plead for him, well. I couldn't help.'

26

MARSHALL

It had only been a few months since Marshall had been here, but the Innocent Railway felt like it had never been the scene of a vicious and brutal murder.

Or an accidental death.

The tunnel's tarmac path seemed freshly laid, climbing beneath Arthur's Seat and Holyrood Park. Edinburgh was still in summer mode, with the city centre calm after the end of the Festival.

The tinkle of a bell reverberated off the brick walls. A group of five cyclists in their sixties pedalled up the hill, a woman at the front, man at the back, with three red faces between them, looking like they'd rather be anywhere than here, pushing uphill.

Marshall waited for them to pass. 'Are you sure it was *this* lamppost?'

'Well, they do move around when we're not looking, don't they?' Taylor couldn't hide his smirk as he checked his tablet. 'It was this one, aye.' He pointed at a giant chip in the black paintwork, revealing the bare metal underneath, then showed it on the tablet screen. 'See?'

'Right. The victim was Beverley Richardson.'

'Indeed. Female. Fifty-three.' Taylor looked up at Marshall. 'You deemed her to have accidentally killed herself by drunkenly stumbling and smashing her head off the lamppost.'

'I didn't do that.' Marshall folded his arms, trying to ignore him while also conjuring up the memories of visiting the crime scene a few months ago, when Beverley's body lay there. But he came up mostly blank, just remembered her bright red hair and the sickening patch of blood. 'That was the Edinburgh pathologist's assessment.'

Taylor rasped the stubble on his chin. 'Weird that, eh?'

'What is?'

'Callum?' A voice echoed around the tunnel.

Marshall swung around.

A man jogged towards them, hands in pockets. He pulled out a paw to give a wave. 'Morning, Cal.'

'Morning, Jordan boy.' Taylor clenched him in a hug, then broke off and gestured to Marshall. 'DC Jordan Russell. DI Rob Marshall.'

Russell held out a hand. 'I led the investigation into Ms Richardson's death.'

Marshall shook his hand hard and gave him a wide grin. 'A DC leading a murder investigation, eh?'

Russell scratched at his neck, nervous eyes dancing between them. Late thirties, but one of those cops who seemed happy with his lot as a constable. Or just incapable of rising any higher. 'Me leading is just the way the cookie crumbled, sir.'

Taylor barked out a laugh, which rattled around the tunnel. 'More like the Edinburgh MIT didn't want to bring in another area to show them up.' He waved to his side. 'Rob's consulting on the case from the—' He rolled his eyes. 'What's your area called again?'

'Behavioural Sciences Unit.'

Russell smirked. 'Isn't that from *The Silence of the Lambs*?'

'It is.' Marshall winced like he always did. 'Not my idea. And it's not much of a unit – just me and my part-time PhD student assistant.'

Russell looked away. 'Sorry about running late, but the gaffer called me ten minutes ago, saying you were on your way here.'

Taylor laughed. 'So you do have adult oversight?'

'I do and she's busy with a case up in Colinton, so can't spare the time.' Russell checked his watch. 'And nor can I, really. Can we get this over and done with?'

'You'll be here as long as we need you, son.' Taylor clamped his arm to assert dominance. 'But the quicker we get the necessary info out of you, the earlier you can fuck off.'

'Fine by me.' Russell looked at the lamppost, then winced. 'What's there to say? A DI Marshall and a DI Taylor passed on the case back in April.' He raised his thick eyebrows. 'So you tubes probably know just as much as I do.'

'Assume we know bugger all, Jordan.'

'Right. Well, in the end we had to put it down to being an accident.'

Taylor glowered at him. 'Even though someone's head got rammed into—'

'The pathologist said it was an accident.'

'Someone doesn't trip up and land with that level of force, do they?'

Russell shifted his gaze between them. 'Listen, Cal, I'm not the expert on these things. I'm just a bam from Niddrie who became a cop. I'm good at what I do, but I rely on experts to help me. The pathologist said it was *likely* to be an accidental death, so I can't argue with that, can I?' His nostrils flared. 'Besides, you two passed on the case. If you wanted to take a run at it, the time was in April, not now.'

'I get it, Jordan.' Taylor gave a friendly smile. 'You're overworked and inexperienced.'

'Eh?'

'It's easy to just crumble in the face of your DI's pressure. Easy to just palm off the case and bury it in the long grass, yet another cold case. Meanwhile, Beverley Richardson gets no justice for her murder.'

'You're still assuming it's a murder.' Russell stepped out of the way of another clutch of cyclists. 'You're here because you think this is the work of a serial killer, right?'

Marshall hushed Taylor with a glance. He needed to take over – Taylor's bullying of a supposed friend was getting them nowhere. 'Our work back in April was to assess whether it was the work of a serial killer, yes. And it's why we're here again now.'

'So there's another victim like Beverley?'

'We've been tasked with investigating a few possibly related crimes. This just happens to be in the cohort we're investigating.'

'What's a cohort?'

Marshall took a deep breath. 'Let's just say this murder bears the same hallmarks as another two deaths in Scotland. Our job is to assess whether there are any connections.'

'Right.' But Russell didn't seem to be reassured. Probably feared being hauled away from Edinburgh to work a cold case. 'So what do you want from me?'

'I'm asking you, in your opinion, could this case have been a murder?'

Russell stared up at the lights, burning away in the middle of the day, then back at Marshall. 'That kind of decision is *way* above my pay grade, as I'm sure you'll understand. But I've seen plenty of accidental deaths like this. Weird shit. And the boss wouldn't leave a bam like me to investigate if she thought this was a murder.'

'I'm paid to play devil's advocate.' Marshall stuffed his hands in his pockets. 'That means I need to ask questions which may seem annoying or trivial. Or both. It's not personal, okay? I'm not here to audit your work. The other two cases had connections with the drug trade. A pharmacist who prescribed drugs to people she shouldn't have done. A DJ who dealt drugs to people who went to his clubs. Is there any of that work there?'

'Nope. No drugs at all.' Russell leaned against the side wall and folded his arms. 'The blood tox came back saying she had drunk enough booze to banjax an aircraft carrier full of sailors. Hence us thinking she stumbled and cracked her bonce off this lamppost.'

'No hint of drugs in her private life?'

'Nope. She worked in John Lewis.' Russell's forehead twitched. 'Weird thing, though. I had to go to her flat to check her stuff. She had *nine* cats.'

'Nine?'

'Right. All older ones. All healthy. But if she had a drug, it was that.'

Marshall felt something needling at the back of his head. 'Hang on. Am I right in thinking she embezzled funds from a cat charity?'

'Aye. We've got the evidence of it in the case file. She took sixteen grand. Not a *lot* of money, maybe, but still a decent sum. And from a charity too.' Russell tutted. 'Her embezzlement meant the charity folded. I've seen people killed over less.'

'What did she do with the cash?'

'She bought a van. Second-hand, but it wasn't cheap. Used it for driving around on her errands. Took money out of the charity for the fuel. Wasn't a national one, but it caused a bit of a stink locally.'

'What kind of stink?'

'A local community journalist got hold of the story. Ran with it.'

'Oh, that's interesting.'

'But if you ask me, I think she was pissed, fell over and was unlucky enough to scone her bonce off metal hard enough to smash her skull in.'

Marshall looked over at Taylor. 'We should speak to the pathologist.'

'You won't get anywhere. I picked up the case two weeks ago and spoke to him again. He reaffirmed the initial findings. The official line is it's "death by misadventure".'

'Did he consider the possibility of the victim's head being rammed into the lamppost by someone?'

'He did. But said it was unlikely.'

'Go on.'

'Eh?'

'When someone says something's unlikely, any detective worth his salt has a wee root around in the unlikely side, don't they? Just to make sure there's no dangling threads you can tug at.'

Russell scratched at the back of his head. 'I didn't do that, sorry.'

'Come on, Jordan...' Taylor looked like he was going to punch him. Or smash his head against the lamppost. 'What did he say about the injury?'

'That's the interesting part, I guess. He said if it was an attack, it'd have to be caused by someone with superhuman strength.'

'Superhuman strength?'

'He was exaggerating for effect, I think. But you guys must realise that literally nobody outside of Marvel or DC comics has superhuman strength. So I stopped asking him.'

'Jordan, what exactly did he say?'

Russell pointed at the lamppost. 'We had blood all over that, do you remember? He said it explains the double fracture.'

Taylor glanced at Marshall. '*Double*?'

'Indeed. Why?'

'What did he say?'

'To quote him, "twice on the same spot could do it, I suppose". Like a rapid-fire machine-gun thing.'

'Wait. So you're saying someone *could've* murdered her?'

Russell was blushing. 'He said it was extremely unlikely.'

'So you keep saying.' Taylor shook his head, then focused on Marshall. 'Rob, this matches what we have with Rebecca.'

'Who's Rebecca?'

Taylor rounded on Russell. 'Listen, Jordan, this information would've been useful back in April.'

'He only told me it two weeks ago!'

'Even so, you should've gone to DI Marshall with it.'

'Like I have the time...'

'It's your fucking *job* to have the time!'

Russell squared up to Taylor. 'Look, mate, when you hear hoof-beats you think horses, not zebras. This seems like an accident to me and to every other prick.'

'I'm telling you, son, you're in the Serengeti now with a pack of hungry tigers on your tail.'

'Then I'd better lace up my running shoes and hope I'm faster than you fannies.' Russell snorted. 'If you want to bully a lowly DC into agreeing this could've been murder, then fine. It could've been. That make you happy?'

'Off you fuck, Jordan.' Taylor waved a hand back up the tunnel. 'Get back to Colinton.'

'Fine. I will. And next time you need someone to rewire your brother's house, you can fuck right off too.' Russell dipped his head to Marshall. 'See you around.' He marched off up the tunnel, chased by an old man in Lycra on a fancy-looking bike, but Russell's walking pace outstripped the cyclist.

Marshall watched him go, then shook his head at Taylor. 'Charming...'

'Ach, he's not bad, just completely out of his depth. I'll send him an apology later.'

'Assuming you've something to apologise for.' Marshall focused on the lamppost with fresh eyes. 'So, I'll ask you this once. Could this be the same killer as Rebecca?'

Taylor let out a long, slow breath. 'What links them?'

'Both are female. Both were intoxicated at the time of their attacks in tunnels.'

'Okay. But Beverley was twice Rebecca's age.'

'So age doesn't have to be a factor in victim selection.'

'And sex is? Does that mean Malkmus is out?'

'I thought you'd be trying to push him *into* my scope, not prise him out?'

Taylor smiled. 'Just trying to make sure we cover all angles.'

'Good idea. Which is why I'm doing it.' Marshall looked back the way and saw the group of cyclists from earlier now hurtling down towards them. He eased Taylor out of the way, then waited for them to pass. 'That stuff about the van got me thinking, though. Ripping off a charity. I'm starting to wonder if this is an avenging angel.'

'Go on.'

'Well, it's that or this is a series of thrill-kills, i.e. how many skulls can I burst and not get caught?'

'Right. But this avenging angel thing?'

'Malkmus had been dealing drugs. Rebecca had her drug thing too, but fentanyl rather than party drugs. Beverley stole money from a cat charity.'

'Sounds a bit tenuous, doesn't it?'

'Does it?'

Taylor screwed up his face. 'You honestly think that's possible?'

'It gives my profile another axis to explore, that's for sure.'

'What, which tunnel-related blunt-force trauma victims had a mark on their record but got off easy?'

'Something like that.'

Taylor shook his head. 'Mate, you're welcome to the case. I

still think it's much more likely to be the drug dealing for both of them.'

'I know. But we can't exclude the possibility of it all being related. My job is to assume they're connected and that we have three cases – Kelvingrove, Innocent Railway and Neidpath.'

'Okay, so what's the plan now?'

'I need to do a full profile for an assumptive murderer of all three.'

Taylor grinned. 'That mean you're going to love me and leave me?'

'I'll do the latter, Cal. Better get back to Gartcosh and see if anything can come from this.'

'Rather you than me, mate.'

Marshall smiled at that. 'Any chance you could drop me in Gorgie?'

27

STRUAN

Struan stopped in the doorway to the Gala nick kitchen. The room had the dusty, earthy smell of stale instant coffee.

Graeme Veitch whistled a Taylor Swift song as the kettle rumbled away next to him.

Struan cleared his throat.

Graeme looked around, then his eyes widened. 'Sarge. Just having a cup of tea before I come on shift.' He opened the fridge and frowned into it. 'Can I get you one?'

'I'm good, ta.' Struan leaned against the counter and folded his arms. 'What are you looking for?'

'The milk.'

'Just the powdered stuff behind the mugs.' Struan waited until he found it. 'There is a canteen here, you know?'

'Is there?'

'You're based in Peebles, right?'

'We don't have a canteen there.' Graeme tipped a couple of heaped spoonfuls of coffee whitener into his tea. 'Sure I can't get you anything?'

It looked all lumpy and rank – the last thing Struan would

want, especially not before a shift. 'Need to ask you a few more questions about Iain Hogg. Won't be long.'

Graeme blew on the surface of his drink. It looked like soup. 'Of course.'

'We've just been up to the university and spoke to his lecturer. The story sort of checks out.'

Took Graeme a few seconds to clock it. 'Sort of?'

'There are a couple of gaps.'

'Like what?'

'The infraction we discussed was the stag's head incident.'

'Right?'

'Your father failed to mention the matter of Iain failing his end-of-year exams, then not even showing for the resits.'

'Are you serious?'

'You don't know anything about it?'

'No.'

'He was drunk too. Chased the lecturer through the university.'

'Wow.'

Struan left a pause. 'You definitely hadn't heard?'

'No. I mean, I knew Iain liked a drink. Ran in the family. Picked up his old man a few times, but I had no idea it was that bad. Lot of people struggle at uni, don't they? Being away from home for the first time or, like me, wishing you were. It's really tough.'

'Obviously, I'd love to chat to your dad—'

'—but it's like chatting to a brick wall. I get it.' Graeme sipped at his minging tea. 'Sorry. I asked him more about Iain after you guys went, but his brain's Swiss cheese these days.'

'He didn't talk about this?'

'No. He just talked about that stag's head thing. He got really annoying about it. Like he thought it was funny, you know?'

'I can imagine.' Struan grinned. 'Do you remember anything about him coming back here?'

'Not much, sorry. Just that Dad asked Iain to stand down from being Cornet's right hand in their third year.'

'Stand down?'

'Dad was secretary of the Beltane committee. He made sure it happened swiftly and effectively.'

'I know that. What I don't know is why.'

'Don't know exactly why, but I thought it was something to do with Iain dropping out of uni and breaking up with Rebecca. Like they'd agreed to not put her through the ordeal of seeing her ex there.'

'Doesn't seem strong enough to me.'

'Sorry. I'm just guessing what happened.'

'I could do without guessing. Let's just stick to the facts, eh?' Struan held his gaze, but the stink of his tea was churning his stomach. 'But you're implying Iain wasn't so much stood down as your dad suggested it?'

'Something like that, aye.'

'Okay.' Struan stood up tall. 'Enjoy your cup of tea and give me a shout if you need any overtime approved on this case.'

'Sure thing, Sarge.'

Struan clapped his arm and left the room. Good lad to have in his pocket – knew where the bodies were buried and knew Peebles.

28

MARSHALL

Marshall tossed his pen down and yawned. 'Time for another coffee…'

Hardeep Singh looked at the pen like Marshall had just stabbed him in the throat with it. He touched his bold orange turban and seemed to take some comfort from that. '*Another?*'

Marshall stood up. Then sat back down again. 'You're right. I've had too many already.' He looked around his office, but didn't see anything inspiring. Another yawn dug into him – that coffee felt very, very tempting. 'Okay.' He grabbed a bottle of water from his drawer and unscrewed the cap – maybe hydration would work better. 'Let's recap what we've got so far. You first.'

'Sir.' Hardeep took a few seconds to consult his notes. Then more seconds as he touched his turban again. Then even more. When he turned back to the first page, the clock said two minutes had passed. 'Okay. There's not a lot to go on, is there? But we're assuming these three are all connected, which may draw out concrete connections, but we have to be open to the likelihood they're not connected in any way.'

'Agreed. But the purpose of this exercise is to draw out any potential links that may lead us forward.'

'First, there's no sign of escalation here. The crimes are all the same level of severity, from last July to April to now. Also, the suspect isn't acting in a frantic manner, but appears to be very controlled, organised and opportunistic.'

'Can you be both opportunistic and organised?'

'Indeed you can.'

'I would've said it's the opposite of that.'

'Which is why it's good discussing these things.' Hardeep let out a sigh. 'The reason I say opportunistic is because he appears to be a patient man who stalks his victims and waits for the right opportunity to kill them. And in a location where he won't be overseen killing them. With minimal chance of immediate discovery of the victims.'

Marshall played it through slowly and couldn't find anything he disagreed with. 'Go on.'

'Adam is the outlier, if we assume he was killed elsewhere and moved into the tunnel at Kelvingrove.' Hardeep frowned at something. 'Forgot to say, I went through their list of Patreon backers and subscribers with one of your officers. Ash Paton?'

'She's good.'

'I'm not sufficiently experienced to be able to judge that. But we can't find Rebecca on their subscriber list, either to their podcast or to the nightclub. We've confirmed that they had a mandatory mailing list to even get into the club. Managed by an app. They were so select and incredibly popular with it. Have you been, sir?'

'Not my scene, Hardeep, no.'

'It's pretty good.'

'You've been?'

Hardeep frowned. 'Are you surprised?'

'A bit. You don't strike me as a fan of banging techno.'

'Massive. But it's more on the dub techno end. Bit of deep house. Minimal. It's good.'

'You'll have to take me there someday.'

'I can't, sir. It's *that* exclusive.'

Not that Marshall even wanted to bloody go. 'Continue?'

'Well, there's definitely no connection between Adam and Rebecca. The drugs angle.'

'Did you get anything on the victim of the drugs she'd sold?'

'It's something I need to pick up. Sorry.'

'Don't worry. Continue?'

'While they appear to be connected, Rebecca and Beverley have a shared MO. Both were killed in situ, in a tunnel. Blunt-force trauma to the head on two planes. And the reason I think he's opportunistic is he didn't know where Rebecca would be. He followed her there and struck when he knew she was alone.'

'Whereas he knew Beverley would walk home that way?'

'Indeed. That's the organised side of things. He'd maybe even been monitoring her in the pub. Maybe he was even drinking with her.'

'The cops spoke with everyone in the pubs she'd visited, didn't they?'

'They did. All subsequent movements accounted for. But my point still stands, sir. Above all else, our killer appears to be organised but he has flexibility to strike when he knows he can with complete impunity. Unlike other types of serial killer, he is able to control his impulses. He can plan and predict, but also he can improvise where necessary. And assuming these are connections between these victims, we can infer that he's not on a downward spiral, because he is executing a slow, steady pace of murders. He's found something that works and he's running with it.'

'Big assumption there.'

'What, you think there may be others to bridge the gap between July and April?'

'Right. Cases we haven't discovered yet.'

'But equally there may not.'

Marshall nodded slowly, then compared his thoughts with his notes. 'You keep saying "he".'

'Indeed. My assessment of the probability of him being male is ninety-eight percent likely.'

'What's that based on?'

'Default gender characteristics in the population coupled with distribution of genders among known populations of murderers with similar characteristics.'

'Like who?'

'My catalogue is currently eighty-seven offenders. Nineteen in this country, with—'

'Okay, I get it. That's good work. Are you able to cross-reference—?'

'No. Already done it. There are no other victims who share this exact pattern.'

'Okay. Good.'

'But I think he's demonstrated flexibility, such as the way he killed Adam Malkmus elsewhere and transported him.' Hardeep raised a finger. 'Assuming these are all the work of the same man.'

'Of course.'

'I will investigate for looser links that may connect more solidly in other domains.'

'Good idea.' Marshall flicked through his notes. 'That there might be a common thread between the three cases is what I want us to focus on. Aside from the tunnels, which has to be significant to the killer – if indeed it is at all significant – then all three victims appear to have done something that blew up on social media or in the local press. Some infraction which got them into trouble. Rebecca's drug dealing, Malkmus's drugs too, and Beverley's stuff with that cat charity. And how they all got away with it. Malkmus's drugs investigation stalled. Rebecca got a suspended sentence. Beverley was investigated, but got a slap on the wrist. Meanwhile the charity went down the tubes.'

Hardeep sat back and tapped his pen off his notepad. 'Hmm.'

Marshall laughed. 'All feels a bit woolly, doesn't it?'

'Very much so.' Hardeep sipped some water. 'But at the same time, it's still very plausible, isn't it? Just because it appears trivial, doesn't mean it's not the reason they have been killed. People who have escaped justice, however small.'

'This is the bit where this assumption trips up, Hardeep. Feels like it's all just... Us trying to join the dots to make it work. But still, this is why this unit was set up, wasn't it? Unit...' Marshall laughed. 'Okay, let's go with that as a likely motivation.'

'I've also worked something on the killer side, which focuses on execution methods, rather than motivations. I agree those are the weakest aspects, if we're looking at connections. Both Neidpath and Innocent are wildly violent acts, which both happened in situ. But they're also sneak attacks.'

'You think we're dealing with someone cowardly?'

'Cowardly's one interpretation, sir. Small, infirm, well-known, shy, female or potentially disabled are all other possibilities.'

'Hardeep, can you be a bit more careful with your words?'

'Am I not allowed to say disabled?'

'No. It's not that, it's just... Cops are very literal. They will go tripping over the other alternatives to find the one you described. If you go in saying things like that to Callum Taylor or Ryan Gashkori, you'll be having to stand up in court to give expert testimony to what you've suggested.'

'I see.'

Marshall waited for him to look up. 'I've known lots of tall cowards, Hardeep. And big ones too. You don't have to be small or disabled to be that way. Especially if our killer is a hunter.'

'Okay. Sorry.'

'No need to apologise. These are good questions to raise. Trouble is, because we don't have a murder site in Glasgow, we can't draw any further inferences.'

Hardeep touched his turban again. 'Adam Malkmus was killed elsewhere and moved there. Nobody really saw anything?'

'Correct.'

'How can that be?'

'Because of the time of night, I suspect. The case file shows a lot of canvassing in the neighbourhood. Many residents were in and a few people passing the site came forward, but nobody saw anything. We don't even have a potential murder location. Probably killed in a car or a van, which was then cleaned or torched.'

'But we don't have anything similar in the other cases.' Hardeep pulled out a sheet of A3, covered in a map of central Scotland, going just south enough to feature Peebles. 'Neidpath and the Innocent Railway are both far from roads. Kelvingrove wasn't.'

'I pointed that out earlier. Still doesn't get us any further forward, does it?'

'No.' Hardeep cleared his throat. 'Another thing I'd like to point out is we have a potential witness.'

'Iain Hogg?'

'Indeed. He claims he was attacked outside of Neidpath Tunnel. But he wasn't killed.'

'Go on.'

'Maybe I'm clutching at straws here, sir, but the others were all murdered. Clear as day. Violent acts against people who caught public attention. Hogg didn't fit that, so he wasn't murdered.'

'Good point.' Marshall leaned back and looked up at the ceiling. He had to consider Hogg being spared as a distinct possibility. But he also had to recognise this whole enterprise was probably Potter trying to show up Gashkori.

Or Marshall trying to justify his existence on the payroll…

He looked back at Hardeep. 'Not a lot to be going on with, is there?'

'I think there's more than enough.' Hardeep checked his watch. 'Anyway, my time's up. I'm meeting a friend for dinner. Can we reconvene in the morning?'

'I'd love to, but I'm heading down to the Borders first thing to attend the briefing. Let's pick up after that. I'll call you.'

29

STRUAN

Struan walked along the corridor, but it wasn't exactly far to the interview room – Gala station was, after all, ridiculously tiny.

Elliot stood outside the room, talking on the phone to someone. She locked eyes with Struan, then muttered something and hung up. 'You get anything from the stooge?'

'The stooge?'

'What they call Graeme Veitch in Peebles.'

'Any idea why?'

'Most nicknames don't have a reason.' Elliot gave a flash of her eyebrows. 'Unless I come up with them.'

Struan returned it with a smile – those were the most words he'd heard from her in months. 'Veitch confirmed that Hogg was stood down, but he says he knows nothing.'

'Sounds like mince to me.'

'Agreed. He reckoned it was because they'd split up.'

'Hmmm. You believe him?'

'I wouldn't go that far, no.'

She drilled her gaze into the door, like the wood could

reveal the truth about the man inside the room. 'Why do *you* think he was stood down?'

'Your guess is as good as mine. Seems like the only two people who know are Hogg himself and Gordon Veitch. One isn't talking and the other... can't.'

'Right.' Elliot let out a slow sigh. 'You grew up in a wee town, didn't you? Everyone knows everybody else's business.'

'True. So you're saying someone else must know what happened to make him drop out?'

'Maybe.' Elliot straightened herself up and cracked her neck, a sickening grinding noise. 'But let's start with the man himself, eh?'

'You okay, ma'am?'

'I'm fine, why?'

'It's just... You've been really quiet.'

'Lot going on, Struan. Wouldn't want to bore you with it.'

'The stuff about—'

'Aye, and a few other things I won't bore you with.'

'I'm actually a pretty good listener. If you need to bounce stuff off someone.'

Elliot looked him up and down. 'The day I need to talk to you, Struan, it'll be after a plague has wiped out the rest of civilisation.' She pushed into the interview room.

Struan watched the door shut behind her. Heard her words rumbling through the wood.

He'd known grief like that. Knew how corrosive it was. Knew how the only solution was talking about it. Knew how you had to *want* to talk first. And most avoided it.

Just like she was.

Struan sucked in a deep breath and entered the room.

Elliot was already on the attack, leaning across the small table. 'So, we gather you failed your exams at uni.'

Hogg sat back and folded his arms. His gaze tightened as he looked right at Struan. Then back to Elliot. 'Right.'

'And you were doing resits?'

'Was supposed to be, aye.'

'Supposed to be... Fancy way of saying you didn't show up for them.'

'That's not what happened.'

'What did?'

Hogg smoothed a hand down his face. His stubble was already thick – this was a man who'd have to shave several times a day. 'I was drunk. Missed my alarm.'

'So, you thought the best prep for your exams was to get so blootered you slept through your alarm?'

'That's not what happened.'

'So what was?'

Hogg shrugged. 'Said I missed my alarm.'

'I'm not following.'

Hogg sat back again and sighed. 'When am I getting out of here?'

'Two options for when you get out of this room. First is when we're satisfied you didn't kill her.'

'I swear I didn't do it.'

'And that don't give me no satisfaction.' Elliot left a pause for her joke to sink in. 'Second, you'll get out of this room when we take you to get charged, then you'll get out of the building when we take you to plead in court.' She checked her watch. 'By my calculations that won't be tomorrow now, so it'll be another day.'

'So you're holding me here without charge?'

'No, son. You've been charged for *some* of your crimes. You were asked if you understood the charges.'

'Right. Thought it was a joke, or something.'

'This is very serious, Mr Hogg. There'll be more charges hitting you soon. As for the court stuff, that's outside of my remit, I'm afraid. And you can blame either the Westminster or Holyrood governments, but the criminal justice system is on its knees. So basic things like your initial hearing are taking way longer than they should.'

'But I *didn't* kill her.'

'And we *don't* believe you. I want to. But you need to persuade us. Because all you've done so far is lie, as far as I can tell.'

'Look.' Hogg slapped his forehead. 'When I left uni, I was a complete mess. But I've cleaned up since. I mean, I still drink. Who doesn't? But... I haven't been as bad as I was on Saturday for a long, long time.'

'Did you black out?'

'Bits of it, aye. Can sort of remember the Highland Games and me trying to steal a caber. Couldn't even lift it.' Hogg laughed. 'Then I can remember waking up with my head in the urinal. Remember chatting to Becky in the tunnel.'

'Do you remember murdering her?'

'No!'

Struan felt a nudge on his thigh – Elliot ordering him to take over. 'Just so happened to get that drunk when Erin happened to be out of town, eh?'

The name seemed to jolt him like someone had shoved a cattle prod up his jacksie. 'Is there any word from her?'

'Her flight's been delayed.'

'Right. Okay. Look, what can I tell you apart from the truth?'

'Don't leave anything out, just give us it straight. That's all.'

'Fine.' Hogg looked at his lawyer and got a nod, then stared into his lap. 'When they kicked me out, I didn't take it well. I mean, it felt really malicious. I was a wee bit late for the exam and they kicked me out.'

'What did you do?'

'That coward... What was his name?'

'Are you talking about your lecturer?'

'Aye. Alistair Henry?'

Hogg nodded. 'Right. Him. He told me that was it. I'd screwed up my last chance. And he just walked away.'

'What did you do?'

'What do you think I did? I ran through the place. Chased after him, asking him for another chance. Begging him for one. Got down on my fucking hands and knees. He said I'd had my second chance and that was it. Time to move on with my life.'

Struan could picture it. The desperation of the student, the cold pomposity of the lecturer. 'Why did you have to get drunk before the exam?'

'I needed a bit of Dutch courage. I felt so much pressure to pass them.'

'Pressure from who? Your folks?'

'Them.'

'And who else?'

'Felt like everyone in the town was laughing at me. I was the Cornet in 2017. You're supposed to be respected, but nobody did. I became the butt of every joke. Heard all these stories about stuff I'd done when I was drunk.'

'Were they true?'

'That's not the point.' Hogg was blushing. 'You do stuff to get a laugh, right? Everyone does… But it comes back to bite you, doesn't it? You become the joke. Or at least the punchline. And I was pretty much an alcoholic. Needed a drink every night. My flatmate suggested going for one. And I couldn't say no. And that first pint didn't just stay at that. I thought it'd be a right laugh. Back then, I thought everything was a laugh. Don't really remember much about that night, to be honest. Where we were. What we did. One of those nights like Saturday where I didn't remember much. Just fragments, you know? Can still remember the fragments, but they're just that.'

'Did you kill someone that night?'

'Of course not. Only thing I killed was my future. I learned a hard lesson, you know? Publicly humiliated.'

'By the university?'

'No. I was stripped of my Cornet title back home.'

'You were *stripped* of it?'

'The term Gordon Veitch used was "stood down". Made Rebecca look like an arse as she had to do it on her own. I'm such a waster.'

'Why did Mr Veitch do that?'

'He's a bully, you know? Makes you feel like shite. I was the one who went to him and told him how I got into trouble.'

'Wasn't the first time you got in trouble with the university, was it?'

'Eh?'

'The stag's head.'

'You heard?' Hogg scratched at his cheek. 'Me and a pal got pissed one night and stole the stag's head from the union at Edinburgh Uni. Planned it all out like in *Ocean's Eleven*, you know? And we got the head off the wall and *almost* got it out of there. But we got caught. Threatened us both with expulsion. I was the Cornet, so Gordon wrote a letter.'

'Are you saying you—'

'Aye. I asked him to step in after what happened with my exams and he called Professor Henry, but it did nothing. Probably didn't bother – I wasn't the Cornet anymore, just some waster who used to be.'

'One thing I can't get my head around here. Perhaps you can help me?'

'What's that?'

'The exams were in August, right? And that's when you were kicked out.'

'Right?'

'But Beltane is in the middle of June.'

'And?'

'It's not like you were immediately embarrassed.'

'No, but I was immediately stood down. It was made known

to people in the town that the Cornet would only have a left hand the next summer, but there'd be a left and right hand for the Lasses. It's the cruellest part, you know? It's one thing for me to pretend to be ill or away on business for the Beltane, but another for people to *know*.'

'Did you speak to Rebecca about it?'

'Haven't seen her since.'

'Were you still going out then?'

'If you can call what we were doing that... She broke up with me just after. And it hit me hard. Thought we'd get married. And that's when my drinking took over. And I didn't see her again until Saturday.'

'Did you blame her for your drinking taking over?'

'No. Of course I didn't.'

'But you were speaking to Rebecca on Saturday night in the tunnel.'

'I don't really remember what she said. She wasn't happy.'

'About you leaving her to do her duties solo?'

'No. We didn't talk about that. About her life. Said she'd made mistakes. Did things she'd regretted.'

Elliot brushed Struan's knee with hers. 'And then you killed her?'

'No!'

'Come on, Iain, just confess to killing her. It'll save us all a lot of hassle.'

'But I *didn't*. Do. It!'

30

SHUNTY

Shunty stared hard at Bob Milne and hoped the words were sinking in like he'd practised and intended them to. 'The bottom line, sir, is it looks like you are the only one who knew where Davie was heading.'

Milne looked all puffy and fed up. 'Right.'

'You split the transport into three. First from Edinburgh to Kirkcaldy, then up to Dundee, then down to Glasgow before the final stretch to Glenochil. That made this not a simple case of someone following a van. Or of guards or court officers leaking information – they knew the first leg. And the drivers didn't know who they had in the back, as you'd switched the names too with each stretch.'

'Thing is, Shunty, it could be just as simple as that.' Milne raised his eyebrows. 'Following a single van isn't hard, even a series of single vans.'

'But someone would surely spot them.'

'Indeed, but they'd have to be looking. A multi-stop operation will deter the basic types, right? I mean, anyone could tail someone and those drivers have no training in counter-surveillance like we have. Or certainly I do. My point stands, though.' Milne got up and walked over to the window, the bright light silhouetting him. 'Thing I keep trying to drill into you, Shunty, is most people don't take their jobs as seriously as you or I do. The guards are just working. They do it because they get decent pay and a generous pension. Maybe a feeling of power. Don't kid yourself and think they take their work home with them. When the drivers are in that van, they're spending most of their time talking or, if they're not driving, twatting about on their phones.'

'I see your point.'

'Good. And you're no closer to the answer, are you?'

Siyal tried to fight against it, but it was true. 'No, sir, I'm not.'

'But you're doing the work and, boy, are you doing it.' Milne laughed then clutched his back and let out a sharp breath. 'Thanks for your work. It's good stuff.'

'Not a problem, sir.'

'No. Indeed.' Milne sat behind the desk again and winced. 'Thing is, Shunty... Rakesh... DS Siyal... I'm afraid your Complaints tenure is coming to an end.'

The words hit Siyal like a cricket ball in the teeth. 'What?'

'Not because I don't rate you, son, but because I'm retiring. Just got my papers through this afternoon.'

'I... I had no idea you were...'

'No. But it's not like you followed me. I just happened to find you here. And you're an excellent investigator. But I'm afraid you won't be renewed, either.'

Siyal felt his blood pumping through his veins like an angry torrent. 'Why not?'

'The powers that be see you as basically my assistant, so if there isn't a me here, there isn't a position for you.'

'But I'm much more than that.'

'Of course you are, but such are the joys of resourcing spreadsheets and headcount management, Shunty. The new super starts on Monday. They want to pick someone familiar to them, someone they can trust. They'll build up their own team and bring in people they know and trust. Different approach to me – I wanted nobody familiar to anyone, so I had complete objectivity. And you've given me that. I saw you sitting apart from your peers at lunchtime – a pariah in a squad full of the buggers. I knew you'd be perfect. And you have been.'

Siyal felt like he was dribbling down the drain. 'So what's going to happen to me?'

'Oh, you won't be let go, Rakesh, if that's what you're worried about. They're short of officers everywhere.'

'Do you mean I'll be in uniform?'

'That's likely. But you can put in for any other position. The advantage you have is you'll be able to shift across anywhere without an existing caseload. That's to your advantage. And you've got a few weeks until I retire.'

'What do you mean?'

'I'm going on a brief holiday, starting on Friday. Had it all stacked up.'

'So my tenure ends when you come back?'

'Right. And it'll be a uniform assignment by default.'

'I see.'

Milne patted his arm. 'You'd be good on the street, Shunty.'

'I was a direct entry. I've never done that before.'

'The last, I gather. Well, now's as good a time as any. The squad will like you, Shunty. You're a good guy. But I'll have my phone with me on holiday, so if you need me to put a word in with anyone in another area...'

Siyal stood up and nodded. 'Thank you for informing me, sir.'

'Don't thank me, Shunty. I should've told you I was thinking of leaving yonks ago. Should've kept you informed. But the truth was, I didn't know it was definite until today.'

31

MARSHALL

While he unlocked the door, Marshall struggled to hold both his laptop bag and the bottle of very nice wine he'd bought to apologise for having to work so late, without dropping the bottle.

The laptop bag thudded to the floor.

Could've been a lot worse.

Marshall managed to get the door open, then crouched down to pick up the laptop bag. He took a breath then walked into the flat. 'Honey, I'm home.'

Silence.

He dumped his bag by the door and hung up his coat.

Zlatan ran through and stopped right in front of him. '*Meow!*' He scurried off into the bedroom.

The light was on in the living room.

Marshall kicked off his shoes and carried the wine through to the living room.

Rakesh Siyal sat on the armchair, staring at the floor.

Kirsten was on the sofa next to him, looking at Marshall with wide eyes. She got up, tilted her head to the side, then led him through to the kitchen.

Marshall handed her the wine. 'Here, this is for me working late.'

'We've got more than enou— Oh, it's a Cairanne...' She kissed him on the cheek. 'Thank you.'

'Least I could do.' Marshall pointed at the living room. 'What's up with Rakesh?'

Kirsten shrugged. 'Search me.'

'But he's sitting there.'

'I know. He just showed up. Didn't say anything, just sat down. And he's been sitting there in an almost catatonic state ever since.'

'How long?'

'Long enough to make me search for directions to the Royal Ed.'

'He doesn't need psychiatric help, does he?'

'God knows what he needs, Rob. Been here for over an hour.'

Marshall blew air up his face. 'Let me have a word with him.'

'Sure. Fill your boots. I'll uncork the wine.'

'I love you.' Marshall kissed her on the lips, then went back into the living room.

Siyal had at least moved and was now standing up so as to give the window a good stare.

Marshall joined him, but tried not to crowd him. 'You okay there, Rakesh?'

No response.

Down below, a cyclist weaved through the heavy traffic filing towards the lights by the latest set of roadworks.

Nothing else of note that required such attention.

'What's up, Rakesh?'

Nothing.

'You want to talk about whatever's happened?'

'I'm fine.'

There we go...

'Rakesh, with all due respect, you're not fine. Or you don't seem fine, anyway. You just turned up and sat there, not talking to Kirsten, so I don't think you—'

'I've been fired.' Siyal looked at Marshall briefly, long enough for him to see the snail trails of tears on his cheeks, then back out of the window.

'You've been *fired*?'

Siyal nodded. 'Today.'

'Who by? My father?'

'Him.'

'What did he say?'

But Marshall had lost him again.

'Stay there, Rakesh.' Marshall brushed a hand on his arm, then walked over to the door. He fished his phone out of his pocket and dialled his dad's personal mobile, all the time watching Siyal standing by the window.

'*Holá*, Roberto! You had to rush off so quickly yesterday. What's up?'

'I need a word.'

'About that case? Because if it is we should—'

'No, it's not about the case.' Marshall turned away so Siyal wouldn't hear him. 'It's... It's about Rakesh.'

'Ah. So he's told you?'

'Kind of. Said he's been sacked.'

'Sacked?' Milne laughed. 'He's been reassigned. That's all.'

'He's not in a good way.'

'Ah, crap. I'm sorry you're having to bear the brunt of that.'

'It's okay. He's a friend. It's what people do for friends, Dad.'

Shite.

Marshall was getting into the habit of using the D-word. He just had to hope he hadn't heard it. 'Is it true?'

'It's true, aye. You remember on Sunday, how I told you I'm retiring? Well, the papers came through. Didn't realise how quickly things were moving, but I'm out at the end of the week. New broom starts. Came up from West Yorkshire to oversee some strategic thing, but she's being given my gig.'

'Makes sense. They need to know they've got full impartiality, right?'

'Exactamundo, Roberto. Exactamundo. And Rakesh... he's unfortunately collateral damage from that.'

'I don't understand. Why won't he be kept on?'

'It's a difficult situation, son. With me going, the new broom doesn't want half the team. Already saddled with them for the rest of their tenures, unless they agree to move on. And I didn't know that young Shunty's tenure was tied to mine.'

'Can't you stay on?'

'I mean, I can. But I won't, Rob.'

'But you could?'

'As of two o'clock today, that ship has now sailed off. I was up at Tulliallan to finalise it. Believe me, they were trying to keep me on. Even sent Miranda Potter down to have a chat. But I have to go, Rob. I've done so much for other people in my life. It's time I did something for myself. And Grumpy.'

Marshall had to bite his tongue. The daft bastard really didn't think, did he? He was completely delusional.

Everything he'd done in his life was for his own gain.

Leaving Marshall and Jen when they were kids, for starters...

And how the hell was it okay to focus on your father, but to leave your kids...?

Marshall clenched the phone tighter. 'I suppose I can understand that.' Best to leave those thoughts unvoiced. 'Is there something going on?'

'What do you mean?'

'Something you're not telling us?'

'I'm not dying, Rob, no. You don't get away from me that easily.' Milne laughed down the line, but it shifted to a sigh.

'Would just rather spend the rest of my life in some form of health, while I've still got it. I've been through so much, son. I need to retire in peace and put my feet up. Rather than die in pieces. I've messed up so many things in my life, like my relationship with you and your sister, but now it's time I made reparations for them.'

At least he was aware he'd screwed up, anyway. 'What about our half-sister?'

'I see plenty of her, don't you worry. More than enough!' Milne laughed. 'But it was fantastic to see you and Jen on Sunday. And Kirsten. She's a cracker, Rob. Brilliant person.'

Marshall didn't want to take a compliment from him. 'Right. I don't appreciate what you said about her not drinking.'

'What are you talking about?'

'How she's not drinking because she's pregnant.'

'That was Grumpy.'

'I don't believe you.'

'Fine. Your choice, Rob. But you know what your grandfather's like. Everything's a joke to him. Since he was seventy, he just stopped giving a shit about what people thought about him. The filter came off.'

Marshall didn't know whether to believe him. He knew he should start to trust him, but he definitely wasn't anywhere near ready to open up about their difficulties.

'I want to do more of that, son. Family stuff is super-important.'

'Sure. I get that.' Marshall gritted his teeth, trying to avoid letting the words out. 'Listen, is there anything that can be done for Rakesh?'

Another rasping sigh. 'I wish there was more, but I tried it all.'

'You didn't tell Rakesh before today?'

'Rob, I wasn't sure I'd actually go. The charm offensive has been ridiculous. And I wasn't sure they'd let me. The truth is, most of the time up at bloody Tulliallan today was spent trying to secure his future.' A pause. 'No dice, I'm afraid.'

'Okay, so what's going to happen to him?'

'Uniform. He'll retain his rank of sergeant. They're looking for two in Craigmillar, so I guess it'll be there.'

'Lovely place...' Marshall would do anything to not be based there.

And Siyal...

He wouldn't last five minutes – and that was just in the staff room.

'You know he was never in uniform, right?'

'Indeed. One of the last direct entry cops in Police Scotland. Daft sods.'

'I was one.'

'Right.' Milne coughed. 'Sure. But you've got particular skills, right?'

'So does Rakesh.'

'There was a big review last year, Rob. We don't let in direct entrants anymore, especially not to detective. The prevailing view is people need to earn their stripes. Sure, you can get a fast track to DS, but you've got to do your time. As much as I like Rakesh, this is a good chance for him to do that work. Plus I told Shunty I'll put in a word for any job he applies for.'

'That's big of you.'

'This kind of nonsense happens all the time, Rob. It's not the end of the world for the lad, just a speed bump. It'll make him a much better cop for it.'

'Sure it will...' Marshall took another look at him – still giving the window a solid stare. Nowhere near high enough to injure himself if he jumped out of it... But the thought was probably crossing his mind. 'Okay. I'll let you get on with your evening, Bob. Catch you later.'

'Just wondered if you—'

Marshall hung up before he could finish the thought.

Time to focus on the task at hand – talking Siyal down from the ledge.

Marshall stepped into the living room. 'Rakesh, can I get you a cup of tea?'

Siyal turned around briefly. 'I've had plenty of cups today. Practically shaking.'

Marshall could tell – it was as though he was phasing in and out of existence, like in some sci-fi show. 'How about a glass of water? Glass of wine?'

'I'm fine.'

Marshall went back over to the window. 'I just spoke to my father. He says he tried to fight your corner.'

'Did he.' Siyal rolled his eyes. 'I'm used to having to fight my own battles, but you can thank him for me.'

'I will. He said you'll likely be a uniform sergeant.'

'Exactly. How can I do that, Rob?'

'Many a career has been enhanced by a stint in uniform. Knew a few in London who stepped back in, climbed the ranks there, and moved back into being a detective. It'll give you that street credibility everyone says you're lacking.'

'Do they?'

'Come on, Rakesh. If you were analysing your own development needs, you'd surely admit that?'

'I would. But the thought of...' Siyal shook his head. 'I can't cope with it. Craigmillar is *Niddrie*.'

'You've coped with working in the Complaints for over a year now. Takes a special type of cop to do that. This won't be as hard as that.'

'But my face didn't fit there, either. Nobody would sit with me at lunch.'

'Cops can be bastards, Rakesh. Even the ones who investigate their own. It's okay.'

'No. It's not.'

'Rakesh, for crying out loud – you worked for *Andrea Elliot*.'

That got a laugh.

'You can handle a few uniform constables.'

'Can I?'

'Of course you can. I was down in the Borders for most of that stint. Elliot worked you hard. Really hard. Made you wish you'd never signed up a few times, I bet. But she toughened you up and gave you some hard investigative skills that stood you in good stead for the role in Standards. You've thrived there.'

'I wouldn't say I've exactly thrived. And I still don't get why I'm being kicked out.'

'It wasn't personal, Rakesh. You're seen as too close to my dad. That's all.'

'Right.'

'New broom sweeping everything clean.'

'Hmmm.'

'You can always apply for another force. The Met, for instance.'

'I like living in Edinburgh.'

'Northumbria, then.'

'I'm not commuting to Newcastle, Rob.'

'No, but... The elephant in the room is you're still a lawyer. Lots of options on that front as well.'

'So, you're saying I should give up being a cop?'

'If you choose to look at it that way. Another way to think about it would be that you've now got a few years' experience as a cop. Sure a few firms would love that kind of experience in a criminal defence lawyer. Especially if said experience is in the Complaints.'

'Crap.' Siyal checked his watch. 'I'm running late for my date.'

Marshall raised his eyebrows. 'Are you in the right frame of mind to go—'

'I'm *fine*.' Siyal brushed past him then stomped out of the flat. 'Bye, Kirsten. And thank you for sitting with me.'

The door opened then rattled shut again.

Kirsten popped her head into the living room, carrying two generous glasses of red wine. 'Has he gone already?'

'He's going on a date.'

'A *date*? Him?'

Marshall shrugged. 'Guess we don't know him as well as he knows us.'

'Clearly.' She handed him his glass, then sat on the edge of the sofa. 'Very nice stuff this, by the way.'

'Better be at that price.' Marshall sipped and got a full flood of red flavours. 'God, that's spectacular.'

'So, what are you going to do?'

'Drink my wine.' Marshall grinned at her, but it felt false, even to him. 'I'll maybe speak to my dad again, but I doubt there's anything I can do about it.'

'No. But you can at least try, eh?'

32

DAY 3
TUESDAY

Marshall swiped his card through the reader and was surprised it still worked. He opened the door and blocked it with his foot, then checked his watch – just in time for the briefing.

He lugged his laptop bag through into the office space.

Gashkori stood at the far side, one hand in a pocket, the other waving around like he was conducting a choir. 'So, that's where we are. Let's get back out to Peebles and see what we can do. Cal, can I grab a moment of your time after you've fetched us both a coffee?'

Taylor laughed. 'Sure thing, boss.'

'Okay, that's all for this morning. Give me a shout if you need anything.' Gashkori locked eyes with Marshall. 'Be back here at five, unless you hear otherwise. Dismissed.'

The crowd broke up and went about their business.

Leaving Marshall a clear path through to Gashkori. 'Thought I'd make it here in time for the briefing. Thanks for letting me know you've brought it forward.'

'It wasn't personal, Rob.' Gashkori couldn't hide his smirk, could he? 'Aren't you profiling in Gartcosh?'

'I have been. It's what I did all of yesterday afternoon. Do you want to—'

'In a minute.' Gashkori held up his phone. 'Got some calls to make first. And I need to get heavily caffeinated before I go anywhere near them.'

'Sure. Of course.' Marshall tried to grin away his fury as he watched Gashkori walk over to his office.

A wasted journey.

Should've just gone to Gartcosh, like he'd planned to.

Maybe he should mention it to Potter.

Nah, he wasn't that petty.

Or was he?

'Long time, no see.' DS Jolene Archer was grinning at him.

Marshall smiled back at her. 'Am I imagining it, or did the briefings used to be at seven?'

'Always have been, aye. Gashkori brought today's forward.'

'Sneaky sod.'

'Gashkori's not that bad, is he?'

He laughed. 'Nah, he's much worse.'

'C'mere.' She wrapped him in a hug. 'How are you doing?'

'I'm still standing, I guess.' Marshall swallowed another sigh. 'Been a while since I've seen you, Jo. You okay?'

'I'm fine, actually. Work's good. Home life is less mental.' She leaned in close. 'Bit worried about Andrea, though. Have you seen her recently?'

'Saw her yesterday and she seemed a bit... I guess when you lose your husband, it's going to take a while. Especially when it happened like that. Should she be back so soon?'

Jolene flashed up her eyebrows. 'You try stopping her.'

Marshall couldn't help but chuckle. 'Would take an army. And even then...'

'Didn't know you were on this case, Rob.'

'Oh, I've been on since Sunday. Had the joy of working with Callum Taylor.'

'Ah. That'll explain where he's been, then. His update at the briefing was a bit vague.'

Marshall was glad he hadn't tried to claim a load of work as his own, but still – he'd love to have been party to what he'd broadcast to the team. 'Are you working it too?'

'Came on last night. Gashkori's asked to back up Struan's work.'

'Back up?'

'Go through and check he hasn't broken any laws, basically. Last night, him and Andrea went back into interview Iain Hogg. You know, the chief suspect?'

'The one who's been charged.'

'Right. Trouble is, he's not really talking, even though they've charged him.'

'I did warn Gashkori that would be the case. And the interview strategy was a mess, if I'm honest. They don't have much on him, do they?'

'No. According to the boss, they've got a couple of days to back it all up.'

'Fingers crossed for him, then.' Marshall had to let out the sigh again. He gave her a smile. 'I'll see you around, Jo.' He walked over to Gashkori's office, ready to confront him.

Taylor beat him to it, carrying two coffee cups. He spotted Marshall, but didn't say anything as he slipped inside, then shut the door behind him.

Marshall was about to open it, when his phone blasted out. He checked the display:

Hardeep calling...

Marshall stepped away from the office and answered it. 'Hardeep, you okay?'

'Yes, yes. Except I couldn't sleep after our meeting last night, so I've been in early to work. Sir, I've found some other potential cases that match our looser search parameters. In Dundee, Hamilton, Aberdeen, Carlisle and another in Glasgow.'

Marshall vaguely remembered something about that. He'd hoped for a few more days before another wild goose chase. 'Okay, I'll have a look at them when I get back to base.'

'Of course. But there's another case which is, if you ask me, ticking a lot of boxes. I feel mortified to miss it.'

'Forget all of that. What is it?'

'Body found in a tunnel at Penmanshiel near Grantshouse in the Borders. It happened eight years ago, so it massively predated the other murders, which is why I missed it. Is that near you?'

'Grantshouse? No, it's not. It's at the other end of the Borders. Over on the east coast. It's almost in East Lothian.'

'Oh, I'm sorry, sir. I didn't know.'

'It's fine, Hardeep. I do know it, though.' Marshall walked over to the giant map on the wall, surveying the geographic scope of their work, and immediately found Grantshouse.

Stuck on the border of two counties, but not quite on the coast. The only thing going for it was the A1 ran next to it. Trapped in the emptiness on the northern side of the Lammermuirs, which separated the East Lothian coast from the towns and villages along the Tweed.

The railway tunnel was marked on the map with '*dis.*' – disused.

Marshall's antennae started twitching again. 'How does it tick a lot of boxes?'

'The MO matches Beverley and Rebecca, almost note for note. But also has similarities with Adam.'

'I'm not quite following you there, Hardeep.'

'No. Sorry, sir. Listen, it's probably best if I meet you there. I'm on my way.'

33

'Here we go!' Taylor turned onto the A1 and powered up it, clearly relishing the joy of finally hitting a fast road. It might have only been a single carriageway, but it was much better than the series of tight twists and bends they'd had to take to get here across the gorgeous Berwickshire countryside. 'Why are we wasting our time with this?'

'Same reason as why we wasted our time going to Glasgow and Edinburgh. If we uncover another case connected to this, it'll help us profile the killer.'

'But it might not.'

'True.' Marshall reached up to hold on to the handle. 'But it shed some light on stuff. The trouble with my work is I'm having to make assumptions constantly. But the more data we get, the more we validate them. This could be another connection and it might help us prove that some of the others aren't connected. Might help us see that none of them are.'

'See, it just feels like a load of nonsense to me.'

'You won't find any arguments from me.'

Taylor laughed. 'Seriously?'

'Serial murderers mostly don't leave playing cards on their bodies or send notes to the press claiming all of their crimes. They tend to just murder a series of victims. And if we don't want them to get away with it, we have to look for other potential murders they've committed. And it feels like a waste of time, Cal, because most of the time it will be. But it's much better to rule it out than to later discover we should've ruled it in.'

'I get that. Are you saying we should've connected Beverley and Adam?'

'No. We were right not to. We didn't have the full set of information.'

'Right. Right. But... It's just...' Taylor took a hand away from the wheel to brush it through his hair. 'Ach, never mind. You're right.' He slowed for the right turn to Penmanshiel, marked as a T-junction, signifying the pointlessness of visiting the place. He shot across the path of an oncoming coach, then followed the road winding up through mature woodland. 'So we're meeting your man here?'

'Hardeep.'

'He any good?'

'Almost too good. He's doing a PhD.'

'Didn't you?'

'Yeah, but I took five years. He's just about done his in two.'

'You can do that?'

'I couldn't. He can.'

'Wow. Think you'll be able to hold on to him after?'

'I doubt it. But there will be other PhD students.'

'Won't there just.' Taylor stopped halfway up a bank through the woods. 'This must be the place.'

Hardeep's Mini was in the car park next to a monument. Hardeep was inspecting it, a curious frown twisting his forehead.

Taylor pulled in next to his car. 'I'll let you lead, Rob. After all, I'm just a piece of arm candy for you.'

Marshall laughed as he got out, then wandered over to Hardeep. 'Well done for getting here quicker than we did.'

Hardeep shrugged. 'Told you, I was already on my way when I called you. And you had to attend the briefing.'

Marshall sighed at the memory, then of trying to persuade Gashkori of the importance of them visiting. At least he hadn't come along himself. He took in the vista – a brief break in the trees looked back across the A1, but he could only hear the road rather than see it. 'Hardeep, this is DI Callum Taylor.'

Taylor held out a hand. 'Pleased to meet you, mate.'

Hardeep didn't seem too sure of that, but he shook the hand anyway. 'And you, sir.'

Taylor walked over to the monument. 'So what's this thing all about?'

'I had to wait, so I did some research into what transpired here. This is a memorial to the tunnel collapse in 1979. Happened as they were improving it. Two men died, but it could've been a lot worse. Thirteen escaped. They'd planned on rebuilding the tunnel but it was decided to be too costly, so they sealed it up and rerouted the A1 and the railway across... I don't know the technical term for it, but they blew up the hill with dynamite to drive a channel through it.'

'Right.' Taylor was staring at the monument, then he looked around. 'This where the body was?'

'It was, yes.'

'This isn't where the tunnel is, though?'

'No. The tunnel is pretty much a ruin now. Even though that was not much less than fifty years ago. Both entrances are completely inaccessible.'

'But you're saying the body was here.'

'Found in the car park, yes.'

Taylor looked over at his pool car. 'So this isn't the same, is it?'

'No, it's not, but it also is.'

Taylor looked over at Marshall with a sour look on his face. 'Rob, can you decipher this for me?'

Marshall nodded at Hardeep. 'I've got to admit, you've kind of lost me too.'

Hardeep looked right at Marshall. 'You and I are working on the basis that all these cases are connected, correct? Aside from tunnels, the main thing connecting the victims is the brutal force used in their murders. Or apparent suicides. The victim here was Kate McWilliams.' He gestured at the monument Taylor was resting against. 'It appears her head was smashed into the monument with enough force to fracture her skull in two main areas.'

Taylor let go of it. 'So you're saying she was attacked *twice*?'

'It appears that way, yes. She wasn't murdered in a tunnel, but this isn't that far off the MO used in the other cases.'

Taylor puffed up his cheeks and stared at the monument like he could see blood or bits of skull on there, or just that it was haunted. 'When was this?'

'Eight years ago.'

'Okay. So back in 2016. Just before the whole world went to shite, eh? Turning on the Large Hadron Collider ruined everything.' Taylor tapped his nose. 'Mark my words.'

Marshall joined Taylor at the monument. Certainly looked sturdy enough to smash someone's skull against. 'And back then, there wasn't a pseudo-MIT down in the Borders, was there?'

'Nope.' Taylor winced. 'You know, I worked the case that sparked it a couple of years ago. Two numpties in a caravan park near Jedburgh.' He looked at the monument again. 'There were MITs in 2016, though. That's after the formation of Police

Scotland and Specialised Crime. So I'm guessing any confirmed homicides would've been the responsibility of some fud from Edinburgh, correct?'

'Correct.' Hardeep winced. 'In this case, the "fud" was one DI James Pringle from the Edinburgh MIT.'

34

Marshall walked into the office space in Gala nick, phone pressed to his ear.

Third time he'd called, third time it hadn't been answered, second time he'd left a voicemail.

He stopped to give it the respect it deserved. 'Jim, it's Rob. Sorry if my first message was a bit garbled. I was driving through the countryside and think I lost phone reception. Anyway. I'm calling you about an old case you worked, back during your time in Edinburgh. Give me a call back when you get this. Cheers. And I hope you're keeping well. Thanks, Jim.'

Marshall hung up and felt a weight tugging down on his shoulders. It'd been ages since he'd heard from Pringle. Weeks since he'd sent him a message. Calling out of the blue like that just for a case...

It felt a bit cheap. Or just cheeky.

He checked his text messages. Still nothing from Belu Owusu – the messages he'd received since April had been all about him handing over his keys for Pringle's house near Glasgow to the estate agent. All very businesslike.

He wondered if the delay in her response was because they

were the other side of the world, so he checked and remembered Durban was only an hour ahead of them – a totally different deal to Australia or the West Coast of the US.

She should've got the message.

And should read it soon.

And Marshall hoped he could refresh Pringle's non-existent.

As Pringle would say.

A tingle of sadness throbbed in his throat.

Marshall swallowed it down, then knocked on the door and waited, sucking in a deep breath. The office was buzzing like a beehive, all the drones making honey here rather than doing work in Peebles. But they were more like wasps than bees. Maybe those Japanese hornets that were doing so much damage in the USA.

The door opened and Elliot stood there, scowling at him. 'Rob? What are you doing here?'

'Working.' Marshall gave her a kind smile. 'You got a sec?'

'Kind of up against it, you know?'

'It's just… I need to pick your brains on something.'

'I mean, my brains are in a worse state than Jim Pringle's.'

'Which is the problem.'

'Eh?'

'The case is something you both worked. Given he's got early-onset Alzheimer's, I doubt I'll get anything out of him. Besides, he's in South Africa. And you're here.'

She flared her nostrils. 'Seriously, if this is about someone who kills people with chopsticks every Shrove Tuesday…'

'It's about this case.'

Elliot snorted, then looked around the office. She sighed, then opened the door wide. 'In you come.'

Marshall followed her in but didn't take a seat – because she hadn't.

She gave a weak smile. 'What's up?'

'I'm looking into a murder Jim investigated a few years ago. Hoping you might be able to shed light on it.'

'Haven't seen you for ages.'

'I saw you yesterday.'

'Right. I remember now. My memory's not that shot.' She laughed. 'You were mansplaining something at Gashkori.'

'Mansplaining?'

Elliot slapped a hand to her forehead. 'Sorry, Rob... I... I haven't been myself.'

'No, that's very on-brand for you.'

At least she smiled at that. 'How are you doing, Rob?'

'I'm fine. Bit fed up of working at Gartcosh, but it's okay.'

'Fifteen months you've been over there now, isn't it?'

'Give or take, aye.'

'And have you got a single result yet?'

'No. Not a single sausage. But that's not the point in my work. I'm there to check mainstream detectives haven't missed anything.'

'*I* never miss a thing.'

Like your husband leaking to a local drug gang lord...

'Sure.' Marshall knew how to placate her, so didn't fight it. 'But lots of cases don't get solved for various reasons.'

'But you haven't found a single mistake?'

'Oh, I've found hundreds of mistakes. Whether they're corruption or, more likely, incompetence isn't my job. I'm not in Standards.'

'Like Rakesh and your old man.'

Marshall had to look away. 'Right, exactly.'

'But you haven't been able to match up any cold cases to an unknown serial killer, have you?'

'No. It's almost like there aren't any.'

'But there are. You've worked two cases down here. And that one back in April?'

'Okay, but that wasn't as a direct result of my new role. It was part of a murder investigation Gashkori ran.'

'You knew him, though?'

'It dated back to the dim and distant. Criminal profiling is a pretty small field.'

'Bet you've taken credit for it, though.'

'Potter has, aye.'

'Shhh. Don't say her name!'

'People need to get over this nonsense.'

'You started it, Robbie.'

'Even so.' Marshall felt that sharp sting in his gut he only got from Elliot. A particular pain. Time to change tack and stop her derailing stuff with her nonsense. 'Truth is, maybe I belong here in the Borders.'

'We're fully booked, sadly. No room at the inn.'

'Happy to work in the manger.'

Elliot laughed. 'You're a dickhead, you know that?'

'Guilty as charged.' Marshall held her gaze, intense and fizzing with secrets. 'How are *you* doing, Andrea?'

'Are you just being polite?'

'No. I'm actually interested.'

'Right. I'm okay, Rob.'

'Seriously?'

'Seriously.'

'Even with all that's happened?'

'Of course I miss aspects of Davie.'

'Aspects?'

'A lot of him. But I feel like he died when he did what he did. Or when he got caught for it. You know?'

'I can totally understand that.'

'Because of what happened to Anna?'

'Right.' Marshall felt a sting of pain in his nostrils. Like he was going to cry. Even in her weakened state, she'd still managed to pierce his defences. 'Exactly that.'

'If you must know, Robbie, my home life is absolute chaos. Mum and Dad are helping, but it's left a massive gap. And they're not getting any younger. Not to mention that Davie's parents are a bloody nightmare too. Haven't bothered to offer to help. It's like they feel shame for what he did, but... it feels like they're blaming me. Does that make any sense?'

'Makes perfect sense to me.'

'I mean, Sam's stepping up to look after her brothers, which is helpful, but it's tough on her. A difficult time for her.'

'Aren't all ages difficult?'

'True.' She sighed. 'Very true. But Sam... Every age has been a total nightmare. I love her, but...'

Marshall waited for her to fill out the silence, but she just left it. 'Have to say, Andrea, I'm surprised to see you back at work so soon.'

'It's been three months. You barely get a fortnight off. And I'm not made of money. I can't just take time off.'

Marshall frowned at that. 'I thought you'd be signed off?'

'I've been to the doctor, but there's nothing wrong with me. Other than having *repulsive* taste in men.'

Marshall smiled at that, even though it wasn't far from the truth. 'Not even taking time off for a holiday?'

'Taking them away to Florida next month. It'll be a chance for us to put it all behind us. Or at least start to. Distract them with rollercoasters and burgers and milkshakes.' Elliot sat against the edge of her desk and folded her arms. 'Keep thinking I should sell the house and move, but... There's so much emotion attached to that place, you know? The youngest two have only ever lived there.'

'I get it.'

'Right. Thank you for caring, Rob. Or at least pretending to.'

'I do care. Of course I do. How's it been going here?'

'Do you want the truth?'

'No, a pack of lies would be totally fine.'

Elliot smiled. 'The reality is I feel side-lined by Gashkori. It's like he doesn't think I'm up to it.'

'But you're now working this case, right?'

'That's only because She Who Cannot Be Named ordered him to bring me on so you could have Taylor.' She nudged his arm. 'Be thankful you didn't get saddled with me, Robbie.'

He smiled it off but the truth was it would've been a nightmare. 'You know her well?'

'Who, Potter?' Elliot gave a quick shake of her head. 'Met her twice.'

'You must've impressed her, because she asked for you to work this case.'

'Exactly. I'm a bit baffled as to why, but I'll take any allies I can get.'

Marshall was similarly mystified. 'What's your take on Hogg?'

'My take? Am I allowed to have one?' Elliot laughed, but the emotion didn't go anywhere near her eyes. 'We've charged him, so I guess that's good enough for me.'

'Level with me here – do you think he's done it?'

'As in killed her?' Elliot shrugged. 'I don't know, Rob. Why are you asking all these annoying questions?'

'They're not that annoying, are they?'

'Okay. But why are you here, then?'

'Hardeep's found a case going back eight years that might connect to this one.'

'You think this is a serial killer?'

'It might be.'

'Okay, so why does that involve me?'

'Because you worked it with Pringle.'

'Remind me?'

'A woman was murdered at the monument to Penmanshiel Tunnel near Grantshouse. Name of Kate McWilliams. Body was found there. Someone had smashed her head into the monument. Twice.'

'Think I remember it, aye.' Elliot sat down behind her desk and logged in to her machine. 'Kate McWilliams...'

Marshall couldn't see what she was up to.

Only took a few seconds of her typing before she glanced over. 'Here we go, Robbie. Pringle was deputy SIO on it. Think that's because he lived down in the Borders.'

'It was Grantshouse, though. Not *that* local to someone who lived in Kelso.'

'I don't make the rules. Nor did Jim.'

'Does it say who the SIO was?'

'Steve Booth.'

'Never met him.'

'You'd have got on well with him. He was a total arsehole too.'

'Was?'

'Long since retired to Spain. Heard he drunk himself to an early death. Admittedly, took him five years of wine, lager, cognac and so much deep-fried food it was like he was still living in Scotland, but he toppled off his balcony one night and that was all she wrote.'

'Brutal.'

'Heart attack did for him, rather than the fall.'

'Heard of similar with other cops.'

'It's a hard game that does weird stuff to people's brains, Robbie.' She was focusing on the screen again. 'Was just checking to prove I wasn't involved in the case and give you what for, but it turns out I was.'

'Good. Because I'm thinking it might be connected to ours.'

'Why, because it's near a train tunnel? Come on, Robbie...'

'Not just that. A couple of other things.'

'Okay, but it's mainly that, right?' Elliot smiled at him. 'Look, I don't have all the details on the case, Robbie, so—'

'But you've got way more than me.'

'Sure, but I was a mere DS at the time, so I didn't make any of the decisions.'

'You being out means you'll know the background and all of the issues.'

She grinned. 'Boy, did I know them.'

'Go on.'

'Okay, so the thing with that case is we never caught Kate's killer, but we did have a suspect. Or a plausible theory, anyway. It goes something like this. A woman called Stacy Gray went to uni in Newcastle, but was seeing a lad in Edinburgh, so she'd drive up and down the A1 a lot. Then one time, as if by magic, she was in a car crash and died.'

'How does this connect with Kate?'

'She was driving the other car in the crash.'

'Okay.' Marshall could start to visualise the motive. 'Basic revenge, then?'

'Right. We'd caught Kate on the speed camera, doing seventy-five in a national speed limit stretch of single carriageway mere seconds before the crash.'

'Did she get done for dangerous driving?'

'Banned from driving for ten years.'

Something tickled at Marshall's brain. 'That seems a bit odd. No custodial sentence?'

'Doesn't it just? A few reasons, though. First, Stacy was caught by the same set of cameras which caught Kate's speeding. One of those that sneakily does both sides of the road. Clocked her doing ninety on that stretch of sixty *and* caught a photo of her using her phone when it happened. Texting with both hands.'

'So who did you have in the frame for it?'

'Booth thought Stacy's husband killed Kate in revenge.'

'Makes sense as a suspect, certainly. What was Jim's take on it?'

'He thought he was innocent. The husband had a rock-solid alibi for the time of death.'

Marshall tried to map it out in his head. The thing that had a giant klaxon around it was the fact Kate had got away with causing a death.

Mitigating circumstances, maybe, but she had been involved in it.

He couldn't stand still so started pacing around the office. 'Was that in the press?'

'Everywhere, Robbie. Online, in the papers, on the telly. You name it.'

'Right.' Marshall took a deep breath. 'Think I should speak to him?'

'The husband? Sure thing. But can you do me a favour and take Struan with you?'

'Struan? Why?'

'He's annoying me. Like a dog with a pheasant in his mouth. Or maybe a dog who wants to have a pheasant in his mouth and who goes around chasing the poor sods everywhere. Besides, he worked the case too. He was a DC back then, in the middle of his many roles around the country.'

'With you now. I'll take him.'

'Thank you, Rob.'

'Cal Taylor will be glad to be off the hook for a bit.'

'Don't talk to me about that clown.' Elliot blocked him from leaving the office. 'But thank you, Robbie. You're the first person who's shown interest in me in months. Well, that's not true. Jolene's been great. And so has Gashkori. But you're the one who persisted and asked me questions. Thank you.' She gave him a hug. 'I appreciate it.'

35

The vista opened up, giving them the first view of Walkerburn, framed by Plora Rig to the south and Caberston to the north. Hills Marshall had been up and down many times over the years, mostly on foot but sometimes on his bike – and once with an alpaca for Thea's birthday.

Struan was behind the wheel, slowing as they hit the long high street into the town, mostly houses with a shop and a closed pub, the artery narrowed by parked cars.

Struan was taking no prisoners and just ploughed through. 'Thinking about buying a flat here before it gets too expensive.'

'In *Walkerburn*?'

Struan glanced over at him. 'Something wrong with that?'

Marshall shrugged. 'Would've thought it'd be pretty cheap here.'

'That's the thing. It is. But Innerleithen's going right upmarket now and it's just two miles away. Before too long, it'll swallow up Walkerburn, you mark my words.' Struan turned past a row of houses painted in the colours of the Brazilian flag – or at least the football strip. He had to slow to let a car through. 'Staying at the old boy's place over in Kelso just now. Bastard of a drive to Gala in the middle of winter.'

'Can well imagine.'

A long row of stone cottages lurked around the bend, opposite a drying green with some decaying garages dotting the perimeter.

Struan pulled up outside the Henry Ballantyne Memorial, a grand old building that looked like a country pub. 'If my intel is right, he should be in here just now...'

Marshall couldn't remember who Henry Ballantyne was or why he'd need to be remembered. Probably someone who founded the town or its now-defunct mills. 'Drinking or working?'

'Usually both.' Struan looked over at Marshall with a hard stare. 'You wanting me to lead in here?'

'I guess so, otherwise there's no point in you being here.' Marshall held his gaze then grinned. 'Elliot wanted rid of you pretty quickly.'

'To be brutally honest, gaffer, we don't see eye to-eye.' Struan leaned over, like he suspected the pool car was bugged. 'Between you and me, I'm worried about her. She doesn't seem to be...' He looked down at the handbrake, then back up. 'Look, losing her husband is a massive deal. Huge. I'm not expecting her to be over it or anything, but do you honestly think she should be back at work?'

'I don't know. I just spoke to her and... She didn't seem to be the same person I know. She seems to have a lot of grief still to process. She needs to speak to someone. And Andrea's probably the last person to want to do that.'

'It's a hard road to go down, especially for a cop, but you can't force someone to walk it, can you?' Struan nodded slowly, like he'd trodden that path himself. 'Anyway. Thanks for listening to my TED talk.' He opened his door and got out.

Marshall took a few seconds to process the fact Struan had showed concern about another human being.

All anyone seemed to do was talk to him. Not a new phenomenon – it'd been that way most of his life. It was just rare in policing circles.

He stepped out of the car and followed him into the building.

The bar was busy with a morning crowd of old boys at a table in the window, tucking into bacon rolls, their lips smacking together, like they were in a golf club and ready for their tee time.

Struan was up at the counter, leaning on it. 'Looking for Andy?'

'Got three Andrews here.' The barman tilted his head back. 'Which one are you looking for?'

'Brydon.'

'That'll be me, then.' Brydon's gaze shifted between Struan and Marshall. 'You pair look like cops.'

'We are. DS Struan Liddell.' He held out his warrant card. 'Need to speak with you. Is there somewhere private we could do this?'

Brydon shook his head. 'Here's fine. Whatever it is, I've nothing to hide.'

'It's about what happened to Stacy.'

Brydon's nostrils flared – talk about someone with a lot of unprocessed grief... 'What about her?'

'It's related to an open murder investigation.'

'You lot thought I killed that woman. Kate McWilliams. You still think that?'

Struan shrugged. 'We're just looking into a few aspects of the case. And it'd be good to hear it from the horse's mouth.'

Brydon stood up tall. 'Are you trying to stitch me up all over again?'

'No.' Marshall stepped forward and rested against the bar

top. 'Quite the opposite. If this pans out the way I think it could, you'll get closure for what happened back then.'

'Right. But this Kate McWilliams is the one who was killed by someone. Not Stacy.' Brydon's gaze was severe, like the crack of a whip. 'Their cars were involved in a head-on collision. Kate was lucky to survive. Stacy wasn't.' He crouched and started emptying glasses from the steaming dishwasher, then set about drying them with a towel. 'Hit me pretty hard. Because... I just knew it was going to happen. Just expected it. Stacy was twenty when she died.'

'How did you meet?'

'I was working in a bar in Edinburgh. The Debonair on West Port.'

Struan chuckled. 'I know it. Rum place.'

'Aye, that's selling it short. Glad I don't work there anymore, put it that way. Stacy's brother worked the door, so she'd come in with her mates and they'd drink and dance in there. One night when Kieron wasn't on, we got talking. And... one thing led to another.'

'Did he mind?'

'Kieron? Nah, he was a good guy. He didn't mind us seeing each other.'

'Was Stacy from Edinburgh?'

'Sighthill, aye. She was a smart cookie, though. Went to uni in Newcastle. And because she was seeing me, she used to bomb up and down the A1.'

'You go down there much?'

'When I could. Didn't fit in with her new uni mates, mind. Hard not to blame myself for what happened because of that. If she hadn't been driving...' Brydon rubbed at his cheek. 'The cops said Stacy was doing ninety on the A1 at the time of the crash. And there's a photo of her checking her phone.' He swallowed hard. 'She was messaging me, you know? I'd no idea she was driving, so kept replying to her. She was planning on surprising me. If I'd known, I would've told her to stop, but she was addicted to messaging. Addicted to driving too. Absolute petrolhead. Her and Kieron both. Driving like idiots connected them with their old man, God rest his soul. Stacy loved her car. This big American import Ford Mustang her dad had left her in his will. Left-hand drive, with enough horsepower to tear the tyres off and a roar you'd hear from miles away.'

'Had one myself.' Struan was nodding. 'Not an import, but it could shift.'

Brydon shrugged. 'To me cars are just how you get from A to B, you know?'

Marshall nodded – he had the same philosophy, though he'd broken it when he'd had to get a heap of crap that went from A to B through the snow. 'How did Kieron take her death?'

'Not great. Blamed me for what happened. Blamed himself, really. Either way, he just got angrier. And he started out at eleven on a scale of five.'

'You tell the police about this?'

'Oh, aye. They spoke to him. Trouble is, when this Kate woman was killed, he was on a stag weekend in Shagaluf with some other bouncers. Must've been insane.'

'When did you last hear from him?'

'About seven years ago. He's inside, last I heard. Battered someone outside the Deb. Broke their arm.'

'Did what happened make you move back here from Edinburgh?'

'No. The trains did. Figured I could save a packet if I moved back here and got the train in, rather than paying through the nose for a flat in Edinburgh.' Brydon shrugged. 'Got an inheritance off my gran. Grew up around here, but I couldn't afford to live in Innerleithen, so Walkerburn it was. Bought a place just before Stacy died. Figured it'd be a good investment, but now I'm on my own and the place feels so big without her. She'd have loved living here. Haring around all the back lanes by the

Tweed.' He looked at them, shifting his gaze between them. 'This was a few years ago. You probably think I'm mental for still living in the past like that.'

'Not at all.' Marshall held his gaze, showing him he meant every single word. 'Until you go through something like that, you can't say how long grief takes.'

Brydon raised his hands. 'Believe me, I know how long it takes. Piece of string, right?'

'Right.' Marshall teased his way through the sums, scratching at his temples.

Brydon would've been twenty-two when Stacy died eight years ago. Meaning he was thirty now, give or take a few months.

Meaning...

'Do you know someone called Rebecca Yellowlees?'

Brydon frowned. 'Should I?'

'She's from Peebles.'

'Mate. Walkerburn and Peebles don't mix.'

'My niece grew up in Cardrona. Kids from both towns go to the same high school, so I beg to differ.'

'Whatever.' Brydon went back to his glasses. 'Either way, I don't know her.' He set the glasses down with a huff. 'You still think I killed Kate McWilliams, don't you? Even with my alibi?'

'Just because it wasn't you, doesn't mean you couldn't have arranged it.'

'Mate.' Brydon sighed. 'You really need to check out the old case file, because you lot tore my life apart. I was grieving, but you...' He shut his eyes and wiped away a tear. 'You interviewed everyone I'd speak to on a regular basis in the Deb up in Edinburgh. Everyone I drank with down here. Everyone I know. Everyone at the garage.'

'Garage?'

'I work at the garage up on the Peebles road. Every customer I dealt with in that last year was spoken to, in case I'd paid them money to kill that woman. The sad truth was that Stacy was a risk-taker, just like her brother. It was only a matter of time before the inevitable happened, wasn't it?' Brydon returned a wave from the old guys at the table. 'Be over in a second, Douglas.' He focused on Marshall. 'I didn't kill her. My alibi will still check out eight years on.'

'Go on.'

Brydon gasped, like that should've been enough. 'When whoever killed Kate did that... I'd just moved into that house and the place was a right state. Like the inside of my head, to be honest. Fixing the place up was a good way to sort my head out, or so I thought. At the time she was killed, I was knocking down walls. Before you ask, I was with a mate. Skinny Mick. He worked as a builder. Hired a sledgehammer and all the gear. Had an architect on-site. All above board. Then we were going at it and we did a live stream from this app called Periscope. It's still up there and it'll show us doing it at the same time Kate McWilliams was killed.'

Struan looked at Marshall, then sighed as he realised he'd just gained an action. Or so Marshall hoped.

Brydon swallowed hard. 'It's awful what happened to Kate. Thing is, I don't blame her for what happened. Stacy dying was tragic, but she was careless. It was inevitable. I was just always waiting for that call...'

36

SHUNTY

Siyal knocked on the door and waited.

Behind him, the open-plan office area thrummed with activity. By the still-broken photocopier, Jolene Archer was having a heated discussion with Jim McIntyre about something – probably not about who had to fix it.

Siyal didn't want to get involved. He knocked again.

Siyal could see Elliot through the gap between the blinds – sitting at her desk, staring at the wall.

'Bugger off, I'm busy.' Her voice rattled through the wood.

He knocked again, harder this time. 'It's Rakesh.'

A long pause. Her head dipped and she shook it. 'Come in, then.'

Siyal opened the door and walked in.

She swivelled around and stared at him, then her head dipped again. 'What?'

'What you did yesterday was highly inappropriate.'

'Eh, what was?'

'Trying to get information out of me in Edinburgh.'

Elliot clenched her fists in a fighting pose. 'I'll show you inapp—' She held up her hands. 'Sorry. I take that back. I shouldn't even joke about that to the likes of you.'

'The *likes of me*?'

'You *know* I mean officers from Professional Standards, Shunty. Nothing to do with your ethnicity, before you get started down that road.'

'Good, because it could be construed—'

'Why are you here?'

Siyal looked around for somewhere to sit, but all the other chairs had been taken out of the room, so he stayed standing. 'You know why, Andrea.'

'I like people to play their cards face up. Spell it out.'

She didn't get any easier when you'd done an ill-advised favour for her...

'I'm here to investigate the detail surrounding your husband's death.'

'Here, though?'

'What do you mean?'

'I mean, Davie was in court in Edinburgh, then they transferred him to a prison near Stirling. Doesn't make sense for you to be here, Shunty.'

'You could think that but the people who Davie was leaking to live near here.'

Elliot snorted. 'That's *way* outside of your terms of reference, Shunty.'

'Yesterday, you told me you wanted me to give you peace by shutting down the investigation. I'm not going to stop until I find the truth. I want to give you justice.'

'Justice, eh?' She got up and shut the door, then leaned back against it. 'Listen to me, okay? You've done a great job by interviewing the guards who could've been involved in this. Well done. But Gary Hislop and Callum Hume are a different matter. They kill people, Rakesh.'

'Do you think I'm scared?'

'You should be. I went to school with Gary. I know him. And you need to stop, okay? You need to learn when to stop.'

'I won't stop. I can't stop.'

Elliot gave him some side eye. 'Is Bob Milne okay with you being here?'

Siyal looked away. 'I haven't told him I'm here.'

'So you of all people are going rogue?' Her eyes widened. 'Wow.'

'Thing is, I'm on the way out.' Siyal let out a deep breath. 'Bob Milne's retiring and the new superintendent doesn't want me.'

'Oh shit. I didn't know. What will you—'

'Sounds like I'll be a uniformed sergeant in Craigmillar unless someone comes up with a better job.'

'Don't look at me with those big eyes, Shunty.' Elliot held up her thumb. 'First, my name's mud around here.' She raised her forefinger with a sly grin. 'Second, I don't rate you so I don't want you.'

Siyal smiled at that, but he wasn't too sure if it was a joke or just the truth. 'Look, I want to help you. If my time's up, then at least let me bow out by giving you some answers.'

'I don't want them!'

'Okay, but when I ran this past DCS Potter, she—'

'You spoke to She Who Cannot Be Named?'

'Most days, yes.'

'Jesus, Shunty! *How*?'

'I don't know. She likes me.'

'Not enough to keep you on in Standards…'

'Not her department. But she doesn't want me letting go of this, so you helping me is the quickest way to stop it. And it'll buy you some brownie points.'

Elliot stared hard at him for a few long seconds, then let out a deep breath and grabbed her car keys. 'Come on, then.'

'That's it?' Siyal had to jog to keep up with her as she raced through the office, then buzzed them back out into reception. 'That's all the resistance you're giving me?'

'If She Who Cannot Be Named wants this, then of course I'll help.' Elliot walked around the building into the car park. 'Get in. I'm driving.' She got behind the wheel and started the engine.

By the time he'd shut his door, Elliot was reversing, then driving off to merge with the traffic heading into the centre of Gala, not that there were many cars. Ignoring the seatbelt warning sign.

Siyal struggled to get his locked in.

'Biggest thing you can learn, Shunty, is how to approach a case from the other direction.'

'What does that even mean?'

'You're looking at it from the evidence you have, but not from the suspects.'

'We don't need to. We've got who killed him in prison.'

'I know you do. And that's all good. I feel *so* much justice for that.' She rolled her eyes. 'But you know he's just an idiot who's doing that to get some kickback. Maybe looking after his mum or his sister's kids or leaving a lump sum or clearing a massive debt. But you're not looking at who really did it. You've found nothing showing anything going wrong on the inside, except for my husband being killed. As far as I'm aware, nobody could've tailed the transport because of the protocols in place. Multiple trips in multiple vans. Shaking off tails. Using assumed names. Changing Davie's appearance slightly. But the truth is...' She swallowed hard and let out a sigh. 'Davie was killed because someone's let something slip. Could be they have people in all of the prisons, could be the drivers are all on the take. But I don't think so. You'd have shaken that loose, Shunty. And besides, Davie was under an assumed name. They'd even shaved his head to disguise him a bit.'

'That's what Bob Milne has been saying. "Any new baldies today?"'

'But his head was shaved just after he was sentenced, so someone knew that'd happened. Your pal Hooper spoke to me.'

'You went straight to him?'

'Why not? None of the court officers were party to that information. Except one, and his movements are all documented. He didn't call anyone or email anything. The clincher that you don't seem to have grokked is how Davie had been taken to a lesser prison.'

'I don't follow.'

'You can get people in Saughton, Barlinnie, all the greatest hits. But not there. Not easily. It means there was very likely a leak.'

'Where are we going?'

'Oh, you'll see. Reason I asked you to stop investigating this is because I didn't think you'd get anywhere. Because it's obvious who's behind this. Someone in Gary Hislop's orbit did this to Davie. Whoever did it must've had a contact in the police, the courts or the prison. Or all three. But to find out who did it, you need to follow the money and you haven't been.'

'What money? You mean the money Davie received for leaking information?'

Elliot glanced over at him. 'I don't think he was paid.'

'That's not what we understand.'

'No. But the... The last thing he said to me, he made it clear he was being threatened. Not just him. Me, our kids. His parents. There were photos of us at that family park place up by Dunbar. At school races. At the rugby. Me and him in that brewery tap room at Tweedbank.'

'You didn't tell us this during your interviews.'

'No. I didn't. Because it's so raw, Shunty.'

'So what are you saying?'

'I'm saying, if you find out who profited from his death, you find out who had him killed.'

'And who is that?'

'Well, to put it another way, who would lose out with him being alive?' Elliot pulled up just down from an office building in one of the old mills lining Gala Water. The rugby and football stadium was just about visible beyond, next to the shared Heriot-Watt and Borders College campus. '*Et voilà.*'

Siyal didn't know what to make of the place. Most of it seemed to be accessed by a communal door, but a brass plaque segmented half of the ground floor off to the side.

Trimontium Associates

He squinted at her. 'Who are—?'

'Callum Hume.'

Siyal frowned. 'As in, Gary Hislop's right-hand man?'

'He's the one behind this, Shunty. Hislop doesn't get anywhere near wet work.'

'Wet work?'

'Killing someone! Hume arranges for all of that.'

As if by magic, the front door opened and Callum Hume sailed out. A big guy, on the cusp of overweight or just overmuscled. His shaved head exposed cauliflower ears like satellite dishes. Well dressed, though, in a charcoal suit with a purple-and-lime tartan polo shirt. The navy Converse baseball boots ruined the look. He got into a purple Maserati sports car and hurtled off, back the way they'd driven. Didn't seem to spot them as he passed.

Elliot set off and tailed him at a distance. She took her time, following the backs of the old mills, then held back and let him race through the long straight. She bombed it along there and flashed her lights to stop a Toyota trundling towards them. She slowed as they passed the retail park on the outskirts of the town centre. A giant Boots and a Markies Simply Food next to a gym that'd opened since Siyal had last been here.

Up ahead, Hume shot across the roundabout on the A7 and headed into the town centre.

Elliot pulled up at it and waited until the set of lights outside Tesco went to green, then crossed.

Hume followed the one-way system around onto Bank Street, then parked halfway along, his car whizzing back into an empty parking space. He got out and pointed right at them.

Elliot stopped the car and rolled down her window. 'Fancy seeing you here, Callum.'

'Indeed. It's almost like you've tailed me from my business office.' Hume stared right at Siyal. 'Morning, Shunty.' He laughed. 'I'm just here to get some ice cream.' He waved again, then went inside Affogato Joe's.

Elliot set off. 'Well, that was a bit of a disaster.'

'Did you know he was going to be at his office?'

'Of course I didn't. Just planned on staking it out for a while until he showed up. But, either way, that hasn't got us any further forward, has it?'

'Did you expect it to?'

'No. But it's confirmed something to me. He's got eyes on us.' Elliot pulled up at the next set of lights, by the bakers, looking right at the new Tapestry of Scotland building. She drummed her thumbs off the steering wheel. 'Could do with borrowing you for something, Shunty.'

'What is it?'

'Come on, Rakesh, you owe me.'

'No, I don't.'

'You do. All the stuff I helped you with when you worked for me.' She pointed back the way. 'And that too. You *owe* me.'

Siyal didn't feel like he had any choice. 'What is it?'

37

MARSHALL

Some days it just had to be a sausage roll.

As he walked, Marshall wolfed his down like he hadn't eaten for days. Felt like he'd eaten his bowl of porridge days ago, rather than mere hours.

Struan crossed the car park next to him, chuckling. 'Eating that like you've just got out of prison.'

'Feel like I have.'

Struan stopped. 'I'm going to check out Stacy's husband's alibi online.'

'Good stuff.' Marshall checked his phone and had a few texts. 'I'll catch you inside, Struan.'

Struan raised his bakery bag, already soaked with grease, and entered the station.

Marshall leaned against the side wall in the bright sunshine and started sifting through his messages, just as a bank of cloud darkened everything. The warm morning was turning into a cool lunchtime – aye, the weather was on the turn into autumn. He might as well do this inside, ideally with another coffee, so he entered the station.

The new desk clerk gave him a nod.

Marshall couldn't remember his name. Steven? Kevin? Ian? Something like that. Either way, he was dealing with an irate member of the public.

He looked over. 'Inspector Marshall? Can I get you to have a word with Mr Gill here?'

Martin Gill pushed away from the desk with a pained look on his face. He frowned at Marshall, squinting like he was staring into a solar eclipse, then he seemed to recognise him. 'Ah, Inspector. At last, someone who will listen to me and treat me with respect.' He leered at the security officer, then stepped over to Marshall, seeming to stagger and wobble a bit.

Was he drunk? Maybe, but the dark rings under his eyes showed maybe it was probably from a lack of sleep. Or dehydration.

Marshall wrapped a caring arm around his shoulder and led him away from the desk. 'I'll take care of this, eh...'

'Steven.'

'Right, Steven. Thank you.' Marshall led Gill over to the low sofas on the other side of the door and sat next to him, though the springs must've burst sometime in the mid-nineties. 'How can I help, sir?'

'I'm struggling. Absolutely bloody toiling.'

'Okay. I'm sorry to hear that. What's happened?'

'I had a couple of young lads come down to the farm.'

'Did they threaten you?'

'No, no, it's nothing like that. Quite the opposite, really – they were police officers. Graeme something and an Irish lad.'

Marshall knew precisely who that'd be. Graeme Veitch and Liam Warner. 'What did they ask?'

'They were just asking me a few questions about the land around the tunnel, you know, and my relationship with Rebecca Yellowlees.'

'I didn't know there was one?'

'Precisely. It didn't exist. I barely knew her. They kept pressing me. Hard.'

'You knew her mother, right?'

'Only to speak to, you know, which means not particularly well. And these guys couldn't answer *my* questions of them, chiefly around when I'll be able to reopen the tunnel. Which is why I had to get in the car and drive here.' Gill flung a hand in the direction of the desk, now unmanned. 'But that invertebrate over there can't answer me either.'

'Why do you need to reopen the tunnel?'

Gill shut his eyes, like he'd had to answer the question far too many times when the answer was patently obvious. 'We're hosting a cycling competition in a few weeks. Part of it, anyway. The route is roughly the Southern Upland Way from Stranraer to Dunbar, but it diverges slightly to take in certain mountain bike trails. Glentress, Innerleithen, Elibank Forest, Yair. Obviously doesn't go through Galabloodyshiels like the path does. But the tunnel was to be a feature. We were going to get it all lit up and so on.'

This was the first Marshall had heard about that. He needed to look into it, or get someone else to. Struan, probably. 'That sounds good, sir, but I'm not party to the operational side of matters. I'm merely consulting on the case.'

'I gather you know Balf Rattray, don't you?'

Marshall tried to hide his wince. 'I went to school with him, briefly.'

'He speaks highly of you.'

Marshall laughed. 'That's a big surprise to me.'

'Why the devil are you consulting?'

'My role is to assess whether this murder might be related to others across Scotland.'

'Serial killers?'

'Right. Exactly.'

'Aren't they just things from film and books?'

'They're all too real, unfortunately. Bible John, Peter Manuel, Dennis Nilsen. I could go on. Hell, Robert Black was arrested in Stow, just up the road.'

'I see. And you believe this to be the work of a serial murderer?'

'Way too early in my assessment, sir. It'd be premature to speculate at this point, but I'm sure you can see the point in us doing that work.'

'I do see, yes. Anyway.' Gill rubbed his hands together. 'One thing I'd—' He stopped. 'Actually, that's made me think of something. Those two pillocks who came down were asking me questions about my wife. Could that be related to your work?'

'I'm truly sorry, sir, but I've no idea how your wife connects with this case?'

'Kathryn Yellowlees knew Sarah through their churches. Not the same one, of course. Peebles and the Ettrick valley kirk. But they dealt with each other fairly often.'

'Okay.' Marshall gave him an encouraging nod. 'Maybe I could have a word with your wife, then?'

'Good luck with that.' Gill laughed. 'Sarah went missing eight years ago.'

'Oh. I'm sorry, sir, I didn't know that.'

'It's okay.'

'Did they find her body?'

'No. I'm at peace with it.' Gill's rapid fidgeting showed he wasn't. 'But their questions have made me wonder if she could've been killed by this person.'

'Sir, I don't think that's something I can say just now.'

'Doesn't Sarah deserve the same justice as Rebecca?'

'Everyone does.' Marshall got out his notebook and pen. 'How about you tell me what happened to her?'

'Fine. One day, she went for her usual run but she never returned. I waited and waited but she never came back. I called the police. They searched for her, but they drew a blank.'

'And you believe she was murdered?'

'I do. The fact they never found her body...'

'I can see why you might think that. What makes you think it might connect with this case?'

'Well. I mean...' Gill cleared his throat. 'She was dying of cancer.'

'And she was still running?'

'Her oncologist told her to keep doing it as long as she could. It was becoming increasingly difficult, but she insisted she was still well enough. I wish I'd joined her, but I'm no runner, let me assure you.'

Marshall didn't expect there to be any connection, but then again... He clicked his pen and put it away. 'Let me look into it for you, sir, but I have to say I think it's highly unlikely she'll match the scope of our investigation.'

'Just on what I've told you?'

'There's a very low probability we're dealing with a serial killer, sir, but it wouldn't appear she would be a match to our victimology.' Marshall gripped his thighs. 'However, I promise to do due diligence on the matter.'

'Sarah was a very kind woman. People don't deserve their fates, do they?' Gill got to his feet and shook Marshall's hand. 'Thank you. All I ever ask for from anyone is to be treated with respect.' He took his hand back and watched it shake like a demon dog was biting it, then stuffed it away in his pocket. 'Parkinson's is a bitch. The drugs can only do so much.' He walked off out into the dark afternoon like he was a puppet on strings. The stiff walk was a tell-tale sign.

Marshall sat back in the sofa and watched him get into his Range Rover, then blast across the car park. He hoped he wasn't drunk. Certainly hadn't caught any second-hand fumes from him.

He pocketed his notebook and tried to process what he'd

just learnt. Nothing – an old man with an unanswered question looking for answers from anyone.

Time to speak to Elliot again, so he got up.

Just as his phone rang.

Belu Owusu calling...

Talk about a bolt from the blue.

Marshall sat back down again and answered it. 'Hey, Belu.'

'Rob. I just saw you'd called Jim.'

'What's up?'

'He's not good. Nothing's working.'

'Shit, I'm sorry to hear that.'

'It is what it is. It's good for... For us to spend time as a family. Build some memories...' She sniffed. 'What were you calling for?'

'It's to do with a case, that's all. But I've got another source of information on it.'

His phone started ringing again.

'Sorry, I've got another call coming in.' He pulled his phone away from his ear.

Hardeep calling...

He put it back, but Owusu was gone.

'Oh, Rob. Thank you for answering. I think I've found another potential case.'

38

SHUNTY

Elliot drove them along Peebles high street, windows down, shades on despite the sky like a clay oven.

Siyal was in the passenger seat, still trying to figure out what she was up to – and failing.

She glanced over to the side. 'What?'

Siyal looked away. 'Nothing.'

'Aye, shite. Come on. What's up?'

'Just wondering what you're up to.'

She sighed. 'Shunty, I'm up to nothing.'

'And yet you've taken me on a mission into deepest, darkest Peeblesshire.'

She laughed at that. 'The town centre is hardly deepest, darkest Peeblesshire.'

'We could be going anywhere.'

'But we're staying north of the river, Shunty. Relax, I'm not going to kill you and bury your body in a woodland nobody visits.' She slowed at the roundabout. A few cars ahead, with traffic snailing into the town. She was indicating right and trying to nudge the Volvo ahead of her out of the lane. 'Okay, here's my thinking on this. Last time I did this, I had Struan with me. He's a decent cop. Trouble with him is he's very much a stick. A nuclear-powered stick, maybe, but still a stick you'd use to beat someone with. Or he's just a stick covered in squidgy, orange dog shite to make you fear that.' She paused, like she expected Siyal to raise a complaint. 'But right now, Shuntster my pal, I could do with a nuclear-powered carrot.'

He knew he was being used but he still didn't know what for. 'I'm not sure that's a compliment.'

'Of course it is. Who doesn't love carrot cake?'

'Me. I hate it.'

'What? How can you hate carrot cake?'

'I don't like cake.'

'You don't like *cake*? Shunty, it's... it's *cake*! How can you not like cake?'

'Don't like sweet things. Give me a curry or a roast and I'll destroy it. Sweets? Chocolate? Ice cream? No thanks.'

'Wish I had your willpower.' Elliot turned off the Edinburgh road onto a back street running past a small-ish Tesco, then another left away from the supermarket onto a road lined with older houses. She pulled up outside a mid-level cottage. 'Let me lead here, okay?'

'Fill your boots.' Siyal got out of the car, happy to use her catchphrase back on her. Felt like it was going to rain, so he hurried up the drive after her.

Elliot knocked on the door. The house was pretty small and single storey, but looked cosy and welcoming.

The door cracked open immediately, like the opener had been waiting for someone. A man wearing a dark blue tunic and matching trousers. Lime-green crocs. His giant bulbous nose looked like it was going to sprout another one, like a cactus would. He looked them up and down. 'What's up?' His voice was so deep it was hard to pick out the words.

Elliot held out her warrant card. 'Looking to speak to Gordon Veitch.'

The name didn't mean anything to Siyal, but there was a PC Graeme Veitch based in Peebles – not someone he needed to speak to, but it was always good to know the names of everyone in the force. At least, Bob Milne told him that – he'd yet to see the evidence of it being a good thing.

'Take it you're his carer?'

'While his son is at work, yes.' The voice raised up enough to detect a Slavic tone in there, but mixed with enough of the local accent. 'What's this about?'

'An ongoing police matter, sir. Is he lucid?'

'He's just had his pills and a big glass of water, so he's as good as you'll get.' The carer opened the door wide. 'In you come, then. Follow me.'

'We know the way.' Elliot barged past him through the house, out to the conservatory at the back.

An old man sat in a comfy armchair, staring out of the window like he was counting the birds on his lawn. He looked over at them, first at Elliot, then he pointed at Siyal. 'Shunty.'

Siyal frowned at him. 'Do I know you, sir?'

'No, but I know people who know you. I've seen the dashboard camera footage of you battering that car off the bridge by Earlston.' Gordon laughed. 'Brilliant. Then you getting out and... It was like something from Morecambe and Wise.'

Siyal tried to hide his blushing. 'Who was it—'

'My lad showed me. The video was doing the rounds on that... What do you call it? Their phones. What's up or something like that?' Gordon scowled at Elliot. 'And I know you, don't I? You were here earlier.'

'I was, aye.'

'That lad you were with was a bit...'

'DS Struan Liddell. I'm sorry he—'

'Decent guy. I liked him a lot.' Gordon tapped his nose. 'And I know why you're here.'

'Oh, go on.'

'You're here to charge me, aren't you?'

'What's the crime?'

'Being a total fucking cunt.'

Elliot's jaw dropped. Siyal had never seen her even mildly shocked. 'Excuse me?'

'I mean, I'm right. It's why I've ended up with my brains dribbling out of my ears like this. You don't know what it's like.' Gordon shook his head. 'And that one doesn't even look like he belongs in Scotland.'

Siyal ignored the racism. 'I was born in Edinburgh.'

'Doesn't mean you belong here, son. The colour of your skin means you get to pretend you're a respectable police officer. We all know you're shite.'

Siyal showed Gordon his warrant card. 'Do you see that? It shows that I'm a sergeant, which is a higher grade than you ever managed.'

'Cheeky prick. If I'd been brown like you, maybe I'd have made a DCI. But nope. Your sort gets away with shite. Like the way you drive.' Gordon scowled at the warrant card, like he was finally reading it for the first time. 'Says you work for the Complaints?'

'That's right.'

'You investigating me, then?'

'No, but we can.' Elliot latched on to it, but she was smiling. 'We're investigating your son.'

'Graeme? But he hasn't done anything.'

'Then that's what we'll find.' Elliot stood there for a few seconds like she too was watching the birds. 'If he hasn't, of course. But he might've been a bit naughty.'

Gordon looked hard at her for a few seconds. 'What's he done?'

'We'll tell you. But only if you answer a few questions.'

'What about?'

'About why you really vouched for Iain Hogg.'

'*Vouched* for him? What are you talking about?'

'Graeme told us. When he was at university.'

'Iain Hogg, eh? Thought he was a good laddie, but he was guilty as sin. Guilty as sin!'

'For what?'

'You don't know, do you?'

'We've got a pretty good idea.'

'Then why the fuck are you here?'

'We need to hear it from you.'

'Well, you can fuck off. I know a bullshitter when I see one! When one craps all over my feet!'

'You were secretary of the Beltane committee and you asked Iain to stand down from being Cornet's right hand in their third year, didn't you?'

'So? It happens.'

'It does. Why did you do it, Gordon?'

'Can't remember.'

'That's bullshit.'

'Lassie, I've got dementia. It makes things hard to remember.'

'Come on, Gordon. You do remember why you did it. Stop lying to me.'

'I don't.'

'Fine. Come on, Shunty. Let's go and question Graeme Veitch. See what he's got to say about this.'

Gordon sat there, his lips twitching like they'd broken him and he was going to open up. 'Fine. Speak to him. I don't need any of this shite from the likes of you. Or that one! Away you fuck, you awful cunts!'

39

MARSHALL

Marshall powered up the steep bank and felt the sweat trickling off him. The day might be overcast now but bloody hell was it humid.

Close, as Grumpy would call it. Muggy, even.

Felt like he was melting into a puddle.

This was supposed to be the Water of Leith walkway, but Marshall couldn't even hear the river, let alone see it.

Taylor raced ahead, seemingly unaffected by the conditions. He craned his neck to look behind at Marshall. 'You okay back there, Rob?'

'I'm fine.' He wiped sweat from his forehead. 'Why?'

'Nothing. Just...' Taylor grunted, then rounded the bend and stopped dead.

Marshall trudged up to join him, sweating like he was playing rugby again.

Taylor was inspecting a crime scene. Not an active one, though – whoever had died was long since gone to the Edinburgh pathology lab down on the Cowgate. No gangs of CSIs searching the area, but their crime scene tent was still up – its only function was to protect DC Jordan Russell from the rain.

Not that it was raining yet, but those dark clouds threatened to open up.

Russell looked up from his phone and winced at their approach, then put his phone away. 'We three meet again, eh?'

'Indeed we do.' Taylor stopped outside the tent, not that it was easy to get past Russell. 'So, this is what's been keeping you so busy, eh?'

Russell scratched at his neck. 'Sure is.'

Taylor folded his arms. 'Didn't think to tell us down at the Innocent Railway how you were working another murder involving a tunnel?'

Russell looked away from him, then focused on Marshall, but quickly realised he wasn't getting any sympathy from him either. 'This doesn't really involve a tunnel...'

Taylor thumbed back the way. 'There's a tunnel about three hundred metres away.'

'So?'

'So...' Taylor huffed out a sigh then laughed. 'How about you just tell us what's going on here, eh?'

Took Russell a few seconds of fidgeting before he settled on a story. 'A couple. Will and Aileen Greig. Both forty-three. Two weeks ago, hence all this stuff being taken away. Murdered on their way home from an evening drinking in the city centre.'

'Where were they?'

'At a bar in Morningside.'

'The Cannie Man's? The Merlin? Bennets?'

'The Waiting Room.'

Taylor smiled to himself. 'Know the place. And they lived in Colinton?'

'Juniper Green.'

'Investigated a murder up there a fair few years ago. Someone burnt to death.' Taylor looked along the path. 'Not too far to walk back, is it?'

'No, but it's a few miles. We gather they'd tried to hail a cab, but all the taxis were rammed because it was the Edinburgh Festival. Uber and Travis were surge charging, so you're talking a hundred quid just for a few miles, so they told their pals they were walking.'

'What about the bus?'

'Not fans of it, apparently.' Russell clicked his fingers. 'Thing is, they'd expected that kind of malarkey, hence them not venturing too far into town.'

'Still, Morningside to Juniper Green is about an hour's walk, isn't it?'

'Give or take, aye.' Russell laughed. 'And I mean, give or take how many pints or bottles of wine you've had. Their presence was noted a few times on the way. Drunken shenanigans.'

'Did anyone see them entering the tunnel?'

'A cyclist saw them inside it. Will was peeing against the side wall. Didn't stop as the witness passed.'

Marshall looked back the way towards the tunnel. 'Any signs they were attacked in there?'

Russell screwed up his eyes like Marshall had gone insane. 'Eh, we don't think they were attacked.'

'Who killed them, then?'

'Each other.'

Taylor shot Marshall a look, one that read 'thanks for wasting my time', then looked back at Russell. 'Talk to me about it, mate.'

'What's there to say? We've spoken to friends and family. They had a tempestuous relationship over the years. She even hospitalised him once.'

'And they never split up?'

'Nope. Came close, apparently. Seems like they both had a massive drink problem. Enabled each other.' Russell stepped into the tent, which hid the gate into the graveyard for the nearby kirk – Marshall had completely missed it in his pursuit of Taylor. 'Aileen's head had been smashed against the wall there.'

The stone was still dashed with blood, the tent having protected it from the elements.

'Found her body right there in the morning.' Russell walked to the far side and pointed at a patch of flattened-down grass. 'Will was found here. Stabbed in the throat and he bled to death. Took seconds, the pathologist reckons.'

Marshall tried to process that. 'What else did he say?'

'Reckons he'd attacked her first. Hit her head off the stone twice. The second blow was fatal, but she'd have taken minutes to die. But that's only after she'd stabbed him.'

'Has he been able to back that up?'

'Found the knife with his blood and her prints on it.' Russell shrugged. 'Enough for the DCI, aye.'

'She had a knife on her?'

'Had been mugged a few times, apparently. A can of mace and a rape alarm weren't enough.' Russell sniffed. 'Why do you ask?'

'It's just...' Marshall's brain was ticking over, pointing him in strange directions. 'I see it as potentially different.'

'And you're now an expert in pathology, are you?'

'Never said I was. But I collate data from crime scenes and see what they say. This case was flagged because of the proximity to the disused tunnel. We walked through it and it's fascinating. A massive mural. An urban regeneration project. But... What if someone followed them and attacked them in there, but they escaped, only to die here?'

Russell laughed. 'You got any evidence of that, chief?'

'No, but I don't really see anything backing up your theory, either. As far as I can tell, it's possible she was killed in the same way as the others in our scope. Adam, Beverley, Rebecca and Kate.'

'Whoa, whoa. Who the hell is Kate?'

'McWilliams. In a tunnel down by Grantshouse.'

Russell frowned. 'In East Lothian?'

'It's in the Borders, but aye.'

'Because her head's caved in on two locations?'

'Precisely.'

'But he was stabbed.'

Marshall nodded. 'It's possible Will wasn't part of the plan, but maybe he attacked the killer and had to be dispatched.'

Russell kept staring at them, then he shook his head. 'You boys are away with the fairies.'

Taylor pointed at Marshall. 'It's his job to think these things, in case us common or garden detectives miss things. Besides, we've got a victim down in Peebles who's the same.'

'Still.' Russell walked off, clutching his phone. 'I'm calling the boss. And the Ghostbusters.'

Marshall watched him go. 'Good.'

Taylor glowered at him. 'Good? You think him calling his boss is good?'

'Means we can speak to someone with some sense.'

Taylor smirked, then it faded. 'This doesn't feel like one of ours.'

Marshall's turn to grin. 'Ours?'

'Yours.' Taylor shrugged. 'Doesn't feel like it matches.'

'Cal, her head was smashed onto the stone in the same way others were smashed into tunnel walls. Or Kate onto the monument.'

Taylor brushed a hand down his cheek. 'Still not sure, though.'

'Listen, maybe the killer was stopped by her husband. Hence him being killed. And it's a lot busier there, so maybe he couldn't return to the scene of the crime.'

'I think you're seeing stuff that isn't there and using "maybe" way too often.'

'Then you'll soon be proved right, Cal.'

'Rob, do you honestly think this is part of your scope?'

'Right now, I'm about sixty percent certain the others are all connected.'

'And this?'

'I'm about thirty percent sure this is included. But it's my job to think these things, right?'

'Glad it's not mine.' Taylor mopped some sweat from his brow. 'Okay. Try and persuade me.'

'This makes me think about Rebecca's case. How Iain Hogg said he'd been attacked outside the tunnel. We got DNA from under his nails.'

'Okay. So you think he managed to fight off the killer, but this Will Greig didn't?'

'Right. I mean, this is all out-there devil's advocate stuff. But I can see that as a possibility, aye.'

'Problem is, this doesn't link to your avenging angel theory, does it? You and your lad, Hardeep, were going on about public shaming. I don't see anything here.'

'No, but I'll get Hardeep digging into this for us.' Marshall nodded at Russell, walking back with a sour look on his face. 'You speak to your boss?'

'Aye.' Russell scratched his neck again. 'Said his boss told him to help you pair out.'

'What I expected.' Marshall smiled at him. 'I understand this feels daft, but it's my job to do the daft work, okay? Just help us out and I'll put in a good word to *his* boss, who I work directly for.'

'Fine. But it seems like a total waste of time to me.'

'Just because we spend time on something doesn't make it a waste. The chances are this is nothing to do with the other cases, but I need to be sure. I need to know as much as you lot do. Is there any family we can speak to about these two?'

'Aye, her sister lives down in Innerleithen.'

40

Marshall sat in the corner of an L-shaped rattan sofa that was more comfortable than any inside sofas he'd sat on. A stiff chill in the air now, but Mhairi O'Donnell insisted on sitting in her garden in Innerleithen, a stone's throw from the bubbling Tweed at the end. She'd clearly spent a few grand on fancy rattan furniture earlier in the summer – not to mention untold thousands on an expensively landscaped lawn and a patio in the shape of an electric guitar – so was obviously determined to get the maximum usage out of it, despite the weather.

Would probably have her Christmas dinner out on the patio, if she could.

Mhairi stared into her cup of tea. 'So, aye. It's true. They were a nightmare for each other.'

Marshall nodded along with it, notebook poised. 'How long had they been going out?'

'Since university. Aileen went to Edinburgh and met *him* there. I went to St Andrews myself. Came back here afterwards, when our folks passed away. I was happy to commute to work in Edinburgh, but Aileen stayed up there. It's a lot closer now with the railway, but it felt a lot further way back when.' She sipped her tea and set the pristine white cup back on the pristine white saucer. 'They're both accountants and that career can have a certain culture, if you know what I mean.'

'Drinking?'

'Right. And they both worked at the same firm. It was very claustrophobic.'

'Aileen said that?'

'No. She never really said anything about anything, but I got that impression.'

'Were you close?'

'Not in that way.'

'But you thought she felt hemmed in by it?'

'Working in the same firm means everyone knew their business. She'd feel judged if she left him.'

'Did she talk about that?'

'Once.' Mhairi took another slow drink of tea. 'I gather it was a violent relationship.'

'Physically?'

'Aye. And emotionally. Not sure what's worse. No kids, thankfully, but... Aileen could've left at any point, but she didn't.' Mhairi stared hard at Marshall. 'Thing you need to understand is Will and Aileen were both massive drinkers. All started out fine. Everyone's doing it at university. You're young, you're free. All of that. But when you're still drinking like that in your early forties, there's something missing...'

'Would they only argue when they'd been drinking?'

'Hard to say. The only time they weren't drinking was when they were at work. And you know... what I said about the culture at work. Quite often they'd be at a client meeting or whatever and that was all done on the sauce. They'd always be the last ones standing. Their hungry eyes looking for another drink. I mean, they earned a lot of money, but their lives were pretty empty otherwise.'

Taylor almost dropped his cup onto the saucer with a clatter. 'That seems a bit harsh.'

'They earned a lot of money, but they spent it on expensive holidays where they'd just drink all day. Everything was geared around them being functioning alcoholics. And when they drank, most of the time it was fine. But sometimes they'd fight and shout and... stop functioning.'

'Do you have an example of that?'

'We had them here for my eldest's birthday once. Before we laid this patio, you know? All of us sitting out on chairs and rugs and stuff. Sadie tried smashing this piñata thing we had hanging from the eaves there.' Mhairi pointed at her house. 'She couldn't do it, poor thing, but she was six. So Will got stuck in and he'd had a few glasses of rosé. He absolutely melted it. Tore the thing apart with the stick. The sweets fell on Sadie's head and hit her. I mean, I wanted to have a quiet word with him, but Aileen... She was leathered on rosé too. They'd brought their own supply in case we ran out. Six bottles. On top of the stuff I had chilling. And she just started laying into him in front of the kids. Effing this and effing that. I had to take them inside. I came back out and was about to give her a piece of my mind when I saw a big gouge out of his cheek.' She drew a circle on her own skin. 'She'd punched him. Her ring caught him.'

Marshall had seen female-on-male domestic violence before. Much less prevalent in society – or just a much lesser possibility of reporting. How many men wanted to admit to being beaten by their wives? And even when it was, it'd potentially be investigated by biased officers who'd focus on her self-defence as cause. 'Was that the only time you saw anything like that?'

'Nope.' Mhairi looked away. 'About six months ago, I got a call to go to the new hospital in Edinburgh. Aileen had pushed him down the stairs. She was in a real state. Couldn't believe it. I told her she had to put a stop to it, for both of their sakes. She said she couldn't. Had deluded herself that she loved him. But this is when all the stuff about their work came out. About her feeling trapped. Really, she needed psychiatric help. They both did. I mean, our dad was abusive to us. Shouted at us. Screamed. Hit us. I'm a therapist myself and I've had years of therapy for what we went through. Don't drink more than a glass myself. And I'm still not right. But I'm not kicking the shit out of my husband. Aileen saw that as how you behaved. How you loved someone. You get drunk, you argue, you punch them.'

'Did Will ever hit her?'

'A couple of times that I'm aware of.' Mhairi tucked her hair behind her ear. 'I got another call two months ago. Went up to the hospital again, but it was her this time. He'd punched her and she thought she'd broken her arm but hadn't. She was still drunk and we had a chat. She said she knew it was over and she needed to move on, but she didn't know how. Thought her leaving would destroy him. But she accepted their relationship was destroying them both.' She finished her tea and poured herself another cup. 'Can I get you two any more?' Said like this was just a gentle chat, not dissecting a cycle of abuse between two people.

Taylor smiled. 'I'm good, thanks.'

Mhairi refilled Marshall's cup without asking. 'So are you two investigating their deaths?'

'We're not, no. At least, not directly.' Marshall sat back in the chair and cradled his cup before taking a fresh sip. Whatever she made the tea from, it was incredible. 'I'm consulting on a murder in Peebles that DI Taylor's working on.'

Mhairi's lips formed an O. 'That lassie in the half-mile tunnel?'

'Do you know her?'

'Nope. Heard about it, though. Awful business.' She frowned into her cup. 'Why are you here, then?'

'We're looking into possible connections between multiple crimes.'

'So you think Aileen and Will were murdered by a... a serial killer?'

'Like I say, I'm just consulting on the case.'

'Right. Well, you know the cops think they killed each other, right?'

'We do. And I agree that's the likeliest explanation. I just wanted to understand a bit more about their lives, and you've been very kind.' Marshall set his cup back down. 'Do you think they killed each other?'

'After all that stuff I told you? Of course I do. Just expected it to be *her* killing *him*.'

'Why?'

'No. I can't say.'

'Say what?'

'It's just...'

'Mhairi, we need to understand everything about their lives.'

'I didn't tell this to the police who came earlier but... I can't. Sorry, I just can't.'

Marshall knew this kind of thing – secrets taken to the grave which the living didn't feel able to share. Attacking it head-on was a mistake, but letting it slide was worse. 'Why didn't you tell them?'

'I'd sort of forgotten it and Aileen had sworn me to secrecy.'

'She killed her husband. So we—'

'I know.' Mhairi stared into space, chewing the inside of her cheek. 'I *know*. But...'

Marshall sat forward. 'If there's something that might help—'

'Aileen had an affair.' She locked eyes with him. 'A lad from around here. She broke it off months ago, but... Will found out about it and that's what started that fight where he punched her arm. He was going to kill her that night. He was going to kill him too. Because it turns out Will had been stalking him...'

41

SHUNTY

'Is that it?' Elliot strode across the office space to her own little room. 'Of course it is.' She opened it and stepped inside.

Siyal wanted to follow her, but she'd been weird all the way back so maybe letting her stew would work. Another of Bob Milne's pieces of advice. He looked across the office – Jolene was still in that deep discussion with Jim McIntyre. Maybe it was the same one as earlier, maybe a new one. Either way, the photocopier was now functional, flashing green as it worked away.

Jolene noticed him this time and waved.

Siyal returned it, then followed Elliot into her office.

She was behind her desk, jabbing her forefinger off her phone screen. 'You're still here?'

'I'm not going until you speak to me.'

'About what?'

'Gordon Veitch. Graeme Veitch. And what we're going to do about it.'

'About what?'

'You threatened to interview Graeme.'

'Aye. Sometimes you just threaten someone for the sheer hell of it, Shunty. Or to see if they're protecting someone else.'

'So you're not going to speak to Graeme Veitch about why Iain Hogg was stood down?'

'I already did.'

'When?'

'This morning. When he clocked on. Me and his sergeant sat with him. He said it's because he didn't want to do it. Broke up with Rebecca and didn't want to embarrass her in public. So he was stood down.'

'You didn't think to tell me?'

'I took you there to back it up. Problem with private organisations like that is when they go all secret squirrel on us. If you attack them from both sides, you can sometimes prise them wide open. And having one of you lot there—' She raised a finger. '—and I mean a member of the rat squad, okay? The biggest threat an ex-cop can receive is you lot investigating his cop son.'

Siyal tried to process it. 'So I was just a prop?'

'Aye, but props can be very useful. And now we're even – you don't owe me anymore.'

'What did I ever owe you?'

Elliot tapped at her nose. 'You know.'

Siyal didn't, so he turned around to leave.

'Let me know if you need any help with the stuff about Davie.'

Siyal turned back. 'I thought you wanted me to drop it?'

'I did. But I know how thrawn you are, Shunty.'

'Thrawn?'

'It means stubborn. Pig-headed. You'll keep pushing until you get an answer. And maybe I'm past that point of caring.'

Siyal sucked in a deep breath. 'I guess I'll see you around.'

She waved at him. 'Shut the door on your way out, eh?'

Siyal shook his head, then slipped out into the office space.

What a waste of time that was. At least he didn't care what'd happen if Bob Milne found out about it. He could blame it on her. Blame it on trying to help process their case by gaining her confidence.

Jolene was looking at him, head tilted to the side. 'You okay, Rakesh?'

'I'm fine.'

'No, you're not.' She gripped his arm and dragged him into the next office – Taylor's, judging by the amount of Scottish football memorabilia all around the place. 'Talk to me.'

'I'm fine, Jo.'

'You look like you're going to cry.'

'That's just my face. I'm fine, seriously.'

'Where did she take you?'

'Just on a little errand.' Siyal took a spare seat. 'I'm not sure what she got out of it, but she seems pleased with it.'

'Right.' Jolene's eyes twitched. 'Let me know if you need me to have a word with her.'

'Do you think that'll achieve anything?'

'I don't know, Rakesh. She likes me. Or tolerates me, at least.'

Siyal smiled at the joke. That feeling was gnawing at his guts again. 'Could do with your advice on something?'

'Sure.'

Siyal fiddled with his collar. Then his sleeve.

'Go on.'

Siyal sat back and sighed. 'It's about Davie. Bob Milne's got me investigating the details of what happened in April.'

'Aye?'

'But Andrea's asked me to drop it.'

'Why?'

'Said she's got closure and justice. Doesn't need me digging into it.'

'I can understand that. Have you got a solid lead, though?'

'Not really. Sorry. Officially, I'm looking into the death of Roger Dalkeith. The assumed ID Davie had...'

'Don't remind me.' Jolene shook her head. 'It's such an obviously made-up name.' She laughed. 'Someone with a stupid name like Roger Dalkeith shows up in prison the same day he's sent down... Shouldn't laugh, but it's not exactly hard to see why they figured it out, is it?' She frowned.

'What is it?'

'Nothing.'

'Do you think I should close it off?'

'Have you found anything when you've been digging?'

Truth was he hadn't. And he hadn't mentioned it to anyone, just kept on trucking.

'Not yet.'

'Then I think it'd be the right thing to do.'

Siyal nodded. 'I'll see you around, Jolene.'

'Don't be a stranger, Shunty.'

42

MARSHALL

In a couple of hours, they'd gone from Edinburgh's leafy suburbs to the wilds of the southern limits of the Scottish Borders – a few miles west or south and you were into Dumfries and Galloway.

The Ettrick Water cut a groove between two ranges of hills, the only difference being the foresting on one. The other was filled with bleating sheep amongst thick heather. An empty field sat opposite the village, though Marshall couldn't see much sign of houses. Just a church hidden behind some trees.

'Whole heap of sod all here, eh?' Taylor slowed as he entered Ettrick, which seemed to be distributed over a few miles, like the houses were all fed up with each other. 'Why are we here, Rob?'

'What do you mean?'

'What's the big deal with this guy?'

'Not every lead has to pan out, Cal. Most won't get us any closer to the truth, but neither of us can predict which.'

'But you're interested in this guy. Why?'

'Because we've got a theory and we need to test it.'

'*O-kay*. So what is your theory?'

Marshall sat back and shut his eyes. 'You know that quote by Eric Clapton, where he says it's about the notes he *doesn't* play as much as the ones he does? This is about the suspects we exclude. And the victims. There's a distinct possibility this John Wrangham had a sufficient axe to grind to attempt to murder Will and Aileen. And maybe that's all it is. If it's the case, we can exclude Aileen and Will's deaths from our scope.'

'That was Miles Davis, not Clapton.'

'Good.' Marshall opened his eyes again. 'Can't stand him.'

'Not even "Layla"?'

'Especially not that. The verse and chorus are in different keys. It sounds horrible.'

'You play music?'

'Not for a very long time. You?'

'Bass.' Taylor took the right turning at the war memorial, along a track overhung by thriving beech and oaks, then trundled past the church, way bigger than it should be for a settlement of this size.

The old manse sat at the top of the lane, which bent around and continued on past the back of the church, leading to a few more houses.

Taylor pulled up and yawned. 'Okay, Rob, this is your circus and these are your clowns, so you're leading here.'

'Fine by me.' Marshall got out into the cool afternoon, then trudged up the drive to Laverlaw – around here the houses were named rather than numbered. Despite that evocative name, it was a sixties bungalow, with a heavily mossed roof, and harling that was more cracked than solid and could really do with being recoated. Or smoothed over.

No car outside, but Marshall knocked on the door anyway.

No sounds came from inside, just sheep bleating on the hill and some voices talking in the nearby kirkyard.

'Back in a sec.' Taylor slipped around the path to the back of the house.

Marshall peered into the living room. Despite the exterior, it looked modern enough and seemed to be recently decorated. A giant telly faced a decent-sized sofa. A grandfather clock ticked away in the far corner, next to a writing bureau. Double doors opened through to a dining room – Taylor was peering in the patio doors, then he disappeared.

Marshall tried the bell again, but all he heard was Taylor crunching along the gravel path.

Taylor rounded the corner of the house, shaking his head.

'Enjoy your pee?'

Taylor chuckled. 'This, to quote Jordan Russell, is a complete waste of time. We're here because one of two people who murdered each other was having a fling with this lad. Your biggest problem, Rob, is when you see a dangling thread, you need to tug it until the garment falls apart.'

'Fair comment.' Marshall set off down the path, but walked around their car instead of getting in, then entered the gate for the kirkyard.

The gravestones were spread out luxuriously, with enough space for another five hundred years' worth of occupants. At least. Around here, there were whole acres of land where only a few people had stood in the whole history of mankind, so it'd take a long time to fill up.

A man was standing by one of the gravestones, talking out loud. 'We will see. We will see.' He looked over at them. Martin Gill, the local landowner. He pointed a shaking finger at Marshall. 'Fancy meeting you here.'

'Indeed.' Marshall looked back the way – Taylor hadn't followed him. 'I didn't know you lived here.'

'Oh, you would if you actually listened to me.' Gill waved over to the lane. 'I live in the farmhouse over there. Generations of Gills have lived there, but I'll be the last one. No children to inherit. I'm investigating options over what to do, but it'll pass to someone on my late brother's side of the family. Just whether it's the useless one or the corrupt one.' He smiled at his own joke. 'Anyway. If you're looking for James Hogg's grave, I could show you it.'

'It's fine, sir. How are you doing?'

'I'm good. We're in that lull now where we've done what passes for a harvest, and sold off this year's livestock. So I shut the farm down for three weeks and let the men have some well-earned rest. Means I can focus on the preparation for the cycling. How's that going?'

'We've passed that on to operations, sir. They'll be in touch.' Marshall fixed him with a hard stare. 'I mean, how are you really doing?'

'How do you bloody think I'm doing? It's half past three in the afternoon and, once again, I'm standing at my wife's gravestone.'

Marshall walked across the grass towards him, careful to avoid the graves. 'I thought you never found her?'

'We didn't, no, but the minister let me erect a gravestone to her memory. Fergus reckoned it'd give me somewhere to focus my grief.' Gill scratched his head. 'Trouble is, I can't find the bugger.'

'The gravestone?'

'No! Fergus!' Gill stared at him like he'd gone insane. 'We're supposed to be having a wee chat about my grief. This stuff about my wife has knocked me for six, I have to say. The only way I can process it is by speaking to Fergus. He's an incredible listener, but this business with Rebecca has brought it all up again.'

'I'm sorry to hear that, sir.'

'It's not your fault, so why apologise. These things happen.'

'In what way has her murder brought it up again?'

'Och, it's probably just me being selfish, but a lassie getting her head caved in on my land makes me think it's a message from God.'

Marshall frowned. 'A message from God?'

'Aye. Me and the big man have a personal connection. These wee chats, you know? When I pray, God soothes my fears. Fergus helps me decipher what he tells me.'

'What kind of thing?'

'Oh. He's just saying things.' Gill shrugged. 'Have you come here to talk to me about her death?'

'No, sir. We—'

'But you will investigate it, won't you?'

'I have done a bit of work, sure. Before we got called out elsewhere I had a look through your wife's case.'

'And?'

'And I'd say it's highly unlikely to be related to what we're looking into.'

'I see. Are you just saying that to put my mind at ease?'

'No, I'm saying that because I mean it. Your wife's death bears none of the hallmarks of the other cases.'

'Okay.' Gill's shoulders slouched, like he'd expected some form of closure. 'I see.'

Marshall gave him a pause, out of respect, but he needed to get on. 'Listen, do you know John Wrangham?'

'Oh, yes. I know John.' Gill nodded up the lane. 'Lives in Laverlaw just there. Lovely wee place. Haunted, mind.'

'Haunted?'

'Hard not to be after what happened between his parents. John and Irene. John junior had left home by then, of course. Still, he's living there on his own now.' Gill shook his head. 'Brutal existence.'

'What happened?'

'His father killed his mother, didn't he? Then shot himself.'

Marshall tasted a sourness in the air. They didn't yet have a concrete profile, but something like that would match more than a few elements of the abstract one in his head. 'Do you know where we could find him?'

'Of course. John works for a friend of mine. Donald Sinclair-Turnbull. Donald runs DST Surveyors in Selkirk. Do you want the number?'

'Sure.'

Gill patted down his pockets then produced an old Nokia phone from inside his olive Barbour. He put on the pair of glasses dangling from his neck and squinted at the screen. 'Do you want me to read it out for you?'

'Just hold it up, sir.' Marshall read the number and tapped it into his own phone. He nodded his thanks, then set off. 'I'll see you later.'

'Let me know if you need anything else from me, won't you?'

'Of course.' Marshall hit dial as he walked across the pebbles, his path this time leading around the graves.

'Donald Sinclair-Turnbull.'

'Sir, it's DI Rob Marshall. I need to ask you a few—'

'How did you get this number?'

'From Martin Gill.'

'Ah. Of course. What's the matter?'

'It's about John Wrangham. Do you know him?'

'He's my nephew. Works at my firm. What's happened?'

'We just need to speak to him. We're at his address and he's not at home.'

'Of course he's not. It's three o'clock on a bloody Tuesday. Most people are at work.'

Marshall spotted Taylor coming towards him. 'Is he in the office just now?'

'No. He's working on-site.'

'Do you know where?'

'We're surveying for the Borders railway extension to Carlisle. John's looking at the area between Shankend Viaduct and Whitrope Tunnel.'

43

Taylor got out of the car first. 'Have to say, Rob, my spider-sense is tingling now. Whitrope Tunnel... Makes me think we have got ourselves a serial killer.'

Marshall rested against the gate and leaned forward.

Train tracks ran in both directions. Ancient rolling stock sat there, dating back decades. Or longer. The track curved around to the right, presumably heading towards the tunnel.

Yet another disused railway tunnel, but this one hidden past a length of tracks, seemingly in use for a tourist attraction. Must've tunnelled for the best part of a mile under the hill. Back when all they had were picks, shovels and loads of dynamite, not giant machines.

Aye, heading into a pitch-dark tunnel that may or may not have a serial killer in it...

It was one thing reading about them. Another thing interviewing convicted ones. But someone in the wild, in an environment they were in charge of...

'Excuse me?' A large man waddled towards them, giant belly stretching his polo shirt past the point of decency. 'You okay there, lads?'

'DI Callum Taylor.' He held out his warrant card. 'This is DI Rob Marshall.'

'Ah, the man himself.' He thrust out a hand to Marshall. 'Donald Sinclair-Turnbull. We spoke on the phone.'

Marshall shook it. 'Good to meet you, sir.'

'Pleasure's all mine. But if we could make this quick? We've got our work cut out for us here surveying this for structural integrity after that wet winter.'

Taylor frowned. 'It's September, though?'

'Been a busy year.' Sinclair-Turnbull laughed, then pointed up the direction of tracks. 'This tunnel was built for the old Waverley railway line, way back in Victorian times. The daft buggers killed it in the sixties. Hit towns like Selkirk and especially Hawick hard. So we're working on the costing for connecting the new line from Tweedbank to Carlisle.'

'I didn't think that had been approved.'

'It hasn't. The first leg to Tweedbank has reaped such wonders for the area that we've been given approval to commence surveying the two potential routes the line could take, to support their detailed costings.'

'Thought this was supposed to be going along the path of the A7.'

'It is, aye. Well, that's the planning basis. It's a few miles west of this old line, so it'd go through Langholm and Longtown, rather than this way, down through Newcastleton, which is in the middle of nowhere and hardly anybody lives there. Still, this won't be wasted work. Part of the funding will be to repurpose the tunnel for a cycle path tracing the original path of the line from Edinburgh to Carlisle. Between us three, there's talk of them adding a spur of the train line through here, in case anything happens to the main route.'

Marshall looked along the line. 'Is John in the tunnel?'

'Nobody's in the tunnel. It's shut at both ends.'

'Isn't making that good going to be expensive?'

'To be honest with you, I think they'll just have the track go around the hill, but I'm arguing that there's a moral angle to going through the tunnel. Six hundred navvies built it and more than a few of them died doing the work. The air supply was non-existent so they had to pump it in for them. And you look here now, and all that work was for nothing. So let's honour what they achieved.'

'So it's about making sure their sacrifice wasn't for nothing?'

'Correct.' Sinclair-Turnbull looked between them. 'I'm not imagining you two lads are here to discuss railway plans, though, are you?'

'We really need to speak to John Wrangham.'

'Ah, well, he's not here.'

'Don't you survey in pairs?'

'Kind of. My son's up the far end, establishing some trig points for us.'

Marshall felt a slackening-off of tension. 'So where is John?'

'Shankend Viaduct.' Sinclair-Turnbull pointed back the way. 'You probably passed it on your way here.'

44

Taylor marched up the hill, phone to his ear. 'Still no answer from Gashkori.'

Marshall followed, wishing he'd brought his sturdy walking boots rather than worn his trainers. 'That because there's no reception here?'

Taylor looked at his phone. 'Got three bars of 4G, so it's not that. He's just not picking up.'

Marshall had to stop. He sucked in a deep breath, trying his hardest to catch it, and looked back down at the road, at their pool car next to the Ford Ranger registered to John Wrangham.

'You okay there, Rob?'

Marshall turned back to look at Taylor. 'I'm good.' He set off again, climbing up the steep bank, then stopped at the top and turned to face Shankend Viaduct, the giant structure lurking behind the hedge. 'Bloody viaducts…'

'Heard about that case two years ago near Melrose.'

'That's what brought me back.'

'Aha, here we go.' Taylor disappeared behind the hedge, then charged off along the path to the viaduct. 'John!'

Marshall jogged to catch up, his feet slapping off the wet ground.

A man was walking towards them and holding out his hands. The harsh daylight made anyone look older than they were, but he seemed really young. Like he was twelve. 'Can I help you?' His voice was deep, though, that of a serious smoker.

'John Wrangham?'

He nodded. 'And you are?'

'DI Callum Taylor.'

'DI Rob Marshall.' He joined them, though it felt precariously close to the edge. 'We need to ask you a few questions about Aileen Greig.'

'Right.' Wrangham wouldn't look at them. 'What about her?'

'We gather you were acquainted?'

'Acquainted.' Wrangham barked out a laugh. 'Big mistake, that. Huge.'

'Go on.'

'I take it you know we, uh, had a fling, then?'

'Right. Why don't you tell us about it?'

'We met through a mutual friend. Went to this charity concert for Ukraine up in Innerleithen. Great night, but I spent a lot of it dancing with her. We ended up... Her mate was being a bit weird, but Aileen came back to mine.'

'Down in Ettrick?'

'Right.'

'Bit of a drive from Innerleithen, isn't it?'

'It was that or she had to head back to Edinburgh.'

'What happened?'

'What do you think? We had sex.'

'I mean to make it a big mistake.'

'Oh, right. That... Turns out Aileen was married. I mean, she's a bit older than me, but I didn't know she had a bloke.

Didn't ask, either. But it meant I was having an affair, which disgusted me. Trouble was, we got on so well and I couldn't stop. Aileen insisted she was going to leave her husband, but she didn't. So I ended it. I had to. I'd given her enough notice. But she kicked off about that. Shouting at me. How I never loved her. How I was just using her for sex. I walked away. Then a few days later, she slashed my tyres. Fucking *psycho*.'

'You know it was her?'

'Watched her do it. She drove up. Showed me the knife, then stabbed it into my tyres and drove off.'

'You call the police?'

'Didn't see the need to involve them. Know how to replace a tyre or four myself.'

'Was that the last time you heard from her?'

'Aye, but not from her husband.'

'Go on.'

'Got a phone call from him, warning me off.'

'Did you heed it?'

'Of course I did. Believe me, I'd received the message loud and clear. If you ask me, he seemed unhinged. Just spoke to me with this coldness in his voice as he threatened to disembowel me and then eat the entrails.'

'Did Aileen ever talk about him?'

'Only the last time we spoke. Said it was over with him. How he beat her up.'

'That's what she said?'

'Aye. Why?'

'She never mentioned attacking him?'

'Are you kidding me?'

'Did she?'

'No.'

'Was Aileen ever violent with you?'

'Violent?'

'Sexually? Or maybe she hit you?'

'No. Why?'

'Her body was found in Edinburgh. We believe she also killed her husband.'

'Fuck.' Wrangham rocked back against the wall at the side. 'Are you serious?'

'Deadly.'

'Fuck.'

Taylor frowned and looked to the side. 'Did you hear that?'

Marshall struggled to listen. Sounded far off and muffled.

'Again.' Taylor swung back around. 'Come on, you must've heard that?'

Wrangham looked at his shoes. 'Haven't heard anything.' He pointed over to the side. 'Shall we do this back at the car? I've got a thermos of coff—'

'Wait.' Taylor stopped dead. 'There it was again.'

'Mate, that road's busy with cars. Loads of wild birds. Heavy traffic for the wind farm. They're using heavy machinery to—'

'*Mmmph! Mmmph!*'

Marshall nodded. 'I heard it.'

Wrangham shook his head. 'No, you didn't.'

'Sounded like someone who—'

'Oh that! It's a badger.'

'A badger?'

'Lots of them out here. It's more like a *brrrl brrl* sound. One of the difficulties with this job, right? Don't want us to build on land where there are badger setts becau—'

'*Mmmf!*"

Marshall definitely heard that. Came from along the viaduct. He looked at Taylor – he had heard it too. 'Stay here, Cal.' He raced off along the brickwork, his feet splashing through the puddles.

Over to the side, a pile of rags lay on the ground.

Marshall slowed to a stop, then leaned down and pushed the rags off.

A man lay there. Tied up. Blood poured from his forehead. His eyes darted around but didn't seem to focus on anything. Something was stuffed into his mouth.

'My name is Rob. I'm a police officer.' Marshall removed a rag from his mouth. 'Are you hurt, sir?'

He could barely focus on Marshall. It must've taken all he had to make that noise. 'Who?'

Marshall spotted the dog collar now, smeared with mud and oil.

A minister?

Was he from Ettrick?

It all slotted into place – Martin Gill had been searching for him but couldn't find him. Because he was here, tied up and... What the hell was Wrangham going to do with him?

Marshall took a long look at him. He didn't want to move him in that condition. He got out his phone to call Control.

'Little help here, Rob!'

Marshall swung around.

Wrangham had Taylor pressed up against the viaduct's half-wall, like he was going to tip him over the side.

Marshall raced over and rugby-tackled him, forcing him down onto the rough surface. He rolled over the damp brickwork, but gripped Wrangham's left arm tight.

His sleeve slid up.

Two scratch marks ran across his skin.

Marshall put his full weight on him.

Wrangham tried to move, but only succeeded in jerking his sleeve up further.

The scratch marks led right up his arm, almost to the elbow. Scabbed over, sure, but they were deep and looked like they were from fingernails.

Human fingernails.

Iain Hogg's?

Marshall tried shifting him over onto his front, but Wrangham was wriggling like an eel.

'Stay down, you wee shite!' Taylor got out his cuffs and knelt on Wrangham's elbow.

Wrangham screamed. 'What the fuck!?'

Taylor slapped the cuffs onto his wrist.

They had their killer...

45

GASHKORI

Gashkori sat back in the driver's seat and didn't know what to say.

The trees surrounding the car park seemed to be closing in on him, like each was a deadly assassin, and all were ready to kill him. If he switched his focus to another one, the first one would step forward.

No getting away.

Even the engine running didn't give him any feeling of security.

He ran a hand down his face and held a grip over his own throat.

His phone rumbled in his pocket. 'Sorry about this.' He took it out and checked the display.

DI Rob Marshall calling...

Gashkori bounced the call, then put his phone on silent and put it away.

Callum Hume sat next to him, more than filling his seat. Too many Callums in Gashkori's life. 'Who was that?'

'Work.'

'Not what I asked. Who was it?'

Gashkori sighed. 'Marshall.'

'Him? But he moved on, didn't he?'

'Aye, he did. But the boss has him looking into these cases to check they're not serial killers.'

Hume laughed. 'Sounds like nonsense to me.'

'It's true. And it is nonsense, if you ask me. Pal of mine up in Aberdeen had Marshall shadowing him for a week, digging into murders he'd had over the last ten years, trying to make them seem like serial killings. They weren't, of course, but it wasted a week of his time and a lot of those in his team.'

'Thing is, though, if I was your boss, I'd be doing the same.' Hume looked over at Gashkori. 'Anyway, that's all by the by, because right now, young feller-me-lad, you need to answer my question. How is the investigation into Davie Elliot going?'

This.

The thing Gashkori wasn't able to get anywhere near, in case it blew his cover. 'It's getting nowhere, as far as I'm aware.'

'You're sure about that?'

'No. I'm not. In the slightest. That's not my department, Callum, and you know that. I can only go on what I can gather by certain means from certain sources. Since they found what Davie was doing – and by that I mean leaking information to you – everything is locked down so much more tightly than before. I can't just look at the case files and I can't ask the investigating officers. And I can no longer trust who I'm asking.'

Hume let out a slow, halting breath. He was getting annoyed. Gashkori didn't want him to get annoyed. 'It appears I'm a lot closer to it than you are, then, because it's getting hot.'

'How hot?'

'For starters, our mutual friend was tailing me at lunchtime. Hence me calling you.'

'Andrea Elliot?'

Hume nodded.

'She's not supposed to be...' Gashkori felt a wave of nausea, like he was on the deck of a boat and it had just pitched to the side. 'She's supposed to be working the case for me, not tailing you.'

'In which case, you're doing a piss-poor job of keeping her on a tight lead, aren't you?'

'I'm sorry, Callum.'

'Sorry? Oh, I can make you very sorry.'

'I won't be any use to you then.'

'You say that like you're of some use to me now.' Hume laughed. 'Are you losing control of this, Ryan?'

'No, I'm still in charge of it. The fact she's running around on her own is a good sign, Callum. If she feels the need to freelance, it means the investigation is shite. Take it as a positive.'

Hume grumbled, then tossed a bag onto Gashkori's lap. 'You don't deserve this.'

Gashkori twisted his fingers into his sleeve and picked it up, then handed it back. 'Told you, I've stopped taking that stuff.'

'Right. And look how effective you are off it.' Hume let the words settle in. 'And you don't get let off the hook because you're not taking it from me now. I've got evidence of you taking it.'

'I know exactly what's going on here.' Gashkori couldn't stop looking at the bag. Sod it – in for a penny... He reached over and took it back. 'Was it just Elliot?'

Hume stared at the bag. 'She was with some guy I didn't recognise. Indian or Pakistani.'

'That'll be DS Rakesh Siyal. He works for the Complaints.'

'The Complains being Internal Affairs, right?'

'Right. The rat squad. We hate them as much as you hate us.'

Hume laughed, then licked his lips slowly. 'That needs to stop.'

'She'll be sorted out. Don't you worry on that score.'

Hume dropped another bag on his lap. 'Remember Elliot's protected by our other mutual friend.'

'I know.' Gashkori held up both bags. Probably enough to get done with intent to supply. He pocketed them both. 'But if she were to be in an accident that wasn't anyone's fault...'

'I'm serious. She's off the table. She stays alive or you don't. Okay?'

'Okay. I'll handle it.'

Hume grumbled. 'Be straight with me here, Ryan – should we be worried?'

'Honestly?'

'No, lie to me.'

'Siyal is about to be dropped from the Complaints.'

'Sacked?'

'Something like that. He's nobody you need to worry about anymore. Next month, he'll be walking the beat in Craigmillar.'

'I appreciate the tip-off. Still a bit worried someone capable might pick it up, though.'

'Don't be. Think of how you got me the info.'

Hume frowned at that. 'I just sat and waited outside the court, then followed a series of unmarked vans until I learned which prison he was being taken to. You gave the name.'

Gashkori swallowed, but his throat was tight.

'Then all I had to was pass along the information you'd given me to the lads we had in that prison... "It's the new guy. Roger Dalkeith. About so high, thin build... Oh, and he's just shaved his head". I passed the location back to make sure we didn't get fingered with it. And we didn't. Or haven't been yet. But I'm worried the fingering is starting now, Ryan.'

'They don't have anything on you.'

'Ryan, that doesn't reassure me. Is Siyal going to finger you?'

'He won't get sweetcorn under his fingernails.'

Hume roared with laughter. 'Sick bastard.'

'Callum, I said I'll sort it out and I'm serious. Give me twenty-four hours. Siyal will no longer be an issue.'

'Deal.' Hume got out into thin rain and walked over to his car. 'Twenty-four hours.'

Gashkori fingered the cocaine in his pocket. A wee toot would go a long way to feeling like he was in control of things again...

46

MARSHALL

John Wrangham was taken away in a squad Volvo SUV.

Marshall held his phone to his head and watched the four-by-four trundle towards the road back to civilisation. He felt a sense of relief, but it was tempered by spotting Liam Warner behind the wheel. Wrangham getting all the way back to Gala in one piece was going to be a long shot...

'We're sorry, but the caller is unavailable. Please leave a message after—'

Marshall hung up. Hopefully the beep had just come in after the call terminated, so Gashkori would have yet another text message and voicemail.

Stop being so petty.

He put his phone away and focused his pettiness on Taylor. 'I keep getting bounced by your boss.'

Taylor watched the CSIs' van arrive, struggling to climb the bank toward the viaduct. 'You say that like I have any influence over him.'

'If he keeps this up, I'll have to contact Potter.'

'That'll make you popular.'

'I'm not here to be popular, Cal.' Marshall spotted Kirsten

behind the wheel of the CSI van as it tugged past them. 'I just wouldn't mind speaking to the SIO on the case I'm attached to, having – you know – caught the killer for him.'

Taylor's phone rang. He checked it and winced. 'Bloody Jim McIntyre now. That's the third one.' He put it to his ear. 'Hi, Jim. No, the briefing's not happening. No. Can you take some initiative and tell the whole team, please? And if you see DCI Gashkori, get him to call me or DI Marshall.' He ended the call and shook his head. 'Can't get the bloody staff.'

Marshall walked over to the ambulance parked precariously close to the edge.

One of the two paramedics stepped down and walked over. 'Marshall, isn't it?' Aussie accent and he was in the early stages of the kind of stringy mullet that'd look at home on an Aussie-rules football pitch. If they even called it a pitch. Shaved on the top and sides, but the back crawled down like spider legs reaching out of an ice cream cone.

Took Marshall a few seconds to recognise him. 'Todd, right?'

'Well done, mate.'

'How's the patient?'

'Your guy...' Todd thumbed behind him. 'Someone's hit him on the head. And I mean *hard*.'

Marshall winced. It was worse than he'd thought – Wrangham had already attacked him. 'Is he going to die?'

'Nah, mate. He's okay.'

Marshall let his breath go. 'But you said he's been hit on the head?'

'Right. Just clonked, like with a torch or something? Knocked out. There's nothing wrong with him other than he's going to have a bruise like a wombat's arsehole for a few days.'

'Okay. Cool. Can I speak to him?'

'Sure thing, mate.'

Marshall nodded his thanks and walked over to the ambulance, but he couldn't help wondering how lumpy wombats' bums actually were. He leaned against the side of the ambulance and waited for the other paramedic to clear off.

The minister was dressed in running gear – tight trousers, flashy trainers, fluorescent yellow jacket open to reveal a dog-collared T-shirt with a sublimated print on it, announcing:

> The
>
> Running
>
> Minister

His bald head didn't hide the bruise on the side of his head, more like a camel's hump than a wombat's back end. He looked up at Marshall. 'You saved me, didn't you?'

Marshall gave a brief smile. 'Glad I got here in time, that's all.'

'Thank you.'

'Can I take your name, sir?'

'Fergus. Fergus McNeill. I'm the minister at Ettrick.'

'Quite a big church for a small place.'

'Such is the state of the kirk these days, but I have to cover three parishes. Yarrow, Ettrick and Kirkhope, down in Ettrickbridge. Even though it's quite a big area, I'm there for my congregation.' Fergus beamed wide. 'And for the wider world.'

'What do you mean by that?'

'I'm the running minister. Probably seen me on Instagram or TikTok?'

'Not really on social media much.'

'Shame. There was a piece on the BBC a while back. Anyway. It lets me reach a global audience. Fifteen thousand followers on Instagram alone.'

Taylor appeared from nowhere. 'What do you do on there?'

'I just run and talk to people, spreading the word of our Lord. It seems to work well. And the Kirk are fully behind it.'

Taylor looked him up and down. 'You're dressed like you were out on a run?'

'Indeed. I was out on a run down past Hawick and I got a call from my housekeeper, Maria. Lives in the manse in Ettrick. She said John had showed up and asked me to meet him. Said it was desperate.'

Which wasn't what Marshall had heard from Martin Gill, but stories changed the more they were told. 'And you ran *here*?'

'It wasn't far off the track, to be honest.'

'How did he seem?'

'Disturbed.'

'Have you seen him like that before?'

'A few times, aye, but not for years. He was all twitchy. Couldn't focus. Said he could hear his parents' voices on the breeze.'

'He said that?'

'Right. He'd been working here on his own for a couple of days. It's pretty exposed out here, isn't it? And lonely. It's partly why I run here. I film myself in this beautiful landscape and it makes me think of the word of the Lord. Anyway. I persuaded John that his parents weren't here. And John attacked me. Brought me here to talk about the death of his parents and he tried to kill me. And he attacked me again. Clubbed me over the head. I thought that was it for me. But then I heard voices. God led you to me.'

Marshall swallowed hard. Saving someone's life was a precarious thing. 'Do you have any idea why he'd attack you?'

'I'm sorry, but no. I've thought about little else while these fine men have tended to me. I mean, I've known John for years. Knew his parents. And what happened to them... It was awful. It broke John. Completely broke him. I can only imagine he's had some sort of psychotic break from reality. If it's all the same with you lot, I won't be pressing charges. Forgive and forget is more my mantra, just want to see he gets the help he needs.'

'Understood, but it's not as simple as you choosing not to prosecute. What made you think he had a psychotic break?'

'He had to get psychiatric help.'

'What happened?'

'One Sunday, he came into the service and started screaming at everyone. I managed to calm him down, then drove him up to the Royal Ed myself. He was in there almost a month. But his condition was deemed not severe and easily managed by drugs.'

'Do you know what his condition was?"

'Sorry, I don't. Thing is, he might've stopped taking his medication.'

'Do you know what he was taking?'

'Sorry, but I'm not party to that. Antipsychotics, as far as I'm aware. It's... They... I... Is he okay?'

'He's fine, aye.'

'Oh, thank heavens.'

'It's you we're worried about, sir.'

Taylor nodded at Marshall, then got out his phone and walked away, hopefully getting someone to dig into Wrangham's medical history.

A warrant would get the actual truth, not whatever truth Wrangham decided to present to the world.

Marshall fixed him with a serious stare. 'Do you have any idea why he'd want to attack you?'

'No. I mean, John had some out-there beliefs...'

'Go on.'

47

It'd been a while since Marshall had been in this interview room.

It smelled like someone had been using it as a makeshift canteen and eating stale meat paste sandwiches in here. Maybe it had always smelled like that and he just didn't remember.

John Wrangham sat next to his lawyer and opposite Taylor, rather than Marshall. His eyes had been closed so long it was like he was asleep.

It made Marshall feel weird to be the one who took down a serial killer. Used to be he'd only speak to them in places called facilities, rather than cop shop interview suites like this, grotty as it was. And he'd been the one to wrestle him to the ground. The one who'd stopped him murdering again.

Up close, Wrangham looked very young in the harsh light cast from the fluorescent strip above them. Unblemished skin. Hair without a hint of silver. No bags under his eyes. Hard to believe he was old enough to have left school, let alone to be working as a surveyor – maybe taking up serial murder was the key to a healthy body.

But his energy was all off. Twitching and jerking. Unable to settle in one position.

The sheer size of him. He looked like he came from generations of farming stock. Fingers as thick as forearms. Bulk everywhere, but not an ounce of fat on him – that would come later in life.

Marshall cleared his throat. 'So they're finally extending the train line?'

Wrangham looked up at him with his dark blue eyes. Maybe something in the blandness of the question piqued him. 'Aye. They've released a tranche of funding to confirm the route is entirely viable.'

'Pretty exciting, right?'

'Right. I mean, it's a huge opportunity to do something big, something that people will remember for years.'

'And murdering people isn't?'

Wrangham looked back down into his lap.

'Is that you denying it, John?'

'My client wishes to exercise his right to maintain silent.'

'Sure.' Marshall sat back and let out a deep breath. 'Do you want to break that silence to discuss your medication?'

Wrangham looked up, but didn't say anything.

'I presume that's for a condition you've been diagnosed with?'

Wrangham just frowned.

'Because if it's *not* something you've been prescribed with, then being in possession of a controlled substance can be a criminal offence.'

'What are you talking about?'

'Antipsychotic medications. We found them in your home. Olanzapine, right? Helps you feel in control, right? To keep a firmer grip on your true self and block out those intrusive thoughts, right?'

'You don't know what you're talking about.'

'I've studied medication for applications in potential criminal cases. But I'm guessing you weren't classified as such by the doctor you saw in the Royal Ed?'

'How did you hear that?'

'Heard from someone close to you.'

'That's nonsense. I'm not saying anything more.'

'We'll speak to whoever assessed you, because they've clearly missed a propensity for violence.'

Wrangham shook his head violently. 'I explicitly refuse you access to my medical records.'

'We will get a warrant for them.'

'So do that, but I'm not happy with releasing them to you.'

'I'm sorry to displease you, Mr Wrangham.' The surname added a distance, but also a bit of respect. Something he'd probably craved all his life. Time to hit him with the main part of it, though. 'I gather you've been espousing some interesting views locally.'

'What?'

'The notion of antinomianism.'

Wrangham looked at him like he was trying to give a blank stare, but there was a twinkle of mischief in his eyes. 'Fergus has been blabbing, hasn't he?'

Marshall ignored that. 'Have to say, I had to look up that term.' He got out his phone but didn't unlock it, just rested it on the table. 'Something like the elect are exempt from moral law as laid out in the Ten Commandments.' He tapped his phone. 'These elect aren't just exempt from those rules, but they're guaranteed salvation by killing those who are already damned by God. Is that right?'

Wrangham offered a meek shrug. 'Pretty much, aye.'

'And you're part of the elect?'

'That's right. I'm executing God's will.'

'Right. By killing people?'

'These people have committed heinous sins.'

'Adam Malkmus, Beverley Richardson, Will and Aileen Greig, Rebecca Yellowl—'

'They all sinned. Of course they had to die.'

'What was Fergus's sin?'

Wrangham shrugged again. 'He was interfering with God's plan for me. He had to die.'

'Killing Rebecca in Peebles, though. That's getting closer to your home, Mr Wrangham. Right?'

'What's that supposed to mean?'

'Well, you've killed a lot further afield. Edinburgh, Glasgow. A few other places we've yet to confirm. And there was Kate up by Grantshouse.'

'Who?'

'Come on, don't start denying it now.'

'I've not killed anyone called Kate. There was a female schoolteacher who abused a male pupil up in Dundee, but she was... something else. Not Kate.'

Marshall struggled to prevent his eyes bulging. He didn't remember that from Hardeep's work. Had they missed a victim? Or was Wrangham just messing with them? 'Who?'

'Told you, I can't remember her name. It was up in Dundee. Place called Finlathen Viaduct.'

'Did you smash her head against the wall?'

'Of course. Got to make sure they're ready to be judged by St Peter.'

Taylor sat back. 'We know about them all, John. We want to make sure you get the full credit, though. How about you make a list and we can check it against ours to make sure they are the same? Wouldn't want some other bloke taking responsibility for something he didn't earn.'

Wrangham nodded, like that was a remotely normal thing to do.

Marshall picked up his phone and googled Finlathen Viaduct. 'Built to transport water into a reservoir for Dundee, then turned into a walkway when it was replaced by other reservoirs. Weird. Because the others are all in train tunnels. Or near.'

'Right. Water. Train tracks. It's all the same.' Wrangham leaned forward, resting on his elbows. 'The thing is they're portals to the next life. Or to damnation.'

'So you're some kind of vigilante who—'

'I am the Sword of the Lord. Appointed by God Himself.' Wrangham sucked in a deep breath. 'The justice system is weak. People get let off every single day without paying for their misdeeds. My victims are all sinners who haven't served the penance they should've done. By separating them from their earthly bonds, I put their fates directly into the hands of God for His justice alone. Nobody escapes God's judgement. My task is just to arrange the meeting.'

'The meeting?'

'With St Peter. He judges them.'

'And you leave them in tunnels...'

'Right. They're pathways in this life, but when they stop being used, they gain power to transport to the next life.'

'What about those old mining tunnels in Midlothian, say?'

'What about them?'

'Have you killed anyone there?'

'Of course not.' Wrangham looked at him like he was a complete idiot. 'Think about it. Train tunnels are like Charon piloting a boat on the River Styx.'

Marshall frowned. 'But that's Ancient Greek religion, not Christianity.'

'I said it's like it. And just because the name of God changes in those stories, it doesn't mean it wasn't Him acting through their mythology.'

'Stories?'

'Right. God planted those ancient stories to educate people about the reality of what would befall them if they didn't live their lives correctly. Hades is a fiction – Hell isn't. He tells me this.'

'He tells you this?'

'Often.'

'Does he talk through Fergus?'

'No. Directly to me.'

'So why did you attack Fergus?'

'I didn't.'

'We caught you red-handed, Mr Wrangham.'

'No, you didn't. I was just there, doing my job. Someone else did that to Fergus. I didn't know he was even there.'

Taylor laughed. 'A big boy did it and ran away, eh?'

Marshall leaned forward, resting on his arms. 'But you admit to committing all the other ones. Except the one in Penmanshiel. Why not that one?'

'Because I didn't do it.'

'You didn't kill Kate?'

'Right. Same with Fergus.'

'Because we interrupted your work with him?'

Wrangham looked at his lap again. 'I was instructed to get rid of him.'

'Who by?'

'I don't know any of the victims. Mine is not to wonder why, just to execute God's plan.' Wrangham shifted his gaze between them. 'Do either of you know the story of Lucifer?'

Taylor nodded. 'Everyone does. He was one of God's angels, but he fell and became the devil.'

'That's what they want you to believe. The truth is, Lucifer didn't fall. He came to Earth by his own volition. And he still works for God. His role is to put temptation and evil in front of the weak, for them to accept or reject. That's the primary method of establishing God's justice.'

'Does Lucifer speak to you as well as God?'

'It's Lucifer who talks to me directly. He delivers the instructions from God.'

'Okay.' Marshall knew he needed to keep him onside, so he nodded like he believed him. 'When did you first meet him?'

'Lucifer visited me at a young age and I sold him my soul.'

Taylor started to laugh.

Marshall cracked his knee off his leg to shut him up. 'Okay. When was this?'

'In 2014.'

'How old were you?'

'Fifteen.'

'How much did you get for your soul?'

'I exchanged it for the No vote in the independence referendum.'

Taylor laughed. 'Son, you need to cut this bullshit.'

Marshall grabbed Taylor by the sleeve. 'Get out.'

Taylor looked him up and down.

'Go.' Marshall pointed at the door. 'Now!'

Taylor brushed his sleeve free, then stood up and walked over to the door, shaking his head.

Marshall watched him go, then focused on Wrangham while he waited for the door to shut. 'Sorry about that, John. I warned him about not showing you sufficient respect.'

That earned him a nod. 'Thank you.'

'So, you were fifteen when you—'

'Right. I was born on the day the Scottish Parliament reconvened for the first time since 1707. Twelfth of May, 1999. It's spooky, isn't it? But I didn't want independence. It'd be a disaster for the country.'

'You were too young to vote at fifteen.'

'Right. Made me feel insignificant. But I won. We won. We remained part of the union.'

'So you sold your soul for the ability to vote in the referendum?'

'No. Lucifer arranged it so No would win.'

'For the whole thing?'

'Correct.' Wrangham believed every word of that. 'And Lucifer has been guiding me ever since, telling me what to do. I'm the Sword of the Lord. My work is to take the damned from this mortal coil to punishment in the next life.'

'And where did you speak to Lucifer?'

'Many places. But mostly an old shepherd's hut near the village.'

'In Ettrick?'

'Near. I had to cycle there. Used to leave my bike under a tree just by the road. We'd meet there when the church was in service. One time I had to hide under the tree for a while – the rain was thundering down so hard. The only tree around for miles, practically. The sheep were all hiding from me. Over time, they got used to me.'

'When was the last time?'

Wrangham rolled up his sleeve and showed off the scars from his attack. 'Sunday morning, after I'd killed Rebecca.'

'And that's when he asked you to target Fergus?'

'No. Fergus was fortunate. He came to me. If he fell from the viaduct, it'd be an accident. And he'd sinned greatly against the Lord. All people in the church do. They ignore the true word of God and instead spread the false word.'

'When were you going to meet Lucifer next?'

'We were supposed to meet again tomorrow so I could take further instructions from him on who to target next.'

'When was that going to be?'

Wrangham stared into his lap again.

Marshall had lost him.

48

Marshall took his seat around the table in Gashkori's office and picked up his coffee. 'Dean's Beans, Melrose' was stamped on the side in a fresh design. He hadn't been there in a while – he needed to pop in and catch up on his old friend at some point. 'My favourite café. Thank you, ma'am.'

'No sweat, Rob.' Potter lifted the lid off her latte, thick and frothy. She checked her smartwatch and looked around the table. 'Does anyone have any idea where Ryan is?'

'Sorry, ma'am.' Taylor slurped at his coffee. 'Been trying to get hold of him for a couple of hours.'

'I was saying to Andrea...' Potter frowned at Elliot, sitting opposite Marshall but just staring into her tea. 'I've been spending so much time down here, I'm getting to know where the good cafés are.' Another check of her watch. 'Even at this time of day.'

Gashkori strolled in, clutching a can of WakeyWakey, with real pep in his stride. He stopped and did a comedy look around the place. 'Is it my birthday or something?'

'No.' Potter pointed at a cup by the empty seat. 'A long black for you, Ryan. A dribble of skimmed milk.'

'Just how I like it. Cheers.' Gashkori took it then sat in the chair nearest his desk. 'So then. What's been going on?'

Elliot finally looked up. 'We're all wondering where you've been, Ryan.'

'Had a bit of a runny tummy after some dodgy chicken I had last night.' Gashkori held up his blingy smartphone. 'Turned this back on and I had all these voicemails from Rob and Cal. Been speaking to young Kirsten Weir.'

Potter pointed at his energy drink can. 'That stuff will go right through you.'

'And it does. That and the chicken.'

'You didn't call either Marshall or Taylor back, did you? Or me, for that matter.'

Gashkori gestured towards them. 'Sounded like they were on top of this Wrangham character, so I thought I'd get on top of the important bit – making sure the evidence stacks up and supports our prosecution.'

Potter narrowed her eyes. 'What, specifically?'

'Kirsten's processed the DNA from Neidpath. Even managed to persuade the idiots in Gartcosh to fast-track it in that new machine of theirs.'

'And?'

Gashkori took a long drink of his coffee. 'Oh, that is good.' He wiped at his lips. 'The person who fought with Hogg has the same blood type as this Wrangham character. His DNA's going to take a while to process, but I've pulled in a favour to get that run overnight.' He winced. 'Bottom line is we need to release Hogg.'

Elliot rolled her eyes at him. 'You've wasted a ton of time on framing the wrong man.'

Gashkori stared at her, long enough to make Marshall

uncomfortable. 'Wrong for this, maybe. But if Iain Hogg hasn't killed his ex, he's done *something*. Won't be the last time he's under caution in a police station.'

Potter slurped at her coffee. 'Ryan, can you let him go, please.'

'Sure thing, ma'am.' Gashkori looked at Taylor. 'Can you get someone to take him home?'

'Not sure who we've got free.'

Potter smiled at Taylor. 'How about Rakesh Siyal?'

'He's not our resource, ma'am.'

'Leave it with me.' Potter got out her phone and tapped out a message, then dropped it on the table and stared hard at Gashkori. 'Ryan, did you listen to *my* voicemail?'

'I did. The kid we've arrested says he's been speaking to the devil and he told him to do it.'

'Not the devil.' Marshall picked up his cup but didn't drink it. 'Lucifer.'

'Same character in the Bible, isn't it?'

'Potentially. Depends on which parts you read.' Marshall took a sip. 'In the mind of John Wrangham, however, there's a huge distinction between the devil and Lucifer.'

'I get it.' Gashkori rubbed at his nostrils. 'Didn't Hogg say his attacker was dressed like the devil?'

'He did, aye.' Marshall rested his cup back down on the table. 'Wrangham says it's someone guiding him. Lucifer, ordering him to murder the damned.'

'Thing is, based on what Kirsten's found...' Gashkori pinched his nose. 'Two things, actually. One, Hogg's attacker isn't Jonty Sandison. Different blood type. Second, the attacker is likely to be Wrangham. I mean, he's admitted to killing Rebecca, but this other figure. What if it's his own psyche?'

Potter scowled at him. 'I'm not following you?'

'He's imagining this figure as a way of dissociating himself from the crimes. If he was ordered to do it, it wasn't his idea.

Probably started with him handling what happened with his parents.' Gashkori nudged Taylor. 'See, I do listen?' He sank the rest of his can, then crushed it and dumped it in the bin. 'Cal's message suggested you think he might even be schizophrenic?'

'That's a loaded term these days, sir.' Marshall finished his coffee and wished he hadn't – it burnt his mouth. 'There's some psychopathology at work, but we do need to get a warrant to access his medical records.'

Gashkori raised an eyebrow at Taylor. 'Cal?'

'Already got Struan on top of it.' Taylor started jotting something down. 'But what if it is the devil? Think of all the good metal bands we'd be upsetting by arresting him.'

Marshall laughed. 'Okay, let's get that warrant processed and we can…'

Everyone was looking at him.

'What?'

Taylor narrowed his eyes at him. 'We should consider it.'

'There's no such thing as gods or angels or devils. This Lucifer, if he exists, isn't a supernatural figure.'

Taylor took a sip of coffee to cover his blushing. 'So what's your big theory, then, brainbox?'

'Two distinct possibilities. First, I can buy that theory about him splitting his psyche. After all, us cops compartmentalise all the shite we go through.' Marshall left a long enough pause for it to be mildly annoying. 'But my favoured theory is I suspect someone is posing as the devil and using Wrangham.'

Potter twisted up her lips. 'You don't think he's acting alone?'

'I'm considering all possibilities, ma'am. The thing I keep going back to is how he denied killing Kate.'

'You don't think he did that?'

'Kate was killed eight years ago. He'd have been seventeen when she was murdered. Probably too young.'

'Sounds like shite to me.' Gashkori was staring at Potter. 'I've known plenty of lads that age capable of murder.'

'But all the way over by Grantshouse? It's some distance from his home, takes way longer than driving to Edinburgh, say.'

'So? He grew up in Ettrick. Round there, he'll be driving on farm tracks from the age of twelve. Pass his test on his seventeenth birthday. Mark my words, Rob. It's only him and it's always been him.' Gashkori held Marshall's gaze. 'The reason he's killing is down to his parents. They sound like a pair of complete arseholes who didn't raise him well. Probably abused him. No wonder his moral compass is all fucked. Easy step for him to kill from a young age. Case closed.'

Marshall smiled. 'You said that about Iain Hogg.'

'Aye, and I was wrong on that, but we had scant evidence to go on. But then *you* caught him in the process of killing that boy, Rob, so we *know* it's him.' Gashkori returned Marshall's smile. 'Now we've got our collar, which I'm grateful for, you can get back to Gartcosh and do the necessary paperwork to celebrate catching a serial killer.'

Potter crumpled her cup into a cylinder. 'No.'

Gashkori pushed his chair back. 'No?'

'I want DI Marshall to remain on the case.'

'Why?'

'For a start, there was another case Wrangham claims to have committed, up in Dundee, which isn't on our radar. And like Rob said, Wrangham denied killing Kate. So I want him to linger here while we let everything settle. You'll charge him for what he did to Fergus McNeill, so there's no rush. No pressure. Let Rob close off the connections with the other cases, then we'll charge him for multiple murders and be out of your hair. Okay?'

Gashkori gave her a warm smile. 'Sure thing, boss.' The brief glower he shot in Marshall's direction would've frozen the warmest of hearts. 'Do you want to speak to the investigating officers up in Dundee?'

Aye, a good way to get Marshall out from under his feet.

'Already asked Struan to do that, sir.' Marshall acted the big man and smiled it off. 'Okay, so I'm going to go and hunt for the devil.' He looked around the room. 'Does anyone want to join me?'

49

SHUNTY

Siyal slowed down to the twenty limit entering Peebles. 'The reason I'm dropping you off is because your home is on my way home.'

And because DCS Potter asked him nicely.

One thing Milne told him was when a senior officer asked, you always nodded, even if it wasn't asked nicely.

'Is it, though?' Iain Hogg was in the passenger seat, folding his arms yet again. Like he couldn't get comfortable. His left hand gripped his bicep. 'Do you live in Penicuik or something?'

'Edinburgh.'

'So, Colinton? Currie?'

'No, just by the Commonwealth Pool.'

'Then this isn't on your way home.'

The most words he'd got out of Hogg since they'd left Galashiels. 'It's not that far out of my way. And resources are otherwise stretched.'

'Half an hour, then you've got to take a worse road north.'

'The A7 is much worse than...' Siyal frowned. 'What's the road called?'

'The A703.' Hogg readjusted his arms yet again. 'Then it's

the A701 until the bypass. You got something to collect from IKEA or something?'

'Something like that, aye.'

'Meatballs from there are awesome, aren't they? Can't get enough.'

'I like the vegan ones.'

'Vegan? Huh. Something we share.'

Siyal scowled at him. 'You're a vegan?'

'You're looking at me like you don't believe me?'

Siyal turned right at the main roundabout, avoiding the town's main drag. 'I do believe you.'

'Sure. Because there aren't many in the town who are.'

'Lot of us everywhere now.'

'Aren't there just.'

Siyal pulled up outside his address, an ex-council house near a river. Lights on inside.

Hogg shifted his arms yet again and didn't seem to want to get out. 'Thank you for asking me how I was when I got in the car.'

'My job in the police service is making sure people are treated with respect.'

'Respect. I'd love to see some of that.'

'You deserve it. Everyone does.'

'Even a rapist? Or a child molester?'

'They deserve the same justice system as everyone else. That's what I mean by respect. A fair trial.'

Hogg looked over at his home, but still didn't get out. He looked back at Siyal. 'Do you believe me that I didn't kill Rebecca?'

Siyal held his gaze. 'I know you didn't.'

'Has someone confessed to it? You know who?'

'I can't tell you that.'

'Right. Trouble is, nobody's believed me my whole life. Nobody has any idea what that's like.'

'I sort of do.'

'How?'

'I've been subjected to racism all my life.'

'Right. Hadn't thought about that.' Hogg focused back on his house. 'I thought I'd get respect when I was the Beltane Cornet, but that turned to shite in my hands, didn't it?' He opened the door. 'Thanks for the lift. Enjoy the meatballs.' He got out into the night and stood there, door hanging open. 'It's nice being outside again.'

'Do you want me to broker your return home?'

'Excuse me?'

'You know, explain to your wife. How you've been helping us with our inquiries. You've maintained your innocence from the start and have been totally exonerated... Stuff like that goes a long way.'

'I'm fine.' Hogg nudged the door shut, then crossed the path to the house.

The front door flew open and a young woman stood there, hands on her hips.

Siyal couldn't hear what she was saying, but Hogg was getting a mouthful from his wife. He just looked defeated and broken. She wrapped him in a cuddle and led him inside.

Siyal put the car back in gear and drove off, wishing he had someone to cuddle him.

But he had a date tonight...

And his phone was ringing...

Jolene calling...

'Evening, Shunty. You heading off?'

'Yes. I've just dropped off Iain Hogg at home.'

'How was he?'

'Quiet. Then he started talking.' Siyal glanced back at the house. 'His wife was there.'

'Oof. Suspect he's got a lot of hard questions to answer. Even if he didn't kill Rebecca, what the hell was he doing in a dark tunnel with her at night when his missus was away?'

'Quite.' Siyal felt himself smile. 'What did you want?'

'Oh, right. It's just… Something you said earlier made me think.'

'Go on.'

'It's better we do this in person.'

50

MARSHALL

Marshall knew this was a stupid idea.

He drove from Selkirk towards Ettrick, following the path of the river with that name. Past steadings, through Ettrickbridge with its tempting pub, glimpsing unnamed grand houses through the trees. But no sign of any shepherds' huts. Or any sole trees – they were either clumped together in plantations like so much of the Borders, or were just bare fields.

Like so much of the Borders.

A different route from the one Taylor took him from Innerleithen earlier. Being back here, it felt like he was so far away from everything, even though it wasn't that far to Hawick or Selkirk.

Marshall slowed to a halt, then got out his phone and found the screenshot he'd taken of the map. Wrangham told them he'd parked his bike under a tree but the land was so barren. Just like murder suspects, Marshall had profiled trees along the road – and there was still the chance Wrangham was lying and there was no tree or no shepherd's hut. Or it was on some other road.

The first candidate was half a mile away – he hadn't missed it, after all.

He tossed his phone onto the passenger seat and set off again, trundling along the road.

There – that one on the right.

Marshall sped up as he approached, then slowed to a halt and pulled in under the tree. Certainly big enough to hide under – it spread across his car. He took a look around the area.

The sun had set behind the hills on the Ettrick valley, just a thin glow hitting the tops of the taller ones to the east. It wouldn't be long before the whole valley was cast in darkness and it wasn't like there was an abundance of street lighting down here. Or any at all.

He should turn around and come back in the morning. Really, he should, but he was here.

The field was filled with sheep, the lambs now long since matured and sold off or ready for next year's generation. A large stone pen was cut into the wall, perfect for driving sheep in for shearing or separating parents from lambs.

Marshall got out his torch and checked his phone – twelve percent. The sodding charger in the car hadn't worked.

Aye, he was a daft bugger and it wasn't like any other bugger wanted to come with him. All thought he was insane.

But this place was just as much a scene of the crime as the actual tunnels or viaducts. Maybe it'd show the source of Wrangham's inspiration. Maybe he kept souvenirs here or a log of his actions.

Or maybe it was just a load of nonsense spewed out by a broken mind.

Marshall needed to see it to rule out those possibilities, so he stepped over the wire fence and crossed the field, hoping the sheep were all ewes. Since he'd moved back to the area, he'd seen many more fields with cattle in than he recalled from his youth, the local farmers finally diversifying from their traditional livestock. And he'd seen the occasional bull or two, giant brutes with swinging testicles bigger than a human head.

Maybe there was one lurking in the dark corner of this field. He swung his beam around but the night swallowed it up.

It caught a spark of something metal.

Marshall took it slowly as he set towards it, scanning the torchlight back across the front of a low building hidden by the walls from the sheep pen. A corrugated iron roof hung over stone walls laid in a tight circle, stuck halfway along the dyke running between two fields. The narrow entrance was open to the elements.

Marshall checked he had reception, then dialled Hardeep.

'Sir?'

'Think I might have found it.'

'Already?'

Marshall kept his phone to his ear as he closed on the building. 'Or something, anyway. I've got a good candidate.'

'The shepherd's hut?' Hardeep's voice was a soothing balm in the darkening evening. 'It's actually there?'

'Yup. First candidate tree.'

'Okay. Pulling it up on Google Maps now.'

'I don't know if this is where Wrangham was meeting Lucifer or not.' Now Marshall was here, in the location, he felt a cold chill run through him. Right up his spine. In an interview room or the bravery of an office surrounded by colleagues, the supernatural felt very abstract. Now in the approaching gloom, it felt all too real – and all too plausible. 'I appreciate you being with me at this time of night.'

Hardeep might not have been able to visit with him in person, but he was here – company.

'This work is important, sir. It's just…'

Marshall wanted to walk into the hut, but couldn't bring himself to. 'Hardeep, it's okay that we missed one.'

'It's not okay. That's a murder, sir. It's someone's life ended. And we didn't pick it up.'

'I know it's not okay... That's not what I meant. But I'm trying to tell you to not beat yourself up, okay? There was no way of us determining whether that case up in Dundee was in scope or not. Unlike the case with Kate, which he denied.'

'I see your point.' Hardeep's sigh rasped down the line. 'It still burns away at me.'

'Burns away at us all. But getting to the truth is why we do this job, isn't it?'

Silence down the line.

'Go back.'

Marshall swung around, casting his torch over the empty hillside.

Nothing moved.

No sounds.

Marshall's breath came in short gasps. His heart was racing.

Someone had spoken, hadn't they?

He couldn't see anyone, but...

'I've been thinking.' Hardeep's voice jerked him out of it.

Marshall tried to keep his voice level. 'Thinking about what?'

'About these theories we're running with. Whether Mr Wrangham believes he's speaking to the devil.'

'To Lucifer.'

'Indeed, yes. I think there might be something in either theory.'

'Either?'

'Either it's an internal psychological phenomenon or it's someone in control of him. It can't be supernatural.'

Marshall didn't feel that sure right now, standing in this dark field outside the shepherd's hut where a man claimed to meet with the devil. Miles from anywhere. 'Or it's bullshit and he's just a psychopath.'

'Sir, I'd class that under "internal psychological phenomenon".'

'I'm not sure, but okay.' Marshall looked at the hut again, but he really didn't want to enter. The way it was wedged between two fields – it was like the kind of portal Wrangham had described. 'We've got three possibilities. One, he's a lying sod and he's killing because he's a psychopath. Two, he's suffering from hallucinations as a result of a neurological condition, which he may have stopped taking his meds for. Three, someone's using said condition to influence him.'

Hardeep laughed. 'That's what I said.'

'But I said it in my own words, so you can tell I understand.'

Hardeep laughed. 'Obviously, you're implying it could be a mix of the two. Say he has a conversation with someone and he later goes into a fugue state, due to his mental illness or possibly to some drugs he's using, and he imagines it was the devil. Then he kills people.'

'Exactly.' Marshall sucked in a deep breath. Enough prevaricating. He walked towards the shepherd's hut. 'Okay, I'm going in.' He stopped and shone his torch across the ground just outside.

A pile of some bones lay there, arranged in a weird pattern. Not quite a pentagram, but not far off. Marshall wasn't an expert on bones, but they seemed to be rabbit or hare. Maybe even a cat. Definitely not large enough to be human.

Marshall crouched low and snapped a photo of it, then sent it to Hardeep. 'I'm sending you something. Could you have a look at that?'

The sharp flash made the photo look professional, like a decent CSI had taken it.

Marshall held on to his phone as he shone the torch inside the building. Empty. Water dripped from the top of the roof. Not a portal, though – the far side was blocked off. Or didn't even have a doorway.

Something caught the beam, though.

Marshall swallowed as he entered the hut and slowly crossed to the far side. A box sat against the stone wall. An industrial-looking flight case, the sort of thing one of Kirsten's CSIs would bring onto a particularly gruesome site to measure something weird and unusual.

A folded-up page of A4 sat on top.

Marshall got out his phone and snapped the box. 'I'm sending you something else.' He opened the page and checked it. Letters and numbers. Looked like they were typewritten, but arranged in a spiral pattern on the left side and in a star on the right. Gibberish. He photographed it and sent it to Hardeep as well. 'Got it yet?'

'Still checking the bones. Seems intriguing. Do you think Wrangham created that?'

'Hard to say.' Marshall felt a wave of heat coming from behind.

The hut walls lit up bright.

He swung around.

The entrance was a wall of fire, flames burning up from the ground.

Marshall ran towards it, but stopped dead. He had to step back. Felt like he was on fire.

The fire cut out.

He moved forward.

Then it blasted out again.

A figure stood there behind the flames. Horns poking up.

The Devil.

Satan.

Lucifer.

Standing right in the way of his exit from the hut.

He had to get out there.

The wall of flame erupted again and pushed him back.

He was going to burn alive in here.

Whatever that thing was... he needed to get past it...

Marshall took a deep breath, the fire burning in his lungs, then rushed forward towards the flames.

He burst through into the cool night air.

Something clattered into him and pushed him back against the wall.

His head cracked off the stone.

Everything went black.

51

SHUNTY

Siyal got back to the station in Gala and pulled into a free space, then left the engine running. No sign of Jolene, so he got out his phone and checked his WhatsApp messages.

Just one from Afri:

> Oh. Okay. Sorry you can't make it. Guess I'll see you around x

Shit. That wasn't what he'd meant...

He quickly tapped out a reply:

> Sorry, it's just that work is super busy. I do want to see you again. Thank you for getting in touch.

He didn't send it, just let it sit there.

It felt cold, indifferent. After all she'd been through, he didn't want to leave her feeling like that.

He deleted it and retyped his reply:

> Sorry, Afri. Work has exploded again. Sure you can understand what that's like. Can we book in some other time this week? I'm free the rest of the week after about six. Maybe Friday? Dinner is my shout x

Was the kiss a mistake?

No.

Sod it.

Send.

He sent it.

And immediately wished he hadn't.

He could edit the message or delete it.

Her single grey tick became two grey ticks then two blue ticks.

She'd read it.

She'd see him editing the message to remove the x.

She'd wonder why.

Too late.

Too late for anything.

Just had to wait for her reply.

Assuming she did.

Maybe she wasn't interested in him in that way and he'd overplayed his hand. After all, he maybe shouldn't be—

He caught a figure running towards the car and flinched.

Jolene opened the passenger door and leaned in. 'There you are.'

Siyal smiled at her. 'I haven't seen you in ages.'

'You saw me earlier.'

'No, I know. I mean properly. To have a chat.'

'Right. Well, here I am.'

Siyal pointed at the seat. 'You're welcome to sit while we have that chat you called me about.'

She shook her head. 'We need to do it inside.'

'One of those, eh?' Siyal opened his door and got out. The night had cooled even further. Felt like rain was on the way. 'What's this about?'

Jolene looked around. 'Like I said, inside.' She sped up.

Siyal followed her into the station.

Struan Liddell was lurking in reception, chatting to someone on his phone. He glanced over and nodded at Siyal, then turned away again.

Jolene was holding the door for Siyal, so he raced over and entered the MIT's office space. She led him to her desk and sat down, facing away from the offices. Voices boomed out of one of them. 'How's your love life?'

'My love life?'

'You said you were dating.'

'Is that what this is about?'

The main door opened and Struan hurried to his desk.

Jolene stood up. 'Can you give us a minute, please?'

'Sure. I'm heading off. Just need to...' Struan crouched, disappearing below the desk. 'Got it.' He held up a gym bag. 'See you both tomorrow. Well, maybe not you, Shunty.'

'Night.' Jolene watched him go, then turned to face him. 'Okay, it's not about you dating.' She leaned in close. 'Like I told you on the phone, that brief chat we had earlier made me think of something.'

Siyal nudged his seat closer. 'Go on.'

'Roger Dalkeith was Davie's assumed name in prison, right?'

'Yes. Why?'

'Well, it's just... I remember hearing it at the time and thinking it was Roger Daltrey of The Who who'd died. It made me sad because my dad was a massive fan. Saw them loads of times in the seventies. Took me to a few of their gigs recently. Like at Edinburgh Castle last summer.'

'So you thought a rock singer had died?'

'You know who The Who are, don't you?'

'Sort of.'

Jolene shook her head. 'I'll educate you one day. But then I later heard it was actually some numpty in jail with a similar name. And then I found out who the numpty actually was. Davie Elliot. And I totally forgot about the Roger Daltrey thing. But when you said that name earlier, it brought it all back to me.'

Siyal sighed. 'You brought me back here because of a rock singer who didn't die?'

'No. The reason I called you, Rakesh, is because I remembered who mentioned that name to me.'

'Who?'

She leaned in a bit closer. 'Gashkori.'

'Okay. So? Is he a fan?'

'Rakesh, he told me before the killing was announced.'

'I'm not following?'

'He shouldn't have known. But he did. He told it to me.'

'Are you sure?'

'I've been through the statements from the time, Rakesh.' Jolene had a case file open, with entries timestamped by the system. She tapped the screen. 'I was entering this record here when he spoke to us.'

'You're sure of this?'

'A hundred percent.' Her eyes were like headlights. 'Gashkori *definitely* already knew Davie's location *and* his custodial identity. Even Andi didn't know. And Gashkori knew all about his in-custody death when he shouldn't have had the first clue about it.'

'So you're saying Gashkori gave up the fake name and location of where Davie was being incarcerated, in exchange for cash or something?'

'I don't know, Rakesh, but it all seems a bit suspicious, doesn't it?'

The one part of his job Siyal hated more than the rest was when he knew who was corrupt.

That sour taste.

That sickening feeling in his stomach.

It gave him no joy to catch a corrupt police officer.

52

STRUAN

Struan slipped back out of the office space and raced through the station's reception, out into the night. He jogged over to his car and got in, waiting for the cabin light to turn off.

Well, well, well...

When he saw them arrive, he'd wondered what they were up to. He'd thought maybe Dirty Old Shunty had been making the beast with two backs with St Jolene.

But now he knew.

Shunty had discovered who the leak was.

Bloody hell.

Struan hadn't expected that. He had a few suspects, but not the gaffer...

He held his phone in his hand and checked the recording had synced with the cloud.

He had no time to waste on reacting to the news. He needed to do something. And he could play this any number of ways.

Doing nothing was always an option – just let the whole thing play out and see what happened, then reap the rewards from the fallout.

Or he could get ahead of it and speak to Marshall's old man about it – always good to get brownie points from the rat squad. But if the whispers about him being on his way out were true, those brownie points were worthless.

But sometimes fate rested a firm hand on your shoulder and pointed its bony finger at a car entering the car park.

Gashkori drove through the empty spaces and parked not far from Struan.

Struan set his phone recording again, then got out just as Gashkori did. 'Evening, gaffer.'

Gashkori seemed to jump. 'Struan.' He puffed out his cheeks. 'Look like you're up to no good there.'

'You know me, gaffer.' Struan stepped right into Gashkori's path and blocked him off. 'Never one to be up to any good.'

'Don't I know it.' Gashkori chuckled and placed a hand on his arm. 'See you tomorrow. Briefing's at seven.' He walked past.

Struan grabbed his arm. 'Need a word, sir.'

'Oh?'

'In the car.'

Gashkori laughed. 'Sure about this, Sergeant?'

'Sure, Ryan.'

'First name, eh? Must be serious.' Gashkori looked hard at him, then raised his eyebrows and got into Struan's car.

Struan felt his pulse slow down. His heart should be thumping, but it was calmer than ever. Weird. He was like one of those Tour de France cyclists whose resting heart rates got under thirty. Except he wasn't a professional cyclist, he was an amateur gambler.

But so many amateurs visited Vegas and cleaned out the house...

He opened the driver door and got in. Kept quiet – time to let Gashkori do the work.

'Okay, Struan. What's this about?'

'What are you getting?'

'What am I getting?'

'Aye. What are you getting?'

'From whom?'

'Is it money? Drugs? Hookers? Rent boys?'

Gashkori laughed. 'What are you talking about?'

'I know.'

'Right. You know. What do you know?'

'I know. I *know*.'

Gashkori sighed. 'What. Do. You. Know?'

'I know you've been leaking to Hislop's people.'

'Shut the fuck up, Sergeant. Of course I haven't.'

'You have been. And I know.'

'You better explain yourself pretty fu—'

Struan prodded his chest. 'You knew where Davie Elliot was being taken when you shouldn't have. And you knew his assumed identity.'

'Of course I didn't.'

'You told two officers before his death had been confirmed.'

'Who?'

'Ah-ah. You slipped up, Ryan. You tipped your hand.'

Gashkori was reddening now.

'You've stopped denying it, I see. So what did they pay you? Cash? Drugs? Hookers?'

Gashkori gritted his teeth, but kept his mouth shut.

'Sorry, gaffer. I said "rent boys" earlier, didn't I? You're supposed to call them "male sex workers" now, aren't you?'

Gashkori sat back in his seat and looked over at Struan, locking eyes. 'What do you want?'

'Who says I want something? I'm just giving you some intel here, Ryan. Some people have figured out what you've done.'

'Some people? You mean, other than you?'

'Right.'

'Who?'

'I'm not saying. But I am suggesting you move on before they tell Bob Milne.'

'Move on?'

'As in, leave the Borders. Bugger off to another part of Police Scotland. I know you've had offers.'

'And leave myself open to this shite from you?'

'Nope. Because I can back up your story. Suggest someone in Hislop's world leaked to us both. Pretend we've been working them. I'm sure they've got people they could sacrifice for this kind of eventuality.'

'Who's Hislop?'

'Don't play me like I'm a fool. Gary Hislop. All I want is for you to move on and for me to get one of the DI slots. And I want a cut of whatever you're getting.'

'A taste, eh?'

Struan laughed, but he felt his heart rate spike. 'Was it cash?'

'No.'

'Drugs, then?'

Gashkori wiped a bead of sweat from his forehead, then brushed his nostrils. 'Do you want some?'

'No. I never dabble in that shite. I want a cash pay-off. Then I'll stay silent and I'll cover your arse for you. Back you up against anyone who comes after you.'

'Thanks for coming forward with this, Struan.' Gashkori dabbed at his nose again. 'I'll speak to the boss about moving on and I'll arrange the payment for you. How much do you need?'

'Twenty grand.'

'That's all?'

'That's the minimum. I'm neither greedy nor stupid. I know that's a drop in a very big bucket for your friend. The more I get, the better my story is to back you up.'

'Right. I'll see what I can do.' Gashkori looked over at him. 'But only if you're honest with me. What's the money for?'

'Debt.'

'What kind of debt are we talking? Divorce? Mortgage? Gambling?'

'One of those three.'

'Gambling?'

'It's my downfall. And the truth is I've had to mortgage myself to the tits on my place in Glasgow. Selling it wouldn't get me the kind of money I need. And I've got power of attorney over my dad and his place, but I've dipped in there too. Pretended it's to pay for his care.'

'But it's not.'

'Nope.'

'Who's the debt to?'

'Nobody bad. Just an online firm.'

'A casino?'

'Spread betting. Got a bit carried away with some football matches. Easy to get yourself deep in the hole with that stuff. The interest rate isn't too bad and there aren't big guys threatening to break my legs.'

'It'll be cash. Delivered in person. Hard to get to the people who you're in debt to.'

'I can pay in cash quite easily.'

'Thought it wasn't dodgy?'

'I said it was online. I didn't say it was clean.' Struan felt a surge of something deep in his guts. 'Once that's clear, I can go back to Gamblers Anonymous and stop this stupid shit, once and for all.'

'You know it's not about the gambling, don't you? Whether it's drugs, drink, food, sex, gambling, it all comes down to the same thing. The thrill of the chase stops you being in the moment with your demons.'

'You know a thing or two about that, do you?'

'You try being a second-generation Pakistani in the police, Struan. You'll see what hatred really is. On both sides.' Gashkori looked down at his hands. 'What is it that's eating away at your soul?'

'Would you believe me if I told you?'

'Of course.'

'I don't know. I've always just been a bit of a dick, I guess. Make one too many risky decisions.'

'You should speak to a psychiatrist.' Gashkori held his gaze. 'I know all about the gambling and—'

'It's all in hand.'

'Wouldn't be so confident on that score. But the other thing...'

'What other thing?'

'You get your kicks from beating people up.'

Struan's heart jabbed in his chest. 'What are you talking about?'

'I'm not talking Taekwondo or Krav Maga here. You find drunk strangers in the street at night and you beat the shit out of them. Why?'

Struan could lie, but he needed that money. He needed Gashkori to believe him. 'Because I can get away with it.'

'How many are we talking?'

'You seem to be the expert.'

'Bathgate, Dunfermline, Dalkeith, Wishaw, Kelso. Once a month. You must get so frustrated with your father and your situation that it all boils over and you need to vent. It's simple, isn't it? You just hit them, hard. Knock them down, then run off.'

'How did you find out?'

'The Kelso one. Never shit where you eat, Struan.'

'So why haven't you done anything about it?'

'Because I don't have any clear evidence it was you. Nothing to send on to the Complaints. I mean, if they were to start looking into me, I could send it on...'

'I've got alibis for it all.'

'Cast-iron alibis? Or some poor bastard who will do time because they lied for you?'

'Cast-iron. You've got nothing on me. Nothing provable. I haven't beaten anyone up.'

'What about the scars on your knuckles?'

'You're right about one thing. I punch walls when I get angry with Dad.'

'That right, aye?'

'I'm aware of that assault in Kelso. Happened seven months ago. And if you're aware of it and you did nothing, it makes it look like you're in on it. That you condoned it. That'll get you fired in the same shout. Maybe you only think you knew something, when in the light of sober second thought, you really didn't.'

Gashkori stuck his tongue in his cheek. 'What do you want, Struan?'

'This isn't about me, Ryan. It's about you.' Struan held his phone tighter. Didn't even glance down to check it was recording – he'd need to edit the shit out of that file. 'How did you get the information to Hislop?'

53

MARSHALL

Marshall woke up and felt like his head had been turned inside out. He was blinking hard, but he couldn't focus on anything. Voices out in the corridor.

A corridor.

Meant there was a door. And walls. That colour. The sound. The smell of disinfectant.

He recognised the place – Borders General. A&E.

He'd spent a lot of time here, but this was the first as a patient in over twenty years – not since he took a tumble off a mountain bike.

He was clothed at least. Wearing what he remembered wearing.

What the hell happened?

Fire.

A door.

The devil.

Shite. He'd finally lost it.

The door opened and Taylor peered in. He nodded at him, then walked off.

Someone else cleared their throat.

Jen entered the room, shaking her head. 'Honestly, Rob. What have you been up to now?'

'Just doing my job.'

'Right.' She smirked. 'See, when *I* do my job, I don't get into trouble. I don't set fire to shepherds' huts.'

Marshall felt his head and he had a big bump. 'Is that what happened?'

'What do you remember?'

'Nothing much. Just followed a lead. Took a few photos.'

'Anything else?'

Marshall looked away. 'The place went on fire.'

'Did you do that?'

'No.'

'See, when you were coming around...' Jen leaned in close. 'The paramedics said you were muttering about the devil.'

'I saw someone. They did this. They cracked my head against the wall.'

'The devil, Rob?'

Marshall sat up. 'Can I go?'

'You were unconscious for a while. Now you're awake, we're going to have to run some concussion tests.'

'I don't feel concussed.'

'Do you know what concussion feels like?'

Marshall looked away. 'Not since I came off my bike.'

'No. You were an idiot for doing that run without a helmet. And you're still an idiot.'

'Guilty as charged.'

She clicked her tongue a few times. 'Good news is your X-ray was clear.'

'I had an X-ray?'

'You were out of it. Sort of awake, but mumbling about devils and Lucifer and God knows what.'

'Right.' Marshall couldn't remember any of that. 'So that means I've not broken my skull?'

'No. You've just got a very thick one. Like an ox's.' She smirked. 'Very much like an ox's.'

'What are you smiling at?'

Someone knocked at the door.

Kirsten stood there, eyebrows raised, leather jacket on, shaking her head. 'You okay there, Rob?'

Marshall couldn't help but smile at the sight of her. 'I'm okay, aye.'

'He's not been cleared. I'll be back and I'll run a few more tests. Then he can go.' Jen walked out of the room, briefly hugging Kirsten as she passed.

Kirsten walked over to the bed and punched him hard on the arm.

'Ow!' Marshall recoiled. 'What was that for?'

'For almost getting yourself killed.' Kirsten ran a hand over his head. 'Christ, that's some lump.'

'It's not broken.'

'Right. Are you sure?'

'Jen says I had an X-ray. I don't remember it.'

'Jesus Christ, Rob. I was really worried. Hardeep called me in a panic, said you were screaming down the phone, then it went silent.'

'I was okay.'

'No, you weren't.'

'Okay, so I wasn't. Did he hear who attacked me?'

'What do you remember?'

'Nothing much.' Marshall avoided her gaze. 'Who found me?'

'I called Callum and he drove out with Andrea Elliot. They found you in this hut at the edge of a field.'

'I'll need to thank them.' Marshall swallowed hard. 'I think I'm going mad, Kirst.'

'Going to a field as it's getting dark is pretty bonkers, aye. But mad? They're saying you said you saw the devil?'

Marshall nodded slowly. 'I know what I saw.'

'Okay, well, I can reassure you that you didn't.'

'How? I saw him with my own eyes.'

'Unfortunately for your insanity, I've got a prosaic Scooby-Doo explanation for what happened.'

'Eh?'

'I'm saying I can lift the sheet up on your ghost and show you it's Old Man Withers from the amusement arcade, who would've got away with it if it wasn't for you meddling kids.' She held his gaze for ages. 'That devil you saw was a bull.'

'A bull?'

Kirsten made horns with her fingers. 'A bull was licking at you.'

Marshall shut his eyes. *Shite*. Through the flames, he'd mistaken a bull for the devil.

Bloody idiot.

'Does Jen know?'

'She does.'

'Bloody hell. But the wall of flames? How did... How?'

'I've visited the site, Rob, and I've got people investigating it. Someone designed a system to make a wall of flame erupt from the ground. We've found a propane tank buried around the back of the hut. A pipe feeds around to a flame emitter at the entrance, triggered by a remote control. You triggered it.'

Marshall didn't know what to say.

'It's like when we saw The Killers at Ingliston last year. Can't remember which song it was, might be "All These Things That I've Done", but do you remember they had this big wall of fire behind them? It's exactly like that, just a lot less elaborate. Who did it, whether it's Old Man Withers or someone else, we don't know. But it wasn't Satan. Or the bull, who is called Dignity.'

'Like the Deacon Blue song?'

'I don't think he was named after it.'

Marshall still clung on to the fear of what he'd seen. And who. 'Was that box I found connected to this?'

'No, I don't think so. Unfortunately, Rob, it's gone.'

'It was there, I swear.'

'I know. Hardeep sent me the photos. But someone took it. Maybe they had a remote sensor for when you triggered their setup. And I've found out what the box is. It's the flight case for a German brand of low fog machine.'

'What's one of them?'

'Basically, it spits out fog. It's used for props in plays or for a nightclub.'

'They didn't use that on me.'

'No. Because it was locked away in a flight case. Anyway, it's gone, but the rest of the gear was still there. From what Callum told me, someone generated the fire to fool Wrangham.'

'And his broken brain did the rest, filling in the details.' Marshall let out a deep breath. 'Have to say, it worked on me.'

'It's a pretty elaborate setup, Rob. Whoever did it knew exactly what they're doing.'

Marshall lay back, resting his head on the pillow. 'So now we're looking for someone with experience of stage props?'

'No, the stuff for the wall of fire at the entrance was pretty easy to rig up. I could do it in half an hour after a trip to B&Q. It's basically the mechanism for a gas barbecue, buried in the ground with a fuel pipe from a decent-sized propane tank. A few minor alterations. Probably cost about two hundred quid, all in.'

'Has Hardeep deciphered the code from the photos yet?'

'Nope. He hasn't. He was worried sick about you.'

The first time Marshall had ever been aware of Hardeep expressing any emotion to anyone. 'I need to speak to Wrangham about this. It's possibly a set of instructions from—'

'Not tonight, Rob. Wrangham's being interviewed by others right now.'

'But—'

'But nothing. I'm getting you home before someone murders you. And you need to get your sister to clear you first.'

54

STRUAN

John Wrangham looked like the sort of man Struan would target.

Young, stupid, naive.

The kind of guy you'd find in any small town across the Central Belt, blootered on a random Tuesday night.

The kind you'd follow and beat the living shit out of.

They wouldn't recognise you.

You wouldn't even know their name.

Close to the perfect crime.

But a very, very good way to get the demons out.

And right now, the demons were forming an orderly queue.

And the way he was twitching, John Wrangham looked like he needed a drink or seventeen. He didn't want to be here.

Struan didn't even want to be, either, but when the boss asked, you did. He had many other places to be. And the recording was burning a hole in his pocket. He'd use that when he needed. The trick he'd learnt was to be patient. Don't force it. Let Gashkori do the work. The recording was a backup. A way to cover his own arse.

'I'm not going to talk to you about my medication.'

'Fine. Let's move on to the devil, then.'

'The devil?'

'About how you met him at a lonely old crossroads. Sold your soul for the blues or just a No vote in the Scottish independence referendum.'

'It's true, but it was Lucifer. Not the devil.'

'Don't understand the difference.'

'There's a colossal one.'

'Sure.' Struan sighed. 'If you don't mind me asking, where do you keep your soul?'

Wrangham looked at him like he was a child who'd just asked why the sky was blue.

'Come on, John. You must know, right? I mean, you sold your soul to the devil.' Struan raised a hand. 'Sorry, to Lucifer. Surely there's got to be a method, right? Do you cut your chest open? Is it in your skull? Does he suck it out through your ear? Does he climb up your bum?'

Wrangham snorted. 'Stop teasing me.'

'I'm genuinely curious.'

'You're not. You're just ridiculing me.'

'You insist you sold your soul to him, but—'

'I did.'

'Okay, but how did he get it from you?'

'He just sort of took it. Asked me to shut my eyes. And I felt it leave my body.'

Struan swallowed down the urge to laugh. He'd got an answer, even if it was absolute gibberish.

Speaking of which...

He reached into his pocket for a print and slid it over the table. 'Does this mean anything to you?'

Wrangham looked at it. 'Where did you get this?'

'A colleague went up to where you met Lucifer and found it. Do you know what it means?'

Wrangham took great care examining it, like deciphering it

could get him out of there, but his sour look suggested he didn't know the first thing about it. 'I don't. Sorry.'

But Struan knew he did. The way his eyes scanned across the symbols, his lips gently moving.

Aye, he knew.

'It's how you receive your instructions, isn't it? Which victim to kill next?'

'I don't have a clue what this is.' Wrangham pushed the paper back but he had a look in his eyes.

Aye, he knew precisely who the next victim was.

'Was this instructing you to kill Fergus McNeill?'

'Like I said, I have no idea what this nonsense means.'

Struan could push him. But he'd keep. Tomorrow morning, he'd go at him full throttle.

After all, John Wrangham wasn't killing anyone else, was he?

55

DAY 4
WEDNESDAY

Kirsten pulled her car into the last free parking space and twisted the key. 'Are you sure you're okay, Rob?'

Marshall shut his eyes, sitting back and listening to the engine dying. He reopened them. The morning sun was bright and low in the sky, smudged with dirt and grease.

Was he okay?

Truth was, he didn't know.

Jen might've cleared him to leave hospital last night, but he wasn't sure he was exactly clear for duty after literally no sleep.

And he could lie to Kirsten, pretending he was fine, but she would see right through it.

He looked over at her. 'I'm not sure if I'm okay. My head's pretty sore.'

'Not surprised. You were wriggling around all night. It was like sleeping next to a pit of snakes.'

'Sorry. I did get up, though, to let you get some sleep. Looked at Fergus the minister's stuff online. It's very Old Testament. All fire and brimstone. Not exactly friendly stuff.'

'That's the kind of thing that's going to get you all rested up, isn't it?'

'I kept thinking it all through. Overthinking it, maybe.'

'Go on.'

'Just a few things. About how Wrangham thought he was dealing with the devil. I saw that figure... the bull... and... It was convincing enough to me and I've not got whatever affliction he has. That fire was... The whole thing was terrifying. Can't help but think about whoever took that flight case did it before they got there to rescue me.'

'Finding you being licked by a bull.'

'Right. The thing I kept wondering is why didn't he try to kill me like the other victims? Was I like Iain Hogg, someone who was in the way? Just in the wrong place at the wrong time?'

'Do you think it's the same person who killed all these people?'

'We know it was Wrangham. We've got him for all of those. Except for one, which he denies.'

'So you think someone's working with him?'

'Right. Maybe. And I'm determined to find out who. Whoever it was can't have known we had Wrangham in custody, because they would surely have cleared the place before I got there.'

'Maybe they didn't expect us to learn about that shepherd's hut and for you to be daft enough to go there on your own.'

Marshall smiled at that. 'I know *how* they're communicating, though.' He got out his phone and struggled to focus on the screen. 'This message on the bit of paper. It's code, but... I can't fathom it. And Hardeep called me while you were in the shower. He wants to use some new AI tech in Gartcosh to decrypt codes like this. It's been used for ancient languages and stuff like that, but he was saying they can understand whale song with it. I'll believe that when I see it, but it's worth a shot, right?'

'Right. I'd say so.'

Marshall tapped out a message, approving the expense. 'Okay. Done.'

'Are you sure you're ready for work?'

'I think I'll be fine. I'm just consulting here, after all.'

'So you won't be going out into fields looking for the place where a serial killer meets the devil?'

Marshall laughed. 'No.' He leaned over and kissed her on the lips. 'Right. We need to get to the briefing.' He got out into the sunny morning and strolled across the car park, trying to ignore the burning in his skull.

Kirsten led through reception to the security door, which hung open for once. 'Odd.'

Marshall followed her into the office space.

The place was empty.

No briefing and no signs of one. No smells of coffee or bacon rolls. No bodies to emit odour.

Marshall was fizzing with rage. 'Has Gashkori pulled the same trick as yesterday?'

Kirsten got out her phone and put it to her ear. 'I'll see where he is.'

'No, sir, I'll sort it out.' A male voice. Then the sound of a desk phone handset being returned to the cradle.

Marshall walked over to the offices at the side.

Taylor was leaning back in his chair, cradling his head in his hands and looking up at the ceiling. He looked over at him. 'Rob? You okay, mate?'

'You seem surprised to see me, Cal.'

'No. Well, aye. Last time I saw you, it wasn't pretty. You were totally out of it.'

'Thanks for finding me.'

'Least I could do, but it's Kirsten and Hardeep who did the hard work in tracking you down.' Taylor got to his feet, but he was looking a few shades whiter than usual. 'And I'd do anything for a mate. You're a mate, right?'

'Well, Kirsten is.' Marshall grinned at him. 'Where is everybody? Was the briefing cancelled?'

'Haven't you heard?'

'Heard what?'

'Wrangham killed himself.'

56

SHUNTY

Elliot stuck her tongue into her cheek, then the other. Something flashed through her brain, but Siyal didn't know quite what. Then she just sagged back in her chair. 'So Gashkori's giving my office to you and Dr Donkey's dad?'

Siyal stayed standing. 'That's my understanding, yes.'

Elliot exhaled slowly, then gave a little chuckle. 'And I'm just to get a desk in amongst the rabble?'

'Again, that's my understanding too.'

She gathered up her things, shaking her head. 'Nice to know where you stand, eh?'

Siyal stepped back to give her space. 'We're making good progress in the other case.'

She looked up with a sharp frown. 'Other case?' She shut her eyes, finally getting it. 'You mean Davie's murder?'

'Indeed.'

She sat back in her chair. 'I thought you'd parked it?'

'We have for now.'

'But you've made a breakthrough?'

'Indeed.'

Elliot sighed. 'Shunty, stop all this theatre and just tell me what it is, would you?'

'I can't. Just wanted to reassure you that you'll get justice for what happened.'

Elliot gave him a withering look. 'Fine.' Another shake of the head. 'Meanwhile, a little birdie tells me you and Dr Donkey Sr are investigating Wrangham's death in custody?'

'Just the initial work while the PIRC come on board, yes.'

Bob Milne stormed into the office, lugging a laptop under his arm. 'Ah, Andi. You got the memo, then?'

Elliot stacked her own laptop on top of a pile of paperwork. 'Hell of a final week for you, Bob.'

'Thought I'd just be able to put my feet up and watch the darts, but no.' Milne sat behind the desk and immediately started fiddling with the settings on her chair, each adjustment making Elliot's look that little bit sourer. He seemed to get it into a position he was happy with and settled back. 'It's good to see you, though. Shunty here passed on a few gems pertaining to—' He did air quotes. '—"the other matter" so please rest assured that we'll make solid progress on that score.'

Elliot shot him a look. 'He won't tell me what it is.'

'Turns out I've managed to train him well. That silence is with very good reason.' Milne gestured around the corners of the room. 'You know as well as I do that the walls in here have had ears. Probably still have someone leaking.' He stared her down until she looked away. 'Is Gashkori about?'

'He was around earlier, but I don't know where he went. He was muttering something about talking to She Who— to DCS Potter.'

'Ah. That'll be where he is.' Milne opened his laptop lid and smiled at her. 'We'll be in touch, Andi.'

'Look forward to it, sir.' Elliot nodded at them both, then scuttled out of the office and closed the door behind her.

Milne stared at the door as he opened his notebook, then looked over at Siyal. 'She likes you.'

'You think?'

'I know so. I've seen your personnel file, Shunty. She put in a rave report.'

'That was to get rid of me.'

'No, this was long after that. Part of your appraisal. And previous line managers can just put in any old bland stuff, but she really went to town on it. She rates you, Shunty. Use that to your advantage.'

'How am I supposed to do that?'

Milne tapped his nose. Then he spent a few seconds writing something down in his notebook, presumably detailed instructions on how Siyal could leverage Elliot's perceived favouring of him. He shut it and wrapped the tie around the long edge – whatever secrets he'd written would remain that way to Siyal. 'Okay, Shunty, the PIRC lot are just boarding their train from Glasgow now, so we need to lay the ground for them.'

'I've started some of the work. I've got a recording of Wrangham chatting with his solicitor.'

Milne's eyes bulged. 'Rakesh! What are you thinking? That's a gross violation of his rights!'

'I know.'

'You daft sod. You'll get fired.'

'Why? It wasn't my fault. His lawyer left the door open and the mic down the hall in the security suite picked up the loud parts of the conversation.'

Milne laughed. 'You're something else, Shunty.'

'I believe that's known in the trade as a schoolboy error?'

'Indeed it is. Have you listened to it?'

'I've started to, yes. Then DI Elliot called me in to moan about desks.'

'Right. Does the lawyer slip him anything?'

'Like what?'

'Anything that'll help him top himself.'

'No. It's not video. But I thought he'd used—'

'We're not prejudging anything here. The local pathologist is still looking at it. Nothing's off the table. Could the solicitor have slipped him anything?'

'No. They just chatted about the weather and the case.'

'So there's nothing?'

'Well...'

'Well?'

'I'll let you be the judge, sir.' Siyal got out his laptop and opened it. 'This is from after Struan and Jolene interviewed him last night.' He set the video playing.

Two men sat in the corridor outside the security station, one of them all patched up. Whatever had happened, Shunty assumed it was a breach of the peace and they were waiting for some uniforms to interview them.

'It's over.' Wrangham's voice.

'What is?'

'This is the end of days. I've achieved everything I set out to.'

'Does that mean you're going to plead guilty?'

'Time to meet the boss.'

'The boss?'

'The boss.'

'John, who is the boss?'

'Every alpha has an omega. I am meeting *Him*.'

The lawyer's voice was too low to pick up.

'Game. Over.'

Siyal stopped it playing. 'Can't hear the next five minutes, then the lawyer goes home. Checked the security cameras downstairs and he left the station in the average amount of time it takes.'

'The average time?'

'I timed it.'

'You've timed how long it takes to leave the station?'

'I got four DCs to do the walk for me. Ten times each. Timed it. Established it takes three minutes and seventeen seconds on average to get from the interview room to the reception area.'

'You never cease to amaze me, Shunty.' Milne laughed. 'Why?'

'I was a lawyer, so I know the dirty tricks. I didn't want any lawyers going missing on their way out of the door.'

Milne scratched the back of his neck. 'This is good stuff, though. How about the CCTV from outside the cell?'

'It confirms the pathologist's take, which you told me I'm not allowed to discuss.'

'Shunty...'

'Sir?'

'Come on. What does it show?'

'Nothing. Hours of it, until Steven opened the cell door and saw Wrangham's corpse. He tried to bring him back but he was long gone.'

'Right. Auto-asphyxiation.' Milne nodded along with his thoughts. 'Seen that done before.' He blew air up his face. 'Wrangham would've been with St Peter at the Pearly Gates in six to seven minutes.'

'You know that was exactly his intent, don't you?'

'What was?'

'Meeting St Peter. Dying, so he could be judged on his way into Heaven.'

'Ah, that stuff. Aye, I listened to some of the interviews on my drive down here.' Milne leaned forward and rubbed his hands together. 'My boy didn't cover himself in glory, I have to say.'

'You mean Rob?'

'Aye. Honestly, dealing with serial killers all day must've melted his brain. At least when we investigate bent cops, it's fairly simple. Bad guys have leverage over bad cops, or just stupid ones. Simple stuff. Then we follow the money, the drugs, the sex workers or identify any other leverage points.' He cleared his throat. 'Serial killers all seem driven by such weird shit. Like killing people who have bought Lego from a particular shop on a Tuesday in November. Or women who look a lot like their Aunt Margaret's pal who once smiled at them when they were thirteen. Or they kill people with lacrosse sticks smeared in peanut butter. Any number of weird motivations.' He drummed his thumbs on the table. 'No, our stuff is much more straightforward. Be glad you're working this beat, Shunty.'

Siyal snapped his laptop shut and got up. 'I won't be for much longer, will I?'

Milne winced, but he didn't say anything as Siyal left the office.

57

MARSHALL

Marshall sipped on his tea and looked around the crime scene lab. 'Truth is, Kirst, I just don't know what to think.'

Kirsten had a machine working away, but didn't seem to be too concerned about what it was doing. 'Aye. It's a bit of a shock.' She took a long drink of her tea and glanced at the box, then back at him. 'You ever had a death in custody before?'

'Not for a while and not since I moved back here. Couple in my time down in London. Not great fun. The IPCC investigated it. Up here, it's the PIRC. Don't even know what it stands for.'

'Police Investigations and Review Commissioner.'

'Got most of that. Thought it was Independent, not Investigations. And no "and".'

'Dealt with them before. They're even more forensic than my lot. And we're called forensics.'

Marshall sipped his tea again. 'Thing is, you do everything you can to secure a suspect but the truth is, when they're caught, that's when the magnitude of the situation hits them. And it hits really hard. Most of them can't face time in prison. Up to that point, they've deluded themselves, think they can handle any amount of time inside or that they'll never get caught. And the delusion fades in the harsh light of day. And...' He took another long drink of tea rather than sighing. 'They know they're guilty and they know they can't pay the price, so they just decide to end it. We put so many measures in place to try to prevent it, but when someone's that determined? They really go for it.'

Kirsten stood there, hands on hips. Looked like she didn't know what to do or say. 'I don't know wha—'

Her phone blasted out.

She picked it up and checked the display. 'Better take this.' She pecked his cheek, then walked off and answered it. 'What's up, Jay?'

The door shut behind her, leaving Marshall on his own, with his cup of dark tea and darker thoughts.

Hard not to think he was to blame.

During the interview, he'd pushed Wrangham hard. And Wrangham was a man with complex psychological issues, though he still didn't know precisely what he'd been diagnosed with.

Hard not to think he was largely responsible for the death.

Sure, Struan and Jolene had spoken to him after, but still it was hard to shake that feeling.

The door opened behind him.

Marshall swung around to smile at Kirsten.

Elliot stood there, smiling away at him. 'There you are, *mein guter Doktor.*'

'Here I am.' Marshall stood up tall. 'Didn't know you spoke German?'

'*Natürlich.* Studied it at uni.'

'Didn't know you went to uni.'

'Don't know a lot of things about me, eh? Dropped out after first year.'

'Sorry to hear that.'

She smiled wide. 'Hated it. Not an environment I wanted to be in. My daughter is dead set on going. What can you do, eh?'

Marshall wished he could dive down that rabbit hole and find out more about it, but she'd shut up as soon as he started. 'What's up?'

'What do you mean, what's up?'

'You're smiling at me, Andrea. It's unsettling.'

'Cheeky bastard.' Elliot collapsed into the chair he'd just given up. 'Have you seen Gashkori?'

'Nope. You look like you want to hit him, though?'

'I've got a whole set of golf clubs in my car. Just trying to decide which one to start with and which part of his anatomy to hit first.' She raised a finger. 'That's a joke, by the way.'

'I get that. What's he done?'

'Cheeky prick has given my office to Shunty and your old man.'

'Death in custody means a major investigation, Andrea. There's not a lot of places in this station for a team that size.'

'No, but why's it always me? Why's it never Callum bloody Taylor?'

Marshall didn't have an answer for that. 'What brings you here?'

'Not you, that's for sure. Came here to speak to your better half, Robbie.'

'She's just nipped out to take a call.'

'Aye, I saw her. She gave me that "two minutes" gesture you often seen just before people sod off and you don't see them for days. Hence me sitting in her chair, waiting.'

'She'll be driving to Edinburgh, then.'

'Seen that move before.' Elliot laughed. 'Don't know if you heard, but we found a shallow grave near where you were attacked by the devil, AKA a raging bull.'

Marshall winced – the good side of not working here was

he'd avoid a new nickname over that. Dr Bullshit or something. 'At the hut?'

'Under those freaky animal bones. Worse, it's human remains. The CSIs looking at it aren't sure how long they've been there. Said it's more like archaeology than forensics. Got half of my team up there investigating it, with most of Kirsten's.'

Marshall looked over at the door and wondered why Kirsten hadn't told him. 'When did she go out there?'

'Kirsten?'

'Aye.'

'She hasn't. That Jay lad is taking lead on it.'

That explained it, maybe. 'You think this is another victim of John Wrangham's?'

'You're the expert, Dr Donkey. You tell me.'

Marshall rested against the edge of the table and tried to think it all through. 'I mean, a shallow grave wouldn't fit the same pattern as the others, which have no signs of burial. Wrangham just left the bodies to be discovered, as though discovery's part of the ritual. When I interviewed him, he talked about tunnels and bridges being portals for the soul – once they were dead, he didn't care about the flesh and bone. So he wouldn't bury them.'

'Even a first murder?'

'Maybe. And it's really close to home, in a place with significance for him.'

'Could just be a coincidence, right?'

'I don't like them.' Marshall folded his arms. 'Do you feel it's connected, Andrea?'

'Seems the only logical explanation, aye. This stuff about him selling his soul. Obviously not to your big bull friend, but what if part of the deal was to murder someone?'

'I can see that.'

'And he's changed his methodology over time.'

Marshall frowned at her. 'What do you know?'

'Why do you think I'm here?'

The door barged open and Kirsten scowled into the lab. She took a look at Elliot and the expression darkened even further. 'Andrea... How can I help?'

'Just looking for an update on the *Time Team* special down at Ettrick.'

'I didn't know anything about that until two minutes ago. We've only just started. It's going to take time.'

'Aye, but you've got all these whizz-bang gizmos that can do a lot of work on-site.'

Kirsten sighed. 'As it happens, I was just on the phone to my lead investigator. He's been using the whizz-bang gizmo already. It appears the grave's about eight to twelve years old, judging by the state of decay.'

'How sure are you about that?'

'Not very. That whizz-bang gizmo can only do so much. We're getting experts from Gartcosh down to deepen the analysis. They'll maybe even nail it down to a more specific range.'

'Twelve years ago would be when Wrangham was thirteen.' Elliot was looking at Marshall. 'Meaning it's unlikely to be his work, isn't it?'

Marshall shook his head. 'We've all seen killers younger than that.'

'Aye, but those are wee fuds with knives getting told what to do by big fuds with knives. Those are kids who get caught in broad daylight, not burying victims in a shallow grave, then stacking bones on top of it.'

'Whoa.' Kirsten glowered at her. 'Who said shallow?'

'Isn't it?'

'It's over a metre deep. Roughly four feet. That's not shallow, by any stretch.'

'How did you find it?'

'The patch of grass under those bones formed a rectangular depression in otherwise flat ground. That made Jay a bit suspicious, so he brought in the ground-penetrating radar and it showed something buried down there. The size of a body. So he started digging.'

'Male or female?'

'Female.'

'Any idea who?'

'We found some clothing, which will help to narrow it down.'

Elliot jotted something in her notebook. 'I'll get that cross-referenced against MisPer reports.'

'Might be able to suggest one place you'd like to start, Andrea.' Kirsten pointed at the corridor. 'Here's the thing – Hardeep called me.' She looked at Marshall. 'It was about the AI.'

'The *AI*?' Elliot laughed. 'What the hell is Dr Donkey's prince doing with an AI?'

'Using it to decipher the code Rob found on a sheet of paper.'

Elliot shook her head. 'Whatever next…'

'The tech moves on. We've been given access to a unit of people in MI6 who work on that kind of thing. Expert code crackers. And they're stacked up for months, so using an AI was the next best thing.' Kirsten focused on Marshall. 'Hardeep's only managed to get a result on a partial chunk of the text. A string of numbers, but they match the exact coordinates of that grave.'

'Right.' Marshall got out his phone and saw a missed call from Hardeep. He'd been too busy to notice it. 'I need to speak to him.'

'One other thing. There's a load of gibberish in there, but there's one word amongst the noise. "Sarah".'

Marshall felt a cold chill run up his spine. 'Martin Gill's wife? Is that *her* grave?'

58

STRUAN

Struan almost got away with it.
Clutching two coffees, heading for Gashkori's office, he heard his name and had to stop dead.

Marshall was standing in Taylor's office door, beckoning him over. 'Need a word.'

Struan felt everything sag. He plastered on a smile and wandered over to him. 'Need to give the gaffer his coffee.'

'I'm in here.' Taylor was behind his desk. 'Absolutely gasping, as it happens.'

'I mean DCI Gashkori.'

Taylor held out a hand. 'Doesn't matter. We take our coffee exactly the same.'

'Right. Course you do.' Struan entered the office and handed over the coffee marked with a G. He needed to get out of there, fast, otherwise he'd get saddled with some stupid shite. Today of all days, he needed to be nimble and flexible – and mostly free. 'I'll just go back to looking through the CCTV for—'

'Not so fast.' Taylor tore off the lid of his coffee and inspected it. 'We've got a wee job for you.'

Struan covered over his groan with a smile. 'What's that, sir?'

'Need you to track down Martin Gill for DI Marshall.'

'Who's he when he's at home?'

'Landowner. Lives down by Ettrick.'

'Ettrick? That's miles away.'

'Aye.' Taylor took another drink of coffee and glowered at it.

Smug twat.

Miles away and deep in the middle of nowhere – with probably terrible phone reception.

Struan looked at Marshall. 'And why can't you go? If you don't mind me asking, sir?'

'Because we've got a separate lead to investigate. We've potentially unearthed the site of his missing wife's grave.'

'And you want *me* to break that news?'

'Not just that.' Marshall walked up to him – he was much taller than Struan thought. 'We need someone with your particular skills to get a read on him.'

'My skills? You mean tact, diplomacy and kindness?'

'Not words I'd associate with you, Sergeant. Just get a read on him when you tell him we might've found his wife's grave.'

'Shouldn't either of you be doing this?'

'We've both dealt with him. We'd appreciate a fresh take.'

Struan felt the coffee burning his hand through the paper, but savoured the pain. 'You think he's killed her?'

'No.' Taylor gasped. 'Can you just do it? Take Ash Paton with you.'

Struan couldn't hide the sigh now. He was sick of people telling him how to do the job he'd done for years. Ash Paton would be a total nightmare, especially in the hour it took to get to bloody Ettrick. At least, he assumed it'd be an hour. All that time, she'd be moaning and nipping his head. 'Are you sure that's wise?'

Taylor took another long sip of Gashkori's coffee. 'Doesn't matter. It's an order.'

'Fine.' Struan raised his own cup. 'Enjoy the gaffer's coffee and don't forget to get him one.' He left the room, but didn't shut the door and instead walked away slowly.

'I swear he gets worse. Didn't think that was possible.'

'We should've sent Jolene instead.'

Aye, they should've done.

Struan couldn't see Paton anywhere in the office, but he checked the clock on the wall. Aye, he knew precisely where to find her at this time of day. He barged through into reception, then out into the cold morning.

The Indian summer had fucked right off and left a horrible dreich behind. He didn't even have a brolly so his hair would go all curly.

Aye, there she was, exactly where he expected.

Ash Paton was vaping with Jolene, Elliot and a couple of female PCs. All clutching coffee cups. Comparing tattoos and laughing.

Maybe he should go and speak to this Martin Gill lad solo.

Nah, that was a daft idea.

'Ash!' He waved at her. 'Paton!'

The surname got her to look over at him. 'What's up, Sarge?'

The nicest name she'd ever used.

'Need to go and break some news to someone. You're to come with me.' Struan held up his cup. 'No rush. You finish your smoke.'

'Sure thing.' Paton went back to her tattoo chat.

Elliot was shaking her head, but Struan couldn't tell if it was at him or the full arm sleeve the uniform was showing.

Struan got into his pool car for the day – always book it first thing, whether you need it or not – and sipped his coffee.

Bloody hell, this was the cup with the G. He had to drink a black coffee.

At least Taylor was having to grimace his way through a latte.

He opened the door, ready to brave the queue again.

His phone rang.

Unknown caller...

Who the hell was that? Any number of berks who had his number, none of them calling would be good news.

Still, he had time to kill, so he answered it. 'Hello.'

'Struan.' Gashkori's voice.

The boss calling him on a burner.

Struan felt a jolt of emotion. Huh. Weird. He savoured it for a second or two, trying to pin it down, something like excitement or hope. 'Morning, sir, I've got your mid-morning coffee but DI Tay—'

'Struan, I'm not fucking talking about fucking cups of fucking coffee. Where are you?'

'In the station car park.'

'Right. I'm just leaving pathology at BGH now. Need a word with you.'

'A word?'

'Aye. I've got a little something for you.'

Hope blossomed in Struan's stomach.

'How about we meet in the Abbotsford car park?'

Struan knew it – the home of Sir Walter Scott, or some other old ponce. 'Okay, I'll see you there.'

'Five mins, Struan.'

'Sure thing, gaffer, but it'll take me closer to ten.'

Gashkori paused. Then he sighed. 'I can wait.'

'See you soon.' Struan ended the call, then wound down his window. 'Ash! I've got to run an errand for the gaffer before we go. Be back in about half an hour.'

'Sure.' She barely looked at him, then went back to tattoo world.

Struan put the car in gear and drove off, looking forward to getting his cut of the money...

Aware that Jolene was watching him drive away.

Nosy cow.

59

MARSHALL

'Nice place, this.' Taylor knocked on the door of the semi-detached cottage that seemed to spread out to fill its generous plot with various extensions out the back. 'This is much bigger than its almost namesake, isn't it?'

Marshall had to agree. The difference between Ettrickbridge and Ettrick was about ten miles, but this felt so much closer to civilisation. He looked back along Ettrickbridge's seemingly unnamed main street, continuing the road they'd driven along – a back road from a back road on the south side of Selkirk's town centre.

Over the road, the Cross Keys pub advertised beer and food, seeming to specialise in pizza. A row of motorbikes with German plates was parked outside. A gang of early-morning hikers tucked into bacon rolls and pots of coffee in the beer garden – brave souls.

Marshall could see himself living here. 'Not bad, eh?'

'Could see myself living here.' Taylor tried the bell again. 'You and Kirsten happy in Edinburgh?'

'We're happy, but not necessarily with Edinburgh.'

'Oh?'

Before Marshall could divulge any more, the front door opened.

A woman rubbed her hands on a dishcloth. Mid-sixties, but with a buzz about her. Like she did yoga or something to keep up her vigour. Long silvery hair in a plait hanging over a well-tanned shoulder. 'Can I help you?'

'Morning.' Taylor smiled at her. 'Looking for a Geraldine Blackhall.'

'You've found her.' Her eagle's gaze shot between them. 'Take it you're police officers?'

'We are. DI Callum Taylor.' He showed her his warrant card. 'This is DI Rob Marshall.'

Geraldine took a while to inspect his credentials, then seemed to be satisfied. 'To what do I owe the pleasure?'

'We understand you're the sister of Sarah Gill?'

'Indeed.' Her gaze sharpened. 'What's happened?'

Taylor gestured behind her. 'We wouldn't mind having a chat inside, if that's okay?'

'Sure. Of course.' She stepped aside to let them into a hallway, the cream walls and white floor tiles making the place glow. 'I'm baking, so if you wouldn't mind me working away...' She led them through the back of the house to a modern kitchen. 'First time I've had this on since April.' She opened the door of a vintage Aga, then pulled out a baking tray and started distributing twelve perfect-looking scones onto a metal rack to cool. The obvious heat of them didn't seem to affect her. 'Can I make you some tea, officers?'

'We're both good. Had some back at the station.'

'Of course.' Geraldine sat at the end of the table and motioned for them to sit, then waited for them to comply. 'I take it you've got an update on Sarah's case?'

Taylor looked over at Marshall, then at Geraldine. 'We've uncovered some remains we believe may belong to her.'

The news seemed to hit her like a block of ice. She seemed

to shiver and shake, despite the heat in the room. Then she snapped back and frowned at them. '*May* belong to Sarah?'

'We found some items matching the Missing Persons report her husband filed at the time.' Marshall held out his phone, showing the photos taken of the items at the grave. 'I gather this—'

'I made that.' Geraldine pointed at the screen, then wiped at her eyes. 'That necklace. I used to make jewellery. Every item was unique. That was one of my first pieces. I gave it to Sarah for her fiftieth birthday. She wore it all the time. I was very touched by that. Trouble with being a maker is you never know when compliments are genuine.'

'Our forensics officers are undertaking DNA tests to confirm it's her, but the clothing found matches what she wore.'

'I see.' Geraldine puckered her lips. 'I still miss her every day.'

'Would you mind going over what happened?'

'Of course I *mind*, but if it'll help you confirm that and bring us some much-needed closure.' Geraldine looked around the room. She walked over to the butler sink and filled a kettle, then set it on to boil. 'Sure I can't make you some tea?'

'We're both good.'

'Of course.' Geraldine snatched a cup from a half-filled oak mug tree then dropped it onto the counter. 'Shuffle.' She righted it, then tossed in a teabag from a pot next to the sink. 'We didn't know what happened to Sarah. One day, she just disappeared.'

'You had no idea where she went?'

'None. She was a homebody. Born in Ettrick, lived most of her days there. Studied in Edinburgh, but that was as far as she ever ventured. She came back and married Martin. Lived her life there, never even going on holiday.'

'How did her husband take it?'

'Martin was beside himself. I...' The kettle boiled and she

tipped the water into the mug. 'Sarah was just the kindest person, you know? She gave up her bone marrow for my own cancer when we were teenagers. I've been in remission for forty years, but the fact I'm still here is all because of her kind act... I tried to do whatever I could to help her but I couldn't return the favour for my sister. Sarah's breast cancer was *vicious*. By the time she was even seen for it, it'd spread everywhere. She was given just months to live. Sarah being Sarah, she just kept on trying to live her life. Didn't stop her running, but it was getting harder and harder for her. Then one day... she just disappeared.'

'What do *you* think happened?'

Geraldine ran her fingers across her eyebrows. 'I thought she had killed herself.'

'Do you have anything to support that?'

'Not really, but I feel it deep in my gut. Like I said, her cancer was terminal. They tried chemotherapy, but it was really tough on her and it just didn't work. The tumours kept growing. She'd hoped it could at least buy her some time. You know, cancer can be a condition these days. It doesn't have to be fatal. But she could see the writing on the wall, so she decided to let nature take its course. She was a big believer in that.'

'Why do you think she took her own life? Did she ever talk to you about that?'

'No. But with terminal cancer there comes a point where the pain becomes intolerable and you're not able to keep doing the things that kept you going. All that lies ahead is more pain... and death. She said the worst part of cancer isn't what it's doing to you, but to your loved ones.'

'She said that?'

'A few times. But the fact we never found a grave left so many questions, you know? So many unanswered questions.'

Marshall stopped nodding along with her words. 'Do you think it's possible she could've been murdered?'

'No.' Geraldine stabbed a spoon into the mug, then flung the teabag into the sink. 'I mean, who by?'

'That's a question I'd ask you.'

'I certainly have no suspects in mind. You asked me what I think happened and I genuinely believe she ended her suffering by taking her life.' Sarah nibbled at her bottom lip. 'That or, she just slipped and lost her footing. Fell and died.'

'There was an organised search, wasn't there? Her husband would know the land around here, wouldn't he?'

'Intimately. Like I said, Sarah and I grew up in Ettrick. It's a wild place. You wouldn't believe you were fifty miles from Edinburgh. It's more remote than lots of the Highlands. And lesser travelled. So it's entirely possible we'd never uncover her body. You get walkers and runners and cyclists and what have you, but there are hundreds of acres nearby where nobody has stood in centuries, if ever.' Geraldine picked up her cup and sat at the head of the table again. 'Sarah knew this. She didn't want Martin to suffer any more. Didn't want to see her decline any further, but she didn't want him to find her body. So I suspect she knew of a few places where she could just slip away.'

'Did that work?'

'How do you mean?'

'You're saying she spared him some pain. Did it?'

'No. Her disappearance hit Martin hard. Very hard. Not knowing what happened to her.' She blew on the surface of her black tea but didn't drink it. 'If you ask me, I'd say he lost his marbles a bit, I'm afraid to say. Martin was ten years older than Sarah, so it's possibly par for the course at his age. And then...' She shut her eyes. 'He started giving stuff away. Possessions, including all their books and LPs. Artworks. Furniture. They'd spent a lifetime collecting it all. But not just that. He had lots of land that'd been in family since forever. Not central to the estate, which runs from Peebles down to Ettrick, but parcels here and there. He threw himself into campaigning for the

Borders rail extension. The Waverley line, he insisted on calling it. Walter Scott country. Some of those bits of land were over past Hawick and he thought it would help things if he donated it to extend the track to Carlisle. Truth is, I think they thought it was more trouble than it was worth as the route wasn't going to run that way, but he insisted they checked if it could.'

Marshall didn't see anything other than a lonely old man, broken by losing his wife. 'Is it possible he—'

'*No*. Martin didn't do this. He's been to hell and back over what happened to Sarah. He's a good man.'

'But?'

'Well...'

'What do you mean?'

'Martin feared it was a serial killer.'

Marshall tried to ignore the goose flesh rising up his arms. So many people had fantasies about serial killers – he knew the mundane reality. 'Did he have any evidence of that?'

'No and that's my point. He started watching and reading all these books and films. Then he found all this stuff on the internet. Even in Ettrick, you could watch YouTube videos. He convinced himself she'd been punished for his sins.'

'*His* sins?'

'Aye.'

Taylor narrowed his eyes. 'People say "for my sins" when they're joking about being a fan of a football team, but I don't think you mean that, do you?'

Geraldine blew on her tea. 'The last time I spoke to Martin was a couple of years ago. He kept muttering about sins.'

'Did he ever explain what they were?'

'No, just that he was being judged by God. Thing is...' She took a halting sip of her tea. 'Around the time of her disappearance, Martin had been speaking to Fergus McNeill a lot.'

'The local minister?'

She nodded. 'And... I think there was a falling out around the time of Sarah's funeral.'

'But you never found the body?'

'Fergus insisted on doing a service. Thought it might help Martin. Might help me too. It didn't. Martin flew off halfway through, shouting at Fergus. It was all very uncomfortable.'

'Do you know what happened between them?'

'I'm not sure. Martin and Fergus used to be incredibly close, but they fell out. And it was very messy.'

'Was it about Sarah?'

'I wondered. I mean, there had been a discussion between them... Sort of a philosophical one. Sarah had talked about whether they would euthanise her when the time came. When she couldn't bear the suffering anymore. She didn't want us to see her going through that. But Martin found it hard, seeing her like that, and he wanted to help her. When Sarah died, she walked off out of our lives, but she'd been in a lot of pain for a long time.'

'Did you help her?'

'No.' She shook her head. 'You're barking up the wrong tree there. The worst part is I was away with my late husband. We were in Chile. On a walking holiday. He'd always wanted to see Patagonia. I lost him a few years later. Fergus spoke so kindly at the funeral.'

'So all you had to go on is Martin saying she went for a run?'

'That's right.'

'Do you believe the story that she went for a run?'

'You mean, do I think Martin killed her?'

'Or he just lied.'

Geraldine stared deep into her mug, then started kneading her forehead. 'I do.' She looked back up at Marshall. 'I think the likeliest thing was she just slipped and injured herself. She was getting weaker and weaker, but still pushed herself hard. She could've lost her footing and...'

'But they didn't find her body?'

'I've told you so many times. It's wild land around here. Could be she's right next to somewhere we looked and we just didn't see her.'

Taylor sat back and folded his arms. 'Do you know where she'd normally run?'

'She was fond of many routes around here, but mostly along the roadside for safety reasons.'

'Did Sarah know a John Wrangham?'

Geraldine covered her mouth with her hand. 'He lived in Ettrick, didn't he? He killed himself, didn't he?'

'We're talking about his son, also called John.'

'Ah, right. Yes. I knew the family. Janice was a kind woman. Awful what happened to them. Sarah said it hit the boy hard.'

'She knew him?'

'Indeed. Sarah taught at the primary school.'

Marshall felt everything clench.

Sarah teaching John Wrangham didn't feel at all good…

60

STRUAN

Struan pulled into the car park at Abbotsford and parked furthest from the entrance, giving him a good view of approaching vehicles. He didn't know what to do. He didn't know if they'd be driving elsewhere or if something else might happen. He didn't know if Gashkori would come to sit with him in this car or he'd have to go to him.

So he left the engine running.

All the same, he felt that flutter of hope deep in his guts.

The money was going to be very useful. Very, very useful. Closing off those debts was precisely what he needed. Getting all of that nonsense under control would sort out his head.

He'd never get back into this stupid situation again.

Trouble was, Gashkori knew all about what he'd been up to. Gave him that sour taste in his mouth when he thought about it. Still, he'd covered it over very well. Implicated him with solid logic.

Turned out he didn't have to wait too long.

A Transit pulled into the car park, then flashed its lights at him before parking alongside.

Gashkori wasn't behind the wheel.

The driver was some nameless mug Struan had seen around but never learned his name. He got out and walked around to slide open the rear door, then stood there. Arms folded. Giant arms that could crush a windpipe.

Of course Gashkori had set a trap. But Struan had kompromat on him, didn't he? A recording of him admitting how he'd covered over Davie Elliot's death. And as he didn't know Struan had recorded it, he'd told him, so Struan knew where the bodies were buried.

Idiot.

Total fucking idiot.

Still, he needed that money.

Struan killed the engine, then got out into the biting wind. He slowly rounded the back of his car, ignoring the voice in his head screaming at him to run as he walked past the brute.

'Stop.' Meaty fingers patted him down, grabbing his phone, his keys and cuffs. The goon tossed Struan's things into the van and pointed into the back.

Struan did as he was told, his heart finally pounding.

Callum Hume was sitting on a seat in the back. He reeked of strong aftershave. Wood and tobacco. He pointed a gun at Struan. 'This is merely for insurance.' He tossed Struan's phone back to him. 'Sodhead there just had to check it wasn't recording.'

Struan took it and checked it. He'd turned it off. He put it in his suit jacket pocket without switching it back on again. 'Sodhead?'

'Everyone's got to have a nickname.' Hume tossed a pair of handcuffs over. 'Cuff yourself.'

'Front or back?'

'Back.'

Struan sighed, then complied, wrapping them around his wrists. He showed them to Hume. 'Happy now?'

Hume held the gun at Struan. 'Drive.'

The van pulled off, pushing Struan back into another seat. 'Weird having chairs in the back of a van.'

'When it's your van, Struan, you can put what you want in the back.'

They pulled up to the junction. To the left, a car sat with its hazards on. Bad place to break down. Sodhead turned right, hitting the back road up towards the A7, taking it slowly.

Hume leaned over as they passed Abbotsford itself. 'Weird how Sir Walter Scott lived there, isn't it? All that seems so long ago. It's just by Tweedbank, when Tweedbank wouldn't have existed. Gala would've been a few houses. On the other hand, Melrose and Selkirk would've been grand towns. Thing with history is it lives with us. Like your gambling debts, eh?'

Struan humoured him with a smile.

'Walter Scott was an interesting character, mind. Might've had a long career as a lawyer and then a judge, but he bought this place with the money he'd made from publishing books. All the other big stately homes around here, a bit of that money came from farming and just owning the land, sure, but the vast majority of it was made from the slave trade in the Caribbean.'

Struan laughed. 'Didn't take you as being woke, Callum.'

'Woke's such a loaded term these days. What's wrong with believing in justice?'

'Man like yourself tries to avoid justice.'

'Touché.' Hume smirked. 'Trouble with that argument is the drug trade should be legalised. Heavily regulated, sure, but legal. Cannabis is much less harmful than alcohol, but we criminalise it and imprison people for it.'

'What about the heroin? Or cocaine? Or ecstasy?'

'I see your point, but we should make them to controlled strengths and qualities, so they're not cut with any old shite and people know what they're taking when they pop a pill or do a line. All I want is for our trade to be treated with respect, like all the others. Take that fancy brewery at Tweedbank. Lovely place, but why do they get to make very tasty artisanal beer and we don't? Why can't we make very tasty artisanal cannabis? Or designer cocaine?'

'Because it's illegal, Callum. It ruins lives.'

'Like gambling does, eh?'

Struan didn't have anything for that.

'When people buy from us, they know they're getting good stuff. We'd more than happily pay tax on what we make. Happily. We'd love to have people like Sodhead here officially on the payroll of a drugs business. But we have to funnel our income and our costs through certain channels. He's a bricklayer, would you believe? Hasn't seen a hod in years.'

'Like those hardware shops.'

'Precisely.'

Struan looked at Sodhead in the front, behind the wheel. Some cottages passed slowly at the side. Struan wished he could get the owners to call for backup. But there was nobody in. Nobody knew where he was going but he was a stupid prick. A greedy prick. A desperate prick. 'Callum, I'm warning you. I've got a dead man's switch.'

'Oh, have you?' Hume didn't seem too bothered.

'If you kill me, I won't be able to log in to my server and everything I have will get emailed out.'

'Kill you? Who said anything about that?'

'Are you trying to pretend this is a nice, friendly drive?'

'Struan. I'm not who you think I am. I'm just a go-between. The reason we're talking is because we need to replace Gashkori. We could use a man like yourself, Struan.'

'I'm a DS. He's a DCI.'

'So? You've both got access to information we need. He's been useful, but I suspect that's coming to an end. You can only do what he's been doing for so long. And you're a lot more resourceful than him.'

'You've been keeping an eye on me?'

'Keep an eye on all of you, Struan.'
'What would I get out of it?'
'Your immediate need is money, correct?'
'That, or someone cancelling my debt. I'm flexible.'
'You'd be a valued member of our organisation, Struan. I mean, there's the risk you'll get made, of course. But we look after people. Like Ryan. If he goes inside and he keeps quiet, then he'll do well out of it.'
'So I'd have to do time for you?'
'Not if you're a good boy.'
'What does that mean?'
'Pass us information, but don't leave a trail.'
'I can do that.'
'Can you? I'm not sure you have the balls for this sort of work, though.'
'Of course I do.'
'Our business is much more ruthless than punching drunks in the street.'

Fuck.

They knew.

Gashkori had passed that on as well.

Idiot.

But this was a game of poker, rather than blackjack. Skill, experience and intuition would trump good fortune any day of the week. 'I've got evidence against Gashkori that'll fuck him over.'
'Your dead man's switch?'
'Right.'
'What service do you use?'
'I'm not telling you.'
'Struan, don't lie to me. Details.'
'I've got three different services. They send me a link to click, which means I've checked in. If I don't, then stuff goes out after three days.'

'Do you have stuff on me?'

'Of course I have. You can't disappear that many people from your organisation without breaking a few eggs. Just took someone to collect enough shells and piece it all back together again. But it's not part of that drop.'

'Why haven't you used any of this against us?'

'Because I always need a bit of leverage. I've built up enough against Ryan to finally make my move.'

'What do you want?'

'Clear my debts. I don't care if that's a big lump of cash or if it's you using your connections in the gambling trade.'

'I don't have any connections with those vermin. Gambling is a vice.'

'And drug dealing isn't?'

'I know I've got a coherent moral argument on my side, Struan. You're just a degenerate thug. I know what you've been doing in Kelso and Dalkeith and Bathgate and other places. Spotting drunks in the street and beating the shite out of them.'

Struan didn't have anything to say to that. Because it was all true.

He was thrown around as they powered onto the A7, heading south towards Selkirk and Hawick. He needed to strap on a seatbelt, but there wasn't one on this seat. He looked past the driver again and clocked the speed at seventy.

On a sixty limit.

And climbing.

Struan didn't know what to do here.

Hume waved the gun at him. 'Thing is, Struan, someone has to pay the price for the difficulties we've faced recently. You thought it was going to be Gashkori, didn't you? Bit of a shame it's you, eh?'

'Please. Callum. Don't kill me. You'll trigger my dead man's switch.'

'Do you think I care? With you gone, they won't be able to

stand up any of that shite against us, will they? Besides, we can blame it all on Gashkori.'

'Please. Don't do this.'

Hume reached over and grabbed Struan by the collar. 'You remember Chunk?'

'Hitman who worked for you, right?'

'The best. The absolute best. Great assassin and very creative for us. Shame about what happened to him. Horrible way to go. Thing is, he was a great teacher too and his methodology was second to none.' Hume reached across and tugged the handle.

The back door slid open.

The wind tugged at Struan.

Hume's strength kept him in place.

Struan lurched forward with his jaw, sinking his teeth into Hume's arm.

He screamed out, but his free hand shifted from Struan's throat to his shoulder. 'Stupid prick.'

He clattered Struan's head against the bare metal of the doorframe then pushed Struan out.

61

MARSHALL

Marshall relished being back behind the wheel and cutting along the country lanes.

It let him chew things over while his body was occupied with the mechanical aspects of driving. And not just focusing on the acrid reek of the brand-new air freshener tree Taylor had hung up when he refuelled the pool car in Selkirk.

He slowed as he approached the field where he'd been attacked.

Where John Wrangham had sold his soul to the devil.

The knackered old vans belonging to Kirsten's team lined the lane, with some squad cars parked opposite.

Marshall squeezed between them like blood through a coated artery, then pulled in past a van from Gartcosh, but didn't get out. 'So Sarah taught John Wrangham. Lots of possibilities there.'

'There are.' Taylor was tapping away on his phone. 'But if you're asking me if I think he killed her?' He put his phone away and looked over. 'It seems like a stretch to me. The kid was fifteen when she died.' He held up a finger. 'Sorry, when she went missing.'

'But age doesn't rule him out. He'd already cycled here to speak to the devil.' Marshall pointed over the road at the shepherd's hut, obscured by crime scene tents and bodies in Smurfs suits. 'He was clearly precocious in some ways. Maybe even sexually too. And physically. He's a big lad, right?'

'You think he was attracted to her?'

'Why not? I've seen it before. A disturbed young man who is obsessed about a teacher from his past.'

'She hadn't taught him for a while.'

'So? Thing with a primary school in Ettrick is it's not like in Glasgow or Peebles where you've got, say, three classes per year. Here you've probably got just one or two teachers for the whole of primary school, which covers a big catchment area.'

'Did a bit of searching just now.' Taylor held up his phone. 'The whole school was mothballed in 2017. Just three pupils, so they moved them to Ettrickbridge, where Sarah's sister lives.'

'But John would've been going to Selkirk High at that time.'

'Right. Exactly. Lots of weird stuff going on in his adolescent head. Think about it. Sarah was known to be a runner. Remember hearing about a case from Andi Elliot from before my time where someone knew the routes people would take and he planned out his attacks on them.'

'I worked it.'

'Right. Well. If Sarah did the same run every day or every week or every third Tuesday...'

'I see your point.' Marshall sat back in his chair and let the thoughts come without trying to force them into a particular shape of hole. 'I guess this was around the time he claimed to have started seeing the devil, after all.'

'Precisely.' Taylor smirked. 'Like you did.' He coughed. 'Bullshit.'

Marshall knew how to defuse it. Ignore it. Humour it. Don't get angry. 'One thing to remember is John Wrangham isn't a rational person. He's a serial killer. A visionary type. But also a missionary type too.'

'I don't know what that means.'

'They're FBI classifications of serial killers.'

'The real Behavioural Sciences Unit?'

'Right. Without the U.' Marshall spotted the journalists up ahead, kept at bay by a pair of uniforms, laughing and joking along with them and hopefully not spilling too many beans. 'Wrangham satisfies criteria for both missionary and visionary. He's seeing visions – the devil – but he's clearly also got a mission, namely killing unpunished sinners so they can receive justice in the next life.'

Taylor scratched at the stubble on his cheek. 'Let's say your attacker was someone pretending to be the devil. He's trying to influence him, right? To use Wrangham as a tool in his game. A pawn, maybe.'

Marshall shrugged. 'Maybe. Hard to tell with Wrangham dead, sadly.'

'Thing is, Rob, you've been trying to figure out if his cognitive distortions were his own or if someone was manipulating him. But maybe they knew all about the visions and used them to manipulate them into killing for him.'

Marshall let out a slow breath. 'That's a good point. Hardeep thinks that's what's happening here.'

Taylor pointed across the road at the hut. 'Do you think whoever has been manipulating him got him to murder Sarah?'

'Makes as much sense to me as him bumping her off because he fancied his teacher and she rebuffed his apple one day.'

Taylor smiled at that. 'Right. We need to speak to Martin Gill and see if he can shed some light on this whole thing. Struan was supposed to track him down.' He got out his phone and called Struan.

Marshall could hear the springy voicemail voice.

Taylor ended the call. 'No answer.'

'Reception is bad out here.' Marshall tried his number.

'We're sorry but the person you've called is unable to take your call. Please leave a message after the tone.'

Beeeep!

'Struan, it's Rob. Give me a call, please. It's urgent.' Marshall killed it and sat back. 'Why do I get a knot in my stomach every time I think about him?'

'Who, Struan?'

'Aye.'

'Get the same one, Rob. He's a sleekit devil.' Taylor gestured down the road. 'Shall we go and see Mr Gill, then?'

'Why not?' Marshall set off away from the crime scene.

His phone rang.

He pulled back in to check the display.

Jolene calling...

Marshall answered the phone. 'Hi, Jolene. You—'

'Someone's thrown Struan out of a van!'

62

Marshall flipped on the indicator and accelerated past the queue of traffic, the pool car's siren blaring away.

A traffic cop held out a hand to them, then spotted Taylor's raised warrant card and looked at it through the wound-down window. He eased them off the carriageway into a long coned-off row of vehicles, not far from the confluence of the Ettrick and the Tweed.

Two ambulances, their lights flashing away.

Marshall got out and jogged over.

Jolene sat on the barrier at the side of the road, staring into space. Covered in blood and clutching something tight.

'I'll see what's what.' Taylor patted Marshall on the arm, then headed for the nearest ambulance.

Marshall approached Jolene slowly. 'Hey, are you okay?'

'Rob?' She focused on him then her eyes went all glassy again. 'It was horrible.'

He perched on the barrier next to her. 'What happened?'

'I told you. Someone chucked him out of a van.'

'Yeah, I get that. Did you see it?'

She shook her head. 'I was driving when the call came over, so I came straight here.' She snorted, then looked down at her bloody clothes. 'Someone stopped just before they hit him.'

'Have you spoken to any of the drivers?'

'A few of them, aye. One of them followed the van from Abbotsford car park. Ash is there just now. Struan's pool car is in the car park there.' Jolene stared right at him. 'They pulled onto this road. As soon as they got up to eighty, they pushed him out. I got here and... He's pretty fucking broken.'

Marshall didn't have any words of kindness or encouragement to offer. 'You used to be a paramedic, right?'

'Briefly. I'm not equipped to save someone in that condition, though. The real paramedics got here quickly, to be honest. They said Struan's unlikely to survive.'

Marshall looked at her bloodstains but decided it didn't warrant any comment. 'Did anyone get plates from the van?'

'Sorry. Maybe a 57. Could be a 67.'

'Whatever it is, it'll be getting crushed somewhere now. Or torched.'

Jolene looked over at the ambulance as it drove off and hurtled towards the hospital by Melrose. She wrapped her arms around her torso and shivered. She started crying and let Marshall hug her, resting her head on his shoulder. She broke off after a few minutes. 'Can't help but think he's been acting weird, Rob.'

'Weird how?'

'Back at the station, he shouted over to Ash Paton, said Gashkori told him to take her with him on some errand. She was chatting away to a few of us. He waited, but I saw him get a phone call, then he drove off in a hurry.' She swallowed hard. 'I mean... He's shady, isn't he? We've had all these leaks and... Him behaving erratically like that...'

'Make sure you pass that on to Rakesh.'

'I will do.' She pushed something into Marshall's hands. 'Here. I can't keep holding on to this.'

Struan's Samsung phone, the screen broken in a spiderweb pattern, and his notebook, soaked with blood.

Jesus.

'He gave them to me, Rob. Didn't say anything.'

His final acts were probably in here. Why he came to be here.

Marshall put on a pair of gloves and took them from her, then started flicking through the pages, but he struggled to read much of it. Cops' handwriting was worse than the average doctor's.

On the latest page, Struan had noted down Martin Gill's address with an instruction that might've been to ask him questions about his wife's grave.

Obviously, he hadn't visited yet.

Marshall wondered if it was all connected…

It probably wasn't, but he needed something to distract himself.

He gave Jolene another hug. 'Go to the hospital, if you want. Okay?'

She looked at him with teary eyes. 'Are you sure?'

'He needs someone there, fighting his corner.'

She got up and let out a snort. 'He's an arsehole, Rob, but I hope he pulls through.'

'Me too.' Marshall handed her the phone and notebook back. 'Do me a favour and put these into evidence.'

She frowned, then took them back. 'I'll see you later, Rob.'

Marshall walked off in the opposite direction, getting out his phone to call Potter.

63

Taylor bombed along the road through the wilds, passing the turning for the caravan park in what passed for the outskirts of Ettrick. 'Anything?'

Marshall checked his phone. 'Still no bars.'

'Bloody typical.'

'That's happened a lot, hasn't it?'

'What, us missing a serial killer?'

'No, Gashkori going off the radar.'

Taylor had to slow for a mail van pulling out of a side lane, but at least he had the good grace to wait for it to pull in before he blasted past. 'He's always been like that.'

'But this is much more, isn't it?'

'Maybe. What can I say, Rob? Ryan marches to his own drumbeat.'

'Cal, he's the SIO on this case. It's taken on multiple victims across the whole country. And he's just buggered off. Where is he?'

'I don't know.'

'You're mates, aren't you?'

'I mean, kind of. A few of us were all in Cologne for the

third Scotland match in the Euros back in June. He was giving it all that with the rest of us. Didn't even bugger off once.' Taylor laughed. 'Even got someone to do a Gashkori tartan. I mean, it was basically the Campbell one, but he pretended it was something new.'

'Mm.'

'You're not a fan?'

'Hard to be a fan of someone who drummed you out of town.'

'A bit harsh, isn't it?'

'I'm not sore, Cal. I get it. If I was in his position, I'd want a team of people I could trust. I'd be moving people on. And I can see why he'd move me on. I'm not your common or garden DI.'

'Saying that like it's a bad thing to be one?'

'Nothing wrong with it. My time is better spent in Gartcosh, at least in his mind.'

'And that of She Who Cannot Be Named?'

'Well, aye. Miranda prefers me doing that work.'

'Miranda...' Taylor slowed at the fork in the road – an old man cycled ahead of them, wobbling around and seemingly oblivious to their presence. 'Not to mention he was seeing your sister, eh?'

'I try not to hold that against him.'

'But?'

'But he didn't treat her very well.'

'Oh?'

'I don't know the details, but their break-up was messy. Jen and I might be twins, but it's fair to say we've both kept secrets back from each other over the years.'

'You think something dodgy happened between them?'

'No, but it makes me uncomfortable.' Marshall got a bar of reception. 'Oh, here we go.' He dialled Gashkori's number.

'We're sorry but the person you're calling—'

He killed it and tried again.

'We're sorry but the—'

He killed it again. 'Where the bloody hell is he?'

A text flashed up from Hardeep.

> The AI has deciphered the rest of the code.
>
> It says if the police catch you, kill yourself.

Marshall read it out to Taylor. 'What do you think of that?'

'It backs up your theory, doesn't it?' Taylor sighed. 'But who wrote it?'

Marshall looked up and they were already in Ettrick, trundling along the single-track lane, past the monument to James Hogg.

Taylor took the hard right up past the kirkyard and stopped at the end. 'You've spoken to Martin Gill before, right? You want to break the news?'

Marshall got out of the car and crunched up the drive.

Gill's farmhouse looked empty. His Range Rover sat on the drive, though, meaning he must be in or nearby.

Marshall knocked on the door and waited, peering in through the bay window. The decor might be dated, but the house was the stuff of dreams. A giant grandfather clock ticked away in the corner. Two huge leather sofas sat opposite each other, either side of a roaring fire, surrounded by a heavy stone fireplace. 'The fire's on, so he's got to be here.'

But Taylor had disappeared, his footsteps crunching from around the side of the house.

Marshall took a look in the other window, but saw no obvious signs of life in the kitchen. No music played. No sounds or smells of cooking. A coffee mug sat at the end of the table, but no steam rose up from it.

He must be in. Or nearby.

Taylor's footsteps crunched towards the front. 'Rob.' He was over by the Range Rover, beckoning him over with his fingers. 'Have a look at this.'

Marshall joined him and peered in.

The back seat was folded down. A flight case sat on the bridge between the boot and the seat.

Taylor pointed at it. 'Isn't that what you said you found?'

Marshall got out his phone and showed him the photo he'd sent to Hardeep. 'Same box, aye.'

So Martin Gill *was* behind it all.

64

SHUNTY

'You're lucky.' Donald Sinclair-Turnbull collapsed into his chair. It was like he was made of jelly. Everything just sort of oozed and dribbled. 'There's a massive tailback on the A7 heading towards Gala, so I cancelled my appointment in the town and came back to do some work here. Very frustrating, but my client was understanding.' He unlocked his laptop. 'Just a sec, lads.' He leaned forward, then plugged in a mouse and fiddled with the keyboard.

Siyal looked over at Milne, legs jogging with deep impatience, then he got out his notebook and dated the page, trying to reflect calmness back.

Sinclair-Turnbull still hadn't finished doing whatever he was up to, so Siyal cleared his throat.

Still nothing, just tapping away at the keyboard, oblivious to the pair of cops sitting in his office.

Then again, it was his name was above the door of DST Surveyors – or his initials, at least – so he probably thought he could behave how he liked, regardless of who was here.

The room was painted in true blue and scarlet, but the Selkirk town colours were so vibrant it would give Siyal a headache sitting in here. The window looked along the Ettrick valley, though the landscape was just a mess of tree-covered hills.

'Now.' Sinclair-Turnbull looked up. 'What's the nature of the emergency, officers?'

Milne gave a lengthy smile. 'It's about John Wrangham.'

'Ah, yes, my nephew. I spoke to a colleague of yours about him. A DI Robert Marshall, I believe?'

'This was yesterday, correct?'

'Late afternoon. Do you need me to find the precise time?'

'No, it's all good.' Milne's smile remained, despite a few signs it was fraying around the edges. 'I gather you've been informed?'

'Of his death? Yes. A DCI Gashkori was in here a few hours ago. I... It's thrown me, but I've got clients' needs to satisfy.'

'My colleague and I are investigating the circumstances pertaining to Mr Wrangham's death in custody.'

'Do you think someone killed him?'

'No. We believe he committed suicide.'

'How? How the... You can still do that? I thought it'd be all locked down nowadays.'

'It should be.' Milne nodded a couple of times, as though that would reassure. 'The Police Investigations and Review Commissioner will be taking charge to identify the circumstances around this tragic event and ascertain whether all necessary precautions were taken.'

'Right, sure they will.' Sinclair-Turnbull laughed. 'Luckily for you lot, his parents are both dead, otherwise they could sue Police Scotland.'

'This isn't a laughing matter, sir.'

'No? It's the only way to cope, to be honest. Sure you lot can understand that.'

Milne gave a flash of his eyebrows. 'I imagine you and Mr Wrangham were close?'

'Aye, a bit. He's a good kid, just... John... He was a junior surveyor here. Did a decent job.'

'How has John seemed over the last few weeks?'

'Hard to say. You can probably tell I'm nearing the end of my time as a useful surveyor. My lad will be taking over in the next five to ten years, meanwhile I'll be spending my days golfing in the Algarve. Got a *beautiful* place out there. Gorgeous. Spend a lot of time over there. And when I'm not there, I'm dreaming of being there. So I haven't really seen him.'

'But when you do?'

'Quiet. But then John's always been quiet. Except when he's not.'

'What do you mean by that?'

Milne's phone rang. He checked the display. 'Ah, jings. They're early. Sorry about this, sir. I'll be back in a sec.' He walked off towards the door. 'Zenna, it's good to hear your voice again.' He shut the door behind him.

Sinclair-Turnbull stared hard at Siyal. 'Are you a religious man?'

'Me? No.'

'But you must've been raised in a faith?'

'I wasn't, no.'

'But you're from the subcontinent, right?'

'My family are Indian, if that's what you're asking. And to answer your question, my ancestors are dual faith. They believe in both Hindu and Sikh teachings.'

'Is that a thing?'

'It's quite common in Punjab, yes. But I've never been there. The furthest east I've been is Berlin.'

'And you don't believe in God?'

'No, sir. I'm an atheist.'

'Right. Right.'

Siyal was a bit stung by the questions. It was like there was a racist element to it, or maybe it was just confusion at his lack of religion. 'Why do you ask?'

'Well, it's just John was a bit of a zealot.'

'A zealot?'

'He wasn't backward in coming forwards about his faith...'

'And you associate religious zealotry with people who look like me?'

Sinclair-Turnbull was blushing. 'God, no. Not at all.' He cleared his throat. 'I don't know what I'm trying to say but, believe me, I wasn't being racist.'

'I didn't say you were.'

'Good.' Sinclair-Turnbull shook his head, with a deep snarl. 'It's a bit of a shock. I'm still reeling. You know what? I think I'll head home. After I've finished with you two.'

'Is that what you meant about being loud?'

'Right. To be honest with you, John was a bit opinionated. We'd sit through in reception every morning for a tea break, you know? Have a chat.' He sighed. 'Around Christmas time, a schoolgirl in the town killed herself. Nice wee lassie. Sort of knew her folks. Awful tragedy. Obviously, there was a lot of chatter in the office about it. People who knew the family, all that jazz. But John... He kept on mouthing off about suicide. Talking about sins. And his reaction to it... I mean, we've got the Samaritans just across the road. He can't be talking about that shite, especially not at that time and in here. I had to take him aside and tell him to STFU, if you catch my drift.'

'And did he?'

'Mercifully, aye.'

'Listen, there are a list of people we needed to speak to Mr Wrangham about, but sadly won't be able to. It'd be useful if you could say whether he ever mentioned them?'

'Sure, of course.'

'How about Adam Malkmus?'

'Nope. Who is he?'

'He lived in Glasgow.'

'Sorry, no.'

'What about Kate McWilliams?'

'Not to my knowledge, sorry.'

'Will Greig?'

'Nope.' But something flickered in his eyebrows. 'Didn't he play football for Northern Ireland?'

'If there's someone with that name, it's not him.'

'Right.'

'Aileen Greig?'

Sinclair-Turnbull clicked his tongue a few times. 'John mentioned an Aileen.'

'In what way?'

'John never discussed much of his personal life, least not with me, but he told me they were romantically involved. Then how they weren't. And he expressed some frustration over the matter, shall we say.'

'Frustration?'

'Just how it ended. I think he liked her a lot. Maybe the feeling wasn't reciprocated.'

'And she finished with him?'

'That's the impression I got. Like I say, he kept his cards very close to his chest.'

'What about Rebecca Yellowlees?'

'Oh yes.'

'So he knew her?'

Sinclair-Turnbull frowned. 'No, I did.'

'You did? How?'

'She was the Cornet's Lass over in Peebles for their Beltane shenanigans one year. 2017? 2018?'

'I don't understand.'

'You're not from around here, are you?' Sinclair-Turnbull raised his hand. 'And I don't mean that in that way.'

'I was born in Scotland, sir.'

'Right. Thought I recognised the accent. Hamilton, right?'

'Correct. What's your point?'

'All the towns around here, we have a Common Riding. And it being the Borders, we all call it something different, right? As it happens, I'm on the committee for the Selkirk Common Riding, so we get to know the representatives from the other towns pretty well. Including the Cornet and Lass from Peebles.'

'So you're confirming you knew Rebecca Yellowlees?'

'That's what I said. As part of their duties, when she was the Lass, her and the Cornet visited Selkirk for our Common Riding. Just like we'd get the Braw Lad and Lass from Gala down here and so on.'

'And your Cornet would go there?'

'We don't have a Cornet. No, us Souters... That's what they call us folk from Selkirk... We've got a Standard Bearer and he has assistants. This is a long-standing tradition, okay? Goes back to the Battle of Flodden in 1513. Eighty lads left the town, but only one returned. Lad called Fletcher, bearing a captured English flag. He held that flag high above his head then swept it low. His way of telling everyone all the others had been cut down. Ever since, the Standard Bearer represents the town. He'd go to Beltane and the Braw Lads Gathering in Gala, plus all the other places. Hawick, Melrose, Lauder. You name it. He'd represent the town.'

'Would John have known her?'

'Not that I'm aware of, no... I mean, that was... Did I say 2017? So, he'd have been twenty-two. Pretty sure he...' Sinclair-Turnbull swallowed hard. 'Aye, that was not long after his folks died. Irene was my sister, you understand? He was staying with us after what happened. But that was before he started working here.' He ran a hand through his hair. 'John wouldn't have known her, no.'

'Sure?'

'Of course. He went to uni in Aberdeen. Him and some pals

went to Australia. Backpacking all summer. So he wasn't even in the country. ' Sinclair-Turnbull smoothed a hand through his hair. He got to his feet and walked over to a grand display cabinet by the window. He flicked through some documents and came back over with a picture. 'Here you go.'

Siyal took it.

A photo of Rebecca Yellowlees as a grinning twenty-something, next to a much younger-looking Donald Sinclair-Turnbull – the few years since had taken a toll on him. Iain Hogg was all rosy-cheeked, his gaze diverted, his left hand cradling Rebecca's shoulder.

'Seeing this reminds me...' Sinclair-Turnbull tapped on Iain Hogg. 'Had a bit of bother with the Cornet. Can't remember his name, but he got a bit pished during the day. She wasn't happy with him. Had a right go at him. They were maybe a bit young, like. Didn't look good for their town, you know? I mean, if our Standard Bearer had got into that state at Beltane or down in Gala, we'd never hear the end of it. Especially in Gala.'

'You know what they argued about?'

'Not sure, no. Rebecca wasn't happy with him, that's for certain. Weirdest thing. I was at the Beltane two years later, as you do. Way it works is you do it over three years, going Cornet, right hand, left hand. Right? Now she was the left hand, but she did it solo. No sign of him. He'd been kicked out.'

'Do you know what happened?'

'Spoke to the boy over there. Veitch. Copper, like yourself. Discreet man – he wouldn't say what happened.' Sinclair-Turnbull leaned forward. 'Between us, though, word on the grapevine is her Cornet had attacked someone.'

65

MARSHALL

Taylor scowled at Marshall. 'So Lucifer is Martin Gill? He was the one guiding Wrangham?'

Marshall felt everything swim around him and had to rest a hand on the Range Rover to steady himself.

He'd screwed up.

Big time.

He should've seen that a mile off. They'd suspected Wrangham had a collaborator, but Martin Gill? How had he missed it?

Stupid, stupid, stupid.

Talking to his wife's grave in the kirkyard was weird behaviour.

Marshall thought about the message again. Someone had been meeting John Wrangham and ordering him to murder.

Could it be Martin Gill?

Could he really be a killer?

Taylor was frowning at him. 'You okay there, Rob?'

'I'm fine.' Marshall tried to steady himself. Tried to make it so he was okay. 'Kirsten said it's a dry ice machine. He used it to…' His mouth was dry. 'He used it to fool Wrangham. Feed his visions. Make him pliable to his instructions. Like the note I found. Struan... He showed it to him. Hardeep's AI deciphered it. It said, if the police catch you, kill yourself. Struan showed him the note and it was exactly like Gill ordering Wrangham to kill himself. And that's our fault.' He tried to focus on practical things. What could be done. 'We need to get forensics here. And a warrant to search his house. And we need to find him.'

'On it.' Taylor walked off, putting his phone to his ear.

Marshall took a look around the place. The farmhouse sat in large grounds, probably a good percentage of the village's footprint, certainly this main section by the kirk. He walked across the pebbles, giving the giant house another careful circuit. He tried each of the four doors, looking through each of the sixteen downstairs windows.

Either Gill wasn't in, or he was very good at hiding.

The farm buildings were over to the side, a respectable distance away from the house. Marshall walked over and did a recce, but it didn't take long – they were all open and he could see right through to Taylor at the far end, giving him a shake of the head.

Marshall walked back to the house, trying to weigh up their options.

A search warrant would be a formality – it just might take a bit of time to arrange, but it would let them get inside and see if Gill was in his home.

Taylor caught up with him by the front door. 'You okay there, Rob?'

'Not really. Feels like we've let him slip through our fingers.'

'These things happen.'

Marshall stopped dead. 'You say that like I've dropped my scones on the floor. I can't just shove these murder victims back in the oven for a few minutes to kill the bacteria.'

'No, but you going all mad here isn't going to solve this. Need you to focus here, Rob. Okay?'

Marshall wanted to swing for him, but he tried to keep calm. Because he was right. 'I'm trying to focus on the main reason we're here. I ordered Struan to track down Gill, while we went and spoke to Gill's sister-in-law. And somehow Struan's gone missing, only to end up getting chucked out of a van.'

'You think Struan's been killed by Gill?'

'I don't know. I don't know what to think. But it all seems to come back to one thing. Sarah Gill. She went missing during a run eight years ago when she was suffering from terminal cancer. And I can't help but think that the first murder happened around then.'

'Kate McWilliams near Grantshouse. Wrangham denied that killing, didn't he?'

'Maybe there were others. But the timeline fits, doesn't it? Wrangham would've only been fifteen at the time, but already in league with the devil.'

Lucifer.

Martin Gill.

A frail man in his seventies. Who needed someone to kill for him.

Marshall returned to the Range Rover. 'Why would he leave his car here?'

Taylor gave a shrug. 'I'm still playing catch-up here, mate. Sorry.'

'Right.' Marshall knew someone who'd know, so he set off away from the house.

'Where are you going?'

'To the church.' Marshall waved towards the giant building. 'In the graveyard, Gill told me God spoke to him. It's all clear, right? His hierarchy is from God's tongue to his ears to Wrangham's actions. Murder is completely justified in his eyes, for those reasons. The rules don't apply to him. Antinomianism.'

'Your profile has the killer as methodical and organised, right?'

'Exactly. It all fits. Say Gill killed at least one victim ten years ago, then maybe even his wife. He didn't want to shit where he ate, so he'd pick up stories across Scotland and those were the ones who he'd punish. Soon enough, he started using John Wrangham to execute people he'd deemed sinners.'

'I can buy all of that, Rob. But my question is, where are you going?'

'Gill isn't here at his farm, so I'm going to speak to Fergus McNeill.' Marshall set off up the lane towards the manse.

'The church minister?'

'Right.'

'Rob, Fergus is in hospital after he was attacked.'

'Of course.' Marshall slapped himself on the head. He got out his phone and called Jolene, trying to avoid Taylor's judgmental gaze as he listened to the ringing sound.

He was making a lot of stupid mistakes. Forgetting a lot of things.

'Hi, Rob.'

Marshall turned away from him. 'How are you doing?'

'Still at the hospital. It's not looking good for Struan. He's... Your sister says he's going into surgery soon, but they don't think he's going to pull through.'

Marshall felt a jolt right in his neck. 'Do you think Martin Gill killed him?'

'*Martin Gill*? Rob, what are you talking about?'

'We think he's behind this whole thing. We sent Struan to speak to him. Next thing we know, he's dumped out of a van.'

'Jesus.'

'You said Struan called someone and drove off. Have we got Struan's phone records?'

'It'll give me something to do while I'm waiting...'

Marshall felt a bit more control over the situation. 'Listen, is Fergus McNeill still there?'

'The minister? Just a sec.' Muffled chat in the background,

then Jolene came back. 'Just spoke to your sister. She says he discharged himself from hospital.'

Marshall felt his throat thicken.

Had Gill taken him to finish the job Wrangham started? Or was Fergus working in league with him? After all, Gill said he was the one who helped him decode the messages from God.

'Okay, keep me updated.' Marshall pocketed his phone and looked over at the manse.

The building stood empty, with no car in the drive – Fergus hadn't returned home yet.

He looked over at Taylor. 'Is Fergus McNeill and Martin Gill working together a crazy theory?'

'Why would you think that?'

'Just... Geraldine Blackhall said there was something going on between them. What if this started out as a simple act of kindness?'

'You mean his wife?'

'Right. Helping someone dying of cancer to euthanise herself, but it soon grew. McNeill and Gill both knew Wrangham, who's younger and more able than both of them.'

'That's a lot of speculation, Rob, without much evidence.'

He was right.

If there was one person who could give him evidence...

Marshall called Kirsten.

'Hey, Rob, what's up?'

'How are you doing with the grave?'

'What do you mean?'

'I mean, is it Martin Gill's wife's remains in there?'

'Slow down there, cowboy. Are you okay?'

'I'm... Fine.'

'Doesn't sound it. Why are you asking?'

'Because... we think it's Martin Gill.'

'What is?'

'Our killer. He's behind this whole thing.'

'Are you sure?'

'We found that smoke machine in his car.'

'Jesus, Rob. Are you keeping yourself safe?'

'I'm with Callum now.'

'Right, good.' She sighed down the line. 'Yes, it's her remains. We've confirmed the DNA just now. And the Gartcosh lot have come good – they've confirmed a dating from eight years and three months ago.'

'That's when Sarah Gill went missing.'

'Indeed. Oh, and the DNA under Iain Hogg's fingernails belonged to John Wrangham.'

'Okay. That's good to know. I love you.'

She chuckled. 'I love you too, Rob. Are you okay?'

'I will be. Catch you later.' Marshall ended the call and tried to think through their next steps. Not easy with Taylor scowling at him. 'What's up?'

Taylor pointed at the manse. 'There's somebody inside.'

'You're sure?'

'Spotted some movement, aye.' Taylor charged across the ancient flagstones, surrounded by pebbles thick with weeds, and he tried the door handle. 'It's open.' He stepped inside without waiting for confirmation.

Leaving Marshall outside. Bloody hell.

He stepped forward and reached for the handle.

'Not so fast.'

Marshall swung around.

Martin Gill was standing there, pointing a shotgun at him.

66

SHUNTY

Siyal pulled up outside the house, knowing he'd solved the case.

Knowing who had murdered Rebecca Yellowlees in Neidpath Tunnel. Everyone thought it was John Wrangham.

But they were wrong.

If he was going to get kicked back to uniform, maybe solving this case would prove them all wrong. Earn him a stint as a detective again.

Siyal got out into the cool lunchtime and walked up the path. The stiff breeze shook the trees, with some stray branches already cast onto the lush lawn. Didn't seem like anyone was inside, but he tried the door anyway.

Maybe he should've come with a partner.

But some incident had dragged all of the local detectives away and most of the uniforms, so who could he have picked?

Besides, Bob Milne was too busy meeting with the PIRC team. That side of things was going to take longer than forever.

One thing Siyal had decided, though, was he wasn't going to play Mr Nice Guy anymore. If he wanted something, he was just going to go for it. Sod diplomacy or worrying about other people's thoughts.

The door slid open and a man stood there, dishevelled and swaying. Took Siyal a few moments to recognise him.

Iain Hogg.

Dressed in long shorts that hid his knees and a tatty old Green Day T-shirt – whoever Green Day were, or whatever it was.

His eyes narrowed at Siyal, but he was struggling to focus on him. 'What do you want?'

'Just need a word.'

'Well, you can fuck right off. You prick. You're the reason she's left me.' Hogg turned around and walked back inside his house.

He hadn't shut the door, so Siyal took that as an invitation. Anyone else would, so the new, bold Shunty certainly had to – he followed him into the kitchen.

White units on three walls with a giant mural on the fourth reading 'Live. Laugh. Love' – it didn't look like a lot of any of the three was happening in there today, though.

Hogg had a giant block of ice in his hands. He laid it in the sink then reached for a pick and stabbed it, breaking the block into shards. He tipped a giant one into a glass, so big it got stuck halfway. He measured out a double shot of cheap gin, then tipped in a can of tonic, which only went up to halfway and barely touched the ice cube. He tipped in another can, then shoogled it all with a spoon, making it fizz and hiss. He sipped the drink right down in one go, then let out a gasp. He tipped more gin onto the partially melted ice cube.

He seemed to notice Siyal for the first time, but didn't say anything.

'I didn't take you as a gin man, Iain.'

That made him chuckle. 'I'm not getting you anything. Why are you here?'

'Because I want you to tell the truth about you and Rebecca.'

'What?'

'Come on, Iain. It's much easier if you just tell me the truth.'

'I've told you lot the truth.' Hogg was still holding the ice pick. 'I haven't done anything to anyone. You didn't believe me. Nobody has, so why should I talk?'

Siyal edged closer to him. 'When you were the Beltane Cornet, you attacked someone.'

'Who did you hear that from?'

'I'm not going to list my sources.'

'Right.' Hogg clenched the pick in his hand. 'You're just like all the rest of you lot, after all. I thought you were different. You think I killed Rebecca, don't you?'

'Where's your wife, Iain?'

Hogg frowned. 'Staying with her sister in Paisley.'

'What happened?'

'After I got back, I discussed what happened on Saturday. She'd heard stories from her pals. And she wouldn't believe my side of it.' Hogg took a sip of his drink then seemed to notice it was just neat gin. 'Lot of that going on.' He barked out a laugh. 'Should've taken you up on your offer to pave the way, or whatever it was you said. Maybe she'd have believed me when I told her the truth.'

'I'll believe you, Iain. As long as you tell me the truth.'

'I've only ever told the truth.' Hogg held the gin bottle like a club. 'You saying I'm a liar?'

Siyal focused on his eyes rather than the potential weapon in the hands of a violent drunk. 'There are two ways to lie, Iain. First, you tell someone something that isn't true. Second, you omit something that *is* true.'

'What have I omitted, then?'

'That you attacked Rebecca.'

'I didn't. And I've told everyone the truth. We just chatted.'

'I'm not talking about Saturday.'

'What?'

'I know the real reason you were stood down, Iain. You attacked Rebecca, didn't you?'

'Attacked her?'

'That's why you broke up, wasn't it?'

'No.'

'How about you tell me the real reason, then we'll both be on the same page.'

'Fucking hell.' Hogg stared at him, hefting the bottle in his hands. Then he rested it on the counter and unscrewed the cap. He poured another very healthy measure in, then tipped in two tonic cans at the same time, missing a good chunk of the glass. 'If it'll get you out of my hair.'

'Oh, it will.'

Hogg picked up the ice pick again then stabbed the block in the sink. He plonked some stray shards into his glass then finally set the pick down by the kettle. Far enough away from him. He looked over at Siyal and sipped his drink. 'Becky and me had been going out since we were fifteen. Everyone in the town loved us. Said we were a great couple, you know? And so I was made the Cornet at a pretty young age, right? And Becky was my Lass. Everyone in the town loved us. We weren't at the same unis, but so what? Uni would finish and we'd live together. I loved her. Really loved her.'

'So what happened?'

'One night I was through at hers in Glasgow, like most weekends. We were drunk, in this club. Something like Bargain. One of her mates got us in. We had great fun. It was fucking *wild* in there. Like, insane. We went back to hers after and God knows what pills I'd been on, but I was so horny.'

'Did you rape her?'

'That's not what happened.' Hogg took a slow sip of his drink. 'You know what? Good fucking riddance to her.'

'Good riddance?'

'Aye. She was bad news.' Hogg took another drink, like he needed one. 'The next morning, she got a message from a mate of hers. Tom. Came from Fife. Said his boyfriend... Keith... he overdosed.'

'On Ecstasy?'

'Right. And those pills... They were mine.'

'Yours?'

'I'd been doing some dealing at the uni. It wasn't much. Just enough to make a wee bit of pocket money...'

'Where did you get the drugs from?'

'Some guy on my course. Thought I was a big shot. Typical idiot from a small town, eh? Get to uni and you're suddenly in amongst all these hard bastards... Easy to get in too deep. And then something like that happens. I'm not proud of what I did, but I didn't kill anyone.'

'Not directly.'

'No. No.'

'But someone died because of pills you'd sold them.'

Hogg grabbed the pick again. 'I didn't kill him, though. I couldn't have known.'

'What did Becky say about it?'

'Dumped me.'

'That's it?'

'Right. And I didn't speak to her in years. Until Saturday. We finally had it out. In that tunnel. I... I apologised for what happened.'

'You *apologised* for killing someone?'

'That wasn't my fault!'

Siyal raised his hands. 'Okay, but why did you apologise?'

'I said sorry because I got her to lie for me. She dumped me, but I'd got her to agree with my story – we'd bought those pills from someone in the club. After that, she told me it was over. Making her lie to the police, man... I've regretted it ever since.

Made me clean up my act.' He held up his glass. 'This is as strong as I'll do anymore.'

'You didn't feel bad about it?'

'How could I? All four of us took those pills. I sold sixteen that night. Just because one of us died, doesn't mean it was because of my drugs. He was taking coke too. Wasn't a student, earned a lot.'

'So you thought it was the cocaine?'

'Right.'

'And Rebecca?'

'She thought it was my fault. And she wanted to end it all.' Hogg laughed, then took another sip. 'Ironic, eh?'

'Sorry, I don't follow.'

'Turns out *she* was into drugs, wasn't she? While I cleaned up my act, she was off her head on pills in clubs in Glasgow. Even heard she got sacked from her job for selling fentanyl to someone. Still, it doesn't change what happened to me, does it? My life was royally fucked after that.'

Siyal stood there and tried to assess the risk of being hit by the bottle or stabbed by the ice pick. Brave Shunty was someone who took risks to get results. 'You know that's a solid motivation to murder someone?'

'What is?'

'I have little sympathy for you, Iain – you sold someone a pill that killed them. You should've been straight about that, but instead you got her to lie. And if she was talking to you about it, all these years later, then who else would she be talking to? You'd have a great motivation to murder her, wouldn't you?'

'How?'

'I'm guessing her pal's boyfriend's death is unexplained. Sure, it happened a few years ago, but we could've used her testimony alongside available evidence to prosecute you. I'm sure other witnesses would come forward, if identified.' And pressured by detectives. 'Like I say, it's a very solid motivation to kill someone.'

Hogg looked up at him, then away. 'Oh, I've paid a price for it. Believe me. I've paid a huge price.'

'I don't think so.'

Hogg looked right back at him. 'See? Nobody believes me.'

'Try me, Iain. I promised to believe you if it was the truth.'

Hogg blew out a deep breath. 'Rebecca told the police what happened.'

'But you weren't prosecuted.'

'Off the record.' Hogg scratched at his neck with his hand. 'She told Gordon Veitch.'

'The Beltane organiser?'

'Right. He was the local police officer. One time she was home and she bumped into him in the street. Asked to speak to him. He told her there was nothing they could do about it as they had no direct evidence of it. Besides, if she'd lied for me, why would they believe she was telling the truth now? So it was all just a bit of he said/she said. And if they prosecuted me, they'd have to do her too. And if you ask me, Veitch didn't want Beltane tarnished by a scandal.'

'So that's why he stood you down?'

'Not even half of it. Sure, he stood me down. But he waited, didn't he? Thought it all through. He'd heard I'd fucked up my exams, right? Everyone in the town did. I was confident over my resits, though. I'd put a lot of stuff behind me and actually knuckled down to do the work. Had a daft job during the day, but every night from the start of June until the end of August, I worked three hours a night to go over the material again. I knew it inside out. I knew I was going to pass. Probably even get a good grade. I'd learnt a hard lesson.' A slow breath slid out. 'And I'd get into my honours years and probably end up coming out of uni with a decent degree, right? Get a job in a bank or whatever. But then...' His shaking hand lifted the glass to his lips. He drank it down, then shook his head and stared into space.

'What happened, Iain?'

Hogg fixed Siyal with a hard stare. 'The night before my resits, I went to the pub with a mate. Bit of Dutch courage, you know? Calm myself down, settle the jitters. And that's when he struck.'

'What happened?'

'He grabbed me on my way back to my flat after that drink. And it was just one. He shoved me into this van and drove off. Held me down and poured vodka down my throat. I couldn't even make myself sick. Just felt myself getting drunker and drunker. And they held me there for hours. I kept passing out and waking up, but they'd pour more vodka down my throat. Next thing I knew, it was light outside. Morning. They tore off all my clothes and dumped me in the Pentlands. I ran back to my flat, all the way home, stark bollock naked. Got to my flat, got in and got changed but... I'd missed my fucking exam. And that was my life fucked.' Hogg dumped the empty glass in the sink. The ice cube rattled across the metal. 'Probably fair enough, all told. Right?'

'Did you see who it was?'

'Veitch and his son.'

'Graeme?'

'Right. So you can see why I didn't go to the police, right?'

Siyal shook his head. 'No, I don't.'

'I'd have to admit what I did, wouldn't I? Or you lot would find out what'd happened. And you'd cover it up.'

'Iain, if an accusation is made against a serving officer, then someone like me investigates it. The department I work in, it's our job to root out corruption. Because that's what this is. Corruption. And abuse of power.'

'Still happens, though, eh?'

'And that's why I have this job.' Siyal fixed him with a hard stare. 'Do you have any proof of this?'

67

MARSHALL

Marshall walked into the manse, hands raised. 'Just take this slowly, Martin. It'll all be okay.'

Taylor was over by the sofa, working away at bonds around Fergus McNeill's wrists. 'Rob, this is the second time he's been—' He glanced over at Marshall, then did a double take. His eyes bulged as he saw Gill and his gun. 'What the hell is going on?'

Something hard cracked off the back of Marshall's knee. He tripped and sprawled forward. His hands caught the floorboards before his face hit them.

Gill edged past him, training the shotgun on Taylor. His hands shook the barrel.

Marshall scampered over and propped himself up against the wall next to the grandfather clock ticking away. He sat there, hands raised. 'Just take it slowly, Martin. It's all going to be fine.'

'Bullshit!' Gill stopped close to Taylor and flicked the barrel towards the ceiling. 'You. On your knees.'

Taylor smiled. 'No.' Despite that, he raised his hands.

Gill laughed. 'Son, I'm the one with the shotgun here. On your knees!'

'Aye, and your hands are shaking like you're on a rollercoaster. Parkinson's, right?'

'Shut your mouth!'

'Are you on any medication for that?'

'On. Your. Knees!'

Taylor just stayed where he was, hands up. 'And you don't have your little helper anymore, do you? John. He killed himself, didn't he? At your instruction. He can't do your work for you now.'

'This is your last warning, arsehole. On your knees now. I *will* shoot you.'

Marshall could use this distraction to get away, but he didn't fancy his chances of getting to the door before Gill could get off his shot. A pistol in the hand of a man with a shaking grip was one thing, but the wide spread of a shotgun changed the probabilities. 'You're not going to kill us.'

Gill swung around and pointed the gun at him. He was sweating and struggling to hold the gun steady – Taylor's gamble was a good one. 'Why would you think that?'

'Because you don't kill people who haven't sinned. You spare anyone who isn't your main target.'

'What are you talking about?'

'Like Iain Hogg. He was there when John Wrangham murdered Rebecca Yellowlees. He wasn't killed. And me last night.'

'You?'

'You must've seen me by the shepherd's hut. You could've killed me. But you just wanted to recover your evidence, didn't you? The fog machine and your instruction to John. You didn't know he'd been arrested then.'

'Think you're very clever, don't you?' A snarl slid across Gill's lips. 'What about Will Greig, though?'

'What about him?'

'Aileen was John's target. He didn't spare him, did he?' The snarl widened. 'Maybe you're not that clever, after all.'

Marshall frowned at that. 'That's not true. They were both targets.'

'Well done. They'd both sinned. She'd broken his heart and Will had threatened him. Even stalked him.'

'That's different to the others. It's personal. They weren't sinners.'

'Don't be so sure of that.' Gill's lips twitched. 'They worked for the accountancy firm which does the books for my farm. Or used to. Previously, I employed a firm in Gala, but they sold up and, well, continuity is important so I shifted to the Edinburgh firm. Worst decision I could've made. They both worked on a contract where they advised us all to sell land down here to an American firm. Let the farmers stay on as tenants. Pretended it was retirement-proofing. I didn't, but I suggested some good friends did. After five years, they were all kicked off their land. And aspects of the contract were declared null and void, so they lost the money they were due. Money that belonged to them. How can that be right?'

'So you judged them to have sinned?'

'They did. And they got off with it. Will Greig even got promoted. I have friends who have lost land their families have farmed for generations.'

Taylor laughed. 'See? You only kill the damned.'

'You're incredibly confident in this theory, aren't you? That I won't shoot either of you before I kill that bastard.' Gill shifted his gun to point at Fergus. 'Or after.' Back to pointing at Taylor.

'Are you confident your aim is good enough to shoot me?' Taylor was grinning. 'Because I'd say there's a ninety percent chance you miss. Meaning I knock you down and grab hold of—'

An eruption of noise filled the room.

Taylor fell back, disappearing behind the sofa.

Gill re-racked his shotgun, spitting the spent cartridge across the floor towards Marshall. He walked over to Fergus and pointed the shotgun at his head. 'Never. Doubt. Me.' Drool dribbled down his cheek. 'I might struggle to hit twenty pheasants in a hunt like I used to, but I fancy my chances at this range.'

'Don't kill me, Martin.' Fergus threw up, vomit dribbling down his black shirt. 'Please.'

Gill shifted his shotgun so it pressed against Fergus's chin, but he was looking over at Marshall. 'He deserves this. Believe me, he actually deserves much, much worse but that's for our Lord and Saviour to decide.'

'You mean he deserves it like all the others you got John to kill for you? Rebecca, Aileen, Will, Kate, Ad—'

'*I* killed Kate. That was my work. I knew the lassie she killed. Stacy. Knew her boyfriend, anyway. He told me what happened. This Kate lassie got off with a driving ban! Couldn't be allowed to happen. She needed to pay. Eye for an eye and all that.'

'That's not your decision to make.'

'It's your job to make her pay. A life sentence for what she did to Stacy. Minimum. Not a year's ban. And you failed to do your job.'

'It was a complicated case. It's not on you to—'

'Of course it's not my place! I'm the Sword of the Lord! It's my job to smite down those who sin and haven't been judged, but I only go on what He tells me.'

Marshall hated to see a theory play out so accurately. A visionary-type killer with a mission. Completely deranged.

'God talks to me and tells me what to do. Who to target. It's my job to set them up for His wrath. I'd read all about these vermin who escaped justice and He would tell me which ones He wanted now and refused to wait for.'

Marshall needed to keep him talking. The longer he stood there, the less chance there was of him going through with this. 'How long have you been doing that for?'

'For too long. Way too long. Decades. Going back to the sixties.'

'You're not just talking locally, are you?'

'God, no. Never within a hundred miles of here. Mostly in England and the Highlands.'

'Give me a list of names.'

'The Strathpeffer Slayer. The Campbeltown Ripper. The Moray Firth Murder Spree.'

'Don't the victims at least deserve to have their names heard?'

'God knows their names and that's enough for me. I just do His bidding. And they all deserved what they got. They've been judged and their souls are being tortured now.'

'But you can't do it anymore, can you? You're too old and infirm, so you had to use John Wrangham.'

Gill laughed, but he shifted his focus to Marshall, pointing the gun right at him. 'You ready to put my infirmity to the test like your friend did?'

Marshall didn't know what to say to that. He had to pick up Taylor's thread and hope it led to a different outcome. 'It is Parkinson's, right?'

'Maybe. I haven't been diagnosed.'

'But you know John had been, didn't you? Paranoid schizophrenia, right?'

'Classic case, apparently. The medication helped him get some normality. What happened to his parents was tragic. It warped John's mind, but he was only ever half a person. God told me he didn't have a soul.'

'Because he sold it to you, didn't he?'

'Of course he didn't.'

'Not to you, but to Lucifer. He believed all of Fergus's fire and brimstone, didn't he? And you let him believe the No vote was all down to him. His condition made him pliable. Did you get him to kill Sarah?'

Gill walked right up to Marshall. 'Don't you *dare* mention her name.'

'We know she's buried at the shepherd hut where you used to meet John.'

Gill flared his nostrils. 'How do you know that?'

'DNA. And she's wearing a unique item of jewellery her sister made for her. I'm guessing you got John to kill her. His first victim, right?'

Gill looked over at the minister, then back at Marshall. 'You know nothing.'

'Did you tell John to kill Fergus to help cover that up?'

'Partly. But the Lord wanted us to make him pay.' The gun shook more violently now. 'Because he wouldn't let me bury Sarah's body in the graveyard.'

'Because you'd killed her?'

'Because she'd killed herself.' The shaking got more violent now. 'We found her body. Ettrick Forest runs from the river here over the hills and north to Peebles. I own it all. My family has done for centuries. I used to play there as a laddie. And Sarah would run across the land every day. Different routes. I even got some of the men to landscape bits of it for her, but she preferred to go off the paths and discover her own. And when she didn't come home that day... I knew where she'd likely go. Fergus came with me and we found her. Looked like she'd taken something. I don't know what, but she was gone from us. A righteous woman who had done good work all her life. The pain had become too much. She'd said she wanted to own the time of her death, but I said only God had that say. And He hadn't spoken to me about it.'

Marshall looked over at Fergus. 'You knew about it?'

He nodded. 'Of course I did.'

'Fergus here refused to let me bury her in the kirkyard because she'd killed herself.'

'But there's a grave there?'

'It's just a gravestone. I let Martin erect it to give him closure, but I couldn't let her body be in there. Suicide is a sin. It's why we didn't go to the police. Her family deserved better.'

Gill stepped forward and pressed the shotgun against Marshall's forehead. 'You see why God needs a sword, now? He's angry at the world, at the lack of natural justice in our society. He needs me to do things to make people pay for their crimes. Adam Malkmus sold drugs to kids who died of overdoses like my Sarah did. Rebecca Yellowlees did the same. Others, it was all... It was all God's work.'

Fergus stared hard at him. 'You're the only sinner in this room, Martin.'

Gill shifted the gun back to point at the minister, turning his back on Marshall. 'Fergus, I'm going to blow—'

Marshall leapt forward, rugby-tackling Gill and using his momentum to knock him over, landing just by the fire.

The gun rolled across the floor and pointed back towards them.

It didn't fire.

Gill caught Marshall with a flying elbow.

Marshall fell back and his head cracked off the fireplace. Everything seemed to swim. He tried to get up again, but fell back.

Gill stood over him, training the gun at his face. 'You don't come for me!'

Marshall lashed out with his left foot and caught Gill's right ankle. He fell to the side and the shotgun fired.

White noise blasted in Marshall's ears.

Took him a few seconds to realise he hadn't been shot.

The grandfather clock was a lump of broken timber, the dull clanging the only sound he could make out.

Gill was on the floor, reaching for the shotgun.

Taylor lay behind him, a trail of blood leading from the sofa. He shut his eyes.

Marshall grabbed Gill by the head and smacked it off the fireplace. Hard enough to make him stop moving. He grabbed his head again, ready to smash him again.

But he didn't.

Gill had suffered enough and would face true justice in a court.

68

SHUNTY

Siyal spotted Graeme Veitch in the office space in Gala nick.

Veitch spotted Siyal. His eyes bulged. His forehead twitched. He opened his mouth to speak, but then turned and sped off away from him, heading for the back exit.

Straight into Elliot.

He spun around but Siyal had closed the gap on him. 'Going somewhere, Graeme?'

McIntyre and Paton flanked Siyal, giving him solid backup.

Veitch stopped and swallowed hard. 'Need the toilet.' He laughed. 'It's up to my eyes.' Another bark of nervous laughter.

'It's okay, Graeme, we'll let you go before we arrest you.'

'What?'

'We know what you and your father did to Iain Hogg.'

Veitch snorted. 'What are you talking about?'

'Your father was smart enough to keep his mouth shut.' Siyal held up a bagged mobile. 'You couldn't help yourself, could you?'

Veitch shifted his gaze between them, his nostrils flaring. 'What the hell are you talking about?'

'This is Iain Hogg's phone.' Siyal tapped the phone. 'You must've been drunk when you sent that text. "Keep your mouth shut". Except you misspelled "your" and your phone autocorrected "shut" to something else, didn't it?'

'This is all my fault.' Veitch's head dipped. 'I did it. All of it. Abducted Iain. Got him drunk. Made him fail his exams.'

'Funny, because your father's said the opposite.'

'What?'

Siyal pointed back the way. 'He's in interview room two right now. I mean, given his condition, I doubt he'll be well enough to appear in court, but he's talking to us very lucidly. Telling us what *he* did to him. Trying to get you off without any charges.'

Veitch glanced over at Elliot, like she could stop this.

She smiled at him. 'Don't look at me with those puppy-dog eyes, Graeme. I can't help you here. I'm just here because I owe DS Siyal a favour. His lot in Professional Standards and Ethics will be investigating you and prosecuting you for what you did to poor Iain Hogg.' She wagged a finger in his face. 'Very, very naughty.'

McIntyre grabbed his arm. 'Thought you were better than this, Graeme. Come on. Let's get you booked, eh?'

Veitch let them lead him through to the cells, head and shoulders bowed.

Elliot watched them go, then smiled at Siyal. 'You're lucky I was there, Rakesh.'

'We would've caught him eventually.' Siyal shrugged. 'Consider that the favour returned.'

'I thought we were already even?'

'No, the investigation into Davie's death is now officially closed. One of Bob Milne's final acts.'

She looked at him with tears twinkling in her eyes, then wrapped her arms around him. 'Thank you, Shunty.'

69

MARSHALL

Marshall watched his sister tend to Gill in the hospital bed.

Deep bruises spread across his cheek already.

Aye, he'd really done a number on him. Maybe went over the score a bit there, but a shotgun wasn't so much a leveller as a huge advantage. And when it's pointing at you…

The only way to stop Gill from killing Fergus and him was for Marshall to take it out of his hands.

The decision was already made when Gill trained the weapon on them.

And saved by Taylor as his dying act…

Marshall left the room, passing the two uniforms on guard duty either side of the door, and walked along the corridor. He collapsed into a chair and rested his head in his hands.

The uniforms weren't looking at him. They just sat there, mucking about on their phones. Just bodies who'd stop anyone getting in there, because Martin Gill was going nowhere.

Not that Marshall figured anyone would go in.

Jen came out of the room and walked over to sit next to him.

'Good news is Mr Gill's going to live, despite you fracturing his skull.'

Marshall let his breath go. 'I didn't think I hit him *that* hard.'

'No, but you did hit him *that* hard. Still.' She stroked his arm. 'It was you or him, right? He'd already shot Callum.'

Marshall swallowed hard. 'How is he?'

'They're fighting to save his leg.'

'He'll live?'

'He'll live.'

Marshall felt a tear slide down his cheek. He wiped it away but more came. 'Jesus. I thought he'd die.'

Jen gave him a tight hug. 'Hey, it's okay. You driving him here saved his life.'

'I barely knew him until the other day. He's a bit of an arse, but he's an okay cop. And his heart's in the right place. He doesn't deserve that.'

Jen broke off from the hug. 'Nobody does, do they?'

Marshall wasn't in the mood to joke about some deserving precisely that fate. 'How likely is it he'll lose the leg?'

'I'm not a surgeon, Rob.' She play-punched his shoulder. 'You and Callum saved the minister, though.'

'Small beer, isn't it?'

'You've got to learn to take a win, Rob.'

'You're right, but... Fergus wasn't exactly an innocent man. Still, he'll face whatever fate's coming his way.' He let out a deep breath, then looked back into the room at Gill.

Battering an old man like that. Hard to believe he was the innocent party in it. He had got the better of him by being younger, bigger, fitter and also a cop.

Callum Taylor was all that and more, but he was in danger of losing a fucking leg.

Jen held his hand. 'You did the right thing, Rob. This isn't on you at all. Okay?'

'I'll try to see it that way.'

'Do, because it's the only way to stay sane.'

Marshall laughed. 'You think I'm sane?'

'Just about, aye. Despite all you've been through, you're not doing too badly.'

'I'll try and take that as a compliment.' Marshall wrapped her in a hug. 'Thanks, Jen. I don't say this often enough, but you're the best.'

'I know I am. But thank you for saying, Rob.'

Marshall let his fingers linger on hers.

Jen smiled. 'Your pal's here.'

Marshall looked up.

Jolene was standing there, head tilted to the side. Looked like she'd been crying. 'Hey.'

Jen gave Marshall's hand a squeeze. 'I'll leave you to it.' She got up and walked off.

Jolene sat next to Marshall. 'Struan didn't make it.'

'Shit.' Grief shuddered back into his throat. Stung his nostrils. He hated Struan. Trusted him as much as a serial killer. But nobody deserved to die like that. 'I'm sorry to hear that.'

'I'm sorry I haven't told anyone. I've been sitting there for, like, six hours and... You'd think dropping someone out of a moving car at eighty miles an hour would be fatal but you need to drop them on their head, not just push them out. Most of the damage is done by other cars hitting them, apparently. He was still alive when he got here. Screaming and shouting. You could hear him in Edinburgh. He had surgery, but didn't pull through. Broke both of his legs and an arm. His chest was like a matchbox, according to the surgeon. Too much internal bleeding and his internal organs were like ketchup.'

Jen was just along the corridor, checking a chart outside a room.

'Jesus.' Marshall had never really seen eye to eye with

Struan, but he wouldn't wish that fate on his worst enemy. 'Did Martin Gill do that to him?'

Jolene looked over at him with weary eyes. 'Who?'

'The man I sent him to see?'

Jolene's eyes shifted away. 'No.'

'Do you know who did?'

'At the roadside, he looked at me, Rob. Told me "Callum did this".'

Marshall swallowed hard. 'Taylor?'

'Hume.'

'He did this?'

Jolene nodded.

Marshall blew air up his face. 'You saw him on the phone to someone. Presumably to arrange a meeting. Must've been Hume.'

'I got Struan's records. That call came from a burner.' Jolene shut her eyes. 'But it was Gashkori.'

'Gashkori?'

'I triangulated the cell location of the burner and his. Matched for the hour the burner was on. Made another call to a burner.' Jolene's eyes swept over Marshall. 'Rob, Gashkori leaked Davie's location to Hume. He covered over what happened to protect Hume.'

Not for the first time that day, Marshall felt everything swim around his head. 'Can you prove it?'

'Not easily. Struan said he has a recording on his phone. But we don't know the passcode.'

Marshall sat there, stunned. Like he'd been shot with Gill's gun. 'You put it in evidence?'

'I haven't yet.' She held up a bag.

'Let me take it.' Marshall took it. 'Are you *sure* it's Gashkori?'

'I know what you're getting at. Struan was a stirrer. Always causing mischief. But he said Gashkori's been doing coke... Gets the stuff from Callum Hume...'

Marshall spotted Jen in the corridor.

Made eye contact with her.

She looked away.

And in that moment, he knew.

He *knew*.

And he knew she fucking knew.

'I'll be back in a sec.' Marshall left her and shut the door. He grabbed Jen by the wrist and pulled her into the cupboard next door. 'You knew.'

'What?'

'You knew, didn't you?'

She couldn't look at him.

'Jen. You knew Ryan was doing drugs.'

She shut her eyes.

'So it's true?'

She nodded. 'I found coke in the freezer. A lot of it. He didn't deny it. So I kicked him out.'

'And you didn't tell anyone?'

'I just wanted him gone, Rob.'

Marshall stared hard at her. 'You should've told me.'

'How the hell could I tell you?'

'Me or Dad. I don't care. We're both cops.'

'Aye, you are, but I'm not. I don't see the world the way you do. What does that say about me, eh? Oh, Jen's a loser. Her loser boyfriend is a cokehead.'

'We can't have DCIs with a *cocaine addiction*!'

Her mouth hung open. Then she snapped it shut.

'You knew he was leaking, didn't you?'

Now she looked at him, fire burning in her eyes. 'What?'

'Jen. He's responsible for what happened to Davie Elliot.'

'Of course I didn't fucking know. Jesus Christ.'

'Don't lie to me, Jen. There's no way you couldn't know. You knew about his drugs, you must've known about—'

'Go fuck yourself, Rob. Think about what I've been through.'

'What *you've* been through? Andrea Elliot's husband was murdered because of this!'

Jen dipped her head, like she was a naughty kid back at school.

'Do you still have the cocaine you found?'

'It's still in the freezer.'

'Call our father. Tell him everything.'

'Rob, I can't—'

'You can. You will.'

She gnawed at her top lip. 'Rob...'

'Fuck this.' Marshall opened the door and set off down the corridor. 'Do it!' He pushed through another door into the main hallway out to the front of the hospital.

What the fuck was she thinking?

70

Marshall knocked on the door, then stepped inside. He smiled at Siyal. 'Rakesh.' He shut the door and shifted his focus back to Bob Milne. 'You wanted to chat this through.'

'I did, but now I regret it.' Milne laughed. 'Bloody hell. And here was me thinking my last week would be simple. Going to have to cancel my holiday.'

Marshall raised an eyebrow. 'I'm sure Butlin's will let you reschedule.'

Milne smiled. 'A cruise up the Nile, Rob. Been meaning to do it for years. Real bucket list stuff. I'll use my travel insurance to get booked on another, don't you worry.'

'You're serious?'

'I'm sure the Nile will still be there in a few weeks. My plan is to take down that gang.'

Siyal looked at him with some kind of hope. 'Does that mean—'

Milne looked at Marshall, then back to Siyal and laughed. 'Relax, son, I'm joking. Believe me, I need to retire. And the force needs me to.' He smiled at Siyal. 'Rakesh, can you do the honours and get things started in that interview room?'

'Of course, sir.'

'I'll see you in there.' Siyal walked over to the door.

Marshall followed him over and blocked it. 'Are you okay?'

'I'm fine. Just...' Siyal looked over Marshall's shoulder. 'He had me thinking I might be able to stay on.'

'Right. Aye.' Marshall gave him a big hug. 'Uniform won't be that bad.'

'No, it'll be terrible.' Siyal smiled. 'But if it'll stop people taking the piss out of me, then it'll be well worth it.'

'People will always take the piss.'

Siyal smiled at that. 'Very true. I'll see you around, Rob.'

Marshall watched him leave the room, then shut the door and turned back to face his father. 'Okay. So what happened?'

'Basically, the reason Iain Hogg missed his resits is Gordon Veitch and his son kidnapped him and got him drunk, then dumped him in the Pentlands and forced him to walk back home.'

Marshall took a seat. 'Do you know why they did it?'

'Hogg had sold some dodgy Ecstasy to one of Rebecca's friends in Glasgow. Said friend died. Hogg made her lie to the cops to cover over his involvement. She told Gordon Veitch about it. He took matters into his own hands.'

'Jesus.' Marshall ran a hand down his face. 'Veitch has Alzheimer's. He won't serve any time.'

'I know, but it's important we get to the bottom of what happened. Poor lad might be tangential to your case, but there's a whole other thing he's been a victim of. Excellent work there from young Shunty. I know Gordon Veitch of old. Worked a case in Peebles years ago and he supported me. He was just a community bobby. Old-fashioned. Joined up late, only got his thirty in his early sixties. Sounds like Rebecca went to him, told him everything and they acted. Bit of Lone Ranger and Tonto action.'

'What evidence do you have?'

'Veitch isn't the type to leave a breadcrumb trail. All the same, we've got him in an interview room singing his heart out, trying to take full credit, so his lad doesn't get the blame. Trouble is, his son's nowhere as good at covering his steps from the witch's house and he's up to his conkers in it.'

Marshall shut his eyes and shook his head. 'You think you've seen everything in this job, right?'

'Even I'm a bit taken aback, have to say.' Milne sucked in a deep breath. He looked his son up and down. 'Your message was a bit intriguing.'

Marshall ran a shaking hand through his hair. 'It's about Gashkori.'

Milne rolled his eyes, then huffed out a deep breath. 'About him being bent?'

'You knew?'

'That's who we're interviewing. Reason he's been missing since first thing this morning is he's under caution. Rakesh told me. My guys backed up a few of the allegations, then I decided we had to act, so I took him aside while we dug into Wrangham's apparent suicide.'

'Apparent? You think Gashkori murdered him?'

'I wondered that myself, but no. It was definitely suicide. Part of me is tempted to stay on and take down that gang, but I do need to put my feet up.'

'I've got some evidence that might help.' Marshall put his hands in his pockets. 'Jen knew he was taking coke.'

'When did she tell you this?'

'About twenty-five minutes ago.' Marshall stared deep into those yellowy eyes. 'Has she told you?'

'Of course she hasn't.'

'The evidence is still in the freezer.'

'Jesus Christ. Right. I'll get her to hand it over in a controlled way and take a statement.' Milne gritted his teeth. 'Did she know he'd been leaking?'

'I don't think so.' Marshall ran a hand over his chin. Felt like he'd hurt his jaw from the fight with Gill. 'I'm guessing not.'

Milne stared up at the ceiling for a few seconds. 'Try not to be too hard on your sister, Rob, eh?'

'Why? It's what brothers and sisters do.'

'I know, but still. You're not kids anymore.'

Marshall held his gaze. 'Okay. I'll try' He held up a phone in an evidence bag. 'You might want this, though. Struan met Gashkori and recorded it on this.'

'Oh.' Milne took it off him. 'This little devil should find its way into forensics and we should listen to that.'

'Just on my way.' Marshall nodded. 'We don't know his code.'

'Fuck.' Milne rubbed his hands together. 'But Gashkori doesn't know that...'

71

SHUNTY

Siyal took the seat opposite the Police Federation rep and tried to avoid eye contact with him. He glanced at Gashkori.

He actually looked sorry. Deep bags under his eyes. A sour stench of sweat emanating from him. He gave a curt smile. 'Hi, Rakesh.'

Siyal looked away. Really uncomfortable having to sit in the same room as an old boss who'd done what he had.

Milne waved a hand in front of Gashkori's face. 'It's me you need to focus on, sunshine.' He was in his favourite seat, sitting directly opposite the interviewee. Considering he was a superintendent, he loved to roll up his sleeves and do the work himself.

Gashkori let out a deep sigh. 'Right, aye.'

'You know why you're here, don't you?'

'Why don't you tell me?'

'Let's start with the coke we found in your pocket. It's enough to charge you with an offence. Same with the stuff you'd stuffed into the wee storage box in the back of your car. But it's not enough proof.'

'Eh?'

'We need more evidence from you.'

'Of what?'

'We know what you did, Ryan. We even know why. But we need to hear it from you.'

'I've no idea what you're talking about here.'

'Just talk to us. Confession's good for the soul, after all.'

'What am I confessing to?'

Milne sniffed. 'Actually, we've already got it recorded.'

'Eh?'

'Your wee chat with Struan last night.'

Gashkori's eyes widened.

'Sneaky devil recorded the whole thing.' Milne tapped the table. 'God rest his soul.'

'Struan died?'

'Funny that. Just so happened that you'd called him before it.'

'I did nothing of the sort.'

'We know you did it. Forensics are unpicking Struan's phone now to get the recording. Why not get ahead of the story?'

'I leaked the information around Davie Elliot's whereabouts in exchange for cocaine.' Gashkori shut his eyes. 'I didn't want to, but I did. I'd love to say I was forced to do it, but there was no pressure applied. I was paid in cocaine. I've no audit trail of that because it all just went straight up my hooter.'

'How did that start?'

'Developed the problem during an undercover case years ago. It's tough living in that world, sure you know precisely how, Bob. Any wrong move could get you killed and then suddenly, you're off the case. You're on the outside. You're clear. Sure, there's the risk of someone from that world seeing you in Tesco but that's why I moved down here. Nobody lives in the Borders, certainly not compared with Glasgow. But being undercover changes your mind-set completely. It makes you empathise with what the arseholes we arrest go through. In order that I didn't just survive in that world but thrived enough to convince them I was legit, I had to act the part. And that meant developing a two-gram-a-day coke habit.'

Milne gasped. 'That's a lot.'

'Right? Getting high on your own supply proves to them you're an idiot, right? An idiot they can leverage. Makes them believe the last thing you are is a copper. And it worked. Eighteen arrests directly attributable to my work. Another thirty based on what that lot spilled under interview.'

'And then you were back on civvy street.'

'Right. And I still wanted it. Needed it. And I couldn't very easily get it anymore. Kept on trying to get hold of it. I was working in Glasgow, but I knew a guy up in Dundee. Used to drive up there to see my nephew at uni.'

'Does he exist?'

'He was doing some computer games course. But this happened over six years, not the four he was there. But it gave me cover and I was buying the stuff by the brick. I moved to the drugs squad in Edinburgh and my guy got killed. I thought it'd be okay on them connecting him to me, but not on needing to score. I was desperate, so I scored off a dealer down in Hawick. Bad move. That's when Hislop got his hooks into me. He had it on video. I couldn't even pretend I was undercover anymore. There was nothing there, just me acting like an absolute idiot and buying coke in a block of flats. And I was useful to Hislop in the drugs squad. Then when Pringle moved on, he needed someone directly in the Borders who could sort things out when it came to murders.'

'So you just gave up people's lives to feed your habit?'

'No.' Gashkori sat back, arms crossed. 'That was all Davie's work. All I did was to cover his arse. Then to cover over what happened to him. And what they did to him.'

'So it's just the one death on your head, then?'

'It's enough, Bob. Believe me, it's enough.' Gashkori stared hard at Milne. 'If I help to bring down Hislop, how about we cut a deal in exchange for leniency on my sentence?'

'What exactly do you want? A chopper on the roof and thirteen virgins in the Maldives?'

'Just a new ID and two years served in a safe prison, Bob. That's it.'

'Aha. You're after the Davie Elliot deal, then?'

'Aye. And I know he got it.' Gashkori laughed. 'I could do without the messy ending, mind.'

Milne sat back. 'You know, this is one of my last acts as a cop.'

'So?'

'So I could do it. Recommend you get a deal. Call up the PF and put in a good word for you personally.' Milne licked his lips slowly. 'But instead, I'm going to tell you to fuck right off, you stupid prick.' He stood up. 'No deal, Ryan. People have died because of you. You're a drug addict who's showing no remorse for your crimes. You're a senior officer. You're supposed to be better than this. Good luck in jail – I'm sure you'll enjoy it. Plenty of drugs in there.'

'I *need* a deal!'

Siyal got up and followed Milne over to the door.

Milne clutched the handle and twisted.

'I know that trick.' Gashkori laughed. 'The door handle of truth, eh? It's not going to work on me.'

Milne turned around, grinning. 'I'm not playing games here. Ryan, I'm going to walk out of that door and there's not another thing you can do to stop me.'

'I can give you—'

'Nope.' Milne waved at him. 'Fuckity bye, arsehole.' He stepped through the door.

72

MARSHALL

Marshall knocked and waited.

'Come in.'

He opened the door and peered in.

Just Kirsten there, head down at her laptop. She looked over at him, frowning. 'Oh, hey. You okay?'

Marshall walked over to sit next to her. 'Got into another fight.'

'Yeah, I heard.'

'Been trying to call, but—'

'Sorry, been so busy.' She clenched her fist and put it to her mouth. 'I heard Cal Taylor got shot.'

Marshall nodded. 'Haven't been able to speak to him. Jen said he might lose his leg.'

'Shit.' Kirsten sighed. 'He's a good guy. A bit daft, but he's got a heart of gold. I should head over to hospital to see him.'

'He won't be out of surgery for ages.'

'Right.'

'Before you go...' Marshall handed the bagged phone to Kirsten. 'Need this processed ASAP.'

She looked at it. 'Whose is it?'

'Struan's. It's apparently got a recording of Gashkori confessing to everything he did.'

'What?'

'He's bent, Kirst.' Marshall looked around the lab at the silent machines. They'd spit out facts, tiny little truths that could make or break a case. They didn't lie. Unlike people. 'He's been taking bungs from Gary Hislop's organisation in the form of cocaine. He covered over Davie's murder and stopped it tracing back to Callum Hume.'

'Jesus. Does your dad know?'

'He does now. Obviously, he's postponed retiring for a few weeks to take him down... Gashkori will rot in jail. Assuming he doesn't get the same treatment as Davie Elliot.'

'My God. I've worked with him for years. I had no idea.'

Marshall looked over at her. 'Jen knew about the coke.'

Kirsten scowled. 'Shite.'

'Said it's why she broke up with him.'

Kirsten let a slow breath slide out. 'Don't be too hard on her, eh?'

'I won't be, but it's knocked me for six, you know?'

Someone knocked on the door.

Marshall looked around.

Potter walked in and smiled at Kirsten. 'I need to borrow your man for a minute, if that's okay.'

'Sure.' Kirsten held up the bag. 'I'll get onto this, Rob, but it's going to take a long time. And even then, we probably won't be able to...'

Marshall nodded his thanks at Kirsten. 'I'll take you to see Callum.' He followed Potter out into the corridor.

Potter led him into a tiny meeting room and handed Marshall a fresh coffee. 'I'd say it's this lovely coffee that's bringing me down here but, sadly, it's this case. Or rather, these cases.'

The cup was stamped with Dean's Beans. He took the lid off

and sipped the coffee, even though it was way too late for that. He could already tell it was going to be a long night. 'I'm sorry you have to deal with them, ma'am.'

'Rob, when you become a DCS, you'll see it's just another part of the job.'

'DCS? I don't think that's for me.'

She frowned at him. 'You don't have ambitions?'

'It's not that... I've been a DI for eleven years now.'

'Never too late to move up.'

'Truth is, ma'am, I don't know what I am. I don't feel like I fit in anywhere.'

'What about in Behavioural Sciences?'

'It's fine. I mean, you've got me doing all that profiling work, which I'm good at, but it's not really getting us any results, is it?'

'Doesn't this case count as a result?'

'Sure, but would it have played out any differently if I was a mainstream detective?'

'Maybe. Maybe not.' She put her cup down on the office table, then tore open a sachet of sugar and tipped it in. 'Of course, after Ryan's antics, he'll be going to prison for a very long time. Meaning there'll be an acting DCI position going here.'

'And if I don't want to take it?'

She laughed, eyebrow raised. 'You're assuming it's open to you?'

'Isn't it?'

She laughed again and the eyebrow lowered back down. 'Rob, the role is yours if you want it. I need someone to shore up the team.'

Marshall let out a deep breath. 'Right.'

She held up a finger. 'But it's only acting. Neither you nor Andrea Elliot have the admin experience to take it full-time.'

'With all due respect, Andrea isn't in a good place psychologically.'

'Does that mean you want to take it?'

Marshall looked around the office. 'Assuming I were to come back here, what would happen to Behavioural Science?'

'You mean, what would happen to Hardeep?'

'That, yes.'

'Hardeep should finish his PhD soon, so maybe he could take over.'

'You think he's up to it?'

'Don't you?'

'He's a bit green. A bit short on actual experience.'

'Then he could do with some coaching. Either yourself or, say, Liana Curtis?'

'I'd be happy to do it, but Liana's a much better fit.'

'That's one problem solved then. Obviously, we'd need to conduct a strategic review of the unit and see what we'd need to do going forward.' She stared right at him. 'So what's your thinking there?'

Marshall took a long drink of his coffee, even though the butterflies were flapping away in his stomach. 'If I was to accept it, there'd be one condition.'

'Oh.' She grinned. 'You think you can raise conditions?'

'I want DS Siyal to work for me.'

'No can do. I've just signed off on his transfer to Craigmillar. Starts in four weeks.'

'But he can apply for a role here, right?' Marshall swallowed hard. 'I mean, Struan's...'

'Rob, these are the kinds of admin chores you'll need to gain experience in, okay?' She patted his arm. 'So what's it to be? Stick with what you've got? Or come back here?'

AFTERWORD

Thank you once again for reading this novel.

It's different in some ways in that the villains are loosely based on James Hogg's *The Private Memoirs and Confessions of a Justified Sinner*, of which a quote gives the title of this book. Published in 1824, it's largely regarded as the first British – or certainly Scottish – serial killer novel. Hogg was known as 'the Ettrick Shepherd' and lived in the area, hence me basing much of the latter half of the book down there. I highly recommend reading it, especially the Oxford edition and its excellent notes on the text, the author and the time it was written in.

The first half of the book, though, centres around Peebles and features its Common Riding, known as Beltane. Beltane is a fire festival in Gaelic countries – Scotland, Ireland, Isle of Man – celebrating the midpoint between equinox and solstice around the start of May. Edinburgh's Beltane festival on Calton Hill is quite the spectacle, if you've never been.

Down in the Borders, though, Peebles has its Beltane Week in early June every year, a month after Edinburgh's. The festival dates back to the fifteenth century, but in the Victorian era it moved back in the calendar to merge with the town's Common

Riding, which all the Borders towns have – I've referenced those in Galashiels and Selkirk in detail in this book – along with their own particular traditions.

Iain Hogg and Rebecca Yellowlees being Cornet and Cornet's Lass is a tradition in Peebles, stretching back to the late 1800s formally, and much earlier informally. Obviously these aren't based on any real people. At Beltane, the Beltane Queen is crowned, which is an award for the day for a local Primary 7 schoolgirl, but the ceremony also features the Cornet and his Lass, who serve for three years.

And Gordon Veitch, as Beltane organiser, isn't based on George Blair, who very kindly gave up a few hours of his time just before Beltane 2024 to explain to this author how the whole thing works. Any mistakes are purely mine!

As part of the planning stage for this, I asked my Facebook page for suggestions regarding names of the pub and hotel in Peebles. Thank you to Detlev Jonentz, Jan Ramsay and Jeni Beasley for Buchan's Steps – inspired! – and to Malcolm Ayze MacGregor, Jan Ramsay, George Blair, Judi Martin, Carolyn Girdwood, Wendy Phoenix, Margaret Hall, Carolyn Pearce, Maggie Toole, Kirsty Allan, Detlev Jonentz and Linda Horsburgh for suggesting variations on Beltane, which used to be a side bar at the Tontine Hotel (a place I highly recommend).

And at the time of writing, sadly the Tweedbank-to-Carlisle extension of the Borders Railway has still not progressed to actual surveying and laying of tracks. The first leg has had a very positive effect on Borders towns like Galashiels and Melrose, not to mention those in Midlothian it passes through, and there's a clear case for towns like Selkirk and Hawick to benefit from the regeneration offered by connections to cities like Edinburgh. And selfishly, I'd like to be able to get the train from near to my house down to Carlisle – and further afield. Reopening the line from Galashiels to Berwick via Greenlaw, Coldstream and Kelso

Afterword

would be a great move too (and save me a lot of hassle getting to London).

Sadly, Peebles is too far from the current route and there are no plans for a rail line across there or down from Edinburgh. If you drive along the A72 from Caddonfoot you can see old railway mounds and spaces for bridges where the train used to run – there's still a bridge over the Tweed at Walkerburn and Innerleithen. Would be nice to reopen that as a spur from Galashiels, wouldn't it?

Thanks as ever go to James Mackay for the help in developing the idea into a synopsis then an outline I could write. And for punching the book hard in the nuts a few times to improve it. Thanks also to John Rickards for copy editing witchcraft, to Julia Gibbs for proofreading wizardry and to Angus King for the god-like audiobook narration (just don't tell him I said that).

And I know I'm a dickhead for leaving you hanging like that again, so here's a little word on what's next in the Marshallverse, which is distinct from the wider Cullenverse, featuring Cullen, Hunter, Dodds and Fenchurch.

Marshall will be back in *This World of Sorrow* around the end of January or February 2025, so not that long to wait, really. I will put it on pre-order once enough of it's done to give me confidence that all the editing and audio work can be completed on schedule. This is a great way for you to support the books early, and my newsletter will always be first to hear of that. You don't get charged until the book comes out too! I might even do the paperback on pre-order too.

Before that, I'm going to try writing a second Shunty novella (or short novel – it'll be longer than any of Agatha Christie's novels), entitled *False Dawn*, about his first day working in Craigmillar. In uniform. I'm eager to do this as it'll let me try a new approach to my outlining/drafting which will hopefully save me a bit of time and a lot of pain. I've had a case idea kicking around for years that could work – though I think the ghost-y bits will come out – and, besides, I haven't written about uniform cops since the first Craig Hunter book, so it's time to show them as professionals rather than comic relief like PC Warner.

I'm aiming for that to come out around 30th November 2024, so it won't be long to wait. If it's going well, there'll be a link to buy it in the back of this edition...

Aside from that, well let's just say there are a few irons in the fire and leave it at that.

Thanks again for reading – please leave a review on Amazon as it massively helps indie authors like me.

Cheers,

Ed

Scottish Borders, July 2024

PS I wrote this in June and July, when it was miserable and hoped against hope that September would be an Indian Summer. I hope it is!

MARSHALL WILL RETURN IN

**This World of Sorrow
Early 2025**

Sign up to my mailing list to be first to know when it's out...

But first, the second Shunty novella, entitled False Dawn, will be out in late November/early December... Watch out for it...

ABOUT THE AUTHOR

Ed James is a Scottish author who writes crime fiction novels across multiple series and in multiple locations.

His latest series is set in the Scottish Borders, where Ed now lives, starring **DI Rob Marshall** – a criminal profiler turned detective, investigating serial murders in a beautiful landscape.

Set four hundred miles south on the gritty streets of East London, his bestselling **DI Fenchurch** series features a cop with little to lose and a kidnapped daughter to find..

His **Police Scotland** books are fronted by multiple detectives based in Edinburgh, including **Scott Cullen**, a young Edinburgh Detective investigating crimes from the bottom rung of the career ladder he's desperate to climb, and **Craig Hunter**, a detective shoved back into uniform who struggles to overcome his PTSD from his time in the army.

Putting Dundee on the tartan noir map, the **DS Vicky Dodds** books feature a driven female detective struggling to combine her complex home life with a heavy caseload.

Formerly an IT project manager, Ed filled his weekly commute to London by writing on planes, trains and automobiles. He now writes full-time and lives in the Scottish Borders with a menagerie of rescued animals.

Connect with Ed online:
Amazon Author page
Website

ED JAMES READERS CLUB

Available now for members of my Readers Club is FALSE START, a prequel ebook to my first new series in six years.

Sign up for FREE and get access to exclusive content and keep up-to-speed with all of my releases on a monthly basis.
https://geni.us/EJM1FS